BREAKING
BADGER

Also by Shelly Laurenston

The Pride Series

The Mane Event

The Beast in Him

The Mane Attraction

The Mane Squeeze

Beast Behaving Badly

Big Bad Beast

Bear Meets Girl

Howl For It

Wolf with Benefits

Bite Me

The Call of Crows Series

The Unleashing

The Undoing

The Unyielding

The Honey Badger Chronicles

Hot and Badgered

In a Badger Way

Badger to the Bone

SHELLY LAURENSTON

BREAKING BADGER

KENSINGTON
PUBLISHING CORP.

www.kensingtonboooks.com

BREAKING BADGER

PROLOGUE

"**H**ey. Hey, kid."

Again the seat jerked forward and Mads Galendotter did what she'd been doing for the last ten minutes: focus on the white, red, and blue basketball she had clutched between her hands.

This was her first day of junior high. She would be trying out for the junior high basketball team later today. She knew she was good enough to make it, but she had to be sure nothing happened between now and tryouts right after school. So she wasn't about to blow it by getting involved. Even though that's exactly what her cousins were hoping she'd do.

They really knew how to get to her, didn't they?

They were two years older than Mads. In ninth grade. By all rights, they should be in the very back of the bus with all the other ninth graders, harassing the nerds like everyone else. But her cousins hated her as much as Mads hated them. So they'd plopped themselves down in the seat right behind her and then this poor kid had put herself right beside Mads. Now, instead of harassing Mads, her cousins were harassing the kid. Because they knew that would bother Mads more than if they harassed her directly. Hell, she was *used* to them harassing her. She'd been tortured by them since birth. It was rumored that when she was a baby, they'd used a stray cat to suffocate her. If her great-grandmother hadn't walked in and found them shoving the screeching animal on top of her face . . .

So, yeah, she'd been emotionally prepared for her cousins to make her entire school year a nightmare until they finally graduated to the high school a few blocks away. But now they had a new victim to abuse. This poor kid. She was a cute little thing—Asian, with pigtails and an actual lunchbox. Her parents hadn't even given her a brown-paper-bag lunch like everyone else in junior high. Or lunch money. Even worse, her lunchbox had Barbie on it. Barbie! She might as well have put an actual target on her back.

"Hey, kid!" Mads's twin cousins pushed the seat again before they kicked the back of it.

Both Mads and the kid jerked forward.

Mads let out a long, slow breath. She could tolerate this sort of thing for ages. All the way to the school's front door. But she knew if she looked at the kid's face, she'd probably see tears welling or something. Hell, by now, those tears could be silently pouring down the poor kid's cheeks.

She glanced around at everybody else on the bus. They were busy talking to each other, tormenting the nerdy kids, or simply praying that no one noticed them. They had no idea what was happening right in front of them. At least not yet. Plus, Mads had picked a seat close to the front of the bus. She'd sat there in the hopes that her cousins would want to sit in the back with everyone else.

They weren't completely alone, though.

Close to them were two other girls sitting in the seat across the aisle. One was reading a book on time management. The other, another Asian girl who appeared way too old to be in junior high, was staring out the window. In the seat in front of them was a third girl, with long brown hair. She sat alone so she was able to sit with her back against the window and her feet up on the seat. She was reading *Vanity Fair* magazine.

And there was definitely no point in talking to the bus driver. None. Mads wouldn't even bother.

Meaning that no one was going to stop her cousins from tormenting the poor kid sitting next to her, and they were still some distance from the school. There was more than enough time for her cousins to give this poor kid years of future therapy needs.

The seat jerked forward again.

"Hey, kid. What's your name? At least tell us that."

"Yeah. Come on. We're just being friendly."

Unable to take any more—because her cousins were never "just being friendly"—Mads finally looked at the twins over her shoulder and said as calmly as she could manage, "Leave her alone."

Two sets of cold brown eyes turned in unison to Mads.

"You say something, cousin?" That came from Tilda. She talked more than Gella. She talked and Gella hit. It was a partnership that worked well for them.

No use in backing down now. Signs of weakness just meant they'd come for her harder. Her cousins always ran down the weakest. They couldn't help themselves. It was instinctual. "I said leave her alone."

Gella giggled and Tilda asked, "Or what?"

"Or I'll rip your face off." That response was instinctual, too. For Mads anyway.

Gella jerked forward, ready to leap on Mads, and Mads was nearly on her feet when the kid next to her spun around, resting on her knees and smiling sweetly at Tilda and Gella as she placed her little Barbie lunchbox on the back of their seat.

It was such a weird development that Mads immediately stopped what she was doing and Tilda blocked Gella with her arm.

"Hi!" the kid said with a sweet smile. "I'm Max."

Mads's cousins just stared, completely confused by what was happening.

The whole thing was so weird that even the other three girls in the seat across the aisle were now watching them.

"If I had lunch money, I'd give it to you," Max went on, "but I'm poor. But I can give you my lunch."

"From your little Barbie lunchbox there?" Gella cruelly teased.

"It's really good. It's my favorite lunch in the whole world."

Christ, this poor kid! She was so innocent. Just a walking victim. She seemed way younger than thirteen. Mads knew her cousins wouldn't be satisfied with this kid's tuna sandwich and Snickers candy bar. She knew they'd want blood. But as Mads listened to the conversation going on between her cousins and the kid, her "other hearing" kicked in. This was the hearing her great-grandmother called her "real" hearing. "The one that makes you better than all those little full-human bastards you are around all day, every day," she'd say. Mads picked up a different sound. A sound coming from inside the kid's Barbie lunchbox. Something scratching against the metal of what Mads realized now was an old metal lunchbox. A more secure lunchbox than the plastic ones made these days.

"My mom always gives me the best stuff," the kid promised Mads's bitchy cousins.

Max unlatched the lunchbox and slipped her hand inside. Mads again glanced around the bus. The only ones paying attention to them were the three other girls across the aisle.

By the time Mads looked back at the kid, she'd pulled her hand out. It was balled around whatever she now held and when Tilda leaned in, openmouthed, to see what the kid held, the kid shoved in something black and moving past Tilda's lips.

She tried to scream, but the kid wrapped her hand around Tilda's face, using her fingers to pin her mouth shut.

Tilda's eyes grew wide in panic, her hands reaching, pawing and slapping at the hand pressed against her face. Gella let out a startled giggle while trying to move the kid's arm, but that "innocent" kid couldn't be budged.

Mads grabbed the lunchbox and opened it. There were at least seven, maybe ten, black scorpions inside the box. This kid was carrying around venomous scorpions in her Barbie lunchbox!

One of the scorpions crawled out and onto Mads's hand. It immediately stung her, but Mads barely blinked. Instead, without really thinking about it, she simply brought her hand to her mouth and scooped the arachnid with her tongue. She was in the middle of eating it when she realized that she was doing something very weird in the middle of a bus filled with full-human children.

Shit.

Everything was so strange at the moment, she'd forgotten to pay attention to her surroundings!

Slowly, she looked up and across the aisle at the three girls who, at the very least, she *knew* had been watching the small drama playing out. They were still watching but now they just appeared . . . curious. And . . . and hungry?

The one sitting alone took a quick glance around before scrambling over and sticking her hand into the lunchbox Mads still held so she could grab her own scorpion. Ignoring the stings she now had all over her hand, she shoved the scorpion into her mouth, crunching on it as if it was peanut brittle and smiling seconds before the other two girls followed suit.

Mads watched, shocked. Like Mads, they were all stung. Multiple times. But none of them had a reaction. Unlike her cousin. Who, by now, was having seizures, foam leaking from the corners of her mouth. Her eyes even rolled to the back of her head so all they could see were the whites.

And the kid? What was she doing? Still holding Tilda's mouth shut. Still ignoring the punches and slaps from both Tilda and Gella. And still smiling. Happily.

Boy, Mads was going to get it tonight when she went home, but she didn't care. For once, she was enjoying herself! How could she not when her cousins were the ones on the receiving end of—*ack!*

A big hand wrapped around Mads's throat and lifted her off the seat. She almost lost control of the still-open lunchbox, but one of the other girls grabbed it and secured the latch, trapping the rest of the scorpions inside.

Mads and the kid were both yanked away from the twins and carried to the front of the bus.

Mads hadn't even realized the bus had been pulled over or that the driver had come to get them. She should have. The bus driver was her aunt. And the twins were her cubs. Not her favorites but she liked them way more than she liked Mads. Her aunt opened the doors and threw Mads and the kid out of her bus. A few minutes later two of the other girls came flying out. But the other Asian girl, who looked too old for junior high, walked off herself. For whatever reason, Mads's aunt didn't lay a finger on this one, even though she appeared to be easy prey in three-inch heels, which seemed highly inappropriate for a thirteen-year-old. Fortunately, she carried everyone's backpacks and lunch bags and even Mads's basketball. A kind gesture they all appreciated.

The bus shifted into gear and rumbled off, leaving the five of them standing on the sidewalk with their stuff by their feet.

"I love breaking in the new bus drivers!" the kid finally announced with a wide smile, throwing her arms up in the air like she'd actually won something.

"Does she know the closest hospital is the other way?" the girl with the long hair asked.

Mads shook her head. "She's not taking them to the hospital. She has other daughters she likes better. So if they don't make it . . ." Mads shrugged. "She'll get over it."

Max wiped away her concern—what there was of it—with a wave of her hand. "Such whining from those two. Those scorpions weren't even that poisonous. I've eaten way more deadly ones."

"*Centruroides sculpturatus*," the reader stated, but when everyone just stared at her she simply added, "Arizona bark scorpion. That's what those were. Poisonous but probably not deadly to a healthy hyena adolescent." She paused a moment before pointing at the watch on her wrist and announcing, "We're going to be late."

"Is that a Minnie Mouse watch?" Mads wanted to know.

The girl quickly covered the watch with her free hand. "For now. But I am saving up for something much better."

"Late for what?" Max asked.

"School."

"That's a big concern for you?"

"Being late is always a big concern for me," the reader explained. "I don't like being late."

The kid shrugged. "I don't like school. We should ditch! How about the mall?"

"Don't you think someone will notice us in the mall?"

"We'll tell 'em we're homeschooled."

"I'm not ditching," Mads told them. "I'm trying out for the basketball team today. I'm not missing it."

"How far is school?" the other Asian chick asked. "I'm not wearing my walking heels."

"How old are you?" Mads had to ask.

"Thirteen."

"Really? Because you look twenty-three."

"Awwww." She smiled warmly. "Thank you."

"We need to start walking if we're going to get to school on time," the reader pushed, tapping her watch face again and again. It was a little . . . obsessive.

"We've got, like, twenty minutes to get there."

"Anything could happen between here and there. Anything." She leaned in closer. "*Anything.*"

"What about the bus driver?" long hair asked.

"What about her?" Max replied.

"You did poison her children."

"Only one."

"She won't say anything," Mads assured them. "It would be too hard to explain why her child survived a Utah meowing tarantula."

"An Arizona bark scorpion."

"We go to school," Mads continued, ignoring the reader's annoying correction, "and act like nothing happened."

"Perfect!" Max cheered. "As long as my sister doesn't find out about this . . . fuck!" She looked down at the ground. "Fuck, fuck, fuck, fuck, fuck!"

"What?" Mads demanded. She felt like the worst thing ever was coming for them. Because this was the first time she'd seen the kid look . . . worried. About anything.

"Tell me your names," she ordered. "Quick!"

"I'm Mads."

"Emily," the reader said. "But my family calls me Tock."

"Cass. Future star of stage and scr—"

"Yeah, yeah, yeah. What about you, supermodel?"

"Gong Zhao. From Hong Kong." When Max just scrunched up her face and shook her head as if completely confused by the simple Asian name, the supermodel rolled her eyes and sighed. "Americans. Just call me Nelle."

"Why?"

"Because I said so. And that's Nelle with two *E*s. N-e-l-l-e. Get it right."

"Fine. Whatever."

Forcing a large smile onto her face, Max turned around as a very old, very battered convertible sputtered to a stop at the curb in front of them. The vehicle was filled to capacity with older teenage girls. It was a mix of girls of all races, but Mads knew from the scent they were all one species. Wolves. A black teen illegally sitting on the top of the backseat—*how did they not get pulled over?*—stared hard at Max for several long seconds.

"Hey!" Max called out.

The teen didn't respond. Instead, she stepped over and around all the teens illegally shoved into the car, and jumped free. She was taller than Max. Bigger. She moved like a wolf, like a stalking animal. Although she did smell a little different. Canine, but also . . . not.

"What'cha doing out here, Max?"

"Just hanging out with my friends," Max easily answered.

She stopped in front of her. "You don't have friends."

"Ouch," Cass said.

"So what did you do?" the teen pushed. "Who did you piss off? Am I going to get a call? Is *Pop* getting a call?"

"*No.*"

What poured out of the older teen next was an explosion of panic and borderline hysteria. "Because if Pop gets a call, I'm going to get really upset. There's already so much going on and Stevie's already stressed out. I had to calm her down this morning because she's worried about taking the SATs. I don't know why. We all know she's going to blow them out of the water, but you know how Stevie is, so if you've already been kicked out—"

"Would you stop! Nothing's wrong! We're just hanging out. Me . . . and my friends."

Eyes narrowing, she leaned back and studied Max. "You . . . and your *friends*?"

"Yeah. I have friends now. It's junior high."

"What kind of friends?"

"Friends."

"What *kind* of friends, Max?"

She shrugged. Sighed. "Honey badgers."

"Honey badgers. You managed to find a group of honey badgers in the middle of *this* town?"

"They're not a group. We just happened to be on the same bus."

"That seems strangely unlikely."

"You make it sound like I set this up! I'm thirteen! Even *I* couldn't manage to arrange something like that. This is just—"

"Luck? We're MacKilligans. We don't have any luck."

"I do. And I found friends who get me."

"You mean friends who'll get you in trouble."

"*No*. They won't! I promised you last night, no more problems."

"Did you bring scorpions to school?"

"No."

"Then where are they? I looked for them in the case under your bed and didn't see them."

"I had breakfast."

It took Mads a second, because they really didn't look alike, but she realized that this teen was the sister Max had been talking about. *Her* sister. They weren't stepsisters either. Half, maybe, but they were definitely blood related. They had the same shoulders. Like fullbacks for the Detroit Lions.

The teen looked over Max's honey badger "friends," and that's when Mads saw Cass hide the lunchbox with the remainder of Max's scorpions behind her back. She almost frowned at that move, confused. Why was Cass protecting this girl? Yeah, they were all honey badgers—well . . . Mads was only half honey badger—but they barely knew one another. Why would they get involved in all this drama?

"So you guys are close?" Max's sister asked.

"Close enough."

"Then what are your friends' names?" the teen questioned. It was like an interrogation.

Max gestured at each of them and correctly remembered their names, "Emily, but we all call her Tock. Cass. Mads. Nelle. With two *E*s."

"Uh-huh."

The teen opened a random backpack, which turned out to be Tock's, and checked out her notebooks. They were completely empty, so she searched out her wallet. It was black and closed with Velcro. It had several forms of ID in it. She also found several passports for different countries. Slowly, the teen looked up at Tock with one raised eyebrow. Tock merely shrugged and asked, "What?"

The teen put everything back in the bag and stood, handing the pack to Tock.

"So what are you and your not-causing-trouble friends planning for today?" the teen asked. But before Max could answer with some lie, the teen pointed her finger at Mads. "You tell me."

Mads blinked and simply replied with the truth. "Basketball tryouts. After school today. That's my plan."

"*Our* plan."

The teen faced her sister. "See? You always go too far, Max MacKilligan. Because even Stevie wouldn't buy that line of bullshit."

"It's true."

"You? You expect me to believe that *you* are going to basketball tryouts? To try out for basketball? *You?*"

"Why do you say it like that? I can play basketball."

"First off, you're a munchkin. And second, you hate team sports. You hate gym. And when Stevie tossed a tennis ball at you, you slammed it back at her and threatened that if she ever threw a ball at you again, you were going to remove all her teeth."

"She *chucked* that ball at me—"

"It was a toss."

"—and she started it. But none of that means I dislike team sports. I am absolutely *dying* to be a team-sports girl. In the wonderful world of . . . um . . ."

"Basketball," Mads prodded.

"Right! Basketball."

"Name one basketball player," her sister tested. "*Any* basketball player."

Mads, trying to help while the teen had her back to her, lifted up her leg and gestured to her foot. Specifically the Nike Air Jordans she was wearing. Everybody knew Michael Jordan, right? Even people who didn't know anything about basketball knew that man. Mads had no idea why she was trying to assist this lying kid, but now she felt as invested in this situation as Cass, who was still hiding that stupid lunchbox behind her back.

And even the others were trying to assist by gesturing to Mads's Jordans and mouthing *Michael Jordan* over and over again.

But the confused look on Max's face told Mads that the kid had no idea who they were talking about.

Her sister, with an exaggerated roll of her eyes, began to turn away when the kid suddenly burst out with, "James!"

The teen turned back around and waited.

"Uh . . . La . . . LaBronnie James."

"Who?"

"LeBron James," Mads corrected. "But close enough." When the teen stared at her, she lowered her still raised leg and said, "He's on the Cleveland Cavaliers. A rookie, but a pretty decent player."

You know . . . for a full-human dude.

"See, Charlie?" Max pushed her sister with a big smile. "I love the basketball."

"Great!" the older teen pushed back. "Then I'll see you guys this afternoon. At the tryouts. Can't wait to watch you *all* try out for the team!"

Without another word, Max's sister got back into the overloaded convertible, and with another smile and a wave, she told the teenage girl in the driver's seat to go.

Once they'd driven far enough away, Tock threw up her arms in frustration. "Why do I have to go to tryouts? I don't want to play basketball!"

"You have to come! She'll be expecting all of us," Max said.

"She's not *my* sister!" Tock blinked, then asked more calmly, "She is your sister, right?"

"Yes, she's my sister. Racist!"

Tock's jaw tightened and she looked at Mads. All Mads could do was quickly look away. Because she had to laugh. Tock appeared part Black, so the accusation was pretty funny.

"And you people don't know my sister," Max went on. "She's crazy. If we're not all there, then we *all* die."

The group gawked at Max for several long seconds, and then Cass asked, "Why would we *all* die?"

"Yes," Nelle agreed. "Why wouldn't just *you* die? You should be the only one who dies."

"Because she's crazy."

"Are you lying?" Tock asked. "I sense you lie a lot."

"Of course I lie a lot. That's how I survive. By lying."

"To your sister?"

"Yes." She shrugged. "And to the government."

Mads frowned. "Why are you lying to the government? You're thirteen."

"You certainly ask a lot of questions."

"Actually, I don't. But what I do know is that I don't care what you guys do. I'm going to be at the tryouts today and I'm going to get on the school team. Because I'm going to be in the WNBA."

"What's the WNBA?" Cass asked.

Mads started walking away. "It's sad you have a vagina."

"So I'm not getting points for remembering LaBronnie James?" Max demanded.

Mads spun around and yelled in Max's face, "It's LeBron!" Of course, the kid didn't even blink. "His name's LeBron James. Not LaBronnie! How did you even know about him anyway? I mean, he's blowing up the NBA, but you are *clearly* not a fan. I mean, you called it *the* basketball and couldn't even pull Michael Jordan's name out of your ass and *everyone on earth* knows him."

"Oh, I needed some extra cash last week and I saw this kid walking around with these brand-new sneakers that I knew I could sell for a really high price. So first, I asked him about them and he bragged they were LaBronn—" She briefly paused when Mads growled and self-corrected. "LeBron James's newest shoes or whatever. So when he separated from his friends, I tackled him, dragged him into the bushes, beat him up, and stole his shoes."

Horrified, Mads gasped. "*You what?*"

"I needed the money!"

"So you had to beat up a child?"

"He wasn't a child. He was, like, seventeen. And I had to bail my father out of jail again, but you can't tell Charlie because if she finds out, she's gonna lose it. *Again*. But Stevie was hysterical. She knew that if Charlie found out Dad was in jail again, she was going to have him killed while he was stuck there."

Tock folded her arms over her chest. "Your sister would have your father killed while he's in jail?"

"She's been a little angry since she discovered Dad used our Social Security numbers to not only steal our identities but also for some long con he was working that eventually and typically blew up in his face."

"Is that why he was in jail?"

"Oh, no. He was in jail because he stole a car with a baby in it, which just happened to belong to the mayor of some little town. Both the car *and* the baby, unfortunately. Honestly, it's just another day with my dad and normally I wouldn't care. I'd leave him there to rot in prison or I'd happily help Charlie hire a dude to hang him from the bars. Either of those options would work for me. But Stevie got really hysterical and when Stevie gets hysterical, Charlie starts freaking out, and when *she* starts freaking out—"

"Okay, okay." Mads held her hands up, palms out. Essentially giving up. "Forget I asked."

"Look, you guys don't owe me anything. But if you come to the tryout this morning—"

"Afternoon."

"Whatever. She just has to see me line up and, I don't know, dribble a ball or something. If she can see me doing something normal, for once, it might actually get Charlie off my back so I can get through the next few days . . ."

"Until you break out the poisonous snakes?" Mads joked.

And that big grin returned. "I did find a couple of timber rattlers on Pack property. If you guys are interested, you can join me for some fine honey badger dining."

"They've probably slithered off by now," Tock warned her.

"No. They're in a duffel bag under my bed."

Max headed off down the street until she seemed to realize that the rest of them weren't right behind her. That's when she stopped and turned to find them all watching her aghast that she'd left a bag of poisonous snakes under a bed in a wolf-pack house. Throwing her arms out at her sides, she asked, "What now?"

chapter ONE

Fourteen years later . . .

The paws landed on her, hitting her upper chest. The legs they were attached to wrapped around her, and a thousand pounds of Siberian tiger flipped her over and took her to the ground.

She'd have been angry and put up a fight if machine-gun fire hadn't lit up the sky moments later, bullets tearing across the ground inches from where they'd landed. The tiger rolled them away from the danger but the bullets came closer.

The cat pulled her in tight and used his thousand-pound body to shield her.

For a brief, panicky moment, Mads almost giggled. Because she felt like she was being shielded by a giant stuffed toy.

Refusing to become a giggling psychotic, Mads pulled herself out of his arms and climbed his body until she could look over his shoulder. She was a nocturnal shifter and she could see deep into the darkness. She caught sight of a good target and resting her bullpup assault rifle against the black-and-white fur—where was the orange?—she took aim with her weapon and opened fire. Her rifle made little noise because her team always used suppressors. They were supposed to get in and out without being seen, but that hadn't happened today.

Because, Mads now realized, they'd been expected.

How the big cat figured into this, she had no clue and absolutely no time to consider.

She sought out another target and opened fire again. She heard her team also returning fire, as well as the tongue clicks and tiny throat growls that told her they were alive and well. It didn't mean they hadn't been shot, just that they were going strong. She wasn't too worried. Honey badgers were hard to kill.

Just as she had that thought, though, something small and metal landed a few feet away from her and the cat. Mads had only a brief second to wonder what it was before her teammate Tock charged past her, grabbed her arm and yanked her up. As she moved, she screamed out, "*Five! Four!*"

Tock was counting down. It was never good when Tock was counting down. She'd gotten her nickname because of her obsession with time. A "nightmarish gift" Tock's father always joked, which had made itself evident when she was still in the "goo-goo, gaa-gaa" phase of babyhood.

But organizing everyone's time wasn't Tock's only area of expertise. She also had a gift for explosive devices. She knew them all. From the lowest kind, made in some mad bomber's basement, to the kind developed by an entire array of scientists run by a government entity. And because Tock was a true info junky, she didn't just know how to build, detonate, and disarm the world's explosives, she'd also forced herself to learn the damage those bombs did. She wanted to understand so she never used them lightly. She never used them just because a boyfriend broke up with her or some cheerleader made her cry.

Which meant that when Tock began counting down out of nowhere, it was for one reason and one reason only.

"*Run!*" Mads yelled, not sure the tiger understood her team's vocal codes.

But he was tiger. Short sprints were their way. He was nearly past them when he abruptly shifted to human and his arms reached out to scoop Mads and Tock up by the waist. She didn't know why. They were two of the fastest girls on their pro basketball team. And even with the extra weight of their equip—

The cat jumped, taking her and Tock straight up. Tock kept counting.

"*Three! Two!*"

Near them, also making the insane straight-up leap, were two more Siberian tigers. One held a screeching Cass, now nicknamed Streep due to her dramatic antics on and off the courts. And an even larger one gripped both Nelle and Max.

"*One! Brace for impact!*"

The blast was so bright, it blinded Mads and sent the cat holding her flipping wildly and freely through the air. Something Mads did not like one bit. Even though she should be used to it by now. She'd been battered by enough predatory players over the years to have experienced this sort of thing before but still . . . she was not enjoying it at all.

At some point, the arm around her turned from human to cat as the man shifted, so when they came screaming back to the ground several million miles away—okay, it wasn't that far—he landed like a cat. That allowed him to flip head over tail over ass so that he landed safely on all four paws. Alive and pissed. Roaring and spitting.

Mads, however, stayed human because it wouldn't matter either way. So when she hit the ground, she hit it hard. On her back. Staring up at the stars.

In all honesty, she should be crushed by the impact. All broken bones and destroyed insides. Brains nothing but pudding. The back of her head something not even a puzzle master could put back together.

But, again, she was honey badger. So her ass was a little singed from the explosion and a couple of her fingers were broken, but they'd been broken before by rough basketball games on street courts. One eye did pop out, but Streep, of all people, crawled over to her, let out a loud, disgusted, "Ewwwww! Madsssss! That is sooooooo grosssssss!" and popped the eye back in, then used a bandana from her pocket to wrap her head.

Max stumbled over to them. Her right arm hung at a weird angle, as did her jaw, but she was alive, too.

She gave them orders but they couldn't understand a word because, again, her jaw . . . weird angle.

"*What?*" Tock asked.

Max repeated her orders.

Nelle approached but seemed unable to figure out where or how to put Max's jaw back into place.

Mads had just decided to take a shot at fixing her teammate when she was roughly pushed aside and a giant of a man stormed over. Two other men were with him and she now recognized all of them. The Malone brothers. Or, as they were called on the streets, The Black Malones.

The oldest, Keane, was also the largest. And the most terrifying. She could see him living his life in Siberia among the few remaining cats of the region. Killing any and all human hunters that came into his territory.

So Mads wasn't exactly shocked when Keane grabbed Max's head between his big hands and slammed her jaw back into place as if he was working on an old carburetor for free. The sound of bone being forced back into place had all the badgers bark-hissing in surprise and poor Max swinging her fists and ready for a life-or-death fight.

Nelle stepped in to calm everything down, quickly moving a livid Max away from the naked Keane before their team leader could rip his cock off with her claws.

Instead of Keane being grateful for their earlier assistance, he bellowed, "*Why are you here?*"

"Should we be running away?" Tock asked, but everyone ignored her. "I feel like we should be running away."

"You—" Max paused, taking a brief second to twist her head one way, then the other with her hands. Finishing the job that Keane had started. "You seem tense," she finally got out without any further difficulty. "You okay, sweetie?"

Mads cringed. Because she knew that Max's friendly, solicitous tone was antagonistic at its core. A tone that caused a brave Nelle to quickly step between the tiger and honey badger. Although ecologists would call only one of these two an apex predator, Mads strongly felt the need to correct the entire field of study. Because Max MacKilligan was an apex predator in her own right.

She could change an entire ecosystem in a night if she set her mind to it. And she would do it all with a smile.

The same smile she was wearing now as she gazed up, wide-eyed, at the Siberian tiger glaring down at her.

"I'm going to go find out if we should be running," Tock told Mads before heading back where they'd come from, motioning Streep to accompany her. The pair skirted the giant crater the explosives had opened up and disappeared into what remained of the surrounding tree line.

"You need to tell me why you're here," the eldest Malone brother ordered, folding his massive arms over his massive chest and then having the nerve to wait for Max to actually answer him.

Mads watched as Max's smile grew wider. She knew a smile like that, coming from Max, would not end well and felt the need to intervene—she had no idea why. As Tock had said, they probably should all be running. She looked at the brother on her left. But he had his mouth open wide, his eyes tightly closed, and his tongue hanging out, as if he was tasting the air. It was weird to look at, so Mads turned to the tiger on her right.

"Your brother is being rude," she said. "And if he expects to get anywhere with Max MacKilligan, he'd better back the fuck up."

Slowly, the cat's head turned her way and bright gold eyes gazed at her, blinking slowly before he replied, "My brother's rude? She had her *fangs* dug into his balls not too long ago."

It took a moment for Mads to remember that particular fight. There had been so many over the years with so many shifters and humans, it was honestly hard to keep them all straight. But once the memory returned in all its vicious, honey badger glory, she fought the urge to grimace and instead shrugged and warned, "Then he may want to take a few steps back. You know, so we don't have a repeat incident."

* * *

Finn smirked a little. Almost chuckled. A surprising response when just a few seconds ago, he was ready to wipe this entire island from the map.

And he was considered the "calm one" of his three brothers. The "rational brother" when others needed to bring something up with the family.

In all honestly, though, they weren't doing too badly.

So far his eldest brother hadn't bitten off Max MacKilligan's head. Something he could easily do in his tiger form. Her head was really tiny, too, and would take just one bite. But Keane had been working hard over the last few years not to be as angry-tiger as he could be. A request from their mother.

"You keep it up," she'd warned a few years back, "and we'll end up having to send you to my cousins. And there are very few MacDonalds on the steppes, my son."

While their father was "Irish down to his toes," as he'd always liked to say, their mother's people were from the Mongolian tribes of the steppes. Tiger shifters whose ancestors had been there long before Genghis Khan had even been born, much less a terror to all the tribes. And although both their parents were several generations American, they'd never lost their connection to the place they'd come from or who they were. And who they were was big cats.

Sure. They were human, too. But in their bones, they felt like tigers first and humans second. An attitude that they'd passed down to their three eldest sons. Which meant that Finn couldn't help but see everyone around him as some form of prey. Not necessarily to be eaten but definitely in his way. An irritant. An annoyance. A pest.

He studied the honey badger next to him. He normally would think of the badgers the same way, except for two things. The first was his baby sister, the light of his life and the lives of his two brothers. True, she'd been a surprise to their mother. A result of that drunken night she'd spent with a honey badger male while mourning the loss of her husband. Yet none of them could regret that it had given them Natalie. Or The Nat, as her big brothers all called her.

Yeah. She was a pain in the ass. And she always found a way to start shit. And when she wasn't starting shit, she was getting into shit. But she was amazing. Smart, funny, beautiful, and too good for the world they all lived in. But she was half honey badger and hardly a pest.

The second reason? The way honey badger shifters fought. The rest of the shifter world had its rules. When fighting your own kind, you kept it to fangs and claws. A rule that worked out for everyone in the end. Wolves and dogs might not have the strength of tigers and jaguars, but they usually had a pack of their own kind right at their back. Smaller cats might not want to go up against lions and hyenas but they were faster than the bigger shifters, and with a tree or building nearby, no She-lion could get near them.

Then there were the bears . . .

Honestly, no one really wanted to mess with the bears.

So it all worked out in the end.

Except for the outliers. The ones the rest of them forgot about. The foxes. The wolverines. The honey badgers.

The foxes were smart. They kept their enemies close, using the bears and wolves as their protection. The wolverines could disappear, making many in the shifter world believe they didn't even exist. But they did. Happily.

The honey badgers, however, they didn't play games. They didn't hide. They were in your face, urging you to just try something. Go ahead! Try it! And rules, apparently, were for suckers. If you came at them with bigger claws and fangs, then they had guns and knives and bombs and the willingness to not only use all that, but to wipe out several blocks around their prey, if that's what it came to.

Nothing stopped a honey badger because they were just so fucking mean.

And despite that smile on Max MacKilligan's face, this particular badger was starting to get a reputation as one of the meanest of them all.

So, yeah, maybe Keane should back up a few hundred feet.

He did hope to have children one day. Couldn't do that without his balls.

"Why are *you* here?" Max asked Finn's brother.

That's when he heard the badger beside him mutter, "Uh-oh."

"What?"

"She's answering a question with a question."

"So?"

"That's never a good sign."

"What is at the moment?" Finn glanced at the badger beside him and tried something. "Why are you guys here?"

And, to his eternal surprise, she answered his calmly asked question. "We heard prey was being moved through here. We came to get them out."

Finn frowned. "That's a lot of firepower to free some monkeys or rabbits used for lipstick testing."

She let out a very soft snort. "Human prey. For shifters."

Finn's muscles tightened in surprise and his jaw clenched. He admitted he didn't like a lot of things in this world, but using humans like Cape buffalo irritated him. And he definitely had his problems with full-humans. He found most of them something to be swatted out of his way like fleas. But just as he didn't want his kind shot down by big-game hunters and left stuffed in their living rooms, he felt the same should not happen to full-humans.

"Keane," Finn called out.

His brother didn't turn around or take his eyes off Max MacKilligan—not that he blamed his brother—but his head tilted a bit so he could hear Finn better.

"They're not here for us. Let's go."

"You sure?"

"I'm sure. Let's—"

Finn stopped talking. He'd heard something come up from behind him and turned to see the two honey badgers who'd walked off earlier now charging back. The one who had counted down to the explosion was chanting something new.

"Run! Run, run, run, run, run!"

Finn shifted back to tiger and ran into the nearby trees. When he stopped and looked back, his brothers had done the same.

The honey badgers, however, didn't run.

They reloaded their weapons.

The cats had shifted and disappeared before Mads could even bother to tell them to do so. Good, she wouldn't have to worry about them.

Streep went underground, literally. The rest of them reloaded and got ready for . . .

A man suddenly appeared from behind a tree. He wore all-black tactical gear, including a helmet and night-vision goggles. All of that for them? Did he know they were honey badgers? No. No way.

Whatever the reason for such heavy gear, he put it to full use, raising his weapon and immediately locking on Max and Mads. He was fast, but Mads's team was faster.

Streep launched herself from the dirt onto the gunman's back. With her legs wrapped around his waist, she raised her arms and unleashed her claws. Growling, she rammed them into the top of the man's shoulders. He let out a muted scream; his knees trembled, but he managed to stay standing. Streep's attack did lock his arms, but his trigger finger was still free. Nelle caught the weapon by its muzzle and lifted up a half second before it started firing. She jerked her head to the side to avoid getting shot and wrenched the gun away.

As Nelle turned, Tock slashed her claws and blood spurted from the gunman's torn throat.

Just as he dropped face-first into the dirt, Mads scented more human males. She saw ten of them racing their way, weapons raised. She sucked her tongue against her teeth and dropped to one knee. Her team lined up beside her, about to start firing, but they had to pause for a moment. Their plan had been to spray the ten men running toward them. Until several of them went down and were dragged off screaming into the darkness.

The military-trained attackers immediately faced the other way with their weapons raised. Max motioned her team to move away from the line of fire. Just as they did, they saw the big cats ease out of the trees again. They'd moved around so that they were again behind the attacking males.

Tigers preferred to attack their prey from behind. So all those men facing in the opposite direction were vulnerable. The cats picked their victims and pounced . . . literally. Each brother grabbed a man by the back of the neck and ran off into the trees like a dog running off with his favorite stuffed toy.

The remaining men began shooting wildly and screaming out for their comrades. But it was too late. There were only four of them left, and Max wanted information.

Mads followed Max to the hysterical men, and when she got to the one she figured was the leader of the group, she nodded. Mads slapped his helmet off and pressed a .45 to the back of his head.

The other men spun around, ready to fire, but Max simply wagged her finger. "Tsk, tsk, tsk," she said.

The men still didn't give up their weapons . . . until they saw the rest of Mads's team surrounding them, a weapon locked on each one of them. Without another word, the men gave up.

Getting them on their knees, Tock and Streep zip-tied the men's wrists and ankles and Max crouched in front of the leader. She held one of her knives in front of his face but he didn't even see it. None of the men did. They were too busy looking all around them, out into the darkness with wide, panicked eyes.

That was pure terror. Because they still didn't know what had grabbed and dragged off their teammates. They just knew whatever it had been had not been human.

"Listen," Max said, and when the man she was talking to ignored her, she snapped her fingers in his face until he turned those panicked eyes directly to her. She raised one of her blades. She was an expert at handling edge weapons. So she wasn't exaggerating when she told him, "I can cut off pieces of you and be chewing on them like an old cigar before you even know they're missing. Or you can simply tell me what I want to—"

Blood splashed across Max's face as white fangs bit down on the head of the man she'd been threatening and tore it off his shoulders.

The remaining men screamed and desperately tried to move away, knocking into each other in their panic.

Max, however, simply wiped the blood and gore from her eyes and sighed deeply as the top of the man's head was spit out and rolled past her.

"That seems aggressive," she muttered.

But now the last of the men were ready to talk. In fact, they were ready to reveal anything her team wanted to know.

"The Malones!" one of them yelled. "We're here for the Malones!"

Max looked off into the darkness and Mads knew she was staring directly into the gold eyes of the Malone brothers. After a brief moment, she nodded and re-focused on the full-humans.

"Why?" Max pushed, grabbing one of the hysterical men and dragging him back by the leg. "*Why?*" she bellowed when he started to scream.

"We were just told to put them down! I don't know why!"

"For how much?"

"Three million."

"For the entire job?" He nodded and Max released his leg so he could continue to drag himself away. It wasn't like he could get far.

She stood and faced the team.

"So why were the rest of us lured here?" Tock asked.

Max shrugged. "Somebody's fuckup?"

"Weird fuckup," Mads remarked. She didn't like weird fuckups. Then again, she was naturally paranoid. It was in her bones. She wouldn't say she was born paranoid, but her family situation had made her paranoid. It was the only way she'd managed to survive her early years.

"True, but it's not like we'll figure anything out here. Let's get back and regroup."

They all nodded in agreement but before they could start moving toward the other side of the island, Mads heard something coming from the nearby beach. She halted her teammates with a raised hand. All of them had enhanced hearing. The benefit of being honey badgers who needed to hear prey underground. But her auditory senses were further enhanced by her hyena hearing and she could hear even the slightest sound if she focused. The turn of a bird's head. A squirrel asleep in a tree. Or rubber rafts easing up to a coastline and men wordlessly jumping out.

"What?" Max asked.

These men, the ones who'd already been wiped out and the ones still trying to drag themselves away, were nothing more than a distraction. Something to keep the Malones and maybe Mads and her team busy until the real forces showed up.

"We need to go," Mads said. "Now."

"What do you want to do about them?" Tock asked, gesturing at the three remaining men with her weapon. They were still trying to crawl away, but they were so busy looking around for whatever had killed their teammates that they weren't getting very far.

"You guys go," Max ordered. She still had her blade in her hand. She pulled out another because she worked faster with two. Stretching her shoulders, she faced the three men, but she'd only taken one step toward them when a paw reached out from the darkness and slammed onto the head of one man, crushing it.

Another paw lashed out, ripping the face off the second. And the third was dragged into the darkness screaming. His screams ended within seconds.

Moments later, the cats trotted toward them.

"Those were *my* toys," Max complained as the brothers passed her.

"Let's move out," Mads pushed, heading toward the location where the copter was waiting to take them back to the city.

They quickly cut through the trees but when they made it to the other side of the small island, they found no copter.

Max walked to where the copter had dropped them off only twenty minutes before. She stood there for long seconds, then faced the rest of her team and the cats, a confused look on her face. "I don't understand. Did those bitches leave us?"

"Do you *see* them?" Nelle asked.

"But . . . they're our transport team. How could they just leave us? No one just leaves."

"Max—"

"I mean . . . I've never been deserted before. Ever."

"Didn't your mother desert you?" Tock asked.

"That was different. She was thrown in prison against her will."

"And your father?"

"He was never there in the first place. I learned never to count on him. But it's the transport team's job to be here. To get us out. Who just leaves?"

Mads watched their team leader and finally noted to the others, "I think we may have lost her."

"She seems so confused by this," Nelle agreed.

"Look!" Max pointed at the cats now loping by her, heading toward the water. "Now *they're* deserting us."

"They're tigers. They can swim back to Jersey from here," Mads pointed out. "Almost five miles with no problem. We do not have that luxury. So we'd better come up with something quick."

"We can tunnel," Streep suggested.

"Tunnel where?" Mads asked. "We don't know what's between us and the city. Or even Jersey." She shuddered at the thought of ending up in that hellscape. "Jersey."

"Fine." Tock pulled her weapon off her shoulder. "Then we kill everybody."

"I scented a lot of sweaty men," Nelle remarked, also

readying her weapon. "Enough to accidentally get a good head-shot on any one of us."

"And don't forget that we do have a game coming up."

The entire team stopped what they were doing and looked at Mads. Even Max finally returned to the moment at hand to gawk at her.

"What?" Mads demanded. "We're in the *playoffs*. We are *this* close to getting into the championships. But not if we're dead."

"Okay, okay, okay." Max shook her head and focused on Tock. "What have you got on you?"

Tock shrugged. "Enough to take out the whole island."

"And bring down every government organization looking for terrorists," Nelle noted.

"Especially if you start blowing up islands near New York and Jersey."

"You're not even trying to help," Max admonished Mads.

Max wasn't wrong. Mads was known for being a bit of a Negative Nancy when it came to Max's "Let's kill everyone now and worry about ramifications later"-type plans. Though in truth, Mads often preferred Nelle's "In, out, no one knew we were there until they realized their shit was missing" plans a little better because Nelle's plans meant that Mads never had to limp onto the basketball court at the beginning of a game. Or have bullets removed from her back and neck.

When it came to Max's plans, Mads never knew how she'd end up when the night was over. Simply black and blue? Or riddled with bullet holes that required some backroom shifter doc to yank the fragments out of her ass?

"Well, they're coming," Streep said, dropping to one knee and aiming her weapon. "So whatever we're going to do . . ."

With a shrug, they all took positions behind trees or an abandoned boat. Nelle, their best sniper, climbed a tree and hid among the leaves so she could take out the best shooters first.

"Get ready!" Tock called out. "They'll be here in five, four, three—"

The sound of an outboard motor had them all turning, their

weapons still raised. The speedboat made a wide arc and pulled to a stop near the shore.

"Get in!" ordered one of the big cats, now in his human form and wearing black sweatpants.

"Huh," Max observed softly next to Mads. "They didn't run."

"Why are you staring?" the cat snarled. "*Move those asses!*"

"Go!" Mads pushed her teammates, her gaze still locked on the men she could see moving through the trees toward them.

Nelle scrambled down the tree and ran toward the speedboat. Tock and Streep had begun to follow her when the gunfire started.

Mads heard a muffled roar and knew one of her teammates had been hit. And knew it was Streep when that muffled roar was followed by, "Dear God! I'm dying! I'm dying!"

"*Get that ass up, drama queen!*" Max bellowed.

Mads returned fire, mowing down a few men who weren't fast enough to take cover.

"*Mads, let's go!*"

She knew better than to turn away, so she started to walk backward, shooting as she went. Hoping to keep the men off her until she could at least reach the shore. If nothing else, she could dive under the water and come up on the other side of the boat. Or meet the others out in the middle of the water somewhere. Moving backward, however, was not easy and she started to stumble in the sand. She caught herself before hitting the ground, steadied her weapon, and was about to unleash more bullets, when screaming from the men stopped her. Two of the tigers had attacked from opposite sides, ripping into the men. They tore off arms and legs, tossing bodies and body parts through the air.

Mads was so fascinated by it all, she froze and simply watched until Max grabbed her from behind and dragged her to the boat by her collar. They were moving so fast that when they jumped into the boat, they landed on their backs and were unable to scramble out of the way before the two cats leaped in moments later. The tigers' big, black tails slapped both Max and Mads in the face.

As the boat powered off across the water, Mads let out three loud sneezes, and one of the cats turned to glare at her with his wide gold eyes.

"What do you expect?" she snapped at him, again vainly pushing away his tail. "It's your cat dander!"

While the rest of the team scoured the island, he stared down at the full-humans dead at his feet.

"Where are they?" the team leader who'd been hired to handle this asked.

"Not here, which is a problem."

"This should have worked."

"But it didn't."

The team leader looked around. "Let me pull everyone to-gether, sir, and re-evaluate our—"

He had the one who had failed him by the throat, dragging him close so he could clearly understand every word. "Stop talking to me."

When he felt the message had been properly received, he shoved the fool away and pulled his phone from his back pocket, speed-dialing a number.

"*Pronto?*"

"They're still breathing," he told his eldest brother and quickly lowered the phone from his ear when the rage-filled roaring began.

chapter TWO

Nat slipped through the open window but she wasn't as graceful as she'd hoped to be and ended up flipping head over ass and landing in a pile of her brother Dale's dirty clothes, which was beyond disgusting but at least muffled any noise she might have made.

It was extremely late but her family was made up of tigers. They were nocturnal. Her brothers were probably out, but her mother was undoubtedly in the kitchen now, watching old episodes of *Star Trek: Deep Space Nine* and *Twilight Zone*.

She tried to be as quiet as possible as she pulled her brother's disgusting dirty clothes off her body but, as she stood, she was faced with The Wall.

That's what she called them when she got caught like this. The Wall. With a capital *T* and a capital *W*, punctuation being all important at this particular moment.

What else could she possibly call them when they stood there like that? All three of them standing side by side with their long, tree-trunk legs braced apart. Their big arms crossed over their massive chests. Their big heads aimed right at her so it seemed as if their gold eyes were part of a targeting system that had locked on her and was waiting to fire directly at her.

She knew she had to act fast, so she quickly produced tears and began to speak in ASL. American Sign Language was her go-to when she wanted to get the most sympathy from her big, caring, and loving bro—

"Don't even try it," Keane shot back. He didn't even uncross his arms so he could respond in ASL. To a family outsider it might seem like a form of punishment, but it wasn't. She could read her brothers' lips because she'd grown up with them.

And when she'd lost her hearing, it was Keane who'd begun learning ASL before anyone else. He'd never allowed anyone to think of Nat's deafness as a problem. A disability. It wasn't to her or to him. It was simply the way she was. Like being born honey badger or growing up to be five-nine rather than five-six. Not having to be overwhelmed by the noises of the world always seemed like a blessing to Nat. It allowed her to focus, and the rest of her senses kept her safe.

Besides, what her senses didn't do for her, her giant, scary brothers did. They'd been protecting her since the day her mother had brought her home from the hospital. After she'd pulled Nat off the nurse who'd been trying to change her diaper. At least that's how the story went every Christmas day. Apparently, Nat had latched onto the cheetah's hand with her baby fangs and wouldn't let go, the entire time growling and staring coldly into the nurse's eyes.

From that moment on, her mother had felt that the only protection her daughter would ever need was from herself. Nat's elder brothers, however, had other opinions.

How could she ever be mad at them, really? They not only took care of her when her mother was out working full time, but they'd gone to afterschool classes to learn ASL. They wound up speaking it so well, many thought they were deaf, too.

"Where have you been?" Keane demanded.

"Uhhhhh . . ."

As Nat desperately scrambled for a believable lie, her rescue party stormed into the room.

"Why are you always so nice to her?" Dale demanded, asking in ASL and out loud.

Nat didn't need to hear her brother's voice to know he was putting in as whiny a tone as humanly possible. Why? Because his whining wore on their elder brothers' every nerve ending.

It showed in the roll of their eyes. The curl of their lips. The baring of their fangs. In fact, Dale could even whine through his hands. That's how good he was at it.

Dale was only seventeen months older than Nat and, in some ways, they might as well be twins. They covered for each other whenever they needed, and she needed him right now.

"We do not—"

"You do!" Dale insisted. "You always baby her and you always come down hard on me! It's not fair! It's not fair how you always give me such a hard time! Why do you always give me such a hard time? What did I do to make you give me such a hard time? *Mom!*" he called out. "Keane is giving me a hard time again! It's not fair!"

When none of her brothers said anything for a moment, Nat assumed her mother was yelling back, "You boys stop giving your baby brother a hard time!"

Nat automatically rolled her eyes because her mother was so protective of Dale and insisted on riding *her* ass all the damn time like she always thought Nat was up to something! As Dale pointed out, it wasn't fair!

Keane pointed at her. "We'll discuss this later," he told her calmly because it was true. Her three oldest brothers totally did baby her and she loved it.

"See what I mean?" Dale went on, his hand gestures getting more extravagant. "'We'll discuss this later,'" he repeated with his hands but the expression on his face had Nat biting her lip so she didn't laugh. "All nice and sweet to *her*! *And all mean to me! Why are you always mean to me?*"

Keane pulled his giant fist back but Dale screamed out, "*Mooooom!*" and seconds later Keane lowered that fist.

"Your weakness sickens me," Keane snapped before shoving past Dale. Shay followed, slamming his elbow into Dale's chest and sending the much smaller brother stumbling back several feet. Finn caught him before he could land on his ass but when he dragged him up, he made sure to slam him into the wall.

Rubbing his forehead, Dale whined, "Owww."

Sorry, Nat mouthed.

Glancing into the hallway first to make sure they were alone, Dale closed the door and faced her.

"Where were you?" he signed.

"Out."

He threw his hands up. His usual "I'm frustrated" move.

Nat held her own hands up and went back to the window she'd come through. She'd been sneaking her way in and out of the house since her brothers had purchased it. Before that, she'd been sneaking in and out of their old house since she was four. She'd learned a long time ago not to bring anything into the house until she was sure her brothers weren't waiting for her.

She leaned out and grabbed the bag she'd left hanging from the hook she'd discreetly stuck to the side of the house.

Bringing the bag inside, she dropped it on her brother's bed and opened it. With a flourish, she swept her hands toward it.

Dale looked inside and, his mouth open, immediately closed the bag, yanked it off the bed, and threw it in his closet. Shutting the door, he stood in front of it like he was trapping a wild animal inside, which was kind of funny since technically . . .

"What?" she asked.

"Where did you get that money from?" he verbally asked. He was so freaked out, he didn't even bother with signing.

"What does that matter?" she shot back. She didn't sign either.

He put a finger in front of his lips to tell her to lower her voice but . . . seriously?

"Are you stealing again?" he signed.

And she signed back, "When did I ever stop?"

That was when he threw his hands up in the air again.

Imani Ako stared at the paperwork on her desk, feeling less than enthusiastic about filling it out as Kip and Millie came into her office.

Millie had her arm around Kip's shoulders and he was holding onto her as if she was about to pass out at any moment.

They both had some blood on them and there seemed to be a wound in Millie's leg.

Imani leaned back in her leather chair and waited for the pair to speak first.

"We have some bad news," Kip said.

Millie was one of the copter pilots but Kip was the one who did the talking for the pair.

Imani nodded and continued to wait.

Kip choked back a breath before announcing, "We lost MacKilligan's team."

Leaning forward, Imani rested her arms on her desk and asked, "All of them?"

"Yeah. All of them."

"Kip . . . are you sure? You need to be sure before I say a word to Charlie."

"I'm sure."

Imani gasped. "My God, that's so shocking. Especially since they're standing right behind you."

Kip turned around so fast he nearly tossed Millie into the wall, but she managed to hang on. Unfortunate, since she only wound up getting punched in the face by Max, who hit her first with a strong right, then hit Kip with an equally strong left.

Was Max ambidextrous?

Max continued to pummel Kip until he was bleeding on the floor. After she had him on the ground, she grabbed Millie, yanked her up, and slammed her onto Imani's desk.

"Oh, no," Imani lazily complained. "All my paperwork is everywhere. Now I'll never get it done on time. What a shame."

Max climbed on top of Millie, straddling her on the desk, knees pinning the other woman's shoulders so she could ram her fist repeatedly into her face without getting hit back. All while the rest of her team stood in the doorway and watched. They'd clearly been through hell. They were covered in blood and bruises and cuts. They smelled of full-human men and, weirdly, alley cats. Millie was canine and Kip a cheetah. So why the team would also smell like tigers seemed strange.

Honestly, though, the pair was lucky. They were lucky because Charlie MacKilligan wasn't here. If they'd come back without Charlie's sister and that lame "We lost the team" line . . . a good, solid beating would be the last thing they'd have to endure.

Charlie didn't really waste time with beatings. Or, as Max liked to put it, "My sister doesn't play with her food."

With both Millie and Kip out cold and bloody, the honey badger crawled off Imani's desk and gave a little shake of her head. Other than her bruised and blood-covered knuckles, Max wasn't even panting from that workout.

"I don't want to ever see them again," she told Imani.

"You won't. I don't keep people who leave their teammates behind."

Max returned to the others but they looked at her as if expecting something else, and she gazed back . . . seemingly confused.

"What?" she finally asked.

Her entire team gestured toward Imani.

"You want to ask about getting a raise *now*?"

"No!" Mads snapped. "The setup, dumbass."

"What setup?" Imani asked.

"Oh." Max faced her again. "When we got to the island, there was no trafficked prey, but their guys were waiting." She frowned. "They wanted the tigers, not us. But something about the whole thing set my teeth on edge. I don't like it."

"I'll make sure to look into that. You guys go home and get some sleep."

"We can't. We're going to get Danish."

Tock frowned. "We are?"

"Yes." Max smiled. "For once, we're going to do something nice for someone. To say thank you for not deserting us, unlike *these bitches on the floor!*"

Mads frowned. "Not sure the yelling is necessary."

"According to Charlie," Max went on, "that's what you do. You say thank-you for that sort of thing."

"With Danish?"

"Everybody loves Danish."

"Yeahhhh," Imani felt the need to point out, "but if you're talking about thanking the alley cats, especially this early in the morning, and after a long night, no less, I'd probably just shoot 'em an email. Or maybe even a text."

Max shrugged. "But everybody loves Danish."

It wasn't until the hand persistently tapping him on his bare back turned into a paw and swiped him across the spine that Finn Malone knew for sure it was his mother attempting to wake him up. That's when he grudgingly turned over and glared at her.

"What, Ma?"

"We have vermin in our home," she informed him.

"'Our'?" he asked.

Finn knew it had been a mistake, inviting his family to move into his house all those years ago when he'd gotten his first payout after being drafted. Sure, the NFL draft got all the ESPN coverage but in his mind the shifter football league was a much bigger deal. He'd been up against guys who'd been born in Alaska and had nothing to do all day but grow big and ram into stuff with their giant bodies. One time he'd rammed into the side of a bodega and the next thing he knew, his mother had to come down to the police station and talk them out of charging him for property damage. They kept insisting he must have done the damage with a car or something, but nope. Shay had just bet him ten bucks he wouldn't run directly into the side of the building and . . . ya know . . . he did. Left a real healthy indent in the brick there, too.

Those full-human kids couldn't do that. Not sober anyway. And not without breaking a bone or two.

All fourteen-year-old Finn did was knock himself out for a few minutes.

It was good to get the new house, though. His family needed a fresh start and the old house held too many memories. But everybody thought they had some kind of financial stake in his house and it was annoying. Sure, Keane and Shay paid part of the mortgage and had tossed in part of the down payment, and according to his grumpy wolf lawyer, because his brothers had their names on the deed, they actually owned the house along with him, but he wasn't sure he agreed with that.

"It's the law," his lawyer had insisted.

"You have proof of that?" Finn had asked.

His lawyer had done that thing dogs do when asked a question that seems to confuse them: the head tilt to the side, eyes staring, expression quizzical. The dog's confusion at such a straightforward query made Finn wonder if the man really had graduated from Columbia Law as he had said.

And his mother also thought she had some investment in his home because, according to her, "I gave your ass life. That's why."

But was that reason enough to allow her to stay here when she insisted on waking him up every time there was the *slightest* issue in *his* home?

"If there's rats, Ma," he grumbled into his pillow, "let those dogs you insisted on buying take care of them. Isn't that their job?"

"They're hiding in the backyard."

Finn finally opened his eyes and rolled onto his back again. He stared up at his mother. "By our blessed ancestors . . . the aunts are here, aren't they?"

"Yes. My sisters are here to visit for a few days."

"How many months does 'a few days' translate into this time?"

His mother's eyes narrowed a bit and he could almost *see* the wheels turning inside her head as she debated how to handle her son. She finally went with guilt.

"The pain and suffering I went through to have you children . . . and this is how you treat me. Like garbage. On the street! What did I do to deserve such awful children?"

"Guilt them whenever you want something?"

She began slapping at him, forcing Finn to cover his head with his arms while he laughed.

"All right! All right! I'll deal with it!"

"Thank you!" She headed toward his bedroom door. "My

sisters already think I'm weak for letting all of you boys still live in my house."

"It's not your house!" But his mother was already gone.

Growling, Finn tossed off the covers and got out of bed. He already had on loose long shorts but grabbed a T-shirt to cover any bruises or scratches left over from the previous night. He wasn't in the mood to field questions from his mother and her sisters. His mother worried enough about her three oldest.

Walking barefoot, he stomped out of his room and past his brothers' rooms, not caring if he woke them up.

"You better be studying," he snarled at the closed bedroom door of his baby brother.

"Stop harassing me!" the kid yelled back.

"You don't know harassment yet," he warned.

They had plans for their baby brother and his future didn't involve guns or tracking down scumbags or being involved in shoot-outs. It involved him being a respectable Malone. There weren't a lot of those. A few priests, maybe a nun or two, and there was at least one librarian who still lived in Ireland, but that was it. The rest of them were . . . well . . . Malones.

Dale Malone would do better even if it meant Finn, Keane, and Shay had to ride him like a pony straight through until he got his PhD and a respectable job.

Finn continued down the stairs to the first floor and, assuming the vermin was in the kitchen, headed down the hallway toward the large room necessary to feed a family of this size and a family of *their* size. They were Amur tigers, after all. A bucket of chicken from the local KFC was not going to feed them. It would barely feed Dale, and that poor kid was skinny and weak. He was barely even six-one. Not even two hundred pounds. Among some other cat families, he would have been abandoned to the elements as a runt and left to die.

The rest of them, though—Finn, Keane, and Shay—all played pro ball on shifter teams. They were constantly eating. Their kitchen had three refrigerators and two standing freezers, and in their garage were three chest freezers. All to supply their weekly and monthly food needs. Because their kind ate a lot.

Even the females. Finn was always hungry. He traveled with a lot of treats. He wasn't really an omnivore but it was less terrifying to fellow passengers to break out the nuts on a subway than it was to break out the big chunks of freshly roasted meats.

He didn't know why he got such stares. It wasn't as if the meat was raw. They were shifters, not barbarians!

As Finn neared his kitchen, he heard music coming from the TV and . . . chatter.

Not his mother and her sisters. They were chatty but they enjoyed chatting in the language of their Mongolian tribe. Something they didn't get a chance to do unless they went to visit, but that could be a challenge. Those who'd spent their entire lives on the steppes tended to mock the cousins' American accents, so his mother and aunts were less confident there. But in each other's kitchens, they were nothing but confident. Besides, he'd just passed them sitting in the living room.

He even walked back to make sure. And the four women were silently perched on the family couches, backs straight, claws out, restlessly tapping their crossed legs. He didn't really find their claws concerning. It was their silence that had Finn heading toward the kitchen with more speed than he had before.

He pushed open the swinging door and froze.

The "vermin" sat in his chairs and on his counters and on his kitchen table. One was painting her toenails, another was eating his cheddar cheese and crackers, a third was writing quickly in a notebook with a pencil, and a fourth changing channels on his TV until she found some reality show that involved people dating and marrying others recently released from prison.

There should be a fifth, but he didn't see her.

It didn't matter either way.

Taking a moment to calm himself down, Finn loudly asked, "Why are you in my kitchen?"

"Hey!" Max jumped off the table to greet him with a big smile. "Look at you . . . mister! First one up."

Finn narrowed his eyes at the middle MacKilligan sister. "You don't know which one I am . . . do you?"

"You're one of the three," she said with a shrug. "Your mother was here with three old ladies."

"Please don't call them old."

"They were friendly."

"No, they weren't."

"Hope we didn't scare them, though. Because they just turned around and walked right out."

Finn couldn't help himself. He snorted a laugh. "Yeahhhh. I don't think that's an issue."

"Great!" She gestured at the table. "We brought Danish. We couldn't agree on what you guys would like, though, so we brought Italian, French, and pastries from that Jewish bakery about two miles from here."

"That was my idea," one of the badgers noted without lifting her head from the notebook in which she was writing copious notes.

Max rolled her eyes. "We know, Tock."

"They weren't even going to go to a Jewish bakery."

"Let it go, Tock."

"Just going to bypass it altogether."

"*Give it up already!*"

"I even made sure it was kosher . . . just in case."

"Yes, because the name Malone makes it obvious these guys are so very kosher."

"You don't know." The one named Tock lifted her head and looked at her friend. "I've actually lived on a kibbutz."

"Weren't you asked to leave?"

"That was *not* my fault. Was it, *Nelle*?"

The one painting her toenails abruptly glanced up. "Need I remind you I was not even there?" she said in what sounded almost like a British accent. "I was in Rome that summer with Streep's family. Having a delightful, innocent time, I might add."

"Innocent? Really? Let's ask the Pope if it was so innocent."

"They proved nothing," another badger announced, pointing a finger. "*Nothing!*"

"See?" Nelle said sweetly, going back to her toenails. "Streep says they proved nothing."

Rolling her eyes, Max explained, "What Tock is really doing is pointing out that she's half Black and half Israeli. But it's New York, so no one actually gives a shit. Anyway," Max continued, "we bring breakfast and good cheer for you and your brothers."

Finn took a moment to rub his eyes and let out a breath. Because, wow, the honey badgers were a lot to take this early in the morning.

Or, quite honestly, any time during the day . . . or night.

"Why?" he finally asked.

"As part of our thank-you."

Oh, no. "Part?"

"Yeah. We owe you. For last night. You could have paddled your giant paws off into the night, but you didn't. You came and saved our asses. And we pay our debts. Or, at the very least, we're starting to try."

Finn shook his head. "No, no. You don't owe us anything. So you can leave." He blinked. "What are you doing?"

The one who'd been painting her toenails had suddenly jumped up and, being careful of the fresh enamel, waddled over to his side, and lifted her phone up.

"I'm taking our picture. I'm Nelle, by the way."

"Yes. I figured that out. Now why are you taking my picture?"

"There's a running thing me and my friends have about guys who look good when they just wake up, and you definitely fit the bill."

"He does, doesn't he?" Streep agreed.

"Eh," Tock muttered, her focus now back on her notebook.

Finn covered the phone with his hand. "Do not take my picture."

"Seriously? But I'll totally win with you. My other friends

are mostly full-human. The late-night partying, extreme diet-
ing, and exhaustive drug use of their supermodel boyfriends almost ensure a lock on this month's contest."

His hand still over the phone, Finn simply turned his head
and glowered at her.

"Got it," she finally said, lowering the device and returning
to her seat and nail painting.

"Right," Max said, gleefully clapping her hands together.
"Now, what do you need from us? A painting you'd like to
have but can't get your hands on? Like a Matisse or a Warhol?
Although I find his work pretentious."

"I'm not having this argument with you again," Nelle sang
while changing nail polish colors.

"Perhaps an extremely rare bottle of wine."

"There's that billionaire Internet guy in Connecticut who
just purchased a case of those bottles from the time of George
Washington," Streep noted. "We can grab a few bottles from
him for ya."

"Oh, wouldn't that be nice?" Max said, grinning at him.

"Grab a few bottles?" Finn asked, confused.

"She means steal, sweetie," Tock clarified. "Max always
means steal."

"Well, I'm not made of money!" Max snapped before plastering on that disturbing smile again. "Or maybe you'd like us
to deal with someone you and your brothers find annoying?"
She wiggled her eyebrows. "We're really good at that."

"No girls, though," Tock said. "We don't handle girls."

Max frowned. "Since when?"

"Let me rephrase. We don't handle girls for guys. It's called
loyalty to the pussy and we honor it."

Max nodded and looked back at Finn. "She's right. We do
have loyalty to the pussy. We don't beat up girls unless they
come at us first."

Dearest ancestors in heaven, how could he end this conversation?

Finn cleared his throat. "Look, this is all great but . . . we
don't want anything. Could you just go?"

"What about a car?" Streep offered. "Some of us . . ." And she let that "us" linger out there for a moment before she continued. ". . . are very good at obtaining vehicles."

"Streep is right," Max said. "We can get you a brand-new Bugatti in about a week."

"You want us to have a three-million-dollar car just sitting in front of our house with no explanation?" Finn had to ask. "Don't you think the neighbors will find that odd?"

"Three million?" Max said with a short laugh. "That's for the basic package. I've met your mother. She'd want that bitch flexed out, so we'd get her the works."

Finn raised his arms, palms facing out. "I'm going to stop you right there. We don't want a car of any price. Nor any paintings, statues, or anything else you've stolen. Nor do we want you to kill anyone for us. But thanks for the offer. Instead, I'd really prefer that you just left. There's the door . . . head for it."

"Why are you being so difficult?"

"I'm not being difficult. I'm just trying to get you out of here before—"

Finn cringed. The heavy, damning thud from upstairs shook the entire house.

"Too late," he muttered seconds before Keane stormed down the stairs and into the kitchen, with Shay right behind him.

"Keane, I'm handling—" was all Finn got out before his eldest brother grabbed the back of his neck and shoved him into Shay so he could stand right in front of the females and unleash the Malone tiger roar with all the subtlety of a rampaging elephant herd.

"*GET OUT OF MY HOUSE!*"

The badgers should have reacted. They should have jumped up in panic. They should have dropped things, fallen over. At least one should have bolted for the door. Finn had used that bellow before himself, and it was always the reaction he'd gotten from shifters and full-humans alike. Except, of course, lions. They just roared back. And grizzlies. You never wanted to use that roar on unsuspecting grizzlies. Because they were startled all right . . . but that just led to maulings. Shay still had the scars from a startled grizzly mauling on his shoulder and back, and you never really knew who'd come out on the winning end of that particular matchup.

But these guys? These honey badgers? They were one of the smallest of shifters while Amur tigers were biggest among cats and only second and third among grizzlies and polar bears. What did these tiny badgers do when faced with the Malone roar?

Nothing. They did nothing.

Well, to clarify, they did do *something* but it wasn't anything meaningful. It definitely wasn't what Finn would call a "normal" reaction. Not by full-human or shifter standards. Not by anyone's standards, really.

Max held up a plate of Danish with a smile. She didn't say anything, though, because she already had one treat stuffed into her mouth. Raspberry filling smeared her nose and, somehow, her forehead. Finn didn't want to know how that happened.

Nelle, who'd been painting her toenails, closed another bottle of polish and put it in a leather bag. Then she proceeded to take pictures. Of her toenails. She didn't even seem to notice that Keane was in the room . . . or on the planet.

Streep had been on her phone when the roar happened and never stopped scrolling.

Tock, still writing in her notebook, casually gestured at a duffel bag by her feet with a tilt of her head and calmly noted, "Wouldn't do all that screaming. Have some sensitive stuff in here."

That comment seemed to garner more of a reaction from the females than anything Finn's brothers had done because the badgers immediately went wide-eyed and Max demanded of Tock, "Are you walking around with explosives in there?"

"Of course not."

"Then what do you have that's so sensitive?"

"Kitten."

"Oh." Max blinked, thought a moment. "Why are you walking around with a kitten in a duffel bag?"

"You with so many questions."

"Oh, my God, Tock!" Streep demanded. *"Are you going to blow up that kitten?"*

Tock rolled her eyes. "Of course not."

The women stared at her, seemingly unwilling to accept that answer.

"It'll be fine," she insisted.

Still didn't seem good enough for her friends.

"I promised you guys I'd never try that again. You know . . . for *moral* reasons."

Try that again?

More staring.

"I can't believe you're still holding that against me! I was fourteen! It was for science!"

Staring.

Now she simply stared back at the others. The standoff lasted a solid two minutes until she could no longer maintain eye contact and turned her gaze to Finn and his brothers. "You guys want a cat?"

"No," Finn immediately replied.

"Fine," Tock snapped. "I'll throw it in the backyard."

"We have dogs in the backyard," Shay pointed out.

Streep frowned. "Why do cats have dogs in the backyard?"

Keane locked gazes with Max. "To deal with all the vermin."

Max blinked, startled. "Why are you looking at me? I'll have you know that honey badgers are an important part of the ecosystem or whatever."

Tock winced a little at that wording but she shook it off like a champ.

"And," Max continued happily, "we came here today with pastry and to thank you."

"We don't need *anything* from you. Not your nasty pastries"—Max gasped at that insult but considering Shay was on his fourth Danish, she shouldn't have taken it so personally—"not your annoying presence, not your weird badger smell!"

"That weird badger smell, as you call it, is the latest French perfume from that designer I can't pronounce—"

"She really can't," Nelle muttered.

"—that costs seven hundred and eighty-nine dollars an ounce and that *I* managed to steal from their Fifth Avenue boutique without getting caught just last week!"

"*Oh, my God!*" Keane exploded. "You're a walking felony and you're in my house! Get out! *Now!*"

Max stood against Keane's rage in a way that Finn had absolutely never seen before: by simply gazing at him, appearing a little shocked and confused.

After a few seconds of silence, she reminded Keane, "But . . . I brought you Danish."

"I don't care."

"I'm being nice."

"Still don't care."

"I offered the services of myself and my teammates to kill your enemies or to steal you cool stuff. Do you have any idea how hard it is to steal a tricked-out Bugatti? It's super hard! And now you come down here and you . . ." She glanced at the floor, the ceiling, then Keane. "You're mean to me? When *I,* Max MacKilligan, was nice. To *you?*"

"Yeah, that's exactly what I did," Keane told her. "Now do you get it?"

And that's when Max went for Finn's elder brother. Not with fang and claw but a giant hunting knife that she pulled out of somewhere on her person. She charged him with such speed and intent that the three of them just stood there, not doing anything. Not fighting back or protecting Keane or even jumping out of the way.

Finn could only assume they were just too shocked by the sudden brutal attack. Over Danish?

Thankfully, her three friends *were* fast and didn't seem nearly as shocked by the move. Nelle caught Max's knife-holding arm while Tock and Streep grabbed her around the waist. With much effort, they dragged her back toward the door.

"Just let it go!" Tock ordered Max.

"Fuck him!" Max screamed. "Fuck all of them! *Kill 'em all!*"

"Don't forget!" Streep reminded her. "He's the half-brother of your half-sister!"

They were by the door and suddenly Max MacKilligan stopped fighting. The change was so abrupt that Finn and his brothers lowered their arms and braced their legs apart, waiting for another random attack. A more vicious one. And they were right to expect it. Because MacKilligan went for the jugular as only a MacKilligan could and would.

Her smile this time was not the off-putting faux-friendly grin that scared so many. This was a smile that Finn was guessing was the last thing on earth many full-humans saw before MacKilligan finished them off.

And, with that slow spreading smile, she said, "One day . . . your baby sister is going to come to me and ask me a question about men and dating"—she leaned away from her friends and toward the brothers—"and I'm going to tell her every. fucking. *thing.*"

Keane was nearly across the room, his hands around MacKilligan's throat when Finn and Shay caught him and tackled him to the ground like they'd just sacked a quarterback.

"*You bitch!*" Keane roared from the floor.

"*You don't deserve that Danish, you ungrateful prick!*" Max screeched back.

"*Your Danish looks dry!*"

MacKilligan gasped. "*You motherfucker!*"

The honey badgers dragged their hysterical friend out the side door and Finn and Shay kept Keane pinned to the ground until he finally threw them off in a burst of tiger strength.

"Get off me!"

The three brothers jumped to their feet and now squared off against each other.

"I was handling that!" Finn told Keane.

"Yeah, I saw how you were handling that. In your usual mealy-mouthed way. Letting those rats walk all over you!"

"But you did such a great fucking job dealing with it your-self!"

"*They're out, aren't they?*"

There was no point in talking to Keane when he was like this. So Finn didn't bother. He just watched his brother storm toward the hallway, turn around, return to the kitchen table, grab a box of Danish, then storm back to the hallway and up-stairs to his room. When Finn heard Keane's bedroom door slam closed, he let out a breath.

"Can you believe—"

Shay held up a hand, another Danish already in his mouth. "I'm not getting in the middle of—"

The rest of Shay's statement was lost to his chewing.

"How did you even get that Danish?" They weren't stand-ing close to the table.

He swallowed. "I was holding it the whole time."

Disgusted, pissed, and a lot of other things, Finn was about to go to his room and try to get some more sleep. But he'd barely taken a few steps when he heard his brother's low whistle.

He turned around and Shay jabbed his thumb toward one of the overhead cabinets.

Finn walked across the kitchen and opened the cabinet door.

That's where he found her. Sound asleep on her right side. A pillow from the couch under her head; one hand tucked under her cheek, the other curled into a fist and pressed against her upper chest. Her hair was still in the two braids she'd worn the night before. He didn't know any honey badgers with blond hair but maybe she dyed hers. The bruises on her face had turned black and blue but the open wounds on her neck that he'd no-ticed had already healed.

Fascinated, Finn leaned close to see how big this woman was. He remembered this She-badger from the night before and he recalled her being, you know . . . normal sized. Defi-nitely bigger than Max MacKilligan, who could easily fit into this cabinet space. But she didn't seem uncomfortable. In fact, she was snoring a little.

"Huh," Finn said softly when he saw that the badger's legs were tucked up and around all his mother's seasoning jars.

How could she possibly be comfortable like that? She looked like a pretzel.

Finn began to pull back when he realized that he was being watched. He lifted his gaze to see that the She-badger was no longer asleep but was now wide awake and studying him closely.

"What'cha doing?" she asked.

"I was just curious to see how you got yourself in there."

"Uh-huh."

"I swear it wasn't weird."

"Okay."

"Your friends already left, by the way."

"Friends?" she asked with a confused frown, but then just as quickly she said, "Oh! My teammates. They left?" She lifted her wrist and glanced at her fitness watch. "That was fast."

"You didn't hear any of what went on out here?"

She snorted. "I grew up in a family of hyenas." She untangled herself from the cabinet with ease, forcing Finn to move back so she could get out. "There was never a quiet moment in my house at any time. Either I learned to sleep through anything or I would have died of sleep deprivation by the time I was three."

She jumped from the cabinet and down to the floor.

"So how did it go?" she asked.

"How did what go?"

"Our Danish-covered thank-you? For saving us last night."

Finn shook his head. "Not too well, I'm afraid. We didn't really want what MacKilligan was offering."

"Really? That's too bad. Having MacKilligans on my team has always worked out for me."

"You have great need for a stolen Bugatti in your driveway?"

"I can steal my own Bugatti. It was one of the first things my family made sure I knew how to do, whether I wanted to know it or not," she said. "But when you need to get rid of that Bugatti because you can hear the police sirens thirty seconds away and you're bleeding from the leg because your cousin just stabbed you to make sure you couldn't run and your aunts have blocked the door so you can't get back into the house and your own mother won't give you bail even though you *know* you're not responsible for this particular felony and you're at that awkward age where you can be tried as an adult but you can't move out of your home because you can't legally sign a lease yet . . . Max MacKilligan is the one you want on your side."

She shrugged, lifting her arms up and letting them drop.

"But, ya know . . . you do you."

And with that, the She-badger walked out.

Finn faced his still-feeding brother and said the only thing he could think of saying in that particular moment . . .

"Huh."

chapter THREE

The SUV stopped in front of the Queens, New York, house that the MacKilligan sisters had been living in for quite a while now.

Well, quite a while for them. The sisters really weren't known for living in any one place for any length of time. The fact that Max had been able to make it through junior high and high school with the rest of them so that she could stay on the basketball team was an absolute triumph and was, Mads finally realized, the work of Charlie. The eldest MacKilligan sister had determined that both her younger sisters would have some kind of normalcy in their childhoods. Impossible at the end of the day, but what she did insist on was that they had a home at least until they finished high school. For Max that was when she was eighteen and graduated with the rest of her team. For Stevie that was the same year because she'd tested out of high school and went to Oxford University for something or other involving science.

Mads truly didn't think she'd ever see Max MacKilligan again after graduation. Or any of her other high school teammates. She'd assumed Tock would head back to Israel and Mossad, since that organization had been secretly working for years to recruit her. Streep would head for Hollywood or Broadway. And Nelle would move to Europe. As for her own plans . . . it had always been the WNBA, but then her high school coach had called and offered her a chance to be on the shifter-only team for Wisconsin. It was a good offer but . . .

but . . . the WNBA had been her lifelong dream. Right? How could she not even try out?

Then, of course, her coach reminded her. In the WNBA, she could never be what she truly was. Sure, Mads could pull her badass moves on a street court in Detroit with no questions asked, but on TV? With full-human women *much* taller than she would ever be?

Mads was only five-eight!

Okay. Fine. She was five-seven-and-three-quarters. But her crazy-ass shifter legs combined with her natural basketball skills gave her moves that would have any regular ref demanding drug tests for everyone involved. She could never be who she truly was among full-humans. Not only that, but how was the WNBA supposed to recruit her? She was never going to college. Mostly because she really didn't want to, and her family would make sure that was not a good experience for her.

So she went in for the Wisconsin Butchers' training camp, unsure of what to expect. There were a number of shifters in her small town: her coach, Max's Pack, her hyena Clan, and some other shifter families. But almost always they'd met in unsafe spaces. Spaces filled with full-humans. At training camp she was with nothing but her own kind. Different species of her own kind but still . . .

Cats, dogs, and so many bears. Thankfully no hyenas, though. She'd had more than enough of them over the last eighteen years of her life. She was ready for anything else. But while she was on the floor, stretching out her legs, a basketball hit her in the back of her head. At first, she was afraid she was going to have to deal with goddamn hyenas!

That did not mean, however, that she would put up with any more shit from hyenas that were not blood relations. That would not be happening! So she'd jumped up, ready not to start shit, but definitely to finish it! Even if it got her kicked out of training camp the first day. But then she saw Max MacKilligan grinning at her . . .

"What the fuck are *you* doing here?" she'd asked, fighting the urge to hug her old teammate.

"Training camp."

"I thought you were in England with your sisters."

"Three months and Stevie suddenly attacked me with a test monkey." She grinned when Mads laughed. "That's when Charlie suggested she take care of Stevie for a while and I head back to the States for a break. But she was adamant that if I got into any trouble, she would not bail me out, which really limited my options as to what I could do. Thankfully, Coach gave me a call. Suggested training camp."

"Did Stevie actually chuck the monkey at you?"

"Who? Little Baby Goody Two-shoes who'd never, *ever* hurt another animal?"

"And to think she threw that monkey at you."

"She trained that monkey to attack me. Then pretended that she didn't."

"Maybe she didn't. Maybe the monkey just hated you. Remember when all those racoons mounted that coordinated assault?"

"That was not a coordinated assault. They all had rabies and . . . Is that Nelle?"

It *was* Nelle. Her family had temporarily moved to San Francisco in order to plan a "family holiday," which they all knew was code for a grand family heist. But as they'd been finalizing their plans, Nelle's father and his brothers had made the decision that Nelle's older sister would run point in Europe. At the time, the message was clear. At least to Nelle. They didn't think she was ready for such a big job, but they did think her slightly older sister was.

Nelle could have stormed out and returned to Wisconsin. Or gone off on her own. She had family still living in Hong Kong, provinces in China, and in Manhattan. She'd be welcome anywhere. She must have spent too much time around the rest of her teammates, though. Because instead of a dramatic storm off, she chose to punch her sister in the face—breaking her nose and jaw—and tossing her off the penthouse balcony of the Shaw Arms Hotel.

As a honey badger, her sister suffered nothing more than a

few broken bones and a temporarily crushed skull, but the family had been shocked. And impressed. Her father and uncles had immediately changed their minds and offered her the chance to go to Europe in her recovering sister's place, but Nelle had surprised them again and turned them down. She didn't want anyone's "day-old dumplings."

So she'd packed up and headed back to Wisconsin and training camp.

"Does this mean you won't get any of that money?" Max asked, always concerned about the dollars when it came to family-related heists.

"My daddy will never let me be poor," Nelle told them. "Ever." She glanced off. "My God, what would that even be like? Mads?"

"What are you asking me for?"

"Well, now you've made it awkward."

"Now *I've* made it awkward?"

"*Hey, bitches!*" Streep announced in her grand entrance, arms stretched wide. She pushed past several annoyed cats and spun around so they could all see her brand-new fringed leather jacket. A style that had not been in fashion since the Donner party set out. "What do ya think? Fancy, right?"

"Perhaps I should ask you," Nelle said to Streep.

"Ask me what?"

"Anyway," Mads cut in, "I thought you'd be headlining on Broadway by now."

"I tried. But every time I attempted to leave home, my parents would start sobbing and rending their clothes. But they couldn't even get any real tears going. I don't even have to try, and look . . ." She pointed at her face. "Just look."

And sure enough, without even changing her expression, tears began to pour out of both her eyes.

"Even without the tears, though . . ."

The tears immediately stopped and she shrugged. "I just love 'em so much. And we work together so well. Plussss . . ." She leaned in and whispered, "I get to do some other stuff I enjoy on my own. It all works out." She straightened up, stopped whispering. "And let's be honest, I am so damn talented, Hollywood will definitely wait for me."

"And humble," Mads noted.

"I am. Because that's important when you accept your many awards."

"Hey."

Tock seemed to come from nowhere, appearing right next to them like a ghost. They'd hissed at her in warning but she didn't budge. None of them startled easily but honey badgers considered other honey badgers dangerous predators, so what exactly did she expect?

"I thought you were in Tel Aviv," Max said.

"Was."

"And?" When she didn't answer right away, Max grinned. "What'cha do?"

"Nothing."

"Oh, come on," Streep pushed, scrunching her nose in an annoyingly adorable way. "You can tell us."

"Really. I didn't do anything."

"Mossad again?" Mads guessed.

Finally, Tock smirked.

"Your mom found out?"

She shook her head. "No. My father's mother."

"*Ohhhhh!*" all Tock's former teammates shouted in unison, arms raised in the air; everyone in the arena turned around to watch beings so small being so loud.

"She was not happy when she found out they'd been recruiting me. Dragged me to someone's office. Still don't know who. No name on the building or on the office door. There was a lot of yelling. At some point, she mentioned Golda Meir. I still don't know why."

"Was Golda a badger?"

"No. A She-lion, but still . . . it was weird. A couple days later . . . I was on a plane back to Wisconsin. Then I got a call from Coach. Figured it had to be better than sitting around my house watching soap operas and arguing with my mother about whether I should go to college."

Streep looked around at the other She-predators warming up. "Think we have a chance to make the team?"

"It isn't whether we can make the team," Max said, catching with one hand a basketball flung at her head.

"Ooops," a cheetah said, giving them all a fake smile. "My fault."

"No problem," Max replied, before whipping the ball back so hard that they all heard the cheetah's eye socket crack from the contact.

"*Owwwwww! You evil bitch!*"

"The question," Max had calmly continued over the cheetah's screams of pain, "is whether we can stay on the team."

"I can," Mads had told them, her teammates all turning to gaze at her. "I'm a nice person. Good teammate. Try not to fling balls into people's faces."

"She started it," Max had insisted. But she'd insisted without anger.

Max was rarely angry. The only time Mads had ever seen Max angry about anything was when it had to do with her sisters or their father.

So now, seeing Max storm past the SUV, through the front yard, up the porch steps, across the porch, and into the house, slamming the front door behind her was, to say the least, unusual.

"We should go home," Tock immediately suggested.

"Back to Wisconsin?" Streep asked.

Tock frowned. "What?"

"I don't really have a home," Mads noted.

"You can't keep living in cabinets."

"I find cabinets comfortable."

"All of you can crash at my family's place in Manhattan," Nelle offered.

"So we can all listen to you and your sister argue every fucking night?" Tock asked. "Thanks! That sounds like such fun for everyone!"

"The sarcasm wasn't necessary."

"Let's just drive into the city and get hotel rooms with the rest of the team," Streep suggested.

"It's Max's SUV," Mads reminded Streep.

"So?"

"Wouldn't it be wrong to steal it?"

Nelle patted her knee. "You're funny."

The front door of the MacKilligan house was snatched open and Max screamed from inside, *"Would you bitches get in here!"*

"You know," Streep noted, "when she screams like that . . . you can really *see* the familial resemblance between her and Charlie."

"That Danish was good, though."

Finn closed his eyes so he only heard the cracking noise as his older brother clenched his jaw.

"If one more person," Keane growled low, "mentions that fucking Danish to me one more time . . ."

"Just commenting," Shay insisted.

They stood in line, waiting to order fresh bagels. Finn always got the poppyseed. Keane the sesame. And Shay the salted. This place had been run by Orthodox Jewish bears since the thirties and although they weren't fans of the cats—what bear was?—they knew that even cats loved a good bagel. And the Malone brothers were faithful customers. They came in at least four times a week. Sometimes twice a day since they also sold, ya know . . . Danish. Although today the Malones just wanted bagels.

They reached the counter and, after the polite shifter nod different species usually exchanged, Keane ordered, "Dozen sesame, dozen salted, dozen poppyseed."

The bear growled in acknowledgment, pulled their order, and slammed the big paper bags on the counter. Keane threw the cash down and walked out, not waiting for change.

He put the bags in the backseat of the SUV with Shay, who liked to stretch out, and drove to their next stop. Once they arrived, he parked and waited for the right moment.

"Sure you want to do this?" Finn asked.

"We needed information and he gave us information. And he fucked us over. That's what we get for trusting full-humans."

"Think they know who set us up?"

"We'll find out."

"What do you think she was going to do with that cat?"

Finn and Keane exchanged glances before looking over their shoulders at Shay.

"What?" Keane asked.

"The cat."

"What cat?"

"The one that honey badger had. Do you really think that badger was going to blow up that cat?"

"I don't know," Finn answered honestly. Because he didn't. No one knew what badgers were going to do.

Keane also answered honestly, but in the worst way possible. "Who cares?"

Finn cringed. "You *have* to know that was the wrong answer."

"What do you mean, 'who cares?'" Shay snapped. "What kind of fucking question is that?"

"It was a *house* cat."

"It was a *cat*. It was one of us."

Slowly, with that glower he'd inherited from their father permanently etched onto his face, Keane snarled, "*We* are not house cats."

"We're all cats, Keane," Shay replied easily, never scared off by Keane's face. "We should be looking out for each other. Protecting each other."

"You want us to look out for house cats?"

"If not us . . . who?"

"Gee, I don't know. Any ten-year-old girl who dreams of unicorns and wants a kitten for Christmas?"

"All I'm saying is we should have taken the cat away from that badger when she offered it up. For all we know, they ate it."

"Don't be . . ." Finn stopped talking. He'd been set to

argue the point but then realized he really couldn't. "He's right. They may have eaten it."

"You know what?" Max asked after nearly an hour of glaring at the kitchen table while they all silently sat watching her glaring at the kitchen table. "I'm over this now."

"Really?" Tock muttered, glancing at Mads.

"No. Really. I did think about sneaking into their home in the middle of the night and puncturing their lungs while they slept but then I thought . . . eh."

"We're all so glad you rethought your plan," Nelle told her.

"It seemed petty."

They all nodded in agreement and made soft, approving sounds but they were probably all thinking the same thing at the moment: There was no way this was over. But at least Max was serious about not puncturing the cats' lungs. Mads was grateful for that much.

Max let out a breath. "It's been a long day."

"It's not even noon, dude," Mads laughed. "And we still have to go to practice tonight in Staten Island, and I'm going to training in the city this afternoon."

"I'll go with you." Max nodded and smiled. "A good workout is just what I need. To soothe me."

"Is that possible?"

"Shut up, Nelle."

The back door opened and a smiling Stevie practically skipped up the stairs and into the kitchen. She'd recently gotten involved with a very cute giant panda and she hadn't really stopped grinning since. Mads remembered her as a stressed-out, easily panicked nine-year-old genius who was regularly startled by squirrels and tormented by the possum population . . . seemingly on purpose. For whatever reason, those little bastards *hated* her. Mads had been sure the poor kid would be dead from a heart attack before she was thirty, but lately she'd had some real hope for Max's sister.

She'd seemed downright . . . happy? A word Mads never would have used for Stevie. Ever.

"Morning, everyone!" Stevie greeted them with a little wave. They all waved back.

"Beautiful day, isn't it?"

As Stevie passed them Max noticed that a regular, non-shifting cat was resting on her shoulder, hiding underneath Stevie's hair.

Max let out a little snarl. "Why is that cat still here?"

Tock suddenly exclaimed, "Oh, shit!" and sprinted away from the table and the room.

"Because I want him to be," Stevie snapped back at her sister. "I happen to like this cat. And Charlie tolerates it."

"That thing has attacked me a bunch of times."

"You started it!"

Tock returned and put the kitten she had in her duffel bag into Stevie's hands.

"Here. I bequeath you another cat."

"But I don't want another . . . awwwww! She's a kitten!"

Max's left eye twitched and the right side of her lip curled. Mads also saw some fang.

"I hate you," she growled at Tock.

"What was I supposed to do with it?"

"Why did you even have a kitten?" Mads wanted to know.

"I heard her cries, which of course attracted the predator in me, but then once I found her—"

"You just couldn't bring yourself to eat her?"

"You're hilarious."

Stevie stuck the kitten in her sister's face. "Isn't she adorable, Max? Look how adorable she is. She's so damn adorable!"

"Move her or she's my breakfast."

"I'm so happy to have her," Stevie said, pulling the kitten closer.

"Now you're going to have two cats?"

"This is perfect for me," Stevie informed Max.

"Why is it perfect for you?"

"I didn't tell you?"

Max rubbed her stomach and got up, looking through the cabinets for any food. "Tell me what?"

"Oh . . . I've decided to have a baby."

Max froze in the middle of opening a cabinet door.

"Now, the downside of that is I had to go off my meds, but I already have a plan for that. I think I can control my stress with diet. Anyway, the cats will be good training for me to be a mother. Because, honestly, who the fuck knows what's going to come out of me . . . right? With these fucked-up MacKilligan genes!"

With that, Stevie laughed and walked out of the kitchen with her two cats.

Not sure how long Max would remain frozen next to that cabinet, the rest of them slowly pushed away from the table and carefully made their way toward the kitchen exit. But before they could reach it, the cabinet slammed shut. That was when they all bolted, trying to make it to freedom. But Mads just wasn't fast enough.

Max grabbed the back of her T-shirt and held her. Mads held her arms out toward her teammates. Tock began to come back toward her but Streep caught her arm and yanked her toward the front of the house.

"Forget her! Just run!"

Treacherous bitches!

Mads was yanked back and shoved into a chair, with Max looming over her.

"She's having a baby?" she said directly into Mads's face. "And has gone off her meds?"

"I . . . uh . . . don't really think this is . . . uh . . . any of my . . . uh . . . business . . ."

Max leaned in closer, forcing Mads to tilt her head back as far as she could. *"Dear God, what is happening?"*

chapter FOUR

Tom O'Connell—Tommy to his friends or anyone who owed him money—came into his bar from the front and before he even turned on the lights, he knew something was wrong.

He should have walked back out, but he decided to turn the overhead lights on first. He did and let out a surprised gasp.

Having been in the bar business since he was a very young man, he'd come into more than one joint to find it fucked up. Usually by gangsters leaving a message. For instance, they hadn't been paid or they wanted to start getting paid. Or maybe some rowdy kids had found a way in and decided to get drunk and do something stupid.

Over the years, he'd seen all sorts of shit.

But this . . . this he'd never seen before.

He couldn't explain the difference, but it was definitely different.

First, it was the scent. A strong, powerful scent that sent him reeling. And it was everywhere. Then he realized that what he was smelling was urine. And that he could *see* the urine because it had been sprayed all over his wood-paneled bar. Not just on the wood floor or as high as a man could lift his penis but . . . ceiling high. *How the hell did anyone get piss up that high?*

Then there were the tables and chairs. They weren't just tossed around. Or merely broken into pieces. They were . . . stripped? Like something had slashed across each item. Again and again. Brutally. And they'd been chewed. He could see fang marks in the wood. Had dogs broken into his bar?

That didn't make sense, though. How could dogs get their piss up on the ceiling? Even a Great Dane wouldn't find that move possible.

Three of his men walked in from the back. The expressions on their faces told him that the back of his bar looked just like the front.

The four of them were staring at one another when he heard the front doors lock and he turned.

Keane Malone stood in front of the doors like a Mac truck parked sideways.

Tall with terrifyingly wide, muscular shoulders, Malone filled any room he entered without saying a word or making a move. It was assumed by anyone who saw him that the man must be on some weird combination of steroids. Something from Russia. Or Ukraine. Because Tommy had never known a man with shoulders like that. Except, of course, Malone's two younger brothers.

Tommy glanced around, expecting to see those two as well. The Malones usually traveled together. Like three mountains in some picture vista, the two younger ones always slightly behind Keane. But nope. He didn't see those two.

And Tommy had to admit that made him more concerned than if the brothers had been standing right next to Keane sporting brass knuckles.

Even worse, these Malones weren't like the other Malones he'd dealt with over the years. Those Malones were Travelers who had done some work for him and his father back in the day. They could be counted on to break some bones, crack some skulls and, when necessary, whip up some amazing soda bread for the church's Christmas bake sale.

These Malones, though . . .

The Black Malones they were called. Even by their own family. Tommy remembered their father. Thought maybe he'd married a Black woman and that's how the sons had gotten the nickname but no. The wife he'd seen at the father's funeral was

Asian or whatever. And all the Malones had black hair with streaks of red and white. Tommy figured it was some family dye job. Like a family tattoo. But these Malones didn't have the red. Just the black hair with some white. That was it. So he didn't understand the nickname . . . until they grew up and came into his bar, looking for information on their father's death. A brutal murder that the Black Malones were not going to forget or forgive.

He knew why Keane Malone was here, though.

"Malone," Tommy said by way of greeting.

"Surprised to see me?" Malone asked. "You know . . . alive?"

Actually, he was surprised. He'd heard that the kid hadn't made it. Neither had his brothers.

Tommy should have known better than to trust rumors.

Still, he shrugged and said, "I don't know what you mean."

"Really?"

"Yeah. Really."

Bobby was the first one dragged off. It happened so fast, Tommy didn't even see it happen. One second Bobby was standing there with the rest of them, the next . . . he was disappearing down the hall, screaming his head off, attempting to dig his fingers into the hardwood floors or grab onto walls or furniture, but before Tommy knew it . . .

They could hear Bobby's desperate, panicked screams coming from down the hall until he suddenly rolled back into the main bar. As if he'd been slapped into it by a big hand.

Bobby was still alive but he was covered in blood from all the lacerations riddling his body. Sobbing, Bobby began to drag himself across the floor, trying to reach the front door.

His remaining men had moved around Tommy, their weapons now drawn, but Malone didn't seem to notice or care.

Instead, he grabbed what seemed to be the only undamaged wooden chair in the whole bar and pulled it to the middle of the room. He turned it so that the back faced Bobby and his men and sat down with his big legs straddling it. The creak of the chair made Bobby wince. Fat guys who did nothing but drink beer and eat nachos while watching football games had sat in those chairs every day for years and they never creaked. How much did this kid weigh? And was all that weight from his muscle alone?

"So let's try this again, and I'll be more direct," Malone said calmly. He didn't pull out his own gun. He didn't have to. Then again, Tommy wasn't even sure if Malone was ever armed. "I got information from you that sent me and my brothers to an island where a bunch of guys tried to kill us. Can't help but think you were somehow involved in that."

He opened his mouth to reply but Malone raised one big, blunt finger. "And before you answer, you should know, I only give two chances to give me an honest response. Poor crying, crawling Bobby there was your first chance."

Look, Tommy had grown up with gangsters. He personally knew made guys. Had let them use the basement of his bar to tear out the teeth of men they felt deserved it. Although he never got actively involved in their business, he was savvy enough that he didn't have to pay too much in protection while managing not to get his face bashed in for saying too much or anything at all. So he knew how to play this game better than some juice head that still whined about his dead daddy.

But the kid wasn't alone. Somewhere in the bar his brothers lurked, which meant he had to play this smarter than usual.

"Look, kid, I get that you're upset but—"

"Wrong answer," Malone calmly cut in.

That's when Gary got snatched off his feet and yanked up into the ceiling. Screaming hysterically, Gary begged for help. Begged for Jesus himself to save him. That went on for some time until poor Gary was tossed back down, landing in a bloody heap. He was still alive, too, but one ear was gone, the fingers on his right hand had been mangled beyond anything . . . useful. His left leg appeared . . . chewed? But the worst part was the opening in his chest. Like something had just ripped across it. Tommy was sure he could actually see the rib cage.

Tommy Jr., Tommy's first born, dropped his gun, went to a corner and sat down. He pulled his legs up and covered his ears with his hands. When he began rocking back and forth and sobbing, Tommy simply blocked him out.

"Now," Malone said, his expression surprisingly neutral for once—he wasn't smiling but he wasn't glowering either, "I'm feeling pretty good today. Like in a giving spirit. So I'm going to break my rule." He lifted one big forefinger. "Just this one time."

Mads watched Max open a cabinet drawer and then proceed to study the bottle of pills she pulled out.

"Oh, my God. These are over a month old. She *has* gone off her meds." She shook her head. "This is crazy. She can't do this."

Mads knew she shouldn't say anything. She'd learned a long time ago not to get between sisters. Long before she'd ever met the MacKilligan sisters. But she found it impossible to just sit there and listen to Max lose her ever-loving mind.

"Don't you think this is a little invasive of your sister's privacy?"

"You don't know my sister."

"I've known her since she was nine. I know she can get . . . moody."

"Moody?" Max gave a harsh laugh, started to say something else, but stopped. "Look, just trust me on this. Going off her meds is not a good idea. I mean, how can she just decide to go off her meds without discussing it with me?"

"Maybe because you insist on asking her, 'Have you had your meds today?' every time she decides to cry."

"Who cries at puppy commercials?"

"Your sister! So what? Who doesn't like puppies? Even I like puppies and I hate almost everything."

"I need to talk to Charlie."

"You really don't."

"I'll be back."

She ran from the room as if she was on fire and Mads pulled out her phone. She downloaded an app that she'd heard was a shifter-run car service. For those drunken nights when fangs might make an appearance and you didn't want to freak out your driver. After ordering a car, she grabbed her training bag from behind the couch and returned to the kitchen.

While she pulled a couple of bottles of water from the refrigerator, Stevie walked in with the kitten.

"We need to get you something to eat," she told the kitten, opening the door of a cabinet that was filled with cans of cat food and big bags of high-end dog food. She grabbed a can of what appeared to be cat food but then paused. "How old do you think this kitten is?"

Mads shrugged. "I have no idea."

"She may be too young for canned food. Or he." Stevie lifted the kitten over her head and studied what Mads liked to call "the undercarriage."

Stevie nodded. "It's a he."

"Why are you whispering?"

"I actually don't know." She dismissed the issue with a hand wave and closed her eyes.

"What are you doing?" Mads asked when Stevie just stood there with her eyes closed.

"Finding what I've previously read on taking care of newborn kittens and looking at it again."

Rearing back a little, Mads asked, "What the hell does that even mean?"

Stevie held up one finger to silence her. After a few more minutes, Stevie finally opened her eyes and let out a breath. "Okay. I'm up to speed. Probably should take him to the vet, though."

"Up to speed with what?"

"How to care for a newborn kitten, which is what he is. Poor thing." She snuggled the kitten close. "Did you lose your momma? I'm so sorry. Well, I'm going to take care of you."

Max returned to the kitchen. "Where's Charlie?"

"Triplet house."

"And the panda?"

"In the backyard, eating his morning bamboo and hanging from trees," Stevie replied. "Just follow the crunching."

Max stormed out the back door.

Mads blew out a breath and, unable to help herself yet again, she said, "I wouldn't worry."

Stevie carefully placed the kitten on the kitchen table. "About what?"

"About Max's reaction to your having a baby. She'll get over it and be a wonderful aunt. I'm sure of it."

She snorted. "I'm not having a baby."

Mads blinked and took a step back. "Wait . . . what?"

Finn and his brothers got back into the SUV and Keane grabbed the bags of bagels, glancing into each one to hand out the correct bagels to Finn and Shay.

Once they each had their food, they began to eat and sip their Starbucks coffee. Shay ate his bagels with big slathers of cream cheese. Keane liked his with just thin layers of butter. But Finn just ate his plain. They didn't speak during their meal. They rarely did. Eating wasn't a time to talk; it was a time to feed.

When the bagels were finished and the brothers gazed out the windows and sipped the remainder of their coffee, Finn asked, "Think we went too far?"

"Nope."

"People are going to be pissed."

Keane glanced at him. "People?"

"Katzenhaus Securities. And those other people."

"What other people?"

"I don't know. And that group run by dogs."

"Who cares?" Shay barked from the backseat. "None of those people have ever cared about what happened to Dad. Why should we care now about anything they have to say? They're just lucky we're not leaving a trail of shredded and half-chewed bodies up and down fucking Fifth Avenue. That's what I feel like doing to the bastards we even *think* had something to do with Dad's murder."

Finn reached into the backseat and wrenched the steel thermos out of his brother's hand. "No more coffee for you before practice."

Stevie picked up the kitten again so it didn't walk off the table and said very definitively, "I am not having a baby." Then she added, "I mean, one day Shen and I plan to have a baby. When I'm in my thirties. By then I'm sure I'll have worked out something very specific and detailed with my doctors regarding my meds, and Shen and I will have our own house. Don't know if we'll be married, though. I personally think marriage is a sham forced upon us by the patriarchy. But, yeah. Marriage, no marriage . . . doesn't matter. We'll have a kid one day. Maybe two. But that's a good decade away."

"Oh." Confused, Mads scratched her head. "Then why did you tell Max . . ."

"The other day there was this ad on TV for a department store and it was about this mom who was taking her daughter to college for the first time. And it was really sweet and at the end, the girl calls her mom from her new dorm room and she says, 'I love you, Mom,' and the mom says, 'I love you, baby,' and I started to cry, and right off the bat, Max goes—"

"'Did you take your meds today?'"

"Yes!" Stevie gasped. "So I decided to fuck with her. Because she pissed me off and I'm sick of it. I manage my mental health quite well, thank you very much, and have since I was seven years old and realized I had some issues. What I *don't* need is my big sister treating me like I have ever been an out-of-control psychotic that she has to hover over. Besides . . . the question was rude."

"You're right. It was rude."

She smirked at Mads. "So are you going to rat me out now? I know how close you five are."

"I learned a long time ago not to get between sisters."

Stevie rolled her eyes. "Is this where you tell me some long, shifter-centric story about that's how you got that scar on your neck?"

Mads pointed at the scar that lashed across the left side of her throat. "This scar? No. This scar I got from my mother when she let my father know that if he ever tried to get custody of me again, she'd make sure to go deep enough to open up the jugular."

Leaning across the table, Mads gently closed Stevie's now open mouth. "Sorry, sweetie. I forget sometimes you're not used to my stories the way Max and my teammates are."

"Do you think O'Connell told us the truth?"

Keane shrugged. "If he did, then we don't really have anywhere to go, do we?"

"I was just thinking that."

"We've run out of contacts. And those we can trust."

"We never had many of those to start with."

Shay leaned forward, resting his arms on the front seats. "So now what?"

"I think I know someone who *might* be able to help. *Maybe*." Finn felt the need to stress.

"A friend?"

"No. Gambler. At least he used to be. Both you guys met him, but trust me . . . you don't remember him. He does know everybody, though, and he's got a lot of contacts."

"Why didn't you ever go to him before?" Keane wanted to know.

"Because he's annoying." Finn snarled. "And a dog."

"Sirens," Shay announced. "We better go."

Keane started the SUV and pulled away from the curb. When he reached the end of the street, he stopped at the red light and looked from Finn to Shay.

"I don't want you guys to worry. We're going to find out who killed Dad. And everyone who was involved, who had a hand in it. We're going to kill 'em all. You have my word on it."

Shay reached between the seats and patted Keane's shoulder. "You give the best pep talks, man."

Finn quickly looked out the passenger window so he wouldn't laugh in Keane's face. His brother hated that. Besides, he knew the sound of Keane's elbow slamming into Shay's face so well by now, he didn't really need to *see* it to know when it happened.

Dez MacDermot had been a cop for a long time. In fact, if you ever talked to her father, he'd say that she'd been born a cop. Still, there was a time when a murder scene like this would have confused and freaked her out. But now . . . ? Not so much.

She always examined a scene like this herself so she knew exactly what she was dealing with . . . because she could already tell it was going to be a massive issue. Especially because no one was dead.

Two men had clearly been mauled by something . . . animal. They were alive but barely and had already been taken away by ambulance.

Usually, shifters kept their shit quiet, and cleaned up after themselves. She knew this from experience. Her husband and son were lions. Two of her best friends were wolves. She'd been part of this world for years now and she knew how careful shifters were. How careful they had to be in order to protect not only themselves but those they loved. Unfortunately, it usually meant that when a full-human saw something he wasn't supposed to see, hard choices had to be made. At least that's how her husband always put it. If possible, the shifters just acted as if the full-human was simply insane or had been drunk or high when they saw whatever they saw. If that didn't work or if they tried to move some video, then things got very difficult.

Thankfully, shifters were positioned everywhere protecting their own. It was something they all had to do in order to ensure that none of them ended up test subjects for government agencies looking for the next super soldier.

That's how Dez had gotten her job. She'd started off just being a cop. An everyday, run-of-the-mill cop. Now here she was . . . staring at an ear on the floor, busy trying to figure out which species had ripped it off a man's head.

My, how things had changed.

She tore her gaze away from that mangled ear and took another look around the bar until it rested on the bar owner, Tommy O'Connell. Dez had known O'Connell a long time.

Dez stepped closer to him as the EMTs tied his screaming son to a gurney; he didn't even bother to look up. "So you're sure you didn't see anything?" she asked. "Absolutely nothing at all?"

O'Connell, who'd inherited this bar from his old man and had been working in it from the early seventies when the Manhattan streets were beyond tough and terrifying, stared blindly across the room and muttered, "I didn't see anything. I got here and . . . it was like this. My guys all fucked up. The bar looking like this. And my guys . . . they won't remember nothin' either. I can promise you that."

Yep. O'Connell was lying. It wasn't just the way he kept repeating that same little speech over and over that gave away his lie either. It was the way his bar had been torn up. She'd seen a lot of destroyed bars in her time. She'd also seen quite a few places destroyed by big guys who shifted into wild animals. This had that wild-animal flavor. Plus, her entire team—made up of varying types of shifters—had done nothing since they'd walked through the door but sniff the air like they were locking on a herd of water buffalo.

Dez, however, didn't have to sniff the air to know this could get messy. They'd sent away the full-human cops who'd arrived first at the crime scene. That had already caused a conflict she would be hearing about later.

"Tigers."

She glanced up at her close friend and former partner, Lou Crushek, who now reported directly to her in their mostly shifter-only precinct. "What?"

"Tigers."

"What about them?"

"They peed everywhere."

"Ewww. What is wrong with you people? You're fucking up the crime scene."

"Not *our* tigers. Other tigers."

Dez scrunched up her face. She couldn't help it. "Why? Why would anyone do that?"

Crushek, a polar bear, shrugged massive shoulders. "Honestly? That's what tigers do when they're really mad." He pointed toward the deep recesses of the building. "There's a load of shit in the back rooms."

She let out a long, painful sigh. "Just lock it all down. Only our people, in or out."

Crushek smirked. "Sometimes you hate this job . . . don't you?"

"You have *no* idea."

chapter FIVE

Mads walked into the Sports Center with her duffel bag and her training plans. She'd be meeting the rest of her team later that evening on Staten Island for practice. This was training just for her. To be the best, one couldn't just show up for the games. Well . . . you could if you were Max. But Mads wasn't a MacKilligan. She didn't have the luck of the Scottish. Or was it Irish? It didn't matter. Whatever it was, she didn't have it.

She took the secret stairs down to the main floor of the shifter-only part of the Sports Center. This set of stairs was monitored by fellow shifters to ensure that full-humans didn't accidentally wander down to locations they shouldn't be in. It wasn't as if they'd necessarily see jaguars romping around with sloth bears right off the bat. It was rarely that obvious. But they would notice some differences right away. Like entire families that stood over seven feet tall chatting with a couple of short, white-haired "friends" who might or might not be picking pockets when the opportunity presented itself. Or maybe they'd notice how fast some of the children could run. Or how high some of the other children could climb when startled. Or how easy it was to get packs of children to howl.

Yeah, it was best to just keep the full-humans away from the many floors that were off-limits to them.

Mads's first plan was to hit the treadmill in the gym. After that, some weight training and then some court time, and then maybe—

She hit the wall and quickly backed up, realizing she hadn't been paying attention again. But when she took several steps back, she noted that she hadn't really walked into a wall.

"Oh. It's you."

The tiger glared down at her.

"Sorry."

"Yeah. Sorry."

They nodded at each other and Mads stepped to the left to go around him. But he also stepped to the left. So Mads stepped to the right, which he also did. She stepped to the left again. But so did he.

She stopped and let out a frustrated breath. Like her, he was carrying a duffel bag but his had a team logo and the team's bright colors. He also hand-carried his helmet and shoulder pads. They were so large, she doubted it would be easy to find a bag large enough for them.

They nodded at each other again and this time Mads took a step to the right. But so did the cat.

Fed up, she finally snapped, "What the fuck are you doing?"

"I was going to ask you the same thing."

Annoyed that he seemed to think it was somehow her fault they were waltzing near the food court, Mads pulled one of her classic court moves. A move she could only do in a shifter league. She leaped onto the cat's chest and climbed up and over him, then continued on her way.

"Did you seriously just do that?" she heard him call out after her.

Grinning, she didn't even bother to turn around. Because, yeah. She'd really just done that.

Finn stood in the middle of the main floor, stunned, realizing that a honey badger had just used him as some kind of ladder. Or bridge.

He hadn't really expected to see any of the badgers that had come to the house that morning. Especially the one so comfortable sleeping in his cabinets. He definitely hadn't expected her to climb over him. Who did that?

"What's wrong with your face?" Keane asked as he walked up to him. He also carried his football gear.

"What?"

"Your face."

"What about it?"

Keane pointed at it. "It looks weird."

Finn jabbed his thumb over his shoulder, about to explain how annoyed he was, when a Black woman on roller skates skidded to a stop and announced, "He's smiling!"

"What?" both Keane and Finn snapped at her.

Seemingly unbothered by their tone, she threw her arms in the air and insisted, "You're smiling! You're happy! Everyone should be so happy!"

With that disturbing performance, she skated away.

"What was that?" Finn asked his brother.

"Some freakish hybrid. Just ignore it." Keane motioned to the elevators. "Let's get to practice."

Charlie MacKilligan expected a few things in life. She expected her father to make her very existence a nightmare. She expected Stevie to screech like a murder victim when squirrels came too close. She expected Max to have access to stolen cars and grenade launchers at any given moment. And being in love with one of triplets meant having three bears around her at all times. Thankfully, she liked all three, but still . . . That was a lot of bear to deal with on any given day.

Anyway, those were things Charlie expected. So when those things happened or she had to deal with those things—like walking out of the shower wearing only a towel to find her mate, Berg, sitting on his bed with his brother and sister, Dag and Britta—she wasn't surprised. What did surprise her was a ranting Max. Because Max didn't rant. She caused others to rant, but Max didn't rant unless she was trying to distract someone from something going on behind them.

It started as soon as they all got into the SUV. It was Charlie, Max, Stevie, Shen, Berg, and a new kitten. Charlie had barely pulled away from the curb when Max suddenly announced, "Those dirty Malones rejected my Danish."

Charlie hit the brakes and asked, "What does *that* mean?"

"I made them a kind gesture, to show them I appreciated what they did for us, and they threw it back in my face!"

"What did they do?"

Max looked at her, stared a moment, before replying, "Nothin'."

"You see, Max, when you start lying to me—"

"Stevie's planning on having a baby," she quickly announced, "and she's gone off her medication."

Charlie watched Max and quickly came to the conclusion her sister was attempting to distract her, but she wasn't lying.

"Well," Max pushed when Charlie only stared at her, "aren't you going to say anything?"

"Okay. Don't get the baby its first knife until it's at least thirteen. There. I said something."

"And that's it?" Max leaned over and said in a very loud whisper, "You're not concerned? Even a little? I mean, just look at her!"

Charlie did. Her baby sister was in the backseat between a giant panda and a grizzly bear. She held a red-and-white kitten so small that she'd used a hand towel to wrap him in, but she could have gotten away with a wash cloth. Stevie was so busy cooing over that cat, she wasn't even paying attention to Max. When she noticed that Charlie was looking at her, she held up the tiny thing for her sister to see and cheered in a squeaky voice, "Kitten!"

Turning back around, Charlie shook her head. "She looks fine."

"Really? Because she just went off her meds. Without any warning!"

Without any warning? Stevie? No way. No way! Stevie could be unpredictable when it came to her work or dealing with nature. But she was never unpredictable when it came to her mental health. She never just "went off her meds." And she

definitely never, ever made unplanned decisions. Charlie remembered when Stevie was eleven and set up a schedule for
therapy three times a week. She put all her appointments on a
massive calendar that she put in the Pack kitchen for all to see.
So that everyone knew when she had to be at her appointments. She had no shame and she kept everyone informed.
Why would that suddenly change?

It wouldn't. Charlie knew that as sure as she was sitting
here. Her baby sister wouldn't change. She feared going to one
of those mental hospitals they'd seen in horror movies when
they were kids. The ones people were forced into against their
will. If she was going to a mental hospital, she wanted to have
complete control over the situation. So, nope. Stevie hadn't
changed. So then where did Max get the idea that . . .

"Kitten!" Stevie said, holding up the cat again.

"And what do you have to say for yourself?" Max demanded of Shen. "Now that you can't drown me out with
your damn bamboo chewing."

Shen looked Max right in the eyes and replied, "I'm just a
male. I want lots of babies. I just want my seed pouring out of
me like I'm a Gatling gun." Then, to get his point across, Shen
made machine-gun sounds with his mouth.

Charlie focused on the street ahead and began driving
again.

"I just can't believe you guys," Max argued. "It's like you
have all lost your minds!"

"That or you don't want to tell me what happened last
night so you're distracting me with Stevie."

Max dismissed Charlie's words by waving her hand in front
of Charlie's face. Normally not an issue except Charlie was
driving.

"You know," Berg noted from the backseat, "my sister
would say that no one has the right to dictate what any grown
woman can do with her body."

"No one is talking to you, Yogi!"

"Okay. But if you bring this up in front of Britta, you're

gonna get a lecture. And remember the last time you tried to walk out on one of her lectures? She just held you in place with her foot."

"I suggest we all not talk until we reach the Sports Center," Charlie told them, reaching for the radio.

"I thought we were going to the vet for that stupid cat."

"The Sports Center has a new vet office in it. Bears love having pet dogs for some reason."

"Dogs help keep invaders away from our beehives," Berg said. "Don't they, Max?"

Without even turning around, Max warned, "I know you're not talking to me."

"Me? Accusing a honey badger of stealing honey from a *beehive*? Why that's crazy talk."

Finn threw the black bear to the ground.

"What was that for?" the bear demanded, getting back to his big feet. "All I asked was—"

Finn again threw the bear to the ground.

"Hey! Cut that out! I can't believe you're acting like this." Once more the bear got up. "All I wanted to know was why—"

Finn threw the black bear to the ground.

"*Stop doing that!*"

"Malone!"

Around the practice field, three heads turned to stare at the defensive line coach but she waved her tablet and changed her bark to, "E.R., come here."

Finn jogged over to Big Julie Farnell. A She-lion from an enormous swamp-cat pride from the West Coast. Julie had taken a job with the team a few years back, leaving her pride behind, and even bringing her cubs with her. A bold move for a lioness and one not really appreciated by her mother and sisters, but Julie was a bold female in many ways. Full-humans had given her the name Big Julie when she joined peewee football as a kid. The parents hated her because she made their sons look bad but they couldn't hate the way she stomped on the other team. She'd continued to play until junior high. She'd been ready to fight it out in court so she could play high school football but some players from the other team decided to "teach" the girl a lesson about playing in a man's sport. They brutally battered her all through a game, using their biggest and meanest guys, with the full approval of the coaching staff.

Julie put up with all of it until one of the guys made the mistake of tackling her after she'd sacked their quarterback. And then he wouldn't let her go. He thought it was funny. Julie didn't. And she proved that point by shoving him off, grabbing his arm, and twisting it until it shattered at the shoulder joint. While he was screaming, one of his teammates tried to yank her off while calling her an "evil cunt." Julie didn't like that either, so she yanked the player's helmet off and beat the hell out of him with it. Mostly around his face and head. Refs tried to step in but that didn't work out for them either and both teams jumped in, fighting each other. It was, in short, a bloodbath when all was said and done. The two boys were in and out of hospitals for months, their future football careers over forever. The parents wanted to file criminal charges but two things backed them off that decision. First, the bruises Julie had all over her body within hours of the game, which the coaching staff had made sure to photograph for posterity. And, of course, Julie's mother and aunts and her father and his brothers. The entire lion pride had walked into the principal's office that Monday and the rage of the full-human fathers, who had such big football dreams for their sons, seemed to wilt in the face of the lion males who stood over them . . . breathing.

That's all it was, just breathing. But when that breathing blew your hair back, and gold eyes bored into your skull like twin suns . . . maybe involving the cops was not such a great idea.

In the end, Julie was transferred to a private school and she started playing for a teen shifter team filled with males and females of all species who knew better than to call a She-lion an "evil cunt." After college, she was drafted to a pro team, where she played for fifteen years until a bad car accident crushed her leg and arm. The accident should have killed her—her sports

car had been decimated by a bus with badly repaired brakes—
but she recuperated just fine in a shifter hospital except for her
elbow. It never healed properly and the only way to fix it was
with a metal joint. A minor surgery for an average shifter but a
major one for a pro player. The prosthetic would give her an
edge over her opponents, making Julie's arm stronger than any
top quarterback's. So she had to choose between the surgery
and her pro career. It wasn't an easy decision but the pain radi-
ating from her elbow to her shoulder made tackling guys twice
her size the last thing she wanted to do despite her very high
tolerance for pain. She'd been tossed around by enough Cape
buffaloes on family vacations to know what real pain was, and
being hit by a couple of grizzlies trying to keep her away from
their quarterback was not it. Which meant if she couldn't suck
up the pain of an elbow injury, it was serious and would only
get worse.

While the surgery had killed one career, it had given her
another. Defensive line coach for the New York Crushers.
She'd been with the team less than a year, but the Malones—so
far—hadn't minded her. And to be honest . . . they minded almost everybody. Especially the last defensive line coach.

Unlike everyone else, Julie used an abbreviation of Finn's
team nickname when calling him. E.R. stood for "Eternal
Rest." A nickname that was well deserved, but that didn't
mean he enjoyed it. Made him feel like a funeral home. And
why nicknames were necessary at all, he didn't know. Weren't
they mostly for the fans?

"You can just call me Finn," he reminded her.

"I'll just call you Malone Three."

Finn let out a long sigh. "Or that."

She gestured in the black bear's direction. "Why are you
throwing Franklin around like a chew toy?"

He shrugged. "No reason."

Franklin stood beside them now. "All I did was ask him—"

Before Finn could even raise his hands, the black bear was
flying forward thirty feet or so as Keane came up behind him.

It was true, what they said . . . tigers really did enjoy attacking a man from behind.

"I know I keep asking this of you both, but I'm going to try again . . . please do not beat up your own teammates."

"What if they deserve it?"

She let out a long breath. "This is why we call your kind alley cats."

"Racist."

Julie let out another breath.

She began to walk away but stopped. "Who is that? He's waving at you."

Finn turned and saw the canine he'd called, hoping he might get some information that could help him and his brothers.

"No outsiders during practice, Malone. You know that. If Coach Bradley sees him . . ."

"I just need to talk to him for five—"

A football slammed into the dog's unsuspecting head, dropping him where he stood.

Finn closed his eyes, but he heard Julie clearly suggest, "Why don't you and your brothers grab your friend there and carry him to my office and we'll all try to convince him not to sue the entire team into oblivion. Okay? Great!"

Julie watched the second oldest Malone brother for nearly a minute before asking, "Could one of you get him down, please?"

Keane Malone slammed his fist on her desk and roared, "*Shay!*"

The sound startled the big cat and Shay fell off the bookshelf he'd been climbing so he landed on his back, leaving a healthy dent in her concrete floor.

She rolled her eyes. She'd always thought dealing with lion males was a lot of work. All the hair conditioner the females needed to provide and feeding them first, even ahead of the kids. It was all so much work. But give her that any day over these cranky tigers. It wasn't just the Black Malones either.

They might be the *crankiest* tigers she'd ever met, but all tigers were grumpy and rude. They just wanted to be left alone to eat and sleep and argue with anyone that happened to walk by.

"How's he doing?" Julie asked Finn, who was hovering over his canine friend.

"He could be dead."

"He's not dead. He's unconscious. Just gently—"

The alley cat reached his arm back and slapped the poor dog as hard as humanly possible.

"Don't hit him!"

"But he's awake now."

He was. The canine woke up swinging and snarling, scrambling backward and looking for who had just struck him.

"Calm him down," Julie ordered. "Calm him down before he starts barking. See, he's barking. That's going to bring Coach Bradley right in here. You know polar bears are attracted to barking because of seals."

"It's okay, Stein," Finn told the dog. "It's okay. Calm down."

"Why am I here again?" Keane asked.

"Because you and your brother were beating up the bears—"

"That wouldn't be possible if you had more bears from Alaska. These tiny Yellowstone bears are holding us back."

"I can't have this bear discussion with you again, Keane."

"What about Russian bears? If they can play stupid hockey, we can teach them to play football."

"Is your brother dead?" she asked about Shay.

"No. Wait." He looked at where his brother had fallen, stared a moment, then finally refocused on her. "No."

"How are we doing, Finn?"

Finn held up a finger and said to his friend, "What do you mean you can't help me?"

"I haven't gambled in years. Thanks to rehab and my cousin's constant threats."

"I thought you had contacts."

His friend finally stood. He was tall. Extremely good looking. A wolf. "What kind of contacts?"

"People who could get me information. You know . . ."
Finn gestured with his hand. "Information information."

"I have no idea what that means."

"Stuff no one else has. About underground shit."

"What makes you think *I* have that kind of contacts?"

"You're a Van Holtz."

"A Van Holtz with a gambling problem. I just made sous
chef for the lunch shift. That is not a show of confidence from
my family. I got miles to go before my cousins and uncles trust
me with anything really important. Although . . ."

Julie watched the canine glance off, staring at her bookshelf.

"What's he doing?" she asked Finn.

"He's thinking."

"Is that what that is? How do they function during the day?
You know, without assistance?"

"I can hear you!" the wolf suddenly barked, glaring at
them. "I'm standing right here!"

"Maybe he can get a dog," Julie suggested, "to assist him.
I've heard border collies are very intelligent."

"Do you want my help or not?"

"I thought you couldn't help," Finn reminded the wolf.

"I can't, but I have a suggestion."

"What suggestion?"

"Your sister."

Julie didn't know too much about the Malones' personal
life. She'd heard things during her time with the team. About
their father's murder. About how the rest of the Malone family
had been no help, putting the three eldest brothers on the outs
with the entire Traveling clan. And about how the brothers had
made it their mission in life to get revenge on those who'd
done the deed.

She'd also heard that any time their baby sister came in to
watch a practice or to stop by and bring the brothers lunch or
just to visit, the other players were very polite. They also never

made eye contact with the kid. The first time Julie saw this behavior, she assumed that maybe they were just uncomfortable
being around a shifter who was deaf. There weren't a lot of
them, but she'd heard there were a few. But she kept seeing the
same reaction each time the pretty shifter came to practice,
which wasn't very often. Still, often enough that the players
should have gotten used to her presence.

Then there was that day . . . the day a rookie smiled at her.
It was a rather innocent smile. Not a leer. Julie knew a leer. So
she hadn't thought much about it. Until the team practiced a
new play. It was just a run-through. Just a quick way to show
each player the moves without anyone actually doing the full
running or tackling. The rookie was a running back. All he
had to do was catch the ball from the quarterback. The offense
would protect him. The defense would go for him, but not
really.

Because it was just a run-through.

Julie remembered watching in horror as the Malone brothers, two on defense, one on offense, mowed down the entire
offensive line and took out that poor rookie just as he caught
the ball. He even had a smile on his face. No idea that he was
about to be taken down by three giant tigers, pissed off that
he'd smiled at their baby sister. Sure, she'd been sixteen at the
time, but it wasn't like he was forty. The poor kid wasn't even
twenty-one and, again, it was a pretty innocent smile. It wasn't
like he'd tried to hump her right on the field! Julie was sure a
simple "Stay away from our sister or we'll kill you," would
have gotten the message across to the young cheetah just as ef-
fectively as turning him into a twisted pretzel did.

When the kid asked to be traded to another team, in another state, across country, the head coach didn't even argue.
How could he?

So the dog's even mentioning the Malones' baby sister
seemed reckless.

Julie cringed when Keane's big fist again slammed on her
desk, and she wondered how much longer the old metal could
last. It wasn't like the team had gotten her a new desk when

she'd taken this job. It had probably been here ever since the team's founding in the seventies.

"*Did you just bring up my baby sister?*" Keane roared.

Surprisingly, the wolf didn't make a run for it. He just rolled his eyes and put his hands in front of him, palms up, and said, "Don't get hysterical. I swear, you cats always get so hysterical."

"Tigers don't get hysterical," Shay warned from the floor he was still lying on. Julie had forgotten he was down there. "We just rip your skin off and eat you whole."

Julie looked at Finn and nodded. "Subtle," she told him.

Wolves were stupid! Even Van Holtzes were stupid!

Because what else would possess Stein Van Holtz to bring Nat into this conversation other than extreme stupidity?

"If ya let me finish . . ."

"We can kill you then?" Shay asked from the floor.

"Prefer you didn't, but thanks for the offer. Instead, I was going to suggest that you talk to her sisters."

"She doesn't have sisters," Finn reminded the wolf.

Stein rubbed his forehead. "Oh, my God. Seriously? Are you guys still doing this shit? Everybody knows she's a MacKilligan."

Keane got up so fast, his metal chair flew backward. All Finn could do was get between the dumb dog and his brother. Even Julie jumped back from her desk, fangs out, a warning growl rolling from her throat. Only Shay didn't bother to move. Why should he, though? Stein was a decent size for a wolf, but nothing Keane couldn't kill on his own.

"She is *not* a MacKilligan!" Keane growled, his voice like crushed gravel. "She's a Malone."

"Whatever gets you through the day, dude," the wolf said with a dismissive wave, forcing Finn to slam his hands against his brother's chest and push him back.

"Are you going to help?" Finn asked Shay.

"Nope."

"Okay, let me put it to you this way so we can get through

this conversation," Stein went on. "Let's pretend the MacKilligans are delusional, and they just *think* your sister is also *their* sister. You can use that."

"Use it how?" Shay asked, his hands behind his head. "To steal us a Porsche?"

"If you want. Or to get you information."

Keane stopped trying to rip Stein's head off and, instead, they all gazed at the wolf.

"What are you talking about?"

"I won't say that honey badgers know everybody. Because they don't. What they do have are connections to almost every badger family worldwide. And by knowing someone in every badger family, they know everyone. It's weird and very honey badger, but it works for them."

Feeling his brother relax beneath his hands, Finn released Keane and turned to face Van Holtz.

"Meaning," the wolf went on, "that if there's one species that can get you information—that can help you solve the murder of your father—it's the honey badger."

Mads wiped the sweat from her face with a dry white towel and grabbed the cold water bottle one of the assistant coaches handed to her. She knew she should sip, but she wasn't really a "sipper." She happily gulped down the cool water until the one-liter bottle was finished and again wiped the fresh bout of sweat from her face.

She was about to take another ball and start a new round of three-point shots when she noticed the four people standing at the entrance of the practice court.

The team practiced on Staten Island so they wouldn't be seen by the opposition, but she practiced by herself at the Sports Center in Manhattan. It had amazing facilities and, even though they were New Yorkers, the people there were surprisingly nice.

Still, these four people stood out from the crowd.

The assistant coach leaned in and said low, "I don't know

who they are or how they got down here without being grabbed by security, but they're full-human and freaky."

Mads handed the basketball over to the assistant, horribly embarrassed.

"Don't worry," she said on a long sigh. "I know who they are."

"Should I call a cleanup crew?"

"No, no. They're fine." Idiots, but fine.

"They're wearing wolf and bear fur . . . in the summer . . . that's just rude on so many levels."

Mads patted the female's shoulder. "I've got this, Tammy."

Slowly, Mads walked over to the four silent people waiting for her.

When she was right in front of them, the four bowed their heads but Mads didn't return the gesture because it was stupid. Maybe if it was the year 910, it would be okay, but it wasn't.

It wasn't!

"What is it?" Mads demanded.

It was the shamaness who spoke. It was always the shamaness who spoke. Of course, she was also the one with a dragon tattoo that went from her left eye, down her cheek to her chin, which gave a gal a certain sense of rank among the fruitcakes the shamaness hung around every day.

"Your great-grandmother—" The shamaness began before lowering her eyes, as did the other three acolytes with her.

"If she has a message for me," Mads said, already running out of patience, "she could have just . . . ya know . . . *called* me. I sent her that cell phone with the big buttons. Didn't she get it?"

"Yes. She received it."

"I made sure it could withstand her throwing it against the wall repeatedly."

"Yes."

"So why didn't she just call? Because she's torturing me?"

Or simply because her great-grandmother always made things hard. And weird. Always so weird.

"That wasn't possible, I'm afraid," the shamaness told her. "Your great-grandmother has entered the gates of Valhalla."

Mads frowned at the statement. "She what?" When the four messengers only gazed at her, Mads blinked and asked, "Wait. Wait. She's dead? Solveig Galendotter is dead?"

"I'm sorry, but yes."

"In battle?"

"No."

"Store robbery?"

"Um—"

"Did the cops shoot her? The Marines? Another blood feud? The old man down the street who said he'd see her dead one day? That militia? They were really gunning for her."

"Ummm. No. She'd already taken care of the militia. The old man died in his sleep months ago. She'd come to a reasonable agreement with the cops and the Marines. And she was managing the blood feuds."

"Then what?"

"It seemed she just died. In her store. Heart attack, apparently."

Mads shook her head. "No way. We're not talking about some everyday . . . This is Solveig Galendotter. She was never *just* going to die. Not now, not ever."

When the shamaness did no more than shrug, Mads blew out a breath, nodded, and worked hard to keep control of her emotions. Her great-grandmother would expect no less from her. Gallendotters didn't get "weepy."

"When did this happen? I'll need to start making calls to—"

"Three weeks ago."

Mads snarled a little. "She died three weeks ago, and you're just telling me now?"

"We just found out now."

A chill went down Mads's back. "How is that possible? Her store—"

"There was always an excuse for why it was closed. Always a reason. We didn't realize anything was wrong until they had already cremated her and placed her ashes in an urn."

"An urn? Solveig is in an urn?"

"And that urn is in Wisconsin."

Mads gasped and stepped back as if she'd been struck. "Dear gods," she whispered. "Not Wisconsin."

Mick had just gotten this job a few months back. He was fresh out of the military and was ready to get to work in the civilian sector. His older brother had hooked him up, which was surprising. Danny had not been in the military. He'd been the smart one. Had done the college track. Had graduated and everything. No one in the family had really seen him much after that. Their mother got the occasional call or email but that was about it. Mick had found out later that boring, always reading in his room, determined to go to the college farthest away from his family, never had time to hunt down a blue sheep Danny had been recruited by the CIA out of college. The siblings had met face-to-face somewhere in the Middle East during an operation they could never speak of to anyone.

Even stranger, both the CIA team Danny was part of and the Navy SEAL team Mick was leading were all shifters. Every last one of them. That meeting had happened four years ago and Mick hadn't seen his brother since, not until he'd decided against re-upping in the military, when suddenly his phone rang.

"Need work?" his brother had asked.

Of course he did. He got bonuses from the government but not anything that would have him living in the lap of luxury until his death of old age.

"The Thursday after you get back to Ma's house, come to this location at two o'clock," Danny had said, spitting out some address in the city, not waiting for Mick to write it down. Must have assumed he'd remember it. "Dress in black jeans, black shirt, and black jacket. That way Ma won't ask any questions but it won't look like you just rolled out of bed either."

Out of habit more than anything, Mick had followed orders. He'd met his brother outside a nice-looking brownstone, but once inside he'd quickly realized what he was about to become a part of: The Group. Unlike Katzenhaus or the Bear Preservation Council, the associations of the Group didn't just "protect their own kind."

Instead, the Group was a nationwide organization that worked with multiple species and breeds of shifters to keep their kind safe. A surprisingly tough job. Like human villages that moved too close to lion territory, the proximity of shifters and full-humans led to all sorts of problems. The Group stepped in before things spun out of control. And if it wasn't battles between shifters and full-humans, it was battles between shifters and shifters. There were far more "wars" that went on between prides and packs and clans than Mick had realized. His species didn't usually worry about that sort of thing. They were all about the hunt and relaxing after a long day of mountain climbing. Who had time for all these blood feuds?

"Hey, y'all."

Mick closed his eyes and fought his urge to leap away from the voice coming from right behind him.

At first, he thought maybe his reaction was PTSD. He'd been through a lot during his time in the military. So being a little jumpy was normal. Some guys got a therapy dog to watch their back for them and help them feel calmer when they were away from home. Then Mick realized that he only got this jumpy when *she* was around. He'd worked with Dee-Ann Smith just a couple of times so far, but there was something about this She-wolf that put him off. He couldn't figure out what it was about her, but he was doing his best to give her the benefit of the doubt. She was a former Marine and their military connection should have put him at ease. But something about her just set his teeth on edge.

"Find anything?" she asked around an apple she was biting with her fangs.

"Yeah," Danny replied, gesturing to the tree line. "There is tiger piss . . . everywhere."

"And I smell honey badger," Mick added. "And blood. Full-human blood."

"Yup. That's what everyone else has been saying, too." She

pushed back her Tennessee Titans baseball cap and looked around the small island not far from New York. Mick didn't even know little islands like this existed near his city. Islands with mansions on them. Rich people got everything! He'd grown up on Staten Island in a four-bedroom walk-up with his parents, his brother, and five bitchy sisters. Forget the cousins who moved in and out when they had nowhere else to go. Maybe he wouldn't have felt the overwhelming desire to make a run for it and join the Marines if he'd grown up in a big mansion like the ones on this island.

"Something very bad happened here. Hell if I know what it was, though." She patted Mick on the shoulder, and it took everything in him not to slap her hand away.

Smith tossed the apple core and sauntered off to talk to some other team members, hiking up her too-loose jeans with apple-juice–covered hands as she moved, and he fought the urge to hiss and attack her from behind, grasping the back of her, dragging her off to a quiet spot, pinning her to the ground, and squeezing her neck until she stopped moving.

He couldn't help it. He was a snow leopard. It's what he did when he was hungry or when he just didn't trust someone.

"You're glaring," his brother warned him.

"What is it about her?" Mick asked. "She's always so nice to me, but . . ."

"Careful, she's the boss's wife."

"What boss?"

"Our boss."

That's what he'd thought his brother had meant, but their boss ought to be able to do better than . . . *her*. Their boss was one of the Van Holtz Pack, a very wealthy, very powerful Pack out of Seattle and Germany. Their bloodline went back centuries, and it was said they'd started the Group with their own money. Not only that, but the man looked like he'd stepped off the pages of GQ magazine. Mick had gone to lunch with him, and women literally swooned around him. Women the man had ignored. Mick had thought maybe his boss simply didn't swing toward females or had his own super-

model at home, but . . . *she* was what he had at home? A rangy
She-wolf who dressed like she was about to go to a Lynyrd
Skynyrd concert in the seventies on the back of some dude's
motorcycle and said "y'all" a lot?

Mick, for as long as he lived, would never understand the
canine mind.

Shaking off what was essentially none of his business, he
turned to his brother.

"So what happens now?"

Danny jerked his head to the north and Mick watched a
chopper land and a dark-haired woman get off. She kept her
body hunched over to avoid the chopper blades, so it wasn't
until she straightened up that Mick recognized her.

"Oh . . . no. What is *she* doing here?"

"There's tiger piss all over the place. What do you think
she's doing here?"

"So? There's tigers all over the five boroughs. Who says it's
one of theirs?"

"Yeah. Sure. There's tigers everywhere. But when it comes
to true shit-startin' . . ." Danny shrugged. "We both know, little brother . . . it's *always* a Malone."

"Why didn't you just eat the pastry?" Stein demanded, and
Julie had to agree. Who wouldn't just say "thank you" and eat
the goddamn pastries while gently leading the annoying honey
badgers out the door? Oh. That's right. Tigers! That's who.
The angriest cats in the land! They made paranoid, rabid alley
cats seem calm and rational.

By now Shay was off Julie's floor and he, along with Finn,
turned to look at Keane.

The bigger, older—and meaner—brother didn't even glance
at them in return, but a growl came from the back of his throat,
vibrating across the room even though he never even opened
his mouth.

"This is bad," Stein said, pacing now. "This is very bad."

With his big arms crossed over his chest like he ruled the
whole world and had complete control of this situation, Keane

cleared his throat and asked, "Can't we just pay them for the information?"

"The same badgers you insulted?" He glanced at Keane from the corner of one eye before rolling both. "You tigers aren't the only ones that can hold a grudge, ya know."

"There are other badgers, right?"

Stein faced the three brothers. "And you can't afford any of them!" He briefly closed his eyes and took a calming breath. "Badgers have an intricate communications system dating back to ancient civilization."

"Is this where you tell us that Julius Caesar was a honey badger?" Shay asked, already sounding bored.

"Julius Caesar was not a honey badger," Stein corrected, clearly annoyed. "Locusta was."

Finn blinked. "Who?"

"Locusta. Poisoner of Ancient Rome. She worked for Nero. Took out Britannicus, heir to the Roman Empire." Julie, who'd been working on some papers, noticed the quiet and glanced up to see the males gazing at her in surprise. She shrugged. "Not surprisingly, there were a lot of lions in Ancient Rome and, when they weren't eating Christians, they used a lot of poisoners. It was a thing."

"Lions," Keane sniffed. "Bunch of snobs."

"Why is my great-grandmother in Wisconsin?" Mads demanded.

"Your mother's family took over everything before we even had a chance—"

Mads tugged at one of her braids and walked away from the shamaness and her acolytes. Then she immediately walked back.

"You let this happen," she accused. "You let those idiots take her body and do exactly what she did not want. Now her soul is trapped in a goddamn urn. In *Wisconsin*."

"We had no rights to Solveig's remains once your grandmother and mother stepped in. Perhaps if you had been more involved in her life—"

Mads pointed a finger, not realizing her claws had come out. She was pointing a lethal claw at a powerful shamaness and she didn't even care, she was so pissed. "Don't. *Even.*"

The shamaness lowered her eyes and raised her hands in supplication.

"Forgive me. I am merely here to tell you what has happened as she had requested. Nothing more."

"Well, you've done your job. Now fuck off."

"Perhaps if we talked to your mother and grand—"

"If you go to Wisconsin, my family will eat you."

"But—"

"Unlike my great-grandmother, their loyalty is not to our Viking blood, so they will show you no respect. They are hyena through and through, always hungry and able to chew and digest *bone.*" Mads stared straight into the shamaness's eyes. "Understand what I'm saying to you?"

"Very clearly."

"Then go. I'm getting tense."

With another annoying head-bow, the four full-humans walked out of the practice court.

Mads couldn't believe her great-grandmother was dead. Solveig Galendotter? Not alive? Sure, she'd been at least one hundred and five years old, but that was nothing. Solveig's own mother had lived until she was one hundred and twenty, and she'd only died because she'd been killed by a blood enemy in battle.

Gallendotter females were long lived not because they were shifters or even because they were Viking . . . but simply because they were too mean to die.

Living was their revenge on all who hated them. And there were many who hated them.

Mads planned to live as long as possible simply to irritate her mother and grandmother. It wasn't a lofty goal but it was better than nothing.

Turning away from the double doors, Mads faced the assistant coach she'd been working with. As soon as she saw the sad expression on the cat's face, she threw up her hands.

"Don't," she ordered, returning to grab the basketball from the female's hands.

"But—"

"No."

"I just want to—"

"No."

"Just let me—"

"No, Tammy. We're not doing this. We're not having the conversation you want to have. So let it go."

"Should I call someone for you?"

"To do what? Raise my great-grandmother from the dead?"

"Uhhhh . . . ?"

"Exactly. So just let it go."

Mads dribbled the ball to the free-throw line and took a couple of shots. When she was about to take a third, she stopped and glanced over her shoulder. Now three of the assistant coaches stood there watching her. They were all cats, so they had the big cat eyes. Not the ones she was used to seeing, narrowed with distrust and plotting, but big and wide and sad.

Eyes filled with pity.

She dropped the ball and walked toward the exit, grabbing her wallet from her open backpack as she moved.

"Where are you going?"

"I need a break," she told the coaches. Not a lie. She really needed a break.

From cats with pity in their eyes.

"You want *me* to talk to them?"

"Well, I can't do it," Keane said calmly, and probably honestly, Julie was guessing. Since, you know, he'd yelled at the honey badgers just that morning.

"And I don't wanna do it," Shay added, also probably honestly.

"I don't want to do it either," Finn practically whined. "They hate us. All of us."

"And with good reason."

The three brothers glared across the room at the Van Holtz wolf.

"Who rejects pastries?" Van Holtz demanded. "*Who?* And they brought you an array of pastries." He pointed an accusing finger. "An *array*. Before we were Van Holtzes, we were just Holtzes in the wilds of Germany, and anyone who turned down our pastries would have started a blood feud."

"Can I hurt him now?" Shay asked, his cat gaze locked on the canine. "I really want to hurt him now."

"No," Finn replied. "His Pack is huge. And one of his uncles makes this amazing Cape buffalo with onion sauce that is to murder for, and I don't want to be banned from their restaurant soooo . . ."

"Fine." Shay walked out of the office without another word, because he had nothing else to say.

Keane stared at his younger brother for a brief moment before following Shay.

"So all this is up to me?" Finn called after Keane.

"Yes!" Keane barked back.

"I hate them," Finn growled before he walked out after his brothers.

Julie went back to the paperwork on her desk, wanting to finish signing a few purchase orders before returning to practice. But then she noticed that the canine hadn't left.

Looking up at him, she asked, "What?"

"I'm waiting."

"For?"

"The box seat tickets you're going to offer me to the first home game so that I don't sue your team into oblivion for hitting me in the head with a football."

Glaring, Julie let out a long, slow breath.

Dogs . . .

chapter SIX

Finn ordered a giant soda and ribs.

He needed to think and when he was brainstorming, he required two things: caffeine and meat.

The bag of food and the big cup of soda appeared on the counter and Finn grabbed them. He looked out over the food court and searched for a table so he could eat and come up with a game plan. He knew that Keane wouldn't let this go. Neither would Shay.

All three of them wanted answers, but to go back to the badgers in the hope they would actually get answers from any of them, especially Max MacKilligan . . . They'd be better off finding a psychic and asking to talk to their dead ancestors.

It was early lunchtime so the food court was already packed but Finn kept swinging his head back and forth, his gaze searching for the first open seat he might spot.

When his gaze swung back to the left for the fourth time, he spotted her. He should have noticed her before. She was sitting at a table by herself with three open seats. Nearly every other table was full, but people seemed to be actively avoiding her. Maybe it was the way she was eating. Slowly, methodically. One honey-covered fry at a time. It was definitely off-putting; he understood why the others were avoiding her. Shifters, among their own, didn't eat like that. They devoured food quickly and with an eye out for a hand or claw that might slip in to steal what was theirs.

This long-legged honey badger, however, didn't seem

worried at all about the predators surrounding her. She appeared too distracted, her gaze locked across the room, one foot on her seat, the drip of the fresh honey from her fries going unnoticed.

With a shrug, Finn made his way to her table. He had to start somewhere, and she seemed the easiest. If nothing else, he could ask her opinion on how to move forward. Maybe she could give him some idea of how to get Max MacKilligan to assist his family.

Forcing a warm smile he did not feel, Finn said, "Hey. Mind if I sit?"

The badger's head slowly turned toward him, and furrowed brows over black eyes glared up at him. After a brief moment of silence, she snarled, "Actually, I do mind . . . fuck off."

The big cat blinked in surprise, then turned and walked away.

Glad to be alone again, Mads went back to her honey-covered fries and her deep thoughts.

The honey was infused with hot Mexican spices and the deep thoughts were infused with misery. She'd been thinking about all the things she hadn't done with her life since she'd left Wisconsin. Other than a few duffel bags filled with tank tops, shorts, basketball shoes, and underwear, Mads didn't have a thing to her name.

Except, of course, the three storage spaces in Minnesota, Washington state, and upstate New York filled with cash, passports, weapons, and other necessary supplies for quick getaways. The storage spaces were in border towns so she could easily slip into Canada if she had to.

Other than that, though . . . she had nothing!

Was this to be her life, then? A life with nothing?

Most honey badgers had a hard time settling down full time, happily moving from cabinet to cabinet so that home-owners never knew a honey badger had been there until they noticed that their supply of honey had been replaced with corn syrup. Yet even those honey badgers still had a place they called "home." A place with a TV set and a closet full of clothes . . . and maybe a kid or two who occasionally called them "mom."

Even Max MacKilligan had begun to settle down. She had a boyfriend now! A male who actually wasn't afraid of her and, Mads was willing to bet, wouldn't leave her in the middle of the night because he was terrified she'd kill him one day for the insurance money. An insurance plan he'd had no idea she'd taken out on his life and that he had not signed.

In fairness, Max only used that move when the guy ignored earlier signals that he should get out. Even her "It's over. Leave me alone!" She was just so cute and small that full-human males didn't take her seriously the way shifter males did. Full-human males thought they could ignore her or push her around and, short of killing them and burying them on hyena land so that Max's adopted grandfather didn't have to deal with the fallout should the law come looking, Max had found that making them watch a few *Dateline* episodes before they "accidentally" found the insurance policy was the only way to get them to go for good.

Mads never had clingy boyfriends like that. She always found that a good, solid basketball right to the face got a guy to leave. "It was an accident!" she always told the cops, and making the move during a friendly game, with all her teammates as "witnesses," had kept her out of jail so far. While any pushy dudes got the message . . . and a broken nose.

But Mads's current dilemma wasn't about past boyfriends. Or past mistakes. Or a combination of both. Her great-grandmother was dead and Mads realized she had nothing to show for her life except a few championship wins and a couple of MVP awards, but would Solveig Galendotter take any of that seriously? No! The first thing she would ask Mads would be, "Do you have a house? A car? A life?"

Mads knew what her great-grandmother had always wanted most for her. A life.

A life she could be proud of and a life she could live without fear.

Not easy when one side of her entire family wanted her—

A tray abruptly slammed down on the table and Mads realized the cat had returned.

"You have the only table with space," he complained, sitting his surprisingly narrow ass down. "So you're just going to have to suck up my presence."

"Then why did you ask me in the first place?"

He picked a boar rib off his plate. "I was being polite."

"A polite tiger? Is that like an honest politician or a charming goat? Maybe a selfless actor?"

"I tried. I failed. Can we get past it?"

"Whatever."

Mads went back to her fries, deciding just to ignore the tiger sitting catty-corner from her.

But he was kind of making that impossible.

"You're getting honey on your knee," he felt he had to point out to her.

"I'll just lick it off later."

"Ewww."

Mads briefly closed her eyes before asking, "What?"

"Can't you just wipe it off?"

"Why would I waste good honey?"

"Why would you lick it off your knees in public?"

"Because tigers are so known for their manners."

"I know not to lick my knees in public!"

"Stop talking to me!"

"Fine!"

"Fine!"

They fell into what Mads could only call a moody silence, and she was grateful. She didn't want to chat with this dude anymore.

"You don't know who I am, do you?"

Mads looked back at the cat. "Am I supposed to?"

With half a boar rib hanging from his mouth, he barked, "You *just* talked to me this morning."

"I did?"

"Yes! And were in my cabinets!"

"I was?"

"Yes! How do you not remember?"

Mads shrugged. "My great-grandmother just died. I'm a little out of it right now. She was one of the few of my mother's family that didn't actively try to kill me at birth. She basically raised me until I was nine. And my family didn't even tell me she was dead. Some Viking shamaness did. The family didn't even give her a proper Viking funeral. They just burned her, put her in a box, and stuck her somewhere in their hoarder house. I don't even know if she'll get to Valhalla now. So I'm just . . . sad."

The tiger didn't say anything, but after a minute of silence he got up from the table and walked away. But he left his food, which most cats wouldn't do. Then again, no one wanted to hear the sad story of Mads Galendotter. So maybe he'd just made a run for it.

She didn't really think about it, just went back to eating her honey-covered fries and staring across the food court.

Mads had no idea how much time had passed when she reached out for a fry and hit hot flesh instead. She looked down at the table and saw that her fries had been moved away and replaced with a *huge* pile of boar ribs.

"You need roasted meat to feed your soul. Not fried foods to destroy it," the tiger said, back in his seat, eating his own ribs. "I got you the lion portion. The tiger and bear portions will make your stomach burst."

As Mads picked up a rib, she also noticed a large bottle of cold water and a carafe of hot tea.

"And don't worry about your great-grandmother's soul," he said between tearing off chunks of meat with his fangs. "When her body was burned, her soul was released to her gods. The ashes are for you. You should get them back. But you don't have to worry about her. The gods always take care of those most loyal to them."

Mads swallowed, although she hadn't taken a bite of food yet. She swallowed to get that lump of tears back down her throat. As she'd heard Max MacKilligan scream at Stevie MacKilligan more than once over the years, *"Honey badgers do not cry!"*

But she wasn't about to cry simply because of what the tiger had said. It was because he'd taken her words and worries seriously. When a girl mentioned Valhalla and "the gods," most people either snickered or headed to the door. But he hadn't. Instead, he'd given her words to soothe her own troubled soul. As if he understood.

His last name might be Malone but she'd heard from Max that his mother was from an ancient and feared Mongolian tribe made up of tiger shifters. They'd existed before even Genghis Khan terrorized Asia. It just hadn't occurred to her that Mongolian-Americans would hold true to their ancestors' beliefs just as Solveig had raised Mads to hold true to hers.

"We are Viking," she would say as Mads watched her replenish stock in her tiny Detroit corner store. "Your mother and that idiot daughter of mine will tell you that we are hyena first, but we were Viking long before we could unleash fang and claw. Remember, it is Odin and Freyja that protect us. They gave us the sword and the axe and the—"

"Basketball!" three-year-old Mads would add, lifting up her mini-ball for her great-grandmother to see.

Solveig would sigh then and complain, "I have *got* to stop taking you to that basketball park for lunch breaks."

The loss of a parent or parent figure was never easy, no matter the age. But when Finn's father was murdered, he'd still had his mother. She'd helped her sons get through the worst time of their lives with the kind of strength that could only come from a woman whose ancestors were born of the hard earth of the Mongolian steppes. When she'd gotten pregnant a year later after a one-night stand with that MacKilligan idiot and her sisters had shaken their heads and clucked their tongues, it was her older sons who'd surrounded her and growled in warning, much to the amusement of their aunts. But if there was one woman who'd needed to find her own way to mourn—a way none of them would hold against her—it was Zaya-Sarnai Selenge.

Or, as she was known in the States, Lisa Malone.

After quite a few generations in the West, Finn's family had grown tired of explaining Mongolian naming to . . . well . . . *everyone*. By the time his great-grandmother came along, she was named Mavis. Her daughter, Deloris. And his mother . . . Lisa. Much easier than explaining that Zaya-Sarnai was *not* his mother's first name, but her tribal name or surname. Actually, the names of the two sisters who'd discovered the ability to shift into Siberian tigers and taught it to other women in their clan. Eventually, they'd become too strong and hated to stay any longer, so they'd gone off and started their own tribe. Found some men who could hunt and didn't irritate them too much. The strongest of the females had babies who could shift without spells or sacrifices as soon as they hit puberty. They soon discovered they could live among the tigers with ease, fighting for food or territory, and surviving the winters more successfully than their all-human clan.

When the summers came and the clan wars began, the shifters were stronger than the full-humans, combining their ability to shift and their skills with bow and arrow and sword. Eventually they went from defense to offense, able to take what they wanted. But Zaya—her name meant "destiny"—and Sarnai—her name meant "rose"—didn't believe in taking just to take. If there was a need, if their tribe might starve or suffer, then they took. If not, they let other clans live in peace. If nothing else, their code yielded "a fat pig for us to devour when we're hungry and desperate, rather than a skinny, weak one we can barely use," as Zaya used to say.

Centuries later, that philosophy had led to a still-strong, family-connected tribe. Most continued to live on the steppes in Mongolia, but some had moved off to cities in France, Thailand, China, Germany, Russia, Great Britain, and the States to bring in new blood to the family.

New blood like the Malones.

The fact that Finn's mother had birthed three strong sons

had brought her quite a bit of respect among the family. It wasn't about race with the Zaya-Sarnai tribe. It was about fangs and claws . . .

It was about power.

The power of the cat within the blood of every Zaya-Sarnai roaming the world.

"Do you live with your entire family in that house?"

Surprised by that non sequitur, Finn looked at the badger and replied, "Not my *entire* family. Just my mother, brothers, and sister."

"You don't feel trapped?"

With a boar's rib in his mouth, Finn asked, "Huh?"

"You don't feel trapped?" she repeated, then continued, "Tigers usually roam hundreds of miles of territory. But you're locked in this tiny house with all these other giant tigers. On this tiny property. In that tiny town on Long Island. Don't you feel like a caged tiger in one of those sideshow zoos?" She raised her hands, fingers curled into mock claws, and began to mime tearing at walls. "Desperately trying to get out. Never to be free again!"

She abruptly stopped and faced him. "Ever feel like that?" she calmly asked.

The boar rib hung from his mouth and his gold eyes were wide, but she still didn't expect him to explode.

"*What is wrong with you?*" the cat demanded, startling a table of bears sitting next to them.

"What?" Mads asked, watching the bears move their table and chairs over so they didn't have to deal with a testy tiger in close quarters.

"Why would you ask me questions like that? And make me think about being trapped? In a zoo? After I just gave you freshly killed and roasted boar!"

"I was just thinking about buying a house."

He gawked at her a long moment before pulling the rib out of his mouth. "What?"

"I don't have my own place. I always hated the idea of it.

But I figured if a tiger could live in a house with other tigers, I could live in a house by myself. Or with my teammates. If they come visit."

"I found you asleep in my cabinets this morning. Shoved in with the condiments."

"I'm not sure what your point is."

"I don't see why you're worried about living in a house if you can survive in a cabinet."

"It's one thing to sleep in a different cabinet of my choosing every night. It's another thing completely to have only one set of cabinets to live in for the rest of your life. That's just sad."

"Where do you live now?"

Mads shrugged.

"What does that shrug mean?"

"Well . . . right now I'm crashing at Max's place until we get through the playoffs and hopefully the championships. I just found out that'll be in New York this year. And I think we have a great chance of getting in. Our team has been on *fire* this season—"

"You don't have your own apartment?" he rudely cut in.

"I don't like a lot of paperwork. Or anyone but my teammates to know where I live. So I don't really live anywhere."

"That's so weird."

"Why's that weird?"

"How is that *not* weird? Just the basics . . . like, how do you pay taxes?"

Mads couldn't help but smile a little. "Taxes?"

"Oh, gods," he muttered. "You don't pay taxes."

"Of course I pay taxes. It's just funny that your first thought was of accounting."

"If there's one thing in this world that can fuck up a shifter or a full-human, it's the goddamn IRS."

"Which is why I pay my taxes. I just have a post office box in Wisconsin. It gets checked regularly and that way I don't miss anything important from the government or anyone else. I don't need a house to get mail."

"Don't you need a base of operation, though?"

"A what?"

"A starting point. My brothers and I meet in the same place, punch each other a little, decide what we need to do, and go from there. When we're done, we come back to the same place—"

"Punch each other?"

"A little. Discuss things. Decompress from the day—"

"By punching each other?"

"A little. And then start again in the morning. It gives us a nice sense of grounding."

Mads rubbed her left eye. "You don't find that boring?"

"No."

"I'm afraid I'd find that boring."

"So you'd rather wake up in a stranger's cabinet if they come home earlier than you expected?"

"It does add excitement."

"And possibly two to four at Rikers for breaking and entering."

"I don't steal anything."

"It doesn't matter!" He let out a breath. "All I'm saying is, it's a good idea to have a place you call home. Your own home. That you legally own. Legally being the big word. *Legally.*"

"I know what it means."

His head tilted to the side, shifting all that gorgeous black hair with white stripes, almost giving her a clear view of his face, as he asked, "Do you?"

She pursed her lips, which Finn realized was a sign of annoyance, and both of them went back to eating their ribs.

But as Finn used his fangs to strip the flesh from the bone and drop the bone back on the plate, he heard crunching from the other side of the table. He glanced over and froze as he saw the honey badger feed rib after rib into her mouth the same way she'd fed the fries.

He didn't know how long he'd been staring until she stopped mid-chomp. Their eyes met, and she shrugged.

"It's a hyena thing," she admitted.

"I thought you were all honey badger."

"Mostly . . . yeah. But I do have a few hyena traits. Well, just a couple. I giggle at inappropriate times. Like in high school, during this old teacher's funeral . . . that was awkward. Got a week's detention for that. And I can crush pretty much anything between my jaws and digest it. Like bone . . . granite . . . steel . . . But before you ask, I do not eat human flesh."

"Why would I *ever* ask you that?"

"Some people ask. But in general, I'm honey badger. When I shift, I'm honey badger. My fangs are honey badger. Temperament . . . honey badger. I can't get enough of actual honey. Most poisons are just a seasoning to me, especially when snake is involved. Although man–made poisons do seem to give me sinus headaches. And that . . . whatchamacallit . . . ricin? It gives me migraines."

"Really? It kills most people."

"Yeah? It just gives me migraines. Max called me a wuss, though."

Unable to help himself, Finn had to ask. "Why were you and Max poisoned with ricin?"

"It's a long story and involves Hungarians, but it wasn't really a big deal. And after a couple of Excedrin and a soda . . . I felt much better."

"Okay." Finn threw up his hands. He couldn't do this anymore. He had come with a purpose. "I just have to ask this and then I'm going to go back to practice—"

"I already told you I do *not* eat human flesh."

"I was not going to ask you that. Ever!" He scrubbed his face with both hands. "I've been told that when it comes to getting information, honey badgers are the best. I thought maybe you could tell me how I could get Max to help me and my brothers."

She frowned. "Do what?"

"Get information that could lead us to the people involved in my father's murder."

"You want Max to help you guys with that?"

"Or you."

"I can't do it."

"Why not?"

"That would be betrayal."

"Betrayal?"

"Of Max."

"Right. Of Max. So I have to go to Max?"

"Yes."

"Fine. I'll go to Max. Since you won't do it."

Her nose briefly crinkled. "Max? Who you just threw out of your house this morning? After your brother yelled at her? And all her teammates? Even though she brought you pastries? That Max?"

Finn let out a sigh. If he had to hear about those damn pastries one more time . . .

"Yes. That Max."

It took a moment, but once she started laughing, she didn't seem able to stop.

"You can stop laughing now," he complained.

But Mads couldn't. She really couldn't. Did he really think, after what had just happened that morning, and the way his older brother had treated Max MacKilligan, that she would ever, *ever* help them with anything? For any reason? Ever?

Max would rather set herself on fire than help these big bastards! Or set the brothers on fire.

The only reason Max MacKilligan hadn't burned the house down with the brothers in it that very morning was because of her half-sister. But the Malone brothers' father was not the father of their young sister. She might legally carry the Malone name, but as far as Max was concerned, Natalie Malone was and always would be a MacKilligan. That connection had kept the brothers physically safe, but it bought them no favors.

They could have called in a huge favor after saving the lives of Max and her teammates just the night before. But they'd been cranky tigers instead and blown that opportunity.

Now, here was younger brother Flynn or Gin or Bry-in—

whatever the dude's name was—asking how he could ask a favor from Max.

And he didn't expect Mads to laugh about that? Laugh a lot? It wasn't even the tiny bit of hyena in her that was laughing. It was all bitter, angry, mean-spirited honey badger that couldn't stop laughing right now.

"Are you going to help me or not? Or are you just going to keep laughing at me?"

Knowing of only one way to answer that, Mads stood up, patted the tiger on his massive shoulder, and walked away.

Still laughing.

It was the clearest way possible to get her point across.

"So is that a 'no' on the helping?" Finn called after her.

When she only laughed harder as she disappeared around a corner toward the elevators, he figured that, yeah, it was a "no."

Noticing that she'd left her food plates behind, Finn cleaned off the table and took his time scraping things off so he could sort stuff in the recycle bins. He stopped by the bathroom to wash his hands and returned to practice.

"Where did you go?" Keane asked, the blood of an offensive lineman splashed across his face.

"I was hungry. And I needed to think."

"You and the thinking." His brother sighed before reaching out his arm, snatching a wide receiver trying to charge past and throwing the poor leopard back a hundred feet.

"I like thinking."

"Why? It never gets you anywhere."

"And you and your mighty instinct do?"

"We're still alive, aren't we?" Keane snapped.

"Barely. But let's not get into a fight."

"Because you know you can't take me?"

"Because I know Ma will beat both our asses if we get into any more fights. So, while I was eating, I saw one of the badgers in the food court."

"Which one?"

"The real blond one. Looks like she just got off the boat from Viking Land."

"What did she say?"

"I'll put it to you this way . . . we'd have a better chance of our ancestors returning to this plane of existence and telling us who murdered our father than getting any help from Max MacKilligan."

A cheetah going at least fifty miles per hour dashed past Keane, but Finn's brother—without even looking—simply reached his arm out and yanked the cat back by his neck, then flung him toward the rest of the offensive line.

"So," Keane reasoned, "we need to find another way to ask MacKilligan nicely."

Shoulders dropping, Finn let out a breath and gave up attempting to understand his eldest brother.

"I'm going to go hit bears," Finn said, moving toward the giant linebackers whose entire job was protecting the quarterback and receiver.

"You should wait thirty minutes after eating," his brother chastised.

Finn was about to tell his brother that was for swimming . . . and for full-humans. But why? Why tell the idiot anything? He'd created the situation they were in; he was the one who had to fix it.

As far as Finn was concerned, he was done dealing with all the MacKilligans. He had a preseason game to think about and murderers to track down.

He did, however, stop long enough to pull his phone out from where he'd tucked it between his hip and his padding and ordered some flowers for the badger who'd just lost her great-grandmother. He knew how hard it was to lose someone you not only loved but who loved you back. And it didn't sound as though she had a lot of family members who loved her back.

With the order in, Finn tossed his phone to Shay, then abruptly charged the unsuspecting linebackers just standing around waiting for Big Julie to give them orders. She saw him coming, too, and didn't say anything until he'd decimated half her line. Then she informed the tryouts, "This isn't the NFL, ladies and gents. You're around real-life predators now. You have to pay attention or you're going to do nothing but get your ass kicked all. Day. Long. By big cats with nothin' better to do."

chapter SEVEN

They didn't say anything until after practice when none of them could take it anymore. Nelle was sitting in the front passenger seat, so they all gestured at her to ask the question, which she attempted to ignore until Streep kicked the back of her seat.

Reaching her arm over the headrest to give Streep the middle finger, Nelle turned and asked Max, "So, um . . . what happened to your face?"

Max stopped behind a car at the light, waited a few seconds, then suddenly pulled out into oncoming traffic, went around the car in front of them, and made a right turn at the corner. Horns blared and the New York drivers cursed up a blue streak. Max didn't even notice.

"My face?" she asked.

Nelle cringed as she gestured at the tiny claw marks that went from one side of their team captain's face to the other and across her chin, nose and lips.

"Oh! That! Yeah. That's from Stevie's new cat." She shook her head. "I can't believe you gave my sister that damn cat, Tock."

"She kind of took it from me."

"And it's not so much a cat as it's a six-month-old kitten."

"Four weeks," Tock corrected Streep. "It's only four weeks old."

Streep gasped. "Why would a four-week-old kitten attack you, Max?"

"I have no idea," Max replied before she made a wild left into oncoming traffic and tore down another street.

"Are we being followed?" Mads wanted to know.

"I don't think so."

"Then what are you doing?"

"Making sure we're not followed."

Mads leaned back into the SUV's leather seats and stared out the window. She was done asking questions. It was too taxing on her brain.

"I still can't believe you were mauled by a kitten," Streep pointed out. "What did you do to it?"

"Nothing! I was just sitting in the vet's waiting room with my sisters, and the next thing I knew it had attached itself to my face and Stevie couldn't get its tiny baby claws out. When Charlie finally pried it loose, it just kept slashing at me. It acted like I owed it money. But I'm pretty sure I don't."

"It doesn't concern you that random animals seem to attack you for what you insist are no obvious reasons?" Nelle asked.

"It's not my fault. I literally was doing nothing." She raised a finger. "Maybe they sense my barely simmering rage."

"You don't have barely simmering rage," Tock reminded her. "You're a sociopath."

"That's borderline at best. According to the psychiatrist I went to."

"Isn't she writing a book on you?"

"No. I'm merely a couple of chapters."

"How to know when you're being conned, or how to know when your spouse is planning to kill you for financial gain?" Streep sweetly asked.

"Something like that."

"That is *not* a definitive answer, Max MacKilligan."

They pulled up to the MacKilligan house in Queens, and everyone got out of the big SUV.

Mads hiked the strap of her duffel bag over her shoulder and started after the rest of the team, but Tock tugged her back by holding onto the bag.

"You okay?" she asked.

"I'm fine. Why?"

"Jaleesa missed that layup at practice and usually you would rip her head off the day before a playoff game. But you didn't say anything. That's not like you."

Mads shook her head. "Nope. I'm cool."

She knew she could tell her teammates what was going on, but she didn't want to. She didn't want to tell anyone. It was her business and she would deal with it on her own. She dealt with everything on her own. No big deal. So she forced a smile, and Tock gave a shrug and walked ahead of her toward the front porch.

Mads glanced across the street and several houses down to the three-story colonial owned by a She-bear widow that Mads hadn't seen around lately. But she could see the She-bear's daughter and son-in-law there now. It looked like they were cleaning out the place. She sighed a little. Another family loss, it seemed.

Turning on her heel, she headed into the MacKilligan house but froze as soon as she stepped inside. Every badger head had turned toward her as soon as Mads entered. That was off-putting enough. But then Max's baby sister suddenly came at her. Arms open wide. And before Mads could make a panicked run for it, she was being hugged.

Hugged.

Against her will.

"I'm so, so, soooo sorry, Mads," Stevie MacKilligan said in a shaky voice that told Mads the woman was barely holding back tears.

Blessed Odin, not the sobbing.

Not knowing what was going on, Mads looked at Tock. Her friend pointed at the dining room table, which could easily be seen from the living room where she was standing. And on that table was an enormous vase of flowers. White lilies mixed with white roses and some other stuff. Mads wasn't really a flower person. But no one had sent her flowers before. Ever. Who the hell would send her flowers? And why would flowers lead to Stevie hugging—

"We are so sorry to hear about your great-grandmother."

Oh, no.

"And before you ask," Stevie went on, "I didn't read the card that came with the flowers. Max did."

"Rat," Max accused before her entire mood changed and she happily noted, "No name on the card but there's a number . . ."

Mads tried to pull away from Stevie but the badger-tiger hybrid merely held on tighter. The MacKilligan sisters were not like other honey badgers. When a badger mated with another breed of shifter, the kids were always honey badger. They might have some slight deviations. Weird hair color or slightly off fangs. Or in Mads's case, the ability to eat and digest steel. But at the end of the day . . . they were really just amped-up honey badgers.

That, however, was not true of the MacKilligan sisters, Charlie and Stevie.

Charlie was half wolf and couldn't even shift. She had fangs and claws whenever she wanted, but that was it. No fur. No changing limbs. But she had a crazy amount of super-shifter strength that would make an entire Navy SEAL team look like three-year-old boys.

And Stevie . . . well, Stevie's abilities were never discussed. By anyone. The team just knew that she wasn't exactly a honey badger; nor was she a Siberian She-tiger. She was something much more terrifying, and if she ever started crying in rage and panic, Max had told her teammates once, they were to start digging escape tunnels and digging them fast. A warning Mads never forgot.

But none of that excused having to put up with hugging. Mads didn't do hugging.

"Awwww," Max teased, coming closer. "Look at all that love."

Mads grabbed her teammate by the hair, yanking and twisting until she stopped laughing and said, "Okay. Okay!"

Mads released her, and Max grabbed her baby sister's shoulders and pulled her away from Mads.

Thankfully, Stevie went willingly, but tears were still shining in her eyes and she kept sniffling.

"Do you need anything, Mads?" Stevie asked. "Would you like some coffee or tea?"

"Vodka?" Tock muttered.

"I'm fine. Thanks."

Stevie's face scrunched up into something Mads couldn't quite explain—she just knew she didn't like it—her head gently tilted to the side, and she said with soft care, "Are you, though, sweetie? Are ya fine?"

Streep immediately covered her mouth, eyes wide. Tock's eyes just rolled. Nelle sniffed once and went back to her phone. Max grinned. Charlie, who'd walked in from the kitchen, grimaced.

And Mads dropped her duffel bag and walked out of the house.

Finn checked his phone again and scowled. She must have gotten the flowers by now. And no thank-you text? Who didn't send a thank-you text after getting a lovely bouquet of "sorry your great-grandmother died" flowers?

Sure, he could imagine his baby sister mouthing her standard *You must be joking* at him. For expecting a thank-you after that morning's blowup in their kitchen. But this wasn't about what had happened between the two groups. This was about the discussion they'd had as two independent, semi-human beings. And his gesture deserved a proper thank-you.

"Hello, cousin!"

Finn looked up from his phone and into gold eyes that matched his own. The gold eyes of a Malone.

Fangs pushed out from his gums and a low growl began to build in the back of his throat, ready to be unleashed so it could take down the entire Sports Center!

A big hand landed on Finn's shoulder as a polar bear sat next to him on the bench.

"Everybody calm down," the bear muttered. "We're just here to talk."

"I don't talk to traitors."

Marcella Malone, one of his many first cousins, put her hands on her hips. "I was a kid when your father died!"

"Murdered! He was murdered! And *your* father, *his* brother, did *nothing*! That makes you the *daughter* of a traitor!"

"What did you say about my father?"

"Do you actually want me to say it louder? Because I will!"

"*Hey!*" the bear bellowed. "This isn't nice! I want nice!"

Finn looked at the polar bear sitting next to him. He looked like an ex-con. Long white hair that reached halfway down his back in a loosely tied ponytail, a threadbare Black Sabbath T-shirt barely covering ten thousand muscles, worn jeans, biker boots, a scar on his neck that was not put there by any claw or fang, and both arms littered with tattoos. But worst of all, he was armed.

"You're hanging around bikers now?" Finn asked his cousin.

Cella pursed her lips. "He's not a biker. He's a cop."

Finn laughed. "Yeah. Right."

Then the cop pulled out his badge.

"Oh." He looked the polar bear over again. "The NYPD's really lowered that dress code."

"I work undercover a lot."

"As what? Old biker or old drug dealer? Or old both?"

"I'm not old," the bear quickly replied. "I'm not old!"

"He just looks old," Cella felt the need to explain. "It's the white hair."

"And that T-shirt. Is it signed by all the original Black Sabbath members?"

"Cella," the polar snarled.

"Shay, I'm here for a reason."

"I'm Finn."

She paused for a moment before faking a laugh. "I knew that. I was just joking." When Finn only stared at her, she went on. "Anyway, there was an incident last night on Denley Island and what seems to be a little tiger-related dust-up at a full-human bar downtown. There's some concern it might have involved you and your brothers."

"Uh-huh."

"Is that all you have to say?"

"What? You're a cop now, too?"

"No. But I do have some involvement with Katzenhaus."

"Katzenhaus. They didn't help us with our father either."

"At some point, cousin, you need to let that go."

"At some point you need to blow me."

"I'm still not hearing nice," the polar complained.

Mads made it to the sidewalk and looked around. She could call a car to take her to a hotel. Just for the night, but that seemed rude. She knew that honey badgers were known for being rude but she wasn't in the mood to be *that* rude. Not after Charlie had been kind enough to open her home to her.

She began pacing but abruptly stopped when she saw the bear couple she'd noticed earlier talking outside the house they were packing up.

Without looking, Mads ran into the street and immediately got slammed into by a taxi. She jumped up just as the full-human driver came around the front to check on her.

"I'm fine," she said.

"But—"

"Really." She pushed him back into the taxi and closed the door for him. "Sorry about that. Totally my fault."

"But—"

"Have a great night!"

She was hoping he wouldn't see the dent she'd left in his front grille until he got back to the garage since it suggested she should be a broken husk under his vehicle but wasn't. And a full-human would find that really strange.

Once the taxi had slowly driven off, the driver looking back at her in his rearview mirror, she rushed across the street to the old She-bear's house.

"Are you okay?" the sow asked. She was a black bear, so she was much nicer than any grizzly would be.

"Oh, I'm fine." Mads shrugged. "Honey badgers are really hard to kill. Sooo"—she pointed—"have you sold this house yet?"

"No. We wanted to get Mom's stuff out before we put it on the market."

"So, your mom . . . ?"

The sow nodded slowly. "It was her time," she said softly. Almost a whisper.

"I understand. And I'm so sorry."

"It had to happen. At some point"—she shrugged—"your mother just wants to move to fucking Florida."

Mads blinked. "Oh."

"But I can't blame her," the sow went on. "She's got everything she wants down there. Her friends are all nearby. An unbelievable number of trees with a whole bee hive colony. Fresh lakes filled with fish. And, of course, bear shuffleboard."

"Bear shuffleboard?"

"Yeah. They just sit around as bears in the Florida heat, sliding that little disc back and forth with their paws. You know, when bears get a certain age, sometimes we just don't feel like shifting back to human that often. So this place is perfect for her."

"Oh. Well . . . that's great!"

"So, are you interested in the house?" the boar asked.

"I am. I can get you cash . . . and a Wassily Kandinsky."

The pair frowned and the sow asked, "Who?"

"An artist. His paintings are worth a good amount. I think. I've had that thing a few years."

The bear couple glanced at each other and the sow finally said, "Not to be rude or anything but . . . you *are* a honey badger and—"

"We don't want to go to prison," the boar finished.

"The cash is clean," Charlie said, walking up behind the three of them with a covered dessert in her hand. "And the Kandinsky has its papers."

"It does," Mads immediately agreed. "My aunt gave it to me in case I needed to make a quick exit. Can't make a quick exit if the painting's authenticity can't be proved."

"You have my word," Charlie said, handing the dessert over to the boar. "We'll get the cash for you in the next . . . ?" She glanced at Mads.

"Ten to twelve hours. And the painting with papers, too."

"You sign the house over to her now with the stipulation that she pays you in the next ten days. The timeline is just a cushion. But she'll get you the cash no later than tomorrow. And you guys will be done moving out of here by . . . ?"

"Tomorrow, actually," the boar replied.

"Perfect. We agreed?"

The sow and Charlie locked gazes, neither breaking the staredown until the boar, who was busy sniffing whatever was under that foil, finally sighed out, "Agreed."

The sow closed her eyes and growled, "What are you doing?"

"Smell this," he ordered, putting the cake under her nose.

"I'm not going to—" She leaned in closer and took several sniffs. "Agreed," she sighed.

The boar gestured to the house. "Would you like to see inside?"

"Nah," Mads replied, turning to walk back to Charlie's house.

"Love to," Charlie said, grabbing Mads's shoulder and steering her toward the front porch. "You should look inside the house," she whispered. "What if they have no cabinets?"

Mads froze mid-step. "By Odin's beard!" she cried, startling the bears. "Who would have no cabinets?"

*   *   *

"Whatever happened on that island is bad enough, but if you and your brothers are attacking full-humans as tigers in the middle of the day in *bars* . . . that's going to be a problem."

"But we're not," Finn lied.

Before his father's murder, Finn had heard a lot about the importance of two things: the Malone family and Katzenhaus. Both would protect their family from the full-human world so they could live their lives as they wanted.

Finn had noticed, though, that his mother hadn't really said anything when his father made those statements. She didn't agree or disagree. She would just keep doing whatever she was doing. Whether she was cooking or reading or breaking up another fight between Keane and Shay.

Then their father had been killed and no one had helped. Not the Malones and not Katzenhaus. Their mother had not seemed surprised. Hurt, but not surprised. But her three sons had been devastated. Everything they'd been taught about their father's side of the family and about Katzenhaus had turned out to be a lie. It was, one of their mother's sisters had noted when she didn't think any of them were around, "the day your sons' hearts turned to stone and their resolve turned to steel."

And she'd been right. Full-blood tigers in the wild were known for their unforgiving nature, and the Black Malones were no different. "To cross a Black Malone is to cross the devil himself," an Irish priest had once said about their great-great-great-grandfather. The first Black Malone.

All the other Malones, when shifted, looked like every other Siberian tiger. With white, orange, and black stripes and big fangs. But not the Black Malones. They had black fur with white stripes. Maybe a little orange or red tossed in for a dash of color, but not much. Usually, the Malones produced only one or two per generation. And they were never brothers. So when one Black Malone had an entire family of Black Malones . . . it was seen as a bad sign among the religious of the family. The nuns turned their eyes away and the priests crossed themselves when the family passed.

A few attempted to blame the Mongolian side of the family and the fact that their father had only picked one mate to breed with, but the Zaya-Sarnai tribe had no black tigers in their long history. Only the occasional white ones with blue eyes, which were usually treated as shamans. And the Malones weren't about to challenge the Zaya-Sarnais since no one had any idea how many of them there were in the world. They kept their overall numbers secret.

The only shifters that Finn and his brothers had any faith in were his mother's side of the family. A large number had come from around the world to attend the funeral. What information they could find about the murder, they'd immediately passed on to Finn's mother. And it became the goal of the tribal elders to teach the three oldest how to protect their immediate family now that their father was gone. They were taught to fight as human and cat, so they would always be ready to stand at their mother's side.

But even with the help of their mother's family, they still had no clue about their father's murderer. Whoever had killed him had a lot of power to keep it quiet for so long. But the Black Malones would not stop. They would never stop.

Something that Cella Malone, of all people, should understand.

"It was you, cousin," Cella pushed. "You and your brothers."

"Prove it."

"You left your piss all over the crime scene."

"Let's test it and find out. Oh, that's right! Do that and the world will wonder why humans are leaving tiger piss everywhere. Can't have that, now can we?"

Cella stepped closer and lowered her voice. "If you're not careful, cousin, there are other ways this could be handled."

"You mean like a shot from a tall building a thousand yards away? Isn't that more your thing . . . *cousin*?"

A tall, lanky woman in loose jeans, worn work boots, and a baseball cap with the Tennessee Titans logo on the front sauntered to a stop in front of them. She was in the middle of eating an ice cream cone. Strawberry, by the looks of it.

"We done?" she asked with a low, gravelly voice.

Finn smirked. "Hanging around dogs now, are we, cousin?"

"We work together."

"That?" Finn asked, incredulous. "I know *that's* not working with Katzenhaus."

"Better watch your mouth, son," the canine said around licks of her ice cream. "I ain't afraid to take on no cat."

"And a hillbilly dog, too!" Finn laughed, gazing at his snarling cousin. "This just gets better!"

"Thanks for helping me out with that."

They walked down the street toward Charlie's rental house. It wasn't very often that Mads was alone with Charlie. Mostly because the team found her terrifying. Not Max, of course, but the rest of them . . . they found her terrifying.

"No problem. Amazing what a honey cinnamon coffee cake can get you, though. When you're dealing with bears anyway. Not polar bears, though. I always have to provide them with something seal or fish based." Charlie wiped her hands on her jeans before adding, "Sorry about your great-grandmother."

"Thanks."

"You okay?"

"I'm fine. A little sad. I always thought she'd outlive most of us. She seemed too mean to die."

"Need me to look into anything for you? Or . . . handle anything?"

Mads stopped walking and shook her head. "No. I'm sure she just died. Or it was a robbery or something. If my mother or grandmother had anything to do with it, they would have let me know by taunting me. Because they're hyena and they can't help themselves."

"Lovely. Well, I'd be happy to go to the funeral with you. I know how that kind of gathering can get with a shitty family and—"

"There won't be a funeral," Mads cut in before this could go any further. "But thanks for the offer."

"No funeral, or you just don't want to go because your family will be a bunch of assholes? I remember them, Mads. I was there." She smiled, but it wasn't a warm, friendly smile. It was the brittle one that Charlie only used with people she hated or when talking about people she hated. "I remember your mother and grandmother extremely well."

"You should. You punched my mother."

"She deserved it."

"Oh, I know," Mads agreed, unable to stop herself from smiling at the memory of what happened after their first junior high team basketball game. "I know. And there won't be a funeral because there isn't a body."

"What do you mean there's no body? Why is there no body? Oh, my God." Charlie grabbed her arm. "Did they eat your great-grandmother?"

"No! My family is fucked up, but we're not *that* fucked up. They do not eat family. They cremated her, stuck her in a box, and put her somewhere in the house."

Charlie released her arm. "The hoarder house?" she asked sadly.

"The hoarder house."

"Why won't they clean that place up?"

"I have no idea. It's so nasty. They don't even live in it anymore. They all have trailers now on the property."

"From what Max has told me about your great-grandmother, that is not how she should go out."

"I know. But her daughter will have it no other way. And my mother does whatever *her* mother tells her. I'm not getting in the middle of that, because I don't want a world war." She stepped closer to Charlie. "And your sisters can't know that, because Max will start a world war. You know it, and I know it."

"So you weren't going to tell anyone?"

"Maybe Tock. She barely speaks."

"And she's your closest friend."

Surprised at the statement, Mads simply stared at Charlie.

"Right?" Charlie pushed when Mads stayed quiet.

"Well . . . she's my teammate. They're all my teammates."

"And your friends." Charlie frowned. "Right?"

"I guess I never really thought about it."

"How could you not think about it? You guys go into fire-fights together. How do you trust each other if you're not friends?"

"We're teammates."

Charlie walked away from Mads then. She thought the eldest MacKilligan would return to her house, but she stopped in front of Mads's teammates, who were lingering outside, and asked, "You guys are all friends . . . right?"

Streep immediately replied, "Of course we are! Best friends forever!"

Tock shrugged and said, "I guess."

Nelle, busy putting on lip gloss in a compact mirror, asked, "Wait . . . what was the question?"

And Max turned to her baby sister and crowed, "Told you I had friends!"

"Wow," Charlie said before she went inside her rental house.

Max motioned to the house across the street and asked, "What were you doing at that old She-bear's house?"

"I just bought it."

"Why?"

"So I can move into it."

"What's wrong with our house?"

"Nothing. Just thought I should buy a place."

"Is this your form of mourning?" Streep asked.

"Okay. We're done." Mads pulled out her phone. "Look, I need to head to my storage—"

"In Wisconsin?"

"No. I can get what I need in my New York storage."

"Oh." Nelle snapped her compact closed. "I'll get one of my father's copters and we'll all go together."

"You guys don't need to do that."

"Are you bringing cash back for the purchase?"

"Yes."

"And one of the real art pieces your aunt gave you?"

"Yes."

Max pulled out one of the knives she kept hidden on her body at all times, but she did it so fast, Mads had no idea which location she took it from. "Then you're gonna need us."

"But we're not friends?" Streep complained.

Mads cleared her throat. "I happen to think teammates are more import—"

"Shut. The fuck. Up."

With that, Streep stomped into the house. Snickering, Nelle and Max followed.

"Don't worry about her," Tock said, resting her elbow on Mads's shoulder. "She'll get over it. And I totally get what you mean about teammates."

"Thank you. Besides, we're not six years old."

"Streep is."

Tock looked up and down the street. "Sure you want to buy a house here? It's bear territory. With lots of cranky grizzlies."

"And even meaner lions a couple of blocks over."

Tock smiled, quickly guessing Mads's logic. "So, doubtful any hyenas will be just dropping by."

"Not any locals anyway. And Charlie shot the out-of-towners. Making me feel relatively safe."

Moving her arm so that it looped around Mads's neck, Tock pressed her head against Mads's.

"Really sorry about Solveig," she whispered.

"Yeah. Me, too."

"Who sent you the flowers anyway?"

"Oh, shit!" Mads lifted her phone up again and Tock handed over the card that had come with the flowers. "I forgot to send a thank-you to that tiger."

"What tiger?"

"Finn Malone. He's the one who sent the flowers."

"Who *sent you flowers?*"

"Uh-oh," Tock muttered before they both lifted their heads to find a now-seething Max standing in front of them in all black, her denim jacket barely hiding all the weapons she now had strapped to her body. Even more than she'd had five minutes ago.

"This has been fun and all, but I'm leaving."

"This isn't over."

Slowly, Finn stood, towering over his six-foot cousin.

"Is that right?"

"You don't scare me."

Finn took a step closer. "I scare ya a little."

Because he was a Black Malone, and no one ever knew what a Black Malone would do next. When they shifted, their eyes turned blue and they were known for playing with their prey.

"I'm still not hearing nice," the polar bear complained.

"You want to come for us," Finn kindly suggested, "just try. I'm sure Keane would love it."

"You know, I'm trying to help you. You're still fam—"

"Don't even." He started to walk away but the hillbilly canine was standing in front of him, blocking his way. "And keep your pet dog away from me."

"Sorry about your daddy," the canine said. "I understand, though. I'm real close to mine . . . maybe one day you'll meet him," she added with a smile.

"Sure. Whatever." He pushed past the female and headed toward the elevators. He texted his brothers, telling them to meet him upstairs by the main exits rather than near the food court. He knew if Keane saw Cella, he'd explode, and Finn wasn't in the mood to calm his brother down. Not when he was more than ready to head over to Mineola, Long Island, and have it out with all his uncles himself. Something he was sure the rest of the Malones wouldn't appreciate one bit. Something the brothers had learned one drunken night when they'd stormed the multiple homes of their uncles. If it hadn't been for their mother and visiting aunts, it might have ended with more serious consequences than a few torn muscles and some artery damage.

He reached the elevators, pressed the button, and again checked his phone.

"Still no thank-you!" he announced to no one in particular, but he managed to startle a grizzly sow, who roared at him.

"Oh, shut up!" he barked back at her.

"Give me that!" Mads ordered, trying to grab the vase of flowers out of Max's hands.

Max dashed around the others, who were trying to take the flowers from her, and jumped up on the dining room table. She raised the big vase of flowers, ready to hurl the whole thing to the ground in a fit of Max-only rage.

"*Betrayal!*" Max bellowed.

"What is wrong with you?" Mads demanded. Only the Malone brothers seemed to get this reaction from Max. Not even Stevie made her this crazy.

Charlie walked out of the kitchen. "What is going on?"

"Your sister is insane!" Mads told her.

"Besides that."

"Mads has betrayed us all!" Max announced.

"Because she got flowers?"

"It's who she got the flowers from."

"Who'd she get the flowers from?"

Max lowered the vase. "No one."

Charlie folded her arms over her chest. "Who'd she get the flowers from, Max?"

"Why do you need to know?"

"Because you've been acting shifty ever since you got back from last night's job, which makes me wonder what the hell happened. So you can tell me the whole story, and I flip out now. Or you can just tell me the name of the person who sent the flowers."

Mads snatched the vase from Max. "These are from Finn Malone. He was in the food court after I found out about my great-grandmother. He was just being nice."

"And we hate him now because . . . ?"

The team looked up at Max, who was still standing on the dining room table.

"Fine!" Max snapped. "We went over there this morning to thank them—"

"Thank them for what?"

"None of your business. Anyway, we had all these fresh pastries and were really nice, and they threw us out of the house."

"Were you invited into their house?"

Max glared down at her sister. "What does that have to do with anything?"

"When people have come uninvited into our house, we've killed them."

"Because they were usually there to kill us! *We* brought pastries."

"You were honey badgers invading their house, Max."

"*Who brought pastries!*"

Eyes wide, Charlie turned her gaze to Mads, but all she could do was protectively hold onto her vase of flowers and shrug.

"Told you," Mads whispered loudly. "Insane."

They were halfway home when Finn's phone vibrated. He glanced at it.

"Finally," he said with a smile.

"What?" Keane asked from the driver's seat.

"Mind your own business."

"Then don't mutter random things while I'm driving."

Ignoring his brother, he looked at the text again.

THX FOR THE FLWERS. MAX STILL HATES YOU & YR BROTHERS, THO. SORRY.

Finn chuckled.

"What now?" Keane demanded.

"Why are you still talking to me?"

"Are you two going to argue all night?" Shay asked from the backseat.

"Shut up!" Finn and Keane barked at the same time.

See? A polite thank-you was all Finn had wanted. Because politeness counted.

chapter EIGHT

As promised, Nelle came through with the private chopper. Her family had a fleet of them on standby, ready for immediate use.

They landed at the closest helipad, then called in an elite car service to take them the rest of the way. There was champagne on ice in what turned out to be a party limo and they indulged, laughing and talking loudly, occasionally flirting with the driver, and asking him inappropriate questions. When they were about a mile from their destination, they told him to stop and stumbled out of the limo, Streep landing on Tock's back before she was shoved off.

Nelle gave the driver a large cash tip and told him to wait.

"Are you sure I shouldn't go with you, ladies?" he asked, appearing more concerned about their state of drunkenness than his desire to get laid. "I don't mind."

"No, no. You just wait here," Nelle said, patting his shoulder. "We'll be back in a little bit. Okay?"

Laughing, they stumbled off into the dark, singing, with their arms around each other's shoulders until they were about a half mile away.

Then, as if on cue, they all immediately stopped performing and continued the last half mile in silence until they reached the high-end self-storage place.

Mads punched in her code, and the large front gate opened. When they'd all walked inside, Mads led them past the outdoor storage containers, then used a different code to enter the building. She led them past the different-sized storage units, took an elevator that required a keycard to make it work and a different code to stop on the correct floor.

When the elevator doors opened, Mads took them down the hall to her storage unit. She needed a keycard, a code, and two different metal keys to get into the space.

"Think this system is a tad paranoid?" Streep asked.

Then they stepped inside the unit and Mads turned on the lights. That's when Tock answered Streep's question with a, "Nooooo. We do not."

Mads, like Solveig, had never really trusted banks. So she kept piles of cash in her storage unit. And since she didn't spend much, she had lots of piles. The artwork had been given to Mads by her honey-badger aunt Sylvie, who wanted to make sure Mads had an escape plan. The jewels were from her father. He also wanted to make sure she had an escape plan. Although Mads didn't feel as confident telling anyone those jewels were *not* stolen as she was with Sylvie's art gifts. But they were pretty and shiny, so she kept them.

"Wow, sweetie," Streep said, her voice filled with awe, "you have a lot of stuff."

"Not that much."

"How did you get an original Rembrandt?"

"I don't have an original Rem—" Mads spotted the painting, which should be somewhere in Vatican City, plopped in the middle of her storage unit. "*Max!*"

Unlike most badgers, Max didn't even bother to lie first. "Sorry. I ran out of space in my own storage . . . and then I forgot I had it here."

"How do you forget you stole a Rembrandt?" Tock wanted to know.

She scratched her head. "At the time I had a lot on my mind."

"Because you were stealing something else?" Nelle guessed.

"Probably."

*   *   *

Finn opened the front door, then just stood and stared. He was too surprised to react.

"You going to invite me in . . . or just gawk at me?" Charlie MacKilligan asked with a smile.

He glanced back at the busy kitchen, which was filled with most of his family. Well not most. Just his brothers. His mother, baby sister, and aunts—oh, and Dale—were scattered throughout the rest of the house as the family meal bubbled on the stove.

But any of them could appear in the kitchen at any time. And his family was a lot to deal with for an outsider.

But Charlie wasn't alone. She had three big grizzly bears standing behind her. Huffing.

Finn was debating whether to let the bears into his house along with Charlie when Keane showed up behind him.

"Who's at the—oh. It's you."

Charlie kept that smile in the face of Keane's cold reception. "Yes. Me! And it's good to see you again, too, Keane."

"You brought security with you?"

Was Keane really blaming her for that? Because Finn didn't.

"No. My boyfriend insisted on coming along." She pointed at one of the bears. "This is my boyfriend, Berg."

"And these are my triplets," the bear introduced. "Britta and Dag."

"There are only two," Keane noted and the bear blinked in confusion.

"What?"

"You said these are your triplets, but there are only two. Where's the third?" His eyes narrowed. "Watching the house?"

The bear shook his head. "No, no. I'm one of triplets. These are my triplets. Britta and Dag."

"Yeah, but there should be a third, right? Because triplets means three. So where is the third?"

The bear cleared his throat, tried again. "If I were a twin, I'd say that this was me and my twin. But I'm a triplet. So there's me and my triplets. Britta and Dag."

"And the third. Why won't you tell me where the third is? Are you hiding him for some reason? Is there an ambush plan?" Keane demanded.

"*Charlie?*" Berg said desperately.

"Why don't we go inside?" she offered, before pushing her way in.

Finn sort of moved out of her way but he was surprised when Keane did. Because Keane didn't move for anybody. But once she'd stepped into the kitchen, Keane leaned over and said, "I didn't move."

"I saw you move."

"No. I mean . . . I didn't get out of her way. She moved me."

The brothers gazed at each other a moment, then leaned around the interior doorway so they could see into the kitchen to get a better look at Charlie MacKilligan.

She had what was universally known among shifters as "She-wolf shoulders." Those were shoulders that were bigger than most female shifters had, even bear sows or She-lions. The rest of her, however, was tiny . . . in comparison to other She-wolves. Yet bigger than any honey badger Finn had ever seen. She was . . . ? What? A good five-eight? Five-nine? That was huge for a honey badger. The Viking honey badger was nearly the same height, but she was lean and her shoulders weren't as wide.

Charlie had a sweet smile, though. But cold eyes. Predator eyes.

Finn and Keane followed her into the kitchen, while the bears stood off to the side.

"What smells so good?" she asked.

"Now you want dinner?" Keane demanded, and Finn shoved his brother into the refrigerator door.

"Ignore him," Finn told the still-smiling badger.

This was when he could see the blood link between the half-sisters. In their smile.

"So what can we do for you?" he asked her.

"What happened last night with my sister and her team?"

"She didn't tell you?"

"She's avoiding telling me, which is never a good sign."

"Yeahhhhh. I'm not sure I want to get in the middle of you—"

Before Finn could finish his very rational thought, Keane shoved him out of the way and into Shay.

"What do we get out of it?" the bastard asked.

"What do you want? More pastries?"

"If I never hear about those fucking pastries again . . ." Finn muttered to Shay.

Shay shrugged. "I thought they were good."

"We need information," Keane told Charlie.

"Information about what?"

Keane held up a finger and a moment later their mother walked into the room. She was sniffing the air, finally asking with disgust, "Why do I smell bear? Oh . . ." She glared at the triplets standing on the other side of the kitchen. "That must be you three funking up my kitchen."

"Ma!" Finn snapped.

Smirking, Keane motioned to their mother. "Ma, could you give us a second?"

"Fine. I don't want my sisters coming in here and being forced to deal with"—she gestured to the triplets with a wave of her hand—"the Hair Bear Bunch over there."

The three bears frowned at the same time, tilted their heads the same exact way—to the left—and then asked in unison, "The what?"

Finn's mother sighed. "Youngsters. I hate all of you," she growled before stomping off.

"She always looks so cute when she marches out of the room like that," Keane noted with a rare smile. But that smile disappeared as soon as he turned back to Charlie MacKilligan.

"We need to find out who killed our father," he told her. "Can you help us get that information?"

"No."

Keane threw up his hands and Shay said, "But we were told that you badgers could get any kind of information."

"Badgers have connections with badgers, which can lead to information."

"Okay . . . and?"

"And . . . I'm the daughter of Freddy MacKilligan. No one's going to tell me shit. That man has burned bridges all over the world, which has put an unfortunate stain on all the MacKilligan sisters."

"Then that doesn't help us and you need to leave," Keane told her. "Just seeing you here with your bears is annoying me."

"There's still Max."

"Isn't she a MacKilligan, too?"

"And a Yang. Her mother's family actually likes her and will help her. But every time you guys are mentioned, Max flips out." She pointed at Finn. "Those flowers you sent Mads were almost slammed to the floor and stomped on. Luckily her basketball player friends are fast and were able to get that very nice vase away from her."

Finn grimaced as Keane and Shay faced him.

"You sent one of those chicks flowers?" Keane demanded

"Chicks?" the female triplet repeated. "Did you really just call them chicks?"

"Don't you have a hive to attack?" Keane shot back.

"Don't you have some knuckles to drag?"

"I sent her flowers," Finn cut in, "because her great-grandmother died. I was being nice."

"You're weak and you disgust me."

"I would be disgusted, too," Shay added, "but she's cute. So I get it."

"You guys shouldn't be disgusted; you should thank him. If it wasn't for those flowers, I wouldn't know the extent to which my sister is hiding shit from me. But you tell me what I want to know . . . and I'll get her to help you."

Keane glanced uneasily at Finn and Shay.

"Why doesn't your sister want to tell you what happened last night?"

"I don't know. If she got herself into trouble . . . she doesn't want to hear me yelling at her about what an idiot she is. Which I totally get. Although I've been working with my therapist not to do that as often. According to her, 'Words hurt.'"

Finn remembered that his baby sister had told him the youngest MacKilligan sister, Stevie, was also in therapy. Did they *all* go to therapy? Did Nat now want to go to therapy? Did just being the daughter of Freddy MacKilligan mean she would *need* to go to therapy one day?

Instead of posing any of those questions, he instead asked, "And if someone else got her into trouble?"

There was that Max-like smile. "Then she worries I'm going to start killing people."

Finn, Shay, and Keane now glanced at each other before saying in unison, "Huh."

"Why is there a Degas here, Max?"

"That's my Degas," Nelle announced. Then she added, "But it's a forgery from my cousin."

"Which cousin?" Tock asked.

"The twelve-year-old. He's getting good. Although his dream—to his mother's eternal sorrow—is to be a fireman."

Mads threw down the duffel bag filled with money. "How many of you have been using my storage for your loot?"

They all raised their hands.

"This is supposed to be a clean space," she reminded them. "Nothing illegal."

"You don't have anything illegal in here," Max reminded her. "We do."

"Then why did you all act like you've never been here before?"

"Wouldn't you have noticed if we hadn't?" Nelle asked in return.

Annoyed at the logical response, Mads grabbed an actual gold bar and held it up for everyone to see. "This better not be from the federal reserve."

"Why are you worried? They don't own the gold they have. They're just holding on to it."

Mads had almost flung the bar directly at Max's face when Tock snatched it from her fist.

"Now, now, ladies," Streep soothed. "No need for everyone to get so upset. If anyone should be upset, it's *me*! Since apparently I'm the only one who thinks of you thankless bitches as friends!"

"Are you still harping on that?" Max asked.

"Yes! Because I feel greatly betrayed. *By all of you!*" She sniffed and a lone tear leaked beautifully from one eye, trailing down between her nose and cheek. "How can you not all love me?"

"Because you're a drama queen?" Tock guessed.

"No one asked you, heifer!"

"Charming."

"I want you *all*"—Mads pointed at each of her teammates—"to get your shit out of here. I am not going to prison for any of you."

"If we went to prison, it's not like we'd have to stay," Max felt the need to point out. "It's only those Russian prisons we have to worry about. They've been built to keep honey badgers in. And that's just the Siberian ones."

"Gulags," Streep said, no longer pretend-crying. "One of the few words that actually strikes fear into the heart of a honey badger."

"Well, Stalin knew how to make our lives hell," Tock muttered.

"Wasn't he one of us?"

"No!" everyone snapped at Streep.

"I don't mean he was honey badger, but wasn't he, like, bear or something?"

"Absolutely not," Tock asserted. "He was appallingly full-human."

"Lenin and Trotsky," Nelle said, removing all the cash from Mads's duffel bags so she could obsessively place it into a black metal briefcase, "they were badgers."

"Remember how hard it was to kill Trotsky?" Max asked. "They had to cave his head in. That wouldn't really work on me, though. I've got a MacKilligan head. It's like a bowling ball."

"It really is," Mads agreed. "I threw a baseball bat once. At this guy. Really winged it, too. But Max got in the way and it hit her in the back of the head. She didn't even yelp."

"Max didn't just get 'in the way,'" Nelle corrected with air quotes. "She jumped in front of that bat."

Confused, Mads asked, "Why the hell would you do that?"

"You don't realize how hard you threw that thing," Max explained. "And that kid wasn't wearing a helmet. You would have definitely done some time. And you were not cut out for life in the system."

"How would you know? You've never been in the system either."

"But half my family has. On both sides. On different continents."

"And?"

Max threw her arms out to her sides. "And can you just appreciate that I have a head as hard as a bowling ball and that I used my hard head to protect you?"

Mads shrugged. "Yeah. I can do that."

"Thank you!"

"Who just leaves their team?" asked Charlie, who now sat at the kitchen table.

Although she really wasn't asking anyone in the kitchen. Finn realized she was actually talking to herself. Or the air. But he was worried that she was somehow expecting an answer.

"When people count on you, you're supposed to be there," she went on. "All they had to do was fly a fucking copter and pick up my sister and her team. Not exactly brain science."

"I think you mean rocket—"

"I know what I mean!"

Shay backed away from her, and Keane insisted on staring down the smirking bears.

"Your sister didn't tell you any of this?" Finn asked Charlie.

"She knew what I'd do."

"What would you do?"

"You don't want to know what I would do."

"Why wouldn't I want to know what you would do?"

"Trust me, you don't want to know."

"I wouldn't have asked if I didn't want—"

"Would you two *stop it!*" Keane growled out, no longer interested in smirking bears. "You're driving me nuts!"

One of the dogs out in the backyard barked a warning and Finn heard his mother bolt toward the front door.

"Ma!" he yelled out. "Don't harass the neighbors!"

"You know that bastard next door is near our property again!"

"He's allowed to be—" Finn sighed, hearing the door slam against the wall after his mother yanked it open. "And she's gone."

"You have dogs?" Charlie asked.

"Yes."

She sniffed the air. Stood. Sniffed the air again. Walked around the kitchen. Sniffed. Walked up to Keane. Sniffed him.

"What are you doing?"

"What *are* you doing?" one of the bears asked.

"If you have dogs, why don't I smell dogs?"

Keane looked around. "What?"

"You have dogs but you don't allow them in the house?"

"Why would we allow dogs in the house?"

One of the bears crossed their eyes and another muttered, "Uh-oh."

Charlie's mouth dropped open as she openly gawked at Keane.

"What's wrong with her?" he asked the bears when her gawking continued for nearly sixty seconds.

"Why would you . . . how could you . . . ." Charlie pointed in the direction of the backyard. "You just leave them out there? All night? *Alone?*"

"They're not alone. They've got each other. And squirrels."

"They're *dogs*. They're meant to be with their people. Kept warm in the house. Cuddled up with you all night."

"I don't want them bringing their funky asses into my house."

"It's my house," Finn corrected. "But he's right. We have a really nice rug in the living room. Our mother brought it back from Mongolia. I don't want them dragging their nasty asses over it."

"If you don't want dogs in the house, why do you have dogs?"

"Basic protection. What else?"

Charlie pointed her finger at Finn and Keane. "I'm going out there to check on those dogs. And if they are in any way neglected or mistreated . . ."

She grabbed them by their T-shirts and with what was a surprising amount of strength for a hybrid canine and badger, yanked them close and whispered, "I will crush you *both*!"

With that, she shoved them away. What shocked Finn was that he couldn't stop himself. His body went back and the only thing he could manage to do was not fall on his ass. But he couldn't stop himself from going back several feet. So did Keane. It was something they were not used to, not even from guys six times bigger than some hybrid. Making it kind of devastating coming from Charlie MacKilligan.

So it was a little terrifying when she walked back into the kitchen a couple of minutes later. Finn couldn't remember the last time he'd even looked at the dogs they kept in the backyard. Hell . . . he hadn't even been in the backyard since the summer began. He'd been too busy. For all he knew, there could be only one dog left and the other dogs dead. Just skeletons.

If that woman found a dead dog back there—

"Okay," Charlie said, smiling as she re-entered the kitchen. "I'll talk to Max. I'll make her help you. Because we're family. Speaking of which . . . is Nat around? I want to say hi."

"Upstairs in her room."

"Cool. I'll be right back."

She slipped out of the kitchen and Finn immediately turned to Shay.

"What did she see?"

Shay shrugged. "I don't know."

"You're the one who feeds those dogs. Because you and I both know we don't care about those dogs. So what did she see?"

"I make sure they're fed. That way they remain loyal."

"Keane," Finn ordered.

Their oldest brother walked out, but he was back in two minutes, his face red.

"*Heated dog houses?*" Keane demanded.

"*Are you kidding me?*" Finn yelled in shock.

"They were cold! In the winter."

"Why are those houses also air conditioned?"

"Summers, they were hot."

"You're pampering those dogs!" Finn accused his brother.

"I like dogs, okay?" Shay admitted. "I like dogs! They're friendly. And they're happy to see me when I go back there. They don't call me stupid when I trip over my own feet, which, if you hadn't noticed, are very large and easy to trip over. And the only time they hit me is accidentally! Not once have they thrown me at a wall *on purpose!*"

"You stole the last brownie!"

"*I was hungry!*" Shay threw his shoulders back. "So, yeah. I like those dogs. And you know what I'm going to do? I'm going to invite them into the house. *My* house! Because they're welcome here!"

"It's *my* house," Finn corrected, "and they're not welcome in here because they're not going to drag their dirty asses over the family rug!"

Shay pushed past Finn but Finn grabbed his brother by his neck and dragged him back. Shay shoved him into the refrigerator but by the time Finn got back to his feet, Keane had Shay in a headlock.

Finn was helping Keane drag the idiot to the ground so they could beat some sense into him when four giant black dogs ran past them and into the house. The She-bear smiled down at them.

"I let the dogs in," she announced with great cheer. "And before you three think about taking me on, I play pro hockey against Russian bears, many of them female with children . . . so please try me."

Keane wisely ignored the She-bear and instead growled at Shay, "You have pit bulls watching our backyard?"

"They are not pit bulls." Shay stood. "Those are one-hundred-and-ten-pound *cane corsos* and descend from Ancient Rome."

"'And descend from Ancient Rome,'" Keane repeated mockingly.

Their mother, having returned at some point from harassing their neighbor, appeared in the kitchen doorway, hands on her hips.

"Why is there a giant pit bull dragging its dirty ass on the rug we got from Mongolia?"

Finn threw his hands up in Shay's face. "*Told you!*"

Nelle, their "money girl," did one more recount of the cash in the case while the rest of them carefully wrapped up the painting. It was a lot more involved than people realized to keep a painting of this caliber safe so that it was not damaged in transport.

Once done, they headed out to the SUV Mads had stashed a mile or so away. She made sure to lock up the storage unit carefully since there was a goddamn Rembrandt in there—possibly more than one. She had spotted several boxes marked with the Vatican logo, but quite honestly she didn't want to think about what else her teammates had been up to—and they all retraced their steps until they were out of the storage compound.

Once they were safely in the SUV and on their way, they would text the limo driver a hefty tip for his wasted time and—

They all froze, midstep. There was a wall of loaded automatic weapons aimed at them.

Mads's immediate response was shaking rage, because she assumed the holders of the weapons were family. But then she scented full-human male.

She knew good and well her family would never send full-humans after her. They were too cheap to hire and arm the kind of full-humans that would actually have a chance in hell of taking the five of them down. So her anger quickly subsided, which led to that damn giggle.

Her team glared at her.

"Sorry," she whispered. "Sorry."

"Put down the money and the painting . . . then walk away."

Now all badger eyes moved to Max. None of them had to say it, but they all knew.

If it wasn't Mads's family, then this obstruction was because of Max's dad. Max knew it. The team knew it. The old Norse gods knew it. *Everybody* knew it.

How did Charlie always put it when talking about her father? "That man could fuck up toilet paper."

Mads never knew what that phrase meant, but she knew Charlie didn't mean it kindly.

Now here they all were. In the middle of nowhere, New York, surrounded by—she quickly counted—thirty-seven heavily armed men with a painting worth a small fortune and a case holding half a million in cash.

So they handled the situation by screaming like little girls and running away.

Finn loved his baby sister but he didn't appreciate how kind she was. She needed to get that Siberian-tiger edge. Or, at the very least, that honey badger–rude edge. He knew the species had it. He'd experienced it more than once. So what had happened to his baby sister? Must be some mutant kindness gene floating through his sister that had prompted her to not only invite Charlie MacKilligan to their dinner table but also those damn bears.

He thought his mother was going to have a stroke when Nat did it. Invited them. In ASL and verbally!

Then that idiot, Dale, followed it up with, "That would be awesome!" Which got him a swift punch to the back of the neck from Shay. That led to much whining. Big baby. Would the kid ever toughen up?

So now they were trapped at the dining room table—they usually ate in the kitchen, in silence, except for the TV—because there were so many of them, forced to eat with strangers they didn't like and share their beef Stroganoff. And based on the way these bears were packing that food away, Finn and his brothers wouldn't have any leftovers for a late-night snack.

"Do you guys do well in school?" MacKilligan asked his baby sister and the idiot.

Nat only shrugged but before Dale could say anything, Keane growled, "He better."

"Why 'he better'?"

"We've got plans for him."

MacKilligan frowned. "What kind of plans? Evil, rule-the-world plans?"

Now Keane frowned. "What?"

"He just means," Finn quickly jumped in, "that we want him to go to college and have a career. Have a better future."

"Oh. I get that. Everything Max and I've done is to ensure that Stevie's brilliance is only used for good. Never for evil."

One of his aunts snorted. "Brilliance? A honey badger? Seriously?"

Charlie's fierce gaze cut across the table without her head moving an inch. She coldly studied Finn's aunt for a long moment before she leaned back in her chair and said, "My sister conducted one of her symphonies in front of the Queen of England by the time she was six. They had to get her a tall box to stand on so the London Symphony Orchestra could see her over the conductor stand. By the time she was nine, she'd finished all her college requirements and had gotten a perfect score on her SATs. By the time she was sixteen, she was running a lab at the University of Oxford, but she was considering a serious offer to move to Switzerland to work at the CERN laboratory. Now, I know you may be worrying that CERN may one day open a black hole, but that's doubtful. And my sister had already done that in her bedroom when she was eleven with her mid-level PC from Circuit City and some other materials she really wasn't supposed to have. Then she almost sucked me and Max into the pits of hell with her, but we really aren't supposed to talk about that because the Russians and Saudis *and* our own government already tried to kidnap her in the hopes that they could use her brilliance for evil. And if they find out that hell is an actual location that one can arrive at through a black hole that my sister has the coordinates to, I'm afraid they'll try to take her yet again. Forcing Max and me to do horrible things that all of you will feel very uncomfortable about. We'll do them, though, to protect our amazing baby sister. But, hey, you go on thinking she's not special."

For a table that was normally silent because—when the aunts weren't there—they only spoke in ASL, this particular silence was unusually awkward. Until Charlie's phone vibrated.

She pulled it out of her back pocket and glanced at it.

"Rude," another aunt muttered.

And Keane had to ask, "Have you learned *nothing*?" Because why would any of them attempt to challenge this woman again? Why?

"Huh," Charlie said after gazing at her phone.

Finn was horrified to see his baby sister point at him and then at Charlie. She wanted him to find out what was wrong. Not because she couldn't but, he knew, she was trying to get her brothers to be friendlier to the woman she considered her half-sister. To be closer. Even though she knew that her family—her *real* family—didn't want that at all.

When he shook his head, she widened her eyes and bared her fangs.

Finn dropped his elbows on the table, buried his hands in his hair, and took in a deep breath, then let it out.

After a few seconds, he unwillingly asked, "Problem?"

"Max is in it again."

"Who did she kill now?" Keane asked around his beer. Quickly followed by, "Owww! Don't kick me!" to their baby sister.

"No one yet," Charlie replied, her fingers quickly moving across the screen of her phone.

Then she added with a wide smile, "But the night is young."

"Do we need to go?" a bear asked.

She sighed. "Yeah, I . . ."

As soon as she lifted her gaze and locked it on Finn, he knew he was in trouble.

"No," he immediately told her. "No, no, *no*."

"If you help now," she told him in a singsong voice, "then I can batter her like a ram until she has no choice but to help you guys."

"No."

"That's Yangs all over the world assisting you," she reminded him, still smiling. "You really can't do better. They know everybody. I mean, it won't be resolved overnight, because Yangs have pissed off almost everybody, too, but still . . . you'll be closer with Max than you would be with anybody else when it comes to getting the information you need."

"Look, I've seen your sister work. Unless she's down the block, by the time we get there—"

She waved off his concerns with her phone-holding hand. "I wouldn't waste your time with that. I know my sister. First she deals with these guys, finds out who sent them, and then she does what she does."

"And then you want my beautiful sons to kill people for your sister?" Finn's mother demanded, tears welling in her gold eyes. Not that Finn believed any of that performance art. Like any true cat, his mother could turn on the tears without much effort. It was a gift for her, but a curse for her sons, who loved her dearly.

"I would never ask someone to kill for my sister. That's what I'm here for." Charlie smirked. "And I'm very good at my job."

Keane knocked his fist on the table and when Nat and Dale had focused on him, he signed, *You two, upstairs.*

"I want to hear the rest of—"

"*Dale!*"

Nat quickly stood and grabbed her brother by the scruff of his neck. She dragged him from his seat and out of the room.

"Look," Charlie kindly said, "if you really want my sister's help, you all need to realize something."

"And what's that?" Keane asked.

"That at the end of the day . . . my sister really only helps family. And right now"—she looked around the table—"y'all ain't family."

chapter NINE

"That was easy," one of his men said low.

Yeah. Too easy. He gave a hand signal for everyone to pull back. They did. Moving away from the items the five women had left behind.

He'd been warned that the main target, Max MacKilligan, was "tricky." That was a word that could have a lot of meanings. She might be a seductress, able to turn his men against each other with great legs and a sexy smile. Or a wise owl, using that briefcase as a decoy with enough explosives to kill half his men as soon as one of them opened it.

Not in the mood to be blown up again—he'd had that experience more times than he cared to think about and the scars that went along with all that—he decided it was better to pull back now and take his time getting control of the five women before making a move on the packages.

He'd rather come out empty-handed and alive than the other way around.

He signaled for five of his men to find the women, assigned a unit to watch the packages from a safe distance, and chose two of his men to go with him. He cut behind his team and circled around to—

He stopped and looked over his left shoulder. Then his right. The men accompanying him were gone. Not down, but gone. And without a sound.

From behind, a blade pressed against the inside of his thigh.

Another blade pressed against his throat. Right against the jugular.

A moment later, someone was . . . climbing him. Wrapped around him like a monkey. A mouth against his ear asked who'd sent him. He didn't know. Money was put into his offshore account. Files were sent about his target. It was all on his phone.

Password?

He hesitated.

The blade against his inner thigh pressed hard. So did the blade against his neck.

He said the password.

He was un-climbed. The phone removed. Password used to prove it worked. Knives slipped away.

He was alone again.

Explosions went off in the distance. He knew his team wouldn't leave the package, though. They wouldn't fall for such a lame distraction.

But when he returned to the packages and his team, he realized it hadn't been a lame distraction. His men were still alive, but they now stood around a giant hole where the packages had been.

"They blew the case up?" he asked.

"No," one of his men replied, his expression confused. "They threw some explosives over there," he said, pointing to a spot several hundred feet away. "We looked but didn't move. But when we turned back . . ." He gestured to the hole. "There was this sinkhole."

"Sinkhole?"

"Yeah. This big sinkhole. And the packages were gone. Few of us guys jumped in and found a tunnel."

"A tunnel? Like an aqueduct?"

"No. A tunnel like a gopher might make. But bigger."

"You're telling me that five women burrowed their way out of here with their hands while carrying a big square package and a case of money?"

"No. I'm just telling you what we saw when we went into the sink hole."

"You hear something?" another one of his men asked.

He listened. He did hear something. An engine. A speeding engine. Racing toward them. A black SUV. They faced the vehicle and raised their weapons but before they could start firing, it stopped with the back end facing them. The back window opened and he quickly lowered his night-vision goggles in time to see a woman lean out of the vehicle and aim something at his team.

"Run," he barked, meaning to say it louder, but so shocked he'd actually whispered it.

"What?"

"*Run!*" he screamed just as the rocket was fired and everything around them exploded in a blaze of blinding light and dirt and human screams.

Nelle shifted the SUV into gear and took off. Mads took the rocket launcher from Max and warned her, "Don't step on the painting!"

"I'm not! Calm down!"

"And why was there a rocket launcher in my SUV?"

"There should always be a rocket launcher in your SUV. It's one of those good-for-all-occasions items."

Mads tucked the weapon back into its case and secured it under the seat.

"We could have just left them, you know. We'd gotten away."

"I'm sure most of them are just fine. I just like to leave a warning behind. To remind them not to fuck with me again."

Max climbed over the seats, over Mads's head—annoying!—until she reached the spot where Tock was reading off the commandeered phone.

"What have you got?"

"The message has everything about you except what you are. And everything about your dad."

Max shook her head. "That man. He could fuck up toilet paper!"

"What does that *mean*?" Mads finally asked, but she didn't get an answer.

"Mads, get my computer out," Tock requested, still on the confiscated phone.

She did as asked, pulling out the computer, booting it up, and getting it online before handing it over to Tock.

While Nelle drove and the rest of them stared out the window, Tock plugged the phone into her system and went to work. Computers weren't really Tock's thing. She'd taken some college courses and learned some things from her grandparents' contacts. But only because a lot of what she did with explosives now started online before moving to putting this thing with that thing and making it do another thing.

But she was great for quick turnaround stuff. Like finding someone who wanted to use Max to get even with her father. A thing that really pissed off the MacKilligan sisters.

After about forty minutes, Tock finally asked, "Max . . . do you know a Balinski?"

Max stared thoughtfully up at the SUV's ceiling. "Huh? Balinski? Balinski? I know a . . . no. There was a . . . no. Nope. No Balinskis. But I'm starting to realize my dad has pissed off a lot of people with Polish names."

"Is this person *in* Poland?" Mads asked. "Because we have—"

"Playoffs!" everyone said together.

"Well, we do. And we're not missing the playoffs to go to Poland. We have a chance to get into the—"

"Championships!" they all said together.

"Well, we do!" Mads insisted. "And you bitches aren't going to ruin this for me."

"Don't you mean for the team?" Streep asked.

"No. I mean for me."

"He's not in Poland. He's in Chinatown. Right now. I have his itinerary. And he's Polish-American. He's from Chicago."

"Chinatown here or in San Francisco?" Max asked.

"Here."

"Oh, that's perfect."

"Are we going to deal with this tonight? I've got a Kandinsky sitting in the back of this SUV."

"No one's stealing that ugly painting," Max shot back.

"That's not a Kandinsky," Nelle said from the front seat.

"What do you mean it's not a Kandinsky?" Mads demanded. "I wrapped it up myself. It's the Kandinsky."

"That Kandinsky you were going to just give away—"

"For a house."

"—was worth a fuck of a lot more than a few hundred thousand. It's worth at least twenty-five million."

Tock turned around to stare at Mads. "You were going to give those people a twenty-five-million-dollar painting for that house?"

"I guess so."

Tock shook her head. "Oh, my God."

"Exactly," Nelle continued on, sounding as haughty as humanely possible. "I was not about to let her give those bears a twenty-five-million-dollar painting for that house. So I had Max switch it out when I asked you about the cash."

"Switch it out with what?"

"That Miquel Barceló painting."

"But I really like that Barceló painting. I was going to put that in my new house."

"Yes, but that painting is worth about half a mil, which is the true cost of that house when combined with the cash. *Not* twenty-five million. So suck it up, tulip."

"Don't call me tulip."

"Don't do stupid shit."

"But I like the Barceló more."

"I will drive us all into a wall!" Nelle yelled.

"Found him!" Max cheered as she lowered her phone.

"Found who?"

"Balinski."

"How the hell did you do that? You never left the car."

"The Yangs *own* Chinatown."

"I love you, Max," Nelle said sweetly, "but the Yangs do *not* own Chinatown."

"Maybe not, but they do like to gamble, and so does Balinski."

"So we're doing this tonight?" Mads asked.

"Now that we don't have a twenty-five-million-dollar painting in the car . . . yeah!"

"You are such a lying cow," Mads told Max. "Even if we had the Kandinsky in the car . . . we would still be doing this tonight."

Max laughed at Mads. "Yeah. We would."

Keane parked next to a building that appeared to be empty, but Finn knew it wasn't. It was the address that Charlie had texted them. She was supposed to be right behind them with her bears but she'd turned off a few streets back and they hadn't seen her since.

Finn looked around. He didn't spot anything except a couple of Asian guys lurking in the dark. Security for the gambling hall that was buried around here somewhere.

"I don't know why we're here," Keane grumbled.

Neither did Finn, but they might as well see this shit through.

"Seems like a waste."

"If it helps us get some information—" Shay began.

"Shut up, dog lover," Keane snapped.

Finn rubbed his nose to stop from laughing. Keane had been giving Shay a hard time since before they'd left the house. Actually, as soon as he'd found one of the dogs asleep on his bed—not next to it, not under it, but *on* his bed—Keane had been on a mission to destroy Shay Malone.

It had been pretty fucking funny.

"You know, if you're just going to be an asshole all—"

The body landed hard on the hood of Keane's SUV, cutting off Shay's potential rant. The three of them leaned forward to study what had dented Keane's ride.

"Is that . . . ?"

"I think it is . . ."

The three of them got out of the SUV and met on the passenger side of the hood, staring down at the physical evidence that would one day be used in a murder trial.

Mads was lying on her side, arms and legs curled in, a knife sticking out just below her left clavicle. Blood flowed from both nostrils and from her mouth.

Finn thought she was dead. He was sure his brothers did, too. She wasn't breathing. He was positive her heart had stopped. The animal inside him knew a carcass when it saw one.

Out of due diligence, though, he reached over to place two fingers against her jugular to check her pulse. Maybe he could get her heart started again. The MacKilligans loved to talk about how hard it was to "kill a honey badger," and he was willing to test that theory.

Finn had barely touched the badger's skin, though, when her eyes opened and she scrambled to her feet.

"Shit!" he barked, stumbling back.

Shay roared and bared his fangs.

Keane just yelled, "Kill it with fire!"

The badger squatted in the dent of Keane's hood, her blood-covered arms resting on her blood-drenched knees. Her eyes rolled to the back of her head as she attempted to focus while more blood poured down a wound under her right eye.

Finn moved closer to the car and Keane immediately grabbed his arm.

"What are you doing?" his brother asked.

"Don't get close to it," Shay warned.

"I'm just going to check on her."

"It doesn't look right," Keane insisted.

"Stop calling her 'it.'"

Finn took another step closer but now both his brothers grabbed his arms and they jerked him back.

She closed her eyes, and he thought she was going to pass out. It might be in her best interest to pass out. Comas happened for a reason.

Her still-crouching body weaved a bit and she pressed her right hand into the hood of the car. After a few seconds, she lifted that hand and Finn noticed the fingertips were covered in blood, too. She pressed them against her forehead and slowly dragged them down the front of her face until she reached her top lip.

"What's happening?" Shay asked.

"War paint," Keane whispered.

She was motionless for another twenty, maybe thirty seconds . . . then her eyes snapped open. They weren't black. Or gold. Or brown. Or even Nordic blue as usual. They were red.

Red with rage.

Then she was moving. Leaving nothing in her wake but blood, a massive dent in Keane's SUV hood, and a giggle.

A really disturbing giggle.

After a moment of stunned silence, Shay said, "Your girl-friend was really mad."

"She's not my girlfriend," Finn growled back. Because she wasn't. "I just sent her flowers because her great-grandmother died."

"You didn't do that when your actual high school girl-friend's great-grandmother died."

"She barely knew that woman."

"Are we supposed to actually do something?" Keane asked Finn and Shay. "Or wait for more falling honey badgers to *fuck up my car*?"

"I don't know if the yelling is necessary," Shay pointed out as they all moved toward the building.

"Shut up, dog lover."

Keane abruptly stopped, opened his mouth, and stuck out his tongue.

"Tigers," he finally said. "Lots of tigers, including females." He sniffed the air a few times. "Bengals. South China. Suma-trans. Whoever those badgers came to get, the guy surrounded himself with cats."

Shay shrugged his lineman shoulders. "Or cats lured the badgers here with that human."

Finn and Keane looked at each other, then slowly turned to Shay.

"What?" he asked when they just stared at him.

Mads dug under the foundation and through the walls until she reached the third floor. She poked her head up, took a quick look around, and hauled herself out when she found it safe.

She was tempted to pull the knife out of her chest, but she wasn't sure if she should. Would she bleed out? Since she wasn't sure, she just left the blade in and kept moving.

This had started out easy. Find Balinski, let Max scare the shit out of him for a few minutes, pick up some McDonald's, buy a house. See? Easy.

But as soon as they'd dug their way into the basement, Tock said, "Something isn't right." She couldn't tell them what wasn't right, but they trusted her instincts. She'd been trained by Mossad operatives since birth. The woman knew when "something isn't right."

Nelle was the only one not with the rest of the team. She'd headed toward the hidden entrance with the rest of the gamblers. Since she spoke both Cantonese and Mandarin, had lots of contacts, and was exceptionally hot and wealthy, they all knew she could get into the establishment without any trouble. Yet they weren't about to desert her while they made a run for it because Tock had a bad feeling; they simply had to handle things differently from their original plan.

Max had sent Mads to the roof to get a look from "higher ground," and the rest went into the walls to track down Nelle.

Mads had just pushed open the door and stepped out onto the roof when big hands grabbed her from behind, yanking her arms back. She started to wrestle herself away from those hands when another big body appeared in front of her. Silver glinted in the city lights and she saw the knife in time to jerk her body just enough so that the blade didn't hit her in the heart but under her left clavicle. Then she'd been punched in the face, punched in the stomach, and tossed over the side of the building.

She thought she'd hit the concrete street below but thankfully that SUV had broken her fall. She'd heard someone talking to her but her ears were ringing so she was unable to make out who it was. And then there was her rage.

She was in a realm of rage that blinded her to anything but finding her teammates and killing anyone who'd had anything to do with this. Mads used to get ambushed by her cousins all the time when she was a kid. It used to set her off then, too, when she was young and weak and couldn't really fight back. And it set her off now, when fighting back was a moral imperative.

Mads moved toward the only door in the small room but she could hear footsteps coming and she quickly pressed her back against the wall. A few seconds later the door flew open, but the knob hit the wall before the door touched her.

Two males stalked in, their footsteps heavy.

"I smell her."

"You threw her from the roof of a twenty-two-story building after stabbing her in the chest. I doubt she'd—"

"I missed the heart."

"Barely."

Mads heard a strange sound and she listened hard to decipher it. She heard it again. And again.

She smiled despite the pain it caused in her broken jaw.

Aluminum against flesh. One of them was slapping an aluminum bat against his palm. She knew the sound because she used to do it all the time that summer Solveig made her join a baseball team. She'd been worried that Mads was "Just too involved in all that basketball shit. Try a little baseball. See if you like that more." She hadn't, but the experience did have its long-term perks.

The door was yanked away from the wall and the Bengal tiger that had tossed her off the building roared down at her. Already crouching, Mads slashed her claws across his upper thigh. The cat dropped to one knee and she grabbed the hand holding the bat and shoved it forward, hitting him in the face. With the tiger stunned, she yanked the bat from him and blocked the other bat a South China tiger was swinging toward her head.

Mads held the cat off with one hand and reached into the sheath attached to the back of her jeans with the other. She jerked the bowie knife out and slammed it into the tiger's boot-covered foot. His roar shook the room as she climbed up and over him. When she landed on the other side, she raised the bat over her shoulder and took her best swing.

The bat connected with his right shoulder, bone splintering. He screamed out and grabbed at it with his other hand.

She danced back several steps; the Bengal tiger was already moving on her. Already swinging at her with his big fist.

Solveig's words had never left her after all these years. The words her great-grandmother had said to her that day when Mads was still in kindergarten and she'd gotten her ass kicked by a couple of shifter boys because she'd made their sister cry. After her great-grandmother had told her to stop crying like some "Weak full-human," she'd proceeded to tell her, "You'll always be weaker because you're nothing but a badger. You're always gonna be smaller than the big cats and the bears, whether they're male or female. You'll be fast, but never faster. You'll be strong, but never stronger. So you'll need to be mean. Meaner than anything they've ever seen before."

Then Solveig had wrapped her hand around her great-granddaughter's throat and lifted her up, feet dangling.

"Because if you're not," she'd warned Mads, "then it'll be me you'll have to deal with. Not some bear or some cat. But me. I'll rip the flesh from your hide and blood-eagle your ass if it'll teach you a lesson."

Years later Mads took a psychology class in community college and discovered that Solveig's idea of "parenting" was actually considered abuse among most specialists, but being a honey badger was not for the faint of heart. To apex predators, badgers were nothing more than an add-on to their value meal. To honey badgers, however . . . their kind *were* apex predators—and damn proud of it. Sadly, though, Mads's mother would never teach her that. So Solveig had decided she would be the one to do it. She just did it in the most hyena-slash-Viking way possible.

Mads ducked under that big fist and swung the bat, hitting the tiger across the gut. He grunted and bent over. She went around him and swung again, smashing the back of his skull. He fell forward, but before she could hit him once more, his friend was coming at her again.

She dropped her body to the ground and rolled away. When she sprang back to her feet, she swung the bat, but he caught it and threw her into the wall. Mads went through the sheetrock and into the next room, landing flat on her back.

Wood posts exploded out as the cat followed behind her through the same wall, big claws swinging down at her. She used the bat to block his claws and kicked her legs out to nail him in the face and chest and, eventually, the groin. When he grunted in pain and had to stop to grit his teeth, Mads rolled backward and came to her feet. She swung the bat, but he caught it and yanked her close. She went with the momentum and ended up climbing onto his shoulders. She wrapped her legs tight around his neck and, still unable to wrest the bat from his hands, simply slammed the end against his face repeatedly.

She was enjoying the moment until hands wrapped around her waist and yanked her off. She flipped across the room and into some old wood furniture, destroying it on impact. She quickly scrambled up, swinging the bat as she did to keep the cats away. She shook the dust and dirt and wood pulp off her face so she could see the two wounded tigers staring at her from a short distance away. Their claws and fangs were unleashed, gold eyes glinting in the weakly lit room. Both males were badly hurt. She ran her gaze over them, examining them for the weakest spots where she could hit them and—hopefully—take them down fast. It wouldn't be easy with both coming at her at the same time but she'd faced worse odds and—

Oh, shit.

An even bigger cat stood in the doorway watching them. Mads had no idea how long he'd been standing there, staring.

But she didn't have time to really think about it because the two males were charging her and the big cat was coming, too.

Lifting the bat over her shoulder, Mads stood her ground as the cats charged her. When the Bengal tiger was only inches from her, she spun out of the way and swung the bat hard at his lower back. The spine cracked from the contact, and he was laid flat out.

She pulled the bat back again to take a swing at the South China tiger but the bigger cat was slamming into him from the side, big jaws wrapping around his neck. The South China tiger shifted to cat as the pair fell to the floor in a desperate fight.

Mads allowed herself a blink of surprise before she turned back to the other cat, who was still in his human form, incapacitated on the floor now that his spine was shattered. If she were in a better mood, a less Viking mood, she would have left him that way. Instead, she brought the bat down on his head over and over again until he stopped screaming and moving.

Raising the bat over her shoulder once more, she spun around and found the bigger cat holding the body of the South China tiger in his mouth like a trophy. After they stared at each other for a few seconds, he spit the corpse at her feet.

She looked at it . . . then back at him.

Then Mads sneezed.

The big tiger shifted back to his human form and Finn Malone stood naked in front of her with all those amazing muscles, covered in the blood of her enemy. And for a Viking female absolutely *nothing* could be sexier.

Until he snapped, "Seriously?" when she sneezed again.

"It's not my fault," she mumbled through her broken jaw. "It's your dander! Hold this." She handed him her bloodied baseball bat, lifted up the right side of her leggings and carefully peeled off the athletic tape that she used for Kinesio taping of her muscles after her workout. After grabbing both sides of her jaw and jamming the pieces back together, she placed the tape carefully around her jaw so that she could move it without so much pain. She wasn't sure how long the tape would hold since it wasn't fresh from a roll, but she could replace it later.

Finn pointed at her chest and she looked down, expecting to see even more blood and damage from her earlier wound. Instead, the blade was being forced out by the healing muscles, and the weapon clattered harmlessly to the ground.

"Is that normal?" he asked.

She shrugged. "How should I know?" She felt around the wound. There was no blood pouring from it. No pain. No lumpiness as if a clot had developed under the skin and muscle.

"Seems good," she said . . . before sneezing again. "Maybe it's your shampoo."

Finn shifted back to cat. That's when she noticed the color of his coat. It's utter blackness with the white streaks throughout. There was no orange. No red. She should have known it was one of the Black Malones as soon as she'd seen him.

The annoyed cat turned away from her, his big, long tail hitting her full in the face. That led to a series of sneezes that forced her to take another length of tape from her leg and re-do her jaw.

"Not cool!" she told the cat stalking back through the doorway. "Not cool at all!"

chapter TEN

Finn made his way down to the gambling hall, which was underground. Mads had gone into the walls, which he found weird but was grateful she could do. He could never hide her scent from an entire population of hungry tigers.

And tigers were *always* hungry.

This whole establishment was owned and run by tigers. He'd heard about places like this but had never been because Finn didn't gamble. He didn't like to lose. He was a poor loser when he played football. Yelling at the defense if they didn't protect the quarterback. Threatening the offense if they didn't take down the other team's running back. His asshole-ness was beaten out by only one other: Keane. So he couldn't even imagine how shitty he'd be if he lost fifty grand at a stupid card game.

Staying in his tiger form, he would probably be ignored if they didn't pay too much attention to his black coat or his size. Even by Siberian tiger standards, he and his brothers were on the enormous side in their cat form. Although compared to the rest of the tigers on the premises, he and his brothers were definitely on the big side. Even by Siberian tiger standards. That was because of their tribe. The Zaya-Sarnai wanted to make sure they could take down bears when they had to. So they found the biggest males to breed with, made more offerings to their gods, added a few spells before copulation and boom! You had giant cats roaming the steppes.

The Malone blood decreased their size a bit but still . . . the

Malone brothers towered over the others standing in the room. The gamblers had formed a big circle around an empty space in the center. So Finn and Keane stayed near the back walls and kept their heads down, hoping to find the rest of the badgers alive.

Finn thought the prayers to his ancestors had been answered when a well-dressed She-tiger dragged in the badger they called Nelle. She must have been their scout. She was dressed in designer everything, it seemed, and had her hair done up. She looked stunning except for the bruise on the right side of her face where someone had punched her. Her hands were cuffed behind her back but she was disturbingly calm. To the point of having no reaction at all. She didn't appear psychotically angry as most honey badgers would be in this situation. Yet she didn't seem weirdly entertained like Max MacKilligan either.

Maybe she was simply waiting for her friends to rescue her. Although that was not how honey badgers usually handled . . . well . . . anything. Ever. In the entirety of their existence on the planet.

Another She-tiger entered and stalked across the room. Finn knew this one. Or, at least, knew of her. Vicky Yun. Her family had been running gambling parlors in New York, Las Vegas, and San Francisco for decades. Full-human law enforcement thought of them as an organized crime family that they'd unsuccessfully been trying to bring down with RICO laws for years. But shifters knew them as an "ambush" of tigers that didn't simply break your legs if you lost money at their gambling tables and didn't pay up. Instead they'd peel off your pelt. It was said the patriarch of the family had hats and coats made for his favorite children and girlfriends from the fur of his enemies. It was also rumored that his eldest daughter had a Louis Vuitton bag made of actual tiger skin! Something most shifters would never, ever do, much less fellow cats.

So seeing an actual Yun here had Finn looking across the room to seek out his big brother's gaze. Their eyes locked and they knew that when they moved, they'd have to move very fast. They'd already figured out all the exits and come up with a hasty escape plan but still . . .

Still.

Yun was on the phone as she stomped her way across the room in ridiculously high heels she didn't need considering her height, loudly speaking to someone in a Bronx accent that set Finn's teeth on edge. He knew that his Long Island accent wasn't a pleasure for a lot of people—as he'd been informed by a slow-drawling Texan teammate once—but wow. This female.

"I got your girl, Zhao. Ya hear me? I got her and if you don't give me what I want, I'm gonna start sending pieces of her back to you in small boxes. Would ya like that? Because I'll do it." She huffed over to Nelle and her guard and held the phone to Nelle's face. "Say hello to your daddy, princess."

"Hi, Daddy," Nelle said to her father in Cantonese. "Everything's fine."

"You sure?" Finn heard Nelle's father calmly reply through the phone's speaker.

"Uh-huh."

Yun lowered the phone and stared at Nelle. "You told him everything's fine?" she asked in English. "Seriously? What? You think your little badger friends are going to save you? Because they're not. I helped drag their corpses to the incinerator myself." She stepped closer to Nelle. "As we speak they are nothing but ashes. Not even worth skinning for their pelts. So beg your father to do what I tell him"—she held the phone up—"or we start finding out what it takes to make a little badger scream."

Shay diligently searched the lower levels of the building while his two brothers went to the main gambling hall to see what the rest of these tigers were up to. He was hoping to find some of the badgers. He knew Finn had tracked down Mads. She was currently in the walls somewhere. But the rest . . . ? He and his brothers didn't have a clue.

Luckily, he didn't have to skulk in the shadows to do what he had to do like his brothers. Although a black-furred tiger like Keane and Finn, Shay was also a chameleon. With a little effort and a good, all-over shake, he could bring out some orange stripes when necessary. He couldn't change his fur completely, but he could change his look enough to temporarily blend in.

At the very least, he wasn't worried anyone was going to immediately point at him and scream, "A Black Malone! Get him!" So that was somewhat comforting.

So far, all he'd gotten was everyone simply nodding at him in greeting, ordering him to do something in Mandarin or English, or ignoring him completely. It was great. Usually, when he had to skulk around full-human buildings, he had a much harder time. It was hard to skulk when six-seven, nearly four hundred pounds, and half-Asian. Just calmly walking through an open door made people react as if he'd busted through the wall like the Kool-Aid Man.

Shay was about to go left down a corridor when he heard several men talking about baseball and their girlfriends. But it was the smell of fire that caught his attention. He turned right and followed the chatter until he reached another hallway. The males had a medium-sized door open to a chute and were shoving the lifeless body of Tock into it. They gave her a good push, made sure she fell, then slammed the door closed. The smell of fire was coming from that area. It was an incinerator. It was designed like an apartment building's garbage chute but in this instance, the tigers had made it into a not-at-all legal incinerator!

He charged down the hall, coming to a stop when one of the cats pushed a red button and he could now *hear* flames from below roaring up, decimating whatever was in the incinerator below.

The tigers didn't flinch when Shay ran at them. They simply glanced his way and one of them said in English, "Sorry, dude. We're done. Maybe next time, though."

Maybe next time? Maybe next time he could burn female bodies like they were trash? What was happening? And what was he going to tell his brothers? And Nat? What was he going to tell Nat about her half-sister? The Malones might not believe the MacKilligan sisters were in any way associated with their beautiful baby sister but she sure did. She liked Max, for some unknown reason. This would devastate her!

Shay sat back on his haunches, unable to think of what to do next.

"You need something, bud?" another tiger asked. "Forget all this. Let's go get a drink. You look like you had a hard day."

A hard day? A hard day? Shay narrowed his eyes on the males. He had just decided he was going to bite their heads off when one of them suddenly stepped closer to the incinerator door.

"Did you guys hear that?" he asked.

"Hear what?" another responded.

The incinerator was shut off and the cat stepped closer, his ear next to it.

"What are you doing?"

"I hear scratching."

"It's probably rats. We have rats all over this building."

"I'm telling you . . . I hear—"

The fist punched out of the wall next to Shay, forcing him to scramble back while the other cats began to roar in panic and surprise.

"*What the fuck?*" one demanded as Max MacKilligan shoved her half-burned head out of the wall and hissed, baring all those tiny but deadly sharp fangs.

Feet smashed through the wall next to Shay's new spot, so he skittered away from there and down the hall. Tock landed on the ground, her entire back burned. She unleashed fangs and claws, caging in the tigers who'd shoved her down the incinerator chute.

Streep barreled her way through the wall above the chute, screaming, "*Look at my hair!*" before she flung herself at the first male she saw. In a full-blown rage, she wrapped her legs around his chest and buried her claws deep into his throat, ripping his jugular out before he could even think to shift into his bigger, stronger form.

"*My hairrrrrrrr!*" she hysterically screamed as the cat crumpled to the ground with Streep still on top of him.

Tock buried her claws into the spine of the cat attempting to run from her. His legs just seemed to give up on him as she severed the nerves that traveled through his body.

The third male had a chance to shift to his tiger form as Max pulled herself from the wall. By the time she had her feet on the ground, he was facing her and had reared up on his hind legs, ready to swat her with one of his giant paws. He was a Siberian. Shay knew just one of his paw swipes could crush her head or chest. That alone could put down even a honey badger. Shay was rearing back so he could leap between the two when Max unleashed her claws and tore them across the other tiger's gut.

Oh . . . wait.

No.

It wasn't his gut.

The stunned look on the cat's face. The way he blinked and staggered back, blood pouring across the floor with no signs of stopping.

The way Max held up her hand in gory triumph . . .

No. It wasn't his gut she'd torn her claw across. It was his groin. Well, his inside thighs and groin.

She'd not only opened up his main arteries, but she'd ripped off his cock. Just out of spite.

Even worse . . . she'd done all that with a smile on her half-burned face.

The tiger continued to stagger back until he hit the opposite wall. Then he slid down to the floor and died.

Max shook the blood—and whatever else—off her hand and, as if on cue, the three badgers abruptly turned to look at Shay. In that moment, he forgot that he was a shifter. That he could turn back into human and tell them he was Shay Malone and was there to help. He even forgot that he could easily shake any orange out of his fur! All he could do was sit there, on his haunches, gawking at them. His mind had literally gone blank except for the one thing he knew . . . he was going to die.

Because Max and Streep were coming toward him.

Until Tock stopped them with two words: "Not him."

"Why not him?" Max asked calmly.

"Yeah. Why not him?" Streep also asked, not remotely calm. She was still hysterical. "They should all die!"

Tock put her hand over Streep's face and pushed her away, speaking directly to Max.

"This is one of the Malones."

Max studied him.

"Are you sure? I see orange. I thought Black Malones didn't have orange."

"Trust me. It's him."

"Why doesn't he shift them?"

"You tore a man's dick off. I think he's freaked out."

"*He deserved it!*" Streep screamed, fighting to get Tock's hand off her face. "They all deserve it! Look at my hair!"

"Would you calm down!"

"*Just look at it!*"

"Which Malone?" Max asked, ignoring Streep.

Tock glanced at him. "The one that always smells like dog."

Annoyed now, Shay remembered who he was, where he was, and why he was there. He immediately shifted back to human simply so he could snarl, "There is nothing wrong with being nice to dogs!"

Gawking at him, Tock replied, "Never said there was."

"I heard tone."

"That sounds like a personal issue. Ewww! She licked my hand!"

"You wouldn't get off my face!" Streep accused.

"We need weapons," Max announced. "We're totally out-numbered. You. Rude brother number three."

"I said I liked the Danish."

"Whatever. Do you know where they keep the weapons?"

"No idea."

"We need to grab somebody, then."

Tock gestured toward the end of the hallway. "What about him?"

It was Tock's victim. She'd only severed his spine. She hadn't killed him. And he was desperately dragging himself down the hall, attempting to get away from the crazy badgers, while leaving a trail of blood and piss in his wake.

Not that Shay could blame him.

Deng debated again whether this was the life for him. He'd had two choices after making his way to America: working here with his cousin in the gambling hall, or in the restaurant with his uncle. His cousin was from his mother's side of the family and, to be blunt, those relatives were a little more comfortable with the criminal way of life. Especially when it involved full-humans. But the money from working here was so much better. If he worked at his uncle's restaurant, he'd have to work harder and longer before he could ever earn as much as he was earning now.

He still had responsibilities back home. Family members relying on him. He had to think about . . .

Deng stopped as he saw one of the lieutenants of the in-house gang attempting to crawl out of the hallway that led to the incinerator. He was sobbing, which was just strange, because one didn't become a lieutenant among the Yuns if one cried over anything. Only the strongest and meanest tigers ever made it that far up the ladder.

Suddenly the lieutenant looked over his shoulder, and whatever he saw must have horrified him because his sobbing became worse and he began begging.

"*No, please! Noooooo!*"

Something dragged the male away and Deng stood there, too shocked to move. A few seconds later a tiny mixed-Asian female stepped into the hallway. Shrewd eyes looked up and down the other hallways but when she saw Deng, she quickly sized him up, then grinned. That's when he realized that she was burned. From the incinerator? No one who went into the incinerator ever came out again. Mostly because when they went into the incinerator they were already dead. But even if someone was into torturing and threw a live human inside the incinerator, there was no way they could get out of it. It was made of metal to contain the flames so that it didn't set the building on fire and was something even strong tigers couldn't dig their way out of. So then how did she . . . ?

Still smiling, she waved at him and he . . . well . . . he waved back.

With that, she returned to the hallway with the lieutenant, and Deng turned and made the final decision that restaurant life was the life for him. His uncle would be happy.

And Deng would be alive.

Nelle glanced at the phone, then at Yun.

The badger's heels were even more ridiculously high than Yun's, so she looked directly into the She-tiger's eyes.

"Tell your daddy to send that twenty-five million to the account I give him, princess," Yun pushed. "Or I'll make this really ugly for you."

Finn and Keane weaved their way through the crowd of cats surrounding the three females. They moved slowly and carefully, making sure not to draw attention to themselves.

"Fine," Nelle said on a long sigh. She held her hand out, wiggled her fingers. "Give me the phone."

Yun began to comply but abruptly stopped, staring at Nelle's hand in confusion.

"Hel-*lo*?" Nelle pushed.

"Your . . . your hand . . . ? Weren't you cuffed?"

"You mean these?" Nelle held up the handcuffs that she'd somehow slipped out of.

"What the fuck?"

"Want them back?" she asked, tossing the metal cuffs at the She-tiger who was supposed to be guarding her before she turned and head-butted Yun.

Yun dropped the phone so she could grab her bleeding forehead and scream curses at Nelle in very Bronx-tainted English.

The guard grabbed Nelle's shoulder and Nelle responded by punching the She-tiger in the throat, grabbing her arm, and flipping her over her hip. Once she had her on the ground, she buried the tip of her right heel in the female's eye.

Brutal but effective.

When Nelle looked up from the damage she'd done, she had a room full of Yun-related tigers and tigers employed by the Yuns glaring at her.

And that's when she threw her arms out in challenge and snarled, "*What?*"

They found the weapons easy enough and Shay watched in fascination as the badgers silently pulled out what they needed, quickly and efficiently checked the equipment, then proceeded to ready themselves for war. If he didn't know better, he'd swear they all had military experience, but he was positive they had none. From what he knew, they'd been playing pro basketball since they graduated high school. So where these military-like skills came from, he had no idea.

Once they had the weapons and ammo they wanted, they found clothes to replace the ones that had been damaged by their time in the incinerator. They were just finishing tugging on the boots that were so small, they were probably for any visiting Yun cubs, when a sound at the front of the room had the females all turning, weapons locked and loaded, and Shay plastering himself against the wall in the hopes of not getting accidentally shot.

But thanks to what had to be some kind of training, not one of the badgers fired a shot at Charlie MacKilligan as she stood in the doorway with a shaking white male Shay didn't recognize.

Max lowered her weapon. "What are you doing here?" she asked her sister with a tone of annoyance that seemed unwarranted considering the situation they were in.

Instead of answering that question, Charlie nodded toward the shaking male. "This is Balinski. Dad owes him money."

"Dad owes everybody money."

"The Yuns used him to lure *you* here."

"Why me? What did I ever do to the Yuns?"

"Nothing. From what I can tell. I think they're working for someone else. We need to find out who."

Max jerked her chin at Balinski. "What about him?"

Charlie barely glanced at the man she was holding by the arm. After a moment, she released him and ordered, "Go away."

He did, sprinting from their small group. Shay had no idea what had happened between Balinski and Charlie but the way the man ran from her . . .

"You need to be more careful," Charlie told Max.

"Are we really going to do this now?"

"Stop being so reactionary."

"Really? This coming from you?"

Charlie studied the badgers for a few seconds before asking, "Why are you all burned like that?"

"The Yuns broke our necks and tossed us down the incinerator."

Tock cringed and glanced at Shay, giving him a little head shake. He just didn't know why.

"Where's Nelle?" Charlie asked.

"They kept her," Max replied. "We can only assume they're trying to sell her back to her father. You know her family is very wealthy. They're going to try and milk that."

"And Mads?"

"The people who tried to murder us told us she got ambushed, stabbed, and thrown off the roof."

After a disturbing grunt, Charlie walked off and Tock slammed her fist into Max's shoulder.

"Oww! What was that for?"

"Why would you tell your terrifying sister *any* of that?"

"Because she gets madder when I lie."

"She should know," Streep snarled. "Let her kill 'em all."

"If this is still about your hair—"

"Look at it!" Streep practically screeched, pointing at her head. "*Look at what they've done!* They should all burn!"

Tock faced Shay. "If I were you . . . I'd warn your brothers."

"Warn them about what?"

"That Charlie may not be able to tell one tiger from an-other."

"Especially if her allergies are acting up." Max suddenly smiled. It was not friendly. It was mean. Really mean. "She won't be able to smell a thing."

Keane leaped from where he stood until he was in front of Nelle and roared. Some of the others shifted to their cat form and roared back. But others pulled out guns and knives. Ready for a more human way of fighting.

Out of any other option, Finn charged through the crowd toward his eldest brother and Nelle but he saw Shay coming through the double doors, heading right for them. It wasn't just his brother running into the room that caught Finn's attention. It was the way his brother was moving. It was a full-blown panic run. But this was not the first time Shay had seen a shit-load of guns pointed at one or both of his siblings. He knew better than to panic.

Panic led to shooting. Shay knew that as well as anyone. So the sight of him sprinting across the room had Finn bringing all four paws forward to stop his momentum as Shay tackled Keane out of the way. Nelle didn't budge. She simply stood there. Even when the shooting started.

The badgers came into the hall like they had military train-ing and with enough weapons and ammunition strapped to their bodies to take down an entire village.

Max burst in through the open double doors and Tock through a side door that led from the kitchen. Streep an-nounced herself by kicking a ceiling panel out and unleashing a volley of shots that cleared space between the cats and a still-unmoving Nelle.

That's when Yun finally entered the fray. Calmly, Finn had to admit, but still with that fucking accent.

"All right, all right!" Yun called out. "Y'all calm the fuck down! Before everybody does somethin' stupid."

The growling and snarling simmered down but the weapons and claws weren't put away; the fangs weren't retracted.

Yun continued to rub her forehead where Nelle had head-butted her; a nice lump was already expanding across that smooth skin. Nelle's forehead, however, appeared perfectly fine. Not even a red spot.

"I know you think," Yun continued on, "that you have some kind of winning position here. What with our guns"—she gestured to the weapons the badgers now held—"and the fact that you somehow managed to survive our incinerator. It's my fault, really. I underestimated the warning when they told me your kind was hard to kill. But you have to see"—she gestured around the room—"that you're outnumbered. No matter how many guns you have. Or additional badgers," she said after Mads pushed her way out of a wall panel, desperately brushing herself off and yelping, "Don't eat *anything* out of this place's kitchen. There're rats everywhere!"

"Or how many bears you may have," Yun added when the Dunn triplets entered through the fire exit, still in their human form, but with their guns drawn.

Yun continued on, although she clearly saw the potential problem, "But I'm sure we can come to some less dramatic approach than an all-out war."

Finn glanced at his brothers and the three of them almost laughed. Because not for a second did they believe that Yun really planned on letting any of them out of here alive. But she was strategic enough to know that losing a bunch of her people in the process of killing her enemies wouldn't do her any good with the rest of her family or her employees, so she was being calm and rational.

Smart. And, if she were up against other cat shifters, this would be a hell of a chess match to see who'd get that checkmate.

But Yun wasn't up against cats. Or dogs. Or even bears that could drop their guns and shift to ten-foot, thousand-pound killing machines at any moment.

She wasn't even up against badgers. Not really.

Because what she was really up against were MacKilligans and the friends of MacKilligans. And who the hell knew what that would lead to? Finn certainly didn't know.

Especially now, with Charlie coming through the double doors, seven cats behind her. One tried to grab her arm as she got close to Yun, but Charlie did something that had the tiger yelping. He snatched his hand back and cradled it against his chest, snarling at the badger as she stood before Yun.

"You must be Charlie MacKilligan," Yun said, smirking. She sized up the smaller but larger-shouldered female and appeared completely unimpressed.

Mads stepped closer to Finn, her face grimacing a bit as he and his brothers shifted back to human.

"Uh-oh," Mads said in a whisper. "Don't smirk, woman. Please don't smirk."

"I was just telling your sister Max," Yun continued, oblivious, "that I was sure we could work this out without further bloodshed."

Charlie gazed at the big cat with a blank, unfriendly expression. After a moment, she asked, "So you're saying we can just walk away?"

"Well—"

"We can just turn our backs and you'll let us go."

"Uhhhh—"

"Let's test that theory."

Charlie turned away from Yun and began to walk away.

"What is she doing?" Keane asked, shocked.

"Testing that theory," Mads replied.

"She has to know," Finn gasped, horrified, "you never turn your back on a tiger. Never."

Tigers ambushed from behind. It was instinctual. Especially when they were already planning to ambush their prey.

So Charlie was only a few feet away when Yun moved on her; arms outstretched, going for Charlie's shoulders or neck. But Charlie turned fast and caught Yun by both her wrists.

They locked gazes. Yun was still wearing that smirk, Charlie continuing to appear blank and unfriendly. But as they remained stuck in position, Charlie holding Yun away from her, they kept looking at each other. Both refusing to look away. Like a lethal staring contest.

Eventually, Yun became frustrated. Finn could see that she tried to push forward, but she couldn't get Charlie to budge. Next she tried to pull away, but Charlie wouldn't release her.

As seconds moved on to minutes and her team watched her closely to see what her next move would be, Yun's nose began to twitch and her eyes narrowed dangerously before changing colors. Then, within seconds, she shifted. From stunningly beautiful woman to stunningly beautiful She-tiger. Seven feet long and six hundred pounds, standing on her hind legs and towering over Charlie MacKilligan, her forelegs still held by Charlie's hands.

A Charlie MacKilligan who couldn't shift.

Yet she didn't back off. She didn't release Yun. She didn't do anything but stand there, holding onto those thick tiger legs that were now too big for Charlie to get her hands around.

The situation grew increasingly tense, especially when Charlie didn't let Yun go and didn't show any signs of fear or weakness. She simply kept her grip and held on. Eventually Yun put her full strength into resisting and so did Charlie, muscles beginning to pop under her black T-shirt.

Finn didn't like this. All Yun had to do was lower her head and she could bite Charlie's face off. So he started to move forward, but Mads's arm shot out and blocked him.

"Don't."

"Yeah, but—"

"Don't."

There was something in Mads's voice. The way she said that one word.

He took a step back and waited.

Then he saw it. Shockingly, Yun's hind claws were forced back as Charlie shoved the bigger, heavier shifter across the hardwood floor of the gambling hall. Yun tried to stop her. Tried to fight her off. Tried to yank her forelegs away from the hybrid holding onto her, but Charlie refused to let go. The worst part now, though, was that Charlie was the one who was smirking. Which made it seem as if holding onto a snarling, snapping She-cat was no strain on her.

How was that even possible?

Finn had known hybrids before. His baby sister was a hybrid. He'd seen her struggle to open a jar of pickles. He'd never known any hybrids with superstrength. Instead, they'd all been . . . quirky. They all chased lights only they could see. The wolf hybrids didn't always know how to howl properly. Bear hybrids could be so easily distracted by butterflies that the Malone brothers made a game of how many in a day or week they could entice into walking face-first into walls, doors, or windows. The cat hybrids sometimes tore up a friend's new wood flooring because they were convinced they heard a mouse underneath—when they didn't. Hybrid antics were always hilarious—especially when they happened to one's teammates—but not remotely terrifying.

Yet watching a non-shifting hybrid shove a She-tiger that was five times bigger across the floor like she was moving an empty refrigerator box by herself . . . ? *That* was terrifying.

Livid and frustrated, Yun leaned forward and snapped her massive jaws at Charlie's face, again and again. But Charlie managed to dodge and weave out of the way without ever losing her grip on Yun's forelegs. She also managed to keep the two of them moving around the floor.

Yun tried to rear farther up and take Charlie with her, but Charlie held her down. No matter how much the She-tiger pulled and heaved.

Then, at some point, Yun seemed to get her right paw free from Charlie's grasp. It shouldn't have surprised Finn, but there was a part of him that felt Charlie had let her go; he just didn't believe the hybrid had run out of steam.

Free, Yun reared back her paw and unleashed a devastating blow to Charlie's head that spun her several feet away. She fell to her knees, her hands covering her face.

Finn and his brothers jerked forward, about to jump in once again, when Mads barked out a sharp, "*No!*"

They all stopped. Even Keane, which was surprising. He usually only stopped so quickly for their mother or Nat. But maybe it was something in the way Mads had warned them off. In her tone. In the way her entire body was rigid and her claws started easing out of her fingertips.

Charlie remained on her knees, her hands still covering her face. Only now blood poured from between her fingers and she seemed afraid to move her hands. Probably afraid that most of her face would go with it.

A blow like the one she'd received from Yun should have crushed her skull. It should have killed her. But Charlie just remained kneeling, cradling her destroyed face.

With Charlie's back to Yun, she didn't see the tiger lowering her head, opening her maw, and charging right toward her.

The room remained silent as they all watched. Not even Charlie's sister called out a warning. And Yun made no sound as she launched herself from about twenty feet away toward Charlie's back. Ears flat against her head. Forelegs spread wide. Lips pulled back over white fangs. Jaws opened wide so she could wrap her fangs around the back of Charlie's neck and crush it on first—

Yun was a hairbreadth away when Charlie spun around to face her, going up on one knee for balance before slamming her fist into the She-tiger's open mouth. With her free hand, she grabbed the back of Yun's head, pulling her forward, closer and closer, which meant that she was sticking more and more of her arm inside the tiger's mouth and down her throat.

Coughing and struggling, Yun tried to unwedge the hybrid's arm. When that didn't work, she tried biting down on it. That brought some blood and some light damage to Charlie's tough badger skin, but the bones . . . the bones didn't break. They didn't bend. They weren't crushed under the strength of desperate tiger jaws. Something Finn had never seen or experienced before. He'd taken down water buffalo that crushed easier than Charlie MacKilligan.

And the entire time that Charlie had her arm down Yun's throat and her hand gripped the back of the She-tiger's head, she stared Victoria Yun directly in the eyes. And she smirked. Just like Vicky Yun had smirked.

Then something happened. Something that had Yun's eyes growing impossibly wide and Charlie's smirk intensifying.

Yun began to fight harder. Her front and back claws slashed at Charlie as Yun struggled to get away from the hybrid with everything she had. But nothing, it seemed, could stop Charlie. Nothing.

Something cracked and Yun's entire body buckled. She fought a little more but it wasn't like before. There was no real determination behind it. Instead, it simply seemed like instinct. The last struggle. Death throes. Something else cracked and air rushed out of Yun seconds before her entire body deflated to the ground.

Charlie still had her arm stuck between Yun's jaws. She tugged once. Then again. With the third, she dragged her arm out and with it, Yun's heart and lungs.

"*Holy shit,*" Shay whispered. He might have said it, but they were all thinking it. Even the badgers in the room. Even Mads, who moved closer to Finn, pressing her arm against his. He understood why, too. They all needed to feel grounded in reality. Because this didn't feel real. A hybrid wolf–honey badger shouldn't be able to do . . . *that*. It wasn't a simple matter of not being normal. It was insane.

He knew just how insane when, in the deafening silence of that room, Max MacKilligan burst out laughing. She was no less shocked than the rest of them, but while they all stood around dazed and disturbed and, quite honestly, freaked the fuck out, Max MacKilligan laughed. Hysterically. Barely able to get out her "Damn, Charlie!" before she started laughing again.

See? That was insane. The MacKilligans were insane.

Mads pressed her arm against Finn's. She knew she shouldn't. They weren't that kind of friends. Or even friendly. But she felt a little dizzy. A little off-center. How could she not with Charlie standing there, holding the major organs of a tiger in her hand?

There was so much blood. Not just from the cat and its

torn-out organs. But from Charlie. Where the cat had struck her with its paw . . . well, that should have crushed her face in. As a honey badger, she probably would have survived anyway, but it would have taken a good week or two for those facial bones to knit themselves back together again. They should have had to carry her out. Instead, Charlie's face wasn't crushed. The skin was torn a bit on the lower jaw. Her nose appeared broken. That wasn't the first time, though . . . and it wouldn't be the last. And she had claw marks across her forehead through part of her scalp. Strangely, they reminded Mads of a stone skipped across a lake. But she'd seen how Yun had hit Charlie. That was one full, powerful strike. She hadn't held back. Yet Charlie was barely injured. That was fucking weird!

Charlie held up the cat's insides.

"It's like some kind of new blood eagle," she whispered to Finn.

"Should I ask what that is?" he whispered back.

"No, you shouldn't." If he didn't already know about the ancient ways Vikings tortured and executed their enemies, it was best he continued not to know.

"If you come after my family," Charlie told the cats gawking at her, "this is what happens to you. All of you. I don't stop. I don't *ever* stop."

With that, Charlie tossed the cat's remains across the ground, shaking the blood and gore off her hand.

One of the male tigers looked around the room and, apparently shocked no one was doing anything to this one crazy woman, took a step forward. He had his gun out, maybe with armor-piercing rounds in the clip. And Charlie was still trying to get the blood off her hands. Maybe he thought he had a shot. He forgot something, though. He forgot Max.

She climbed his back and slammed two blades into his neck before he could even get his finger on the trigger of his gun. She opened up the cat's arteries and scrambled over his head, burying the blades into his chest.

Mads didn't know why Max was stabbing him in the chest. She'd opened up the arteries in his neck while he was human.

He would be dead before he hit the ground. But there Max was . . . stabbing away.

Charlie walked past the pair, the roomful of tigers separating so she and the badgers could leave without any problem. Max was still going, though. Kind of lost in the moment until Charlie yelled, "*Max!*"

Max yanked her blades out of her prey's chest and jumped down from the cat, allowing him to fall dead to the floor.

"Coming!" Max cheerfully called out to her sister before following her.

"Is she . . . is she skipping?" Finn asked Mads about Max.

Mads blew out a breath. "Yeah."

"Why?"

"You know, it's best you don't ask those questions. You will *never* like the answers."

chapter ELEVEN

Finn woke up when he smelled the muffins. They were blue-berry and he really wanted one. Or maybe six. Or a dozen. He wasn't finicky. He just knew he was hungry. It had been hours since he'd eaten. Hours!

They'd left Chinatown the night before, driven to the badger house in Queens, and that was kind of the last thing he remembered. They were all exhausted by the time they got to the house . . . except the two MacKilligan sisters. He recalled both of them being awake enough to still be bickering as he'd stepped out of Keane's battered SUV. How long that had gone on after he'd fallen asleep, he had no idea.

Lifting his head off the back of the couch, Finn realized it wasn't just the smell of muffins that had jogged him awake. It was the sound of crunching. He forced his eyes open despite the bright sunlight in the badger living room and looked around. It looked like people had pretty much dropped wherever they could find a space. Nelle was elegantly curled up on a stuffed chair tucked into the corner opposite the giant sofa he was on. Streep was asleep on the floor, tightly packed into the space between the wall and the chair that Nelle was asleep in. The badger seemed surprisingly comfortable in such a tiny space.

Tock was also asleep on the floor but, unlike her friends, had her back against the wall so she faced the entrance; she had an automatic weapon across her lap, her finger on the trigger.

When Finn's eyes passed over her, she woke up long enough to look at him, judge him nonthreatening, and go back to sleep.

Keane was on the far end of the same couch that Finn was on, his long legs stretched out in front of him, his arms crossed over his chest, his hair covering his face. Shay was next to him in pretty much the same pose except for the loud snoring. It was like sleeping next to a moose. Finn turned his head and found the source of the crunching.

It was Mads. She sat with her back against the armrest of the couch, her bare feet tucked under his thigh as she silently stared at him and chewed something decidedly crunchy now that her broken jaw had healed. He thought maybe cereal or nuts until she opened the wooden box she held in her hand and pulled out a very black, very terrifying-looking scorpion, then put the struggling thing in her mouth. It was a good-sized arachnid, so it didn't go all the way in, the stinger remaining outside her lips. Finn watched in horror as that part jabbed her over and over, most likely injecting her with its venom several times while she chewed and stared . . . at him.

They sat like that for a good—he didn't know—maybe five minutes? Then, unable to help himself, Finn started laughing. Not loudly. He didn't want to wake anybody up. He also didn't want anyone else joining them in this moment. This was their time to be really fucking weird.

Because this was weird, right? Even by shifter standards . . . this was fucking weird.

"What are you doing?" he finally whispered to her.

"Snacking." She held out the wooden box to him. "Want one?"

"No. I prefer my struggling meals to kick me in the head with their hooves."

"There are some scorpions that have poison that can—and will—kick you in the head metaphorically. This, however, is not one of them. It's just an Asian Forest Scorpion. Its venom is very mild. Sure you don't want to try it?"

"Positive." Finn thought a moment. "But give me one."

Mads frowned, then shrugged. She handed over the scorpion and Finn slightly turned so he could carefully place the bug right between Shay's eyes.

Finn tapped his brother's arm and Shay woke up, his eyes crossing to get a better look at what was on his face. Finn had to hand it to his brother. He didn't jump up. He didn't run. He stayed calmly situated on the couch while screaming, "*Get it off me! Get it off me! Get it off me!*"

Chuckling, Mads tried to reach over Finn to get to Shay but Finn blocked her with his arms so his dog-loving brother suffered a little longer.

Keane woke up, and as soon as he saw what was on their brother's face, he shot off the couch, barking, "Fuck! Fuck! *Fuck!*"

By now the other badgers in the room were awake. Nelle and Streep were in hysterical giggles, but Tock simply got to her feet, swung the strap of the automatic weapon she held over her shoulder, and walked across the coffee table so she stood in front of Shay. She easily lifted the scorpion off the panicked cat's nose as Shay swiped at his face a thousand times with both hands. The pair stared at each other for several seconds until Tock simply leaned her head back, opened her mouth wide, and lowered the struggling scorpion in.

As she chewed, Shay finally jumped up and ran out of the room, screaming he needed a washcloth.

"He's going to scrub the skin right off his bones, isn't he?" Mads asked Finn.

"He's going to try."

Finn pointed at the wooden box Mads held. "Do they have a lot of boxes like that around the house?"

"Not really. Stevie is easily—"

"*Squirrel!*"

Outside in the yard, Max's baby sister ran past the living room windows, hands wildly waving over her head.

"—startled," Mads finished. "She's also scared of snakes, racoons, spiders, rats, the occasional thunderstorm if she thinks it has anything to do with climate change, and giant wasp nests but only because she finds the look of them 'aesthetically unappealing'" she said with air quotes.

"What does that mean?"

"I think it means she finds the big nests ugly and they make her skin crawl. But she doesn't know to just say that."

Finn blinked. "Okay."

"Don't be such a snob. I like the MacKilligan sisters," Mads admitted to Finn. "They're good to each other."

Stevie ran back the other way, arms still flailing over her head. But this time, Max ran after her until she abruptly stopped and looked down, up, toward the nearby trees, down again . . . Max finally turned away and that's when Stevie appeared out of nowhere, launching herself at her sister's back. Stevie wrapped her arms around her sister's neck, but couldn't quite manage to take her down. Still, Mads was impressed.

"Wow. Stevie's come a long way."

"Has she?"

"Yeah. That was a full-on ambush. I knew her when she couldn't do that at all. No ambush skills. No fighting skills. Just no skills outside of math and science and fancy music."

"She's definitely got some tiger in that DNA."

"Seems so."

Finn tilted his head to the side. "She's still not quite getting her sister on the ground, though."

"The fact that she could ambush Max MacKilligan at all is impressive. Let's not ask for the moon."

"Muffin?"

Charlie stood over them with a tray of giant blueberry muffins. Before Mads could take one, Finn took the entire tray and placed it in his lap. When silence followed that bold move, he looked up and asked, "What?"

"Not big on sharing?" Tock asked.

"I'm a tiger, so the answer to that is no."

"No problem," Charlie replied. "I have more in the kitchen. But you guys better get what you want before the bears start wandering in."

Keane walked back into the living room holding a platter piled high with blueberry muffins.

Charlie's friendly smile vanished. "Or apparently now, cats."

"You let bears just come into your house?" Keane asked.

"We tried to lock them out," Charlie explained, "but they just took the door down and came right on in. But they did it so nicely, I couldn't even be angry . . . Did you actually take the rest of the muffins?"

"I'm hungry."

"Are you going to share with the rest of us?" Tock asked.

Keane sat down on the far end of the couch, placed the platter on his lap, and finally replied, "No."

Nelle walked barefoot across the room, reached across the coffee table, and snatched a muffin off Keane's platter. The tiger immediately roared in warning and Nelle hissed, bared her fangs, and lunged at him. The move so surprised Keane, he reared back, eyes wide, allowing Nelle to take three more muffins that she tossed to Tock, Streep, and Mads before flashing Keane a smile and taking a big bite out of her own muffin with her fangs still unleashed.

Charlie let out a long sigh. "I guess I have to make more muffins now, before the bears tear the house down."

"And why is that necessary?" Finn asked.

"Bears," all the badgers replied.

"How do you think the MacKilligans get to live here?" Tock asked.

"Because it's America . . . ? Right?"

"What does that matter when there are bears? Hungry, growling bears?"

"A lot of them females with cubs," Streep added. "Even badgers avoid that fight."

"It's just easier to bake them treats and hope for the best."

"Is that why you're baking something already?" Keane asked, nose lifted.

"That cake's for Mads. So she can finalize the papers and buy her house."

Mads had completely forgotten about the house. But she

was also confused. "Was cake part of the deal? I don't remember that." Last night felt as if it had been years ago.

"No. But it's always best to show up to a bear deal with baked goods in hand. I'll go get the cake."

"Do you know how to bake?" Finn asked Mads.

"I can't cook or bake. And I'm not exactly eager to learn."

"Think the bears in the neighborhood will let you stay?"

She knew Finn was only joking, but Mads realized . . . "I hadn't really thought about it."

Charlie returned with a cardboard box that made whatever delicious-smelling thing she had in there look like it came directly from the local bakery. She also had a small container of white cream on top and placed both on the coffee table near Mads.

"It's crumb cake. Tell them when the cake cools, they can drizzle the icing on." For a moment, Charlie's gaze bounced back and forth between Mads and Finn until she finally said, "Go with her, Finn."

"Why?" the pair asked together.

"She's carrying a lot of cash. And a valuable painting. Anything could happen between here and there. Do you want to be responsible for her getting mugged on the cold, heartless streets of Queens?"

"How would I be responsible for that?"

"Because I said so." Charlie gave a smile that was more terrifying than friendly before pointing toward the front door. "Now don't be too long, you two. We still have to discuss—"

There was banging at the living room windows and they all saw Max standing there. Her baby sister still attempting to take her down. It was a sad attempt, but Mads had to give the kid points for sticking it out.

Max jammed her finger against the window and yelled, "Why are those cats still here?"

"Because you're going to be working with them," Charlie informed her younger sister.

"*Like hell I will! I don't owe them anything!*"

"Max—"

"I'd rather set myself on fire!"

"Excuse me, would you?" Charlie walked out of the room.

A few seconds later, she shot past the window, taking down Max and their baby sister in the process.

"Wow," Keane muttered. "That was impressive. Think Charlie would be interested in playing football?"

Finn took the briefcase with the money and carried the cake and icing with his other hand. Mads held the painting. They were just about to head toward the front door when Shay finally returned to the living room, his face bright red from all the scrubbing he must have done after having a scorpion sitting on his nose for half a second. It wasn't just the redness of his face, though, that was the problem . . .

"Uh-oh," Tock said when she turned around and looked up at Finn's brother.

"Wha?" Shay asked seconds before he quickly guessed. "My fay isss wollen, i'n it?"

"Uhhhh . . ."

"Have one of your dogs lick it," Keane unhelpfully suggested, making Finn laugh until Mads glared at him. Then he quickly looked away from her appalled gaze. "Should fix it right up."

Tock slammed her hands against Shay's chest to stop him from going after Keane.

"Your face is a little swollen," Tock said.

A little? It looked like someone had forced a softball into his cheek.

"I'm eye-ing! I 'ow it!"

"You're not dying," Tock told him, somehow understanding his idiot brother. "Even for regular full-humans that scorpion's venom is very mild. You're probably just having an allergic reaction."

"'Ix me, 'oman! 'ow!"

"Calm down." She spun Shay around and shoved him out of the room. "Streep, where do they keep their allergy stuff?"

"Somewhere in the kitchen. I'll come and help you look."

Streep followed them out and Finn followed Mads in the other direction. It wasn't until they had the front door open that Nelle said from behind them, "Just so you're not surprised, I went ahead and ordered some furniture for you."

Mads froze for a second, but then abruptly spun around so fast that Finn had to take a quick step back or find out if they looked good wearing each other's clothes.

"Why?" Mads demanded.

Nelle leaned against the doorjamb separating the living room from the sunroom. "Because you needed furniture and we both know you weren't going to have time to buy any."

She said that so casually it might have sounded like a friendly gesture and not massively presumptuous. But as a tiger that lived with Keane Malone, a massively presumptuous cat, Finn knew the signs when he saw them.

"Oh, my God," Mads snapped. "Seriously?"

"What?"

"You picked my furniture for me?"

"No. Of course not." She slipped one of her high heels on. "I had Sauveterre do it."

"*Who?*"

"Sauveterre."

"Who the fuck is Sauveterre?"

"You know. Charles Sauveterre."

"Do you mean Chuck?"

Nelle put on her other shoe and turned an unsmiling face to her teammate. "You know he hates when you call him that."

"It's his name."

"When he was twelve."

"In Iowa."

"His mother's French."

"Canadian. She's French-Canadian. And I don't need Chuck picking out my furniture either!"

"Look, the reason I had Sauveterre—"

"Chuck."

"—do it is because we all know that it won't just be you hanging out at your house. It'll be all of us. And, quite honestly, you have the taste of a thirteen-year-old boy who really loves basketball."

"I do not."

"You do. Which means you'll get one large TV for the living room that you'll put on top of a cardboard box. A couple of those folding chairs that someone from the neighborhood will give you because they've upgraded their backyard furniture, and some TV trays, so we can all eat. A refrigerator and microwave for the kitchen and a box spring for the bedroom. That'll be it. You know it. I know it." She gestured to Finn. "Even this guy knows it. And I'm sorry, I can't live that way. So I had Sauveterre—"

"Chuck."

"—handle it. That way we can all be comfortable. And happy."

"He designs for those rich sheiks who buy those multimillion-dollar apartments in Manhattan but never live in them. I can't afford the kind of furniture he's going to buy!"

"You have a twenty-five-million-dollar Kandinsky just sitting in a storage locker."

"For emergencies!"

"You were about to give it away!"

"To buy a house!"

"In Queens!"

"Hey! Hey! *Hey!*" Finn finally bellowed as the two females squared off, nose to nose with their fangs out.

"Need some help in there, little brother?" Keane asked. Finn didn't even have to look to know Keane was smirking. He could actually *hear* the smirk in the asshole's voice.

"No, I do *not,*" Finn barked back. "And you," he said to Mads, "out the door. Now!"

Using his body and the cake, he maneuvered the badger through the door, across the stoop, down the stairs, through the fence gate, and out onto the sidewalk.

Once they were free of all the drama, he nodded across the street while asking, "You were really going to give away a twenty-five-million-dollar painting for *that* house?"

"I got the painting, like, a decade ago, and hadn't checked the recent value on it. And, to be quite honest, I'm not that big a fan of his work. I also don't need you giving me shit about this, too."

"Fine. But if you want your friends staying off your back, you need to make smarter financial decisions in the moment."

"Teammates."

"What?"

"They're my teammates."

Finn couldn't help but laugh.

"What's so funny?"

"I said 'friends' because I was being polite. But they're not your friends and they're not your teammates."

"So they're my enemies?"

"Wow." Finn blinked. "No. They're your *family*." When she started to balk, he asked, "Do you think I'd put up with any of the shit I put up with from Keane or Shay if they weren't my brothers? They irritate me in ways you can't even imagine. Chances are I would have killed them a long time ago if we weren't related. But I tolerate them because I love my mother and because our bond is deeper than Keane's annoying habit of humming when he eats bacon. And *only* when he eats bacon. Or Shay's inability to eat rabbits because he finds them cute and fluffy, which we all believed applied only to rabbits but now we see also extends to dogs. I mean, we've never eaten dogs because they're disgusting, unclean beasts but he just finds them . . ." Finn shuddered at the next word he had to say. ". . . cute."

He let out a breath. "But they're my brothers, so I tolerate their bullshit. They're your sisters, so you tolerate their bullshit. That is just how it goes." He gestured with the hand holding the briefcase. "Now let's go buy you this house that is not worth a twenty-five-million-dollar painting."

"You're never going to let that go, are you?"

"I don't know how anyone can let that go. It's the stupidest thing I've ever heard and I live with Shay Malone. Dog lover."

chapter TWELVE

"I've never had my own bed," Mads announced as she stretched out on the double California king in the middle of the master bedroom. A bed that was perfect for a loving pair of grizzly or polar bears but was hilarious for one small badger who looked lost in the middle of it.

"Never?"

"Nope. I took whatever bed was empty or I slept on the couch or outside or crashed at one of my teammate's if their parents didn't care. Luckily they never did since I was such a nice kid."

Finalizing the house deal had taken no time at all because the bears could barely keep their mind on anything once they'd scented Charlie's coffee cake. Even the black bear lawyer they brought along kept drooling while trying to point out where everyone should sign and had to wipe the contract with a paper towel, apologizing profusely, before the group took off with the cake, the lawyer quickly returning to grab up the signed papers. Finn had recorded the whole transaction on his phone so he wasn't too worried about any last-minute double-dealing.

In the end, though, it had all worked out fine. Everyone got what they wanted—Mads a new house and the bears a lot of cash, an expensive painting, and a cake they really desired more than anything else.

The entire transaction took place outside on the hood of the lawyer's car, which turned out to be a good thing. Because even Finn was shocked for a good long while by the way Nelle and her friend had decked out Mads's new house. It wasn't just some nice furniture shoved in so Mads had a place to sleep. The house had been fully decorated. Overnight. Not only the usual matching furniture, but art on the walls, appliances in the kitchen and laundry room, books on the shelves, and one of the bedrooms made into an office with a brand-new computer system and a Wi-Fi network that was already set up through the local cable company. All Mads had to do was enter her email and social media passwords.

How all this had been done in less than twenty-four hours, Finn had no idea. He knew the truly rich had access to things that the "regular guy" simply didn't, but this was impressive. The only room left untouched was the basement. Finn didn't know why. Maybe because it needed so much work or because it was going to be some sort of sports shrine for the sports geek. Those giant cardboard cutouts of history's great basketball players weren't always easy to track down. Especially if she wanted them signed. And Mads would probably want them signed.

After they went through the entire house, saw all the new furniture, Mads didn't say much. Then again, she didn't really need to. Her glaring eyes and low growling pretty much said it all. Still, Mads did seem to like the bed.

"What about when you got older?" Finn asked, his hands stuffed in the front pockets of his jeans. "Where did you sleep then?"

She sat up. "I'm talking about when I got older. When I was younger, I just slept in the cabinets or under the couch. But mostly outside except when temperatures went below zero because I didn't always have access to a warm coat at night and I am made up of two African animals not used to the cold."

"You slept under the couch?"

"Sometimes. I found life easier when I wasn't noticed."

Losing his father when he was pretty young, Finn had always assumed he'd had a hard life. He was starting to realize there was a harder life to have. Especially if he had been raised by hyenas that hated him.

Trying not to give a look of pity, Finn turned away and

quickly opened a closet. Because he'd rather let her think he was a nosey cat instead of a pitying man. But as soon as he had the sliding door open, he gasped.

"They left their mother's clothes here?" he asked.

"She did move to Florida," Mads said, bouncing off the bed. "Maybe she didn't need them and they moved out of the house so fast . . ."

Mads pulled out a medium-sized tank top on a hanger and held it up for both of them to stare at.

"Is that . . . is that . . ." Finn could barely say it, but he finally got it out. "Is that a Scottie Pippen basketball jersey? With his number? From when he was with the Bulls?" Finn was not a basketball fan but before they'd cut off contact with the rest of the Malones, the gamblers—and there were a lot of them among the uncles, aunts, and older cousins—were all sports lovers. Basketball, baseball, soccer. Even rugby. Anything they could bet on. So there was no way he hadn't heard, in detail, about the Chicago Bulls. Especially Michael Jordan and Scottie Pippen. And the constant debate over whether Jordan was possibly a shifter of some kind—which he wasn't.

Mads put the tank back and quickly shuffled through the other tanks and T-shirts. Then she slid open another closet door and found nothing but jeans, basketball shorts, and, on the floor of the closet, an array of basketball sneakers and a bunch of Converse in multiple colors. All in one size. Finn was guessing Mads's size.

"These sneakers are all in my size."

"She got you clothes, too?"

Mads slammed the door so hard that Finn cringed, his superstitious side worried that the attached mirror would shatter, bringing seven years of bad luck to Mads. Something she didn't need at the moment. When the glass held steady, he reached out and slipped his arm around her waist, then pulled her back into the middle of the room.

"Don't do it," he told her.

"I'm going over there right now and tell her to take all her shit back!"

"I know you want to—"

"I have to."

"—but you're not going to."

She stopped trying to pull his arm off her waist and looked up at him.

"And why is that? Exactly?"

"I know this seems—"

"Obsessive? Ridiculous? Like she's throwing her money in my poverty-stricken face?"

"You have a twenty-five-million-dollar painting that she just used against you in an argument . . . she *knows* you are not poverty stricken."

"It's just so presumptuous!"

"She's trying to be helpful. Can't you just appreciate the gesture?"

"*No.*"

She tried again to pull herself out of his arms but then they both saw the coyote walk by the open bedroom door and the struggle immediately stopped. Because that wasn't a shifter coyote. It was a full-blood coyote. Wandering around Mads's new home.

Stepping away from each other, they followed the canine as it walked down the stairs to the first floor, down the hallway, through the big living room, through the dining room, through a swinging door, and into the very large kitchen with the nice breakfast nook and the bar with the seating that separated it from the dining room. It went to the stainless-steel refrigerator and stared at the door until Mads finally went over and opened it.

"Hey," Finn noted, "the refrigerator is stocked."

"And the cabinets. There's a ton of honey in all those cabinets except that set over there," she said, pointing. "Those are empty."

"So you'll have someplace to sleep?"

"Yes."

The coyote pulled out a package of cooked turkey sausage and returned to the dining room.

"Are you going to do something about that?" Finn asked.

Mads shrugged. "About what?"

"You have a wild animal in your house."

"So far you haven't peed anywhere."

Finn glared. "I don't mean *me*. I'm talking about that coyote. You can't let that dirty thing wander around your house."

And the coyote did wander. After quickly devouring the sausage, it started walking again, heading back up the stairs; Finn and Mads followed.

"Charlie says it's good to have a dog around your house." Mads pointed out.

"A *domesticated* dog. Not something that crawled out from under your porch when the last family moved away. For all you know, it could be riddled with rabies."

"It's not."

"How do you know?"

"I can smell it."

"You can *smell* rabies? Really?"

"Well . . . I've had it six times. Eventually you learn to either smell it on others or just lie down and die from it after all the foaming."

"How did you survive having it six times?"

She shrugged. "How did I survive that fight with the Inland Taipan when I was on the school trip at that illegal zoo? I just did."

"What's an Inland Taipan?"

"A poisonous snake. One bite can kill up to a hundred people."

"And you?"

"Passed out for a day. Vomited a lot. Stabbed Max with my claws when she found me in the woods, which I felt really bad about because we had a game coming up over the weekend."

"So you're just going to keep him?"

"Of course not. He's a wild animal." Her phone began to vibrate and she dug into her back pocket to pull it out. "But he lived here before me, so if he can get in . . ."

Finn was going to respond to that bit of insanity but before he could, Mads connected to the call on her phone and as soon as she did, the screaming started.

*   *   *

Mads and Finn leaned away from the phone as her mother's screaming came barreling out of the speaker.

Mads was more than a little shocked. She'd never thought she'd hear from her mother again once Solveig died. The family had gone out of their way *not* to tell Mads her great-grandmother had died. Because they knew how much Solveig had meant to her. It was on purpose. They wanted her to be hurt. Part of that pain—in their minds anyway—was the continued silence. Never understanding that, if nothing else, she reveled in the continued silence of her family. Nothing irritated Mads more than a hyena laugh. She'd started fights in bars, completely sober, because of hyena laughter. Luckily, her fellow honey badgers loved a good random fight.

This wasn't laughter, though. It was hysterical screaming. So hysterical, Mads didn't know what her mother was going on about.

"What are you saying?" she managed to get in at one point. "I don't understand anything you're babbling about."

That just set her mother off all over again. Mads rolled her eyes and glanced at Finn. Poor guy just looked disturbed. Mads was sure Finn's mother was much calmer and more rational. Psychotic in a fight? Of course. She was a tiger, after all. But any other time? Calm and rational whether dealing with her grown cubs or handling some crazed New York driver. Mads was sure Finn never got calls like this.

"I think someone's calling you," he said.

At first Mads didn't know what he was talking about, but then she heard it over her mother's yelling, too, and handed off the phone to him. She went into the master bedroom, walked past the bed where the coyote had made himself at home, and went to one of the windows. She unlatched it and threw it open.

"*What?*" she screamed out.

"*Are you guys coming back or what?*" Tock screamed up at her from the street.

"*Yeah! Sorry! My mother's on the phone!*"

Tock frowned. "*Why the fuck is she on the phone?*"

"*I have no idea! But she's pissed! She's so busy screaming at me I can't make out a word she's saying!*"

"*Hey!*" a She-bear yelled at them from her stoop. "*Are you two going to do that all the time now that you've moved in? All that screaming? This is a quiet neighborhood, ya know!*"

"*We're almost done!*" Tock yelled at the She-bear. She looked up at Mads and yelled, "*Find out what your mother's screaming about and then come over when you're done! I'll let Charlie know you'll be over in a couple of minutes! Okay?*"

"*Yeah! Okay!*"

Tock turned back to the angry She-bear. "*See?*" Tock demanded in a yell. "*Now we're done!*"

Mads turned away from the window to find Finn standing in the doorway, gawking at her while still holding the phone her mother was screaming out of.

"What?" she asked him, no longer yelling since she knew he could hear her.

"The bears on this street are going to *hate* you."

Mads took the phone back from him and began to yell into it, "I don't understand a word you're saying, Mummy. Mummy? I don't understand you!"

"Mummy?" Finn asked.

"She hates when I call her that. Or Mom or Mommy or anything mother related. So I go for the very non-American, full British mother name. Like I'm talking to the Queen of England herself."

"You can't call her mom?" he asked, now ignoring the continued ranting from the phone because he was so annoyed by this horrible female he'd never met. "What does she want you to call her? Bitch?"

Finn cringed. The word was out of his mouth before he could even think to stop it but that had been shitty, even for a tiger. This evil female was still Mads's mother.

"I'm sorry, I shouldn't have—" He stopped talking, because she was waving him off and laughing.

"Mummy, please," she said, still chuckling.

"Stop calling me that!" her mother yelped. But the distraction was enough for Mads to get a word in.

"I don't know what you think I've done but—"

"You've stolen the sword! You didn't think we'd notice?"

All humor left Mads's face and she coldly replied, "I didn't take the sword. Although it's mine by right."

"It's mine by blood! *And we'll get it back!* Do you understand what I'm telling you, girl?"

Mads let that statement sit for a moment before she replied with freezing calm, "Come for me, Freja, and I promise you'll regret it."

Her mother exploded into more hysterical screaming that was unintelligible, and Mads closed her eyes, let out a breath. Finn reached over as if he was attempting to grasp the phone from her. Instead, he simply disconnected the call. When Mads opened her eyes in surprise, he threw up his hands and said, "Ooops. These big, clumsy mitts of mine."

The phone immediately began to ring again but Mads didn't answer. She tapped on her screen, then announced, "Blocked. I've blocked my own mother. How unfortunate."

"And your grandmother?"

"Oh, I blocked her a long time ago. Each time I have to buy a new phone it's one of the first things I do."

"Good. So this sword . . . ?"

"The family sword."

"From ancient Viking times? Pried from the dead hand of one of your ancestors' enemies?"

"No. Purchased from a Renn Faire in Norway back in 1952. But it looks very Viking, and Solveig told them, to their great annoyance, that it was going to me because I—unlike my mother and grandmother—am true Viking rather than just a shifter. They actually stole the damn thing from Solveig and always swore I'd never get it from them and I was always like, 'Whatever.'"

"So you didn't steal it?"

"I would never go back to that hoarder's nest. The sword is in the main house, on the wall so you can easily see it, but you have to *climb* so much crap to reach it . . ." She visibly shuddered. "That's why Solveig never went to get it herself. And I'd rather go to another Renn Faire in Jersey and buy one or travel back in time and fight Erik the Red for his goddamn sword than go back to that goddamn house."

"How do they live there?"

"They don't. They bought a bunch of trailers and they live on the property. At this point, they just use the house as storage."

Finn thought a moment. "If you didn't steal the sword, though . . . who would go in that house and steal it?"

"I think I know, and none of my teammates are going to like it."

"All right, what the hell did you do?"

Max turned away from the kitchen sink to find most of her teammates as well as Charlie, Stevie, and two of those idiot cats staring at her.

"What did I do about what?" Max pointed at the Malones. "The cats are still alive so I've been good."

"Forget the cats, and answer me," Tock pushed. "What did you do?"

She knew she had to be careful here. This could be a trick question. Charlie had caught Max doing all sorts of shit with that line of questioning when she was younger.

"Nothin'," Max instinctively said.

"Max MacKilligan, don't you dare lie to me," Tock barked. "Mads is on the phone with her mother right now getting yelled at. Why is she yelling at her?"

"Why is that evil bitch calling her at all?" Streep chimed in.

Now Max was confused and worried. She knew how cruel that family had been to Mads. Max, for one, had been goddamn gleeful when they'd cut off most contact with Mads. So why were they back now? "I have no idea why Freja's calling her." When that response elicited nothing but glares and arm crossing, she didn't know what to say. "I swear. And let's face it, I would have admitted it by now if I had done something. Under this brutal onslaught of"—she looked around—"whatever this is."

The backdoor opened and Zé came up the short stairway that led into the kitchen. He had bamboo leaves stuck in his black hair, which meant he'd been under the tree where Stevie's panda boyfriend ate his morning bamboo and Zé drank his morning coffee.

He stopped as soon as he saw the inquisition and asked Max, "What did you do now?"

"Is no one on my side?"

"Of course I'm on your side. I . . ." Her eyebrows went up as she waited for Zé to tell her that he loved her in front of all these people. Something she knew he was not comfortable with, just as she was not comfortable with it, but that was okay. They said it to each other at night, when they were alone. That's when it mattered anyway.

". . . tolerate you greatly," he finally finished, which only made her laugh out loud. "But we both know that you love to start shit."

"Not with Mads's family! I don't start shit with them. We all know what they'll do to her."

"What will they do to Mads?" Shay innocently asked.

Tock shook her head. "Nothing good."

The front door opened and before Mads even entered the kitchen, Max was yelling, "It wasn't me! It wasn't me! It wasn't me!"

Mads stood in the kitchen doorway, gazing at her. That other big idiot tiger stood right behind her.

"What are you talking about?" Mads asked.

"Everyone is saying I'm the reason your mother is calling you."

"I know none of you guys would ever purposely engage with my mother. Not after the Tova incident."

"Ahhh. The Tova incident," Tock repeated, a faraway look in her eyes.

"I think that was the last time any of us had any *direct* contact with the females of your family."

"What was the Tova incident?" Zé asked.

Max chuckled.

"Tova is Mads's grandmother," Streep replied before Mads could say a word, "and she didn't want any of us hanging around Mads after basketball practice. So she decided it was a good idea to come to each one of us individually and threaten us that if she saw us around Mads, she'd make us pay. But she was really scary about it. Like mobster kind of scary. Like she'd break our legs or something. And since we were only in seventh grade, we all took it very seriously."

"Why would she do that?"

"She didn't want me to have a safety net," Mads said as she pulled a carton of orange juice from the refrigerator. "A place I could go if things got tough at home. And it was always tough at home."

"We didn't know that at the time," Streep continued. "We'd just started hanging together. But threatening baby honey badgers . . . ? Huge mistake."

"Definite mistake," Nelle said with a little laugh.

"My parents did *not* like some hyena talking to their adored baby on school grounds," Streep explained, "which they told her in no uncertain terms. And then, for some unknown reason, my mother shredded this purse Tova had."

"She did do that," Mads said, dropping into an empty chair next to the kitchen table and opening the orange juice. She took a large swig directly from the carton before adding, "She loved that purse. It was Chanel. Stolen. But Chanel."

"Everyone in Denny's was shocked."

"My father was appalled when he heard she'd had the gall to say a word to me while I was waiting for the family car to pick me up," Nelle said. "So he had a couple of his bodyguards burn down that shed she had with a few of her prized racing cars in it."

"Oh, yeah." Mads grinned. "That really pissed her off."

"She tried to bully me," Tock said. "My parents were going to deal with it, but it got back to my grandparents before they could make a move. They were busy at the time in Belarus, I think. So they asked a few friends of theirs who had some important meeting in DC to take a quick break and handle it for them. You guys met them . . . Moshe, Rachel, Ben."

Mads spit out some of her juice.

As she wiped her chin, she asked, "The *lion* triplets?"

"Yeah. And you know how lions *love* hyenas. From what I understand it was a very nice, polite discussion, though, about how it was in Tova's own best interest never to speak to me again or she would lose her entire face."

Everyone in the room chuckled a bit before turning their attention to Max, but she simply shrugged. "What?"

"So what happened when she talked to you?" Tock asked.

"She never talked to me. Not about Mads. She yelled horrible things to me from moving cars a few times, but that was about it. She kept it up, you know . . . until I left the state. Other than that . . ." Max shrugged again.

"My grandmother didn't talk to you directly at all?" Mads pushed.

"No. I never heard from her." Max thought a moment, then turned and faced her sister. She was busy mixing up batter for a fresh set of muffins for the growing group of work-at-home bears in their yard. Some had even brought their laptops and headphones so they could hold meetings and do work while waiting.

"What?" her sister asked when she looked away from her stainless-steel bowl.

"Did Mads's grandmother say anything to *you*? Back then?"

"When?"

"When I started junior high. Started hanging around Mads. Did she stop you on the street or school or anything?"

"No, actually, she just showed up at the Pack house. When all the adults were out. In fact, everyone was out . . . but me."

Shocked because Charlie had never said a word about it,

Max moved closer to her sister. "Oh, my God! What happened?"

"I . . . uh . . . buried her alive."

Max and Mads quickly covered their mouths. Max, to stop the laughter and Mads, probably to stop herself from spitting out more juice. The rest of Max's teammates stepped as far back from Charlie as they could manage in the small kitchen. The Malones just appeared horrified, which Max really liked. Ungrateful bastards.

Stevie, however, merely grabbed an apple from a bowl on the counter and took a healthy bite; the sound made everyone glare at her. She paused mid-chew to squeak out a "Sorry."

Max refocused on Charlie. "Soooo . . . what happened?"

"I buried her alive. Well . . . first I punched her. Then I hit her with a shovel. Then I dragged her back to hyena territory. *Then* I buried her alive."

"Then . . . you . . . Why?"

"I wasn't going to bury her on Pack territory. Duh, Max."

"I don't mean why did you bury her . . ." Max gritted her teeth. "I mean, why did you do *any* of that?"

"Oh! She clearly came there looking for a fight. And I was kind of in the mood to give her one because Dad had already pissed me off that morning. What really set me off, though, was she grabbed my arm when I tried to walk away. I think she planned to drag me through the house looking for you. But you weren't there. When I tried to explain that, she unleashed her claws in my arm, which I did not like. It hurt and I was already cranky. So I punched her. Now that I think of it"—she glanced off for a moment—"yeah, I punched her a couple of times because she didn't let me go at the first punch. I was still learning my strength, and she was underestimating my strength. But by the third time . . . she was on the ground with a broken jaw and, I think, a broken eye socket. Of course, by then my hand hurt."

"I hate that," Max said and her sister nodded.

"The thing was, as I was shaking out my sore hand and she

was mumbling what sounded like very racist curses at both me and Max, I came to the realization that we were on our own. You, me, Stevie. My grandfather had so much on his mind, and I didn't want to get his Pack involved. They barely tolerated us being there as it was. You'd just started junior high. Stevie was doing her SATs and finding errors in the test booklets and training guides, so she was freaking out. And those hyenas lived right next door to us. Now I didn't know much about hyenas. I knew they had a funny run. I could hear them laughing at night. They either had stripes or spots, and they were matriarchal. And she was an old female. That's when I figured she was probably in charge to some degree, so if I made my point with her . . . I'd make my point."

"Meaning?"

"That if we didn't start letting people know they couldn't fuck with us now, they would be fucking with us forever. So I figured I'd start off with her. And the one thing my mom always told me . . . no one wants to fuck with crazy people. Even shifters. So I grabbed the shovel, because Lucy, one of the elders in our Pack, had been doing a lot of gardening. And I hit the hyena a few times—"

"A few times?" Tock repeated.

"Well, she wouldn't stay down."

"Right."

"And then I dragged her back to hyena territory, dug a hole, dropped her in it, covered it up, went back to the house, made waffles and bacon because I'd missed breakfast. Never heard from her after that, and Max never said a word about her soooo . . ."

Charlie gave a nonchalant shrug and, with an extra-large ice cream scoop, carefully ladled batter into the muffin pans.

"I knew Tova was alive, though," Charlie suddenly added, startling everyone in the room. "Because I'd see her walking around town."

"That must have been comforting for you," one of the Malones said with great sarcasm, which Charlie completely missed.

"It was because I was worried I might have miscalculated. I was only fourteen or fifteen when this happened. I'd gone through puberty, but I was still figuring out how much strength I had. I was desperately trying not to crush her skull. Or take her head off completely. That would have defeated my purpose. It's not like I was positive an old hyena could survive the head wound she already had *and* dig her way out of her own grave. But I was ever hopeful."

She put the bowl aside, opened the oven, and carefully placed the muffin trays inside. When she closed the oven door, she faced the room again.

"I was also surprised, Mads, when Tova or your mother sent those hyena males here to drag you into that heist you didn't want to do. You remember when that happened a little while ago?"

Mads nodded. "I remember."

"I figured she just didn't know I was also here. Because, otherwise, why would she challenge me? As I've gotten older, I've only gotten meaner, angrier, and more willing to bury her alive where she *can't* dig herself out. I assume that shooting her Clan's males in the legs and knees the way I did clearly got my point across. Don't you think?" Gripping the orange juice carton, eyes wide, Mads simply nodded her head. "Yeah. I think so too. But, hey, if you need me to deal with her again, just give me a heads-up. I'd be happy to help."

Max looked at her teammates, grinned, and said, "Hear that, guys? Just give my sister a heads-up! She'd be happy to bury your enemies alive. Owwww, Charlie! I was just joking!"

It was like a herd of cattle stampeding, the way everyone rushed out of that kitchen. Mads wouldn't necessarily say they were trying to get away from Charlie. But she wouldn't say that any of them were trying to hang around her either. Not after the previous night's fight with the Yuns and now hearing how a fourteen-year-old Charlie had handled Tova Galendotter. The reason Mads's other teammates had let the adults in their lives handle Tova was because they'd been too young and scared to stand up to the adult hyena. But Charlie didn't have a choice, so she'd done what none of them would have even thought about at the time. Challenged Tova head-on, but was wise and fast enough not to give Tova time to think. To strategize and plan. By the time the old bitch had dug herself out of that grave, she probably didn't want to ever see Charlie MacKilligan again, much less face her head-on in public. And risk losing one more time, maybe in front of her entire Clan? In front of sisters and nieces who would happily rip the mantle of leadership from her? Nope. She wasn't about to do that.

In the end, Charlie's plan worked brilliantly. She kept Tova away from Max and her grandfather's entire Pack while unknowingly ensuring that Mads always had some place to go when she needed to escape. Whether it was Tock's for the Meyerson-Jackson Seder. Streep's family summer barbeques. Nelle's for Lunar New Year. Or Max's for any American holiday since, according to Max, "Those are the only holidays we know." Her teammates were also there any time Mads needed a bed or a hot meal. They were her escape. Her safety net. Something that drove her grandmother crazy, and that was why Mads was loyal to them to this day.

"Let's make a run for it," Streep suggested when they were in the dining room.

"To where?" Tock asked.

"And why?" Nelle interjected. "If Charlie wanted to kill us, she would have done it a long time ago. We should go to Mads's new place." Nelle smiled at Mads. "I'm sure there's tons of fabulous seating that we can all take advantage of."

Mads jerked forward but someone grabbed her by the back of her T-shirt and yanked her away. She thought it was Max, but she ended up by Finn's side.

"That sounds like a great idea, Nelle," Streep said, smiling.

Unwilling to let this go, Mads told her teammate, "Only a freak buys someone else clothes and—"

Finn's hand covered her mouth, and no matter how she struggled, he wouldn't move it.

"What about the muffins?" Shay asked, his facial swelling

thankfully reduced. The area was still a bright maroon, though, but Mads was sure the redness would go away in a few hours .

"Didn't you get enough muffins?" Keane asked.

"I didn't get *any* muffins. You and Finn ate them all. The only thing I got was scorpions and a near-death experience."

"The swelling wasn't that bad," Tock told him. "We only said we *might* have to do a tracheotomy. *Might*. In the end it was totally unnecessary."

"Forget it!" Max barked into the kitchen as she walked away. "I am not working with these cretins!" She stopped when she saw the group standing in the dining room and said directly to Keane, "And yeah, I'm talking about *you*."

Stevie also exited the kitchen. She moved toward the stairs but stopped long enough to say to Max, "Isn't Charlie amazing? She will make such a wonderful aunt when I have my perfect panda-badger-tiger baby." For emphasis, Stevie gently petted her stomach before heading up the stairs to the second floor.

Mads pulled herself away from Finn and dove onto Max just as Tock did, the pair of them tackling their teammate against the opposite wall to stop her from going after her baby sister. With great effort they pinned her there until she calmed down and ordered them, "Get the fuck off me!"

Motioning to Zé, Shay asked, "Don't I know you?"

"One of you . . . three," he said, gesturing at the Malone brothers, "threw me through the living room window."

"No. I remember that. I mean . . . from years ago. I feel like I . . ." He snapped his fingers. "I sacked you!"

"That sounds weirdly sexual," Streep noted.

"High school football. You were running back. I twisted you up like a pretzel."

"Yeah. I remember that. You sent me to the hospital," Zé accused.

Shay took a step back. "How is that possible?"

"I didn't know what I was."

"You didn't?"

"No. I didn't know until"—he looked at Max over his shoulder—"how long have we known each other?"

"I don't know. Few days? Ten thousand years. Something in that range."

"Yeah. What Max said. You put me in the hospital. Orthopedic surgeon told me I'd probably never walk again. I briefly hated my grandfather because he didn't seem as concerned about his only grandson as I thought he should be. Then I made a miraculous comeback and was the talk of the school year and even got a write-up in the *New York Post*. But, hey. Thanks for trying to destroy me."

"It was my pleasure."

"Do you still play?" Keane asked.

"Football? Not since high school."

"You didn't play in college?"

"Joined the Marines instead."

"Why?"

Zé frowned, as if he'd never heard the question before. "So I could fight for my country."

"Why?"

"I really don't know how to answer that."

"What position did you play? Quarterback?"

"Running back."

"You should come to practice at Sports Center tonight for our pro team. We're having our draft. You can try out."

"For running back? Aren't I a little . . . ?"

"Small?"

"*No*. Old. Not that that's any better. But won't I be up against twenty-somethings?"

"Most of them have barely aged out of sub-adulthood. You'll have experience, strength, and general cat crankiness in your favor. You should stop by. That reminds me . . ."

The eldest Malone brother pulled his phone out of his front pocket and began typing away with big thumbs. When he stopped a few seconds later, Max heard her sister call from the kitchen, "You want me to come to your football practice tonight?"

"Yeah."

"Uh . . . okay."

Annoyed, Max called out, "Charlie, are you coming to *my* game tonight? It's the playoffs."

"What? I have to go to those now?"

"Charlie's going to come to my child's games, Max," Stevie yelled from the second floor, "because she's going to be *such* a great aunt!"

Max was halfway up the stairs when Mads and Tock caught her by the ankles and dragged her back down and toward the front door, with her screaming all the way, "*We aren't done discussing this! I will bring you back to those German docs in Switzerland myself!*"

"Why can't you be nice to your sister?" Mads asked, ignoring the fact that Max's chin was hitting each of the stoop steps.

"She's so sweet," Tock insisted. "And you're just so *mean!*"

"Oww!" Max complained when they slammed her body up against someone's SUV bumper.

"Sorry," the pair said in unison as they dragged her all the way back to Mads's new house.

Evil bitches.

chapter THIRTEEN

"**Y**ou cannot tell your sister what to do with her womb."
Finn buried his head in his hands. "Must we talk about this now?"

"I can if whatever comes out of her womb is going to be a demon," Max said.

Apparently they *did* have to talk about this now.

"A demon?" Shay questioned.

"Yes. A powerful entity bent on destroying the world, and only *I* can stop it."

"Or join forces with it," Mads said.

"There's always that risk."

"There's no proof it'll be a demon," Tock argued. "It could just be a monster. Something vile and disgusting just oozing out of her like—"

"*That's it!*" Keane bellowed. "I am not here to talk about your sister's womb. I'm here to find out if you're going to help us or not."

"*Never!*" Max bellowed back. "I'm never going to help you!"

Mads, with her elbow resting on the dining room table and her chin resting on her fist, raised her phone with her other hand. She'd already dialed someone, and one word came out of the phone's speaker . . .

"*Max!*" came her eldest sister's voice, snapping orders. "You're doing this!"

With the drapes pulled back from the big bay window, they all had a clear view of the MacKilligan rental house across the street. It was now surrounded by bears. All waiting for morning muffins. For most people, this vision would be something out of a nightmare. For those who had actually come face-to-face with a bear in the wilderness and had survived, it was a horror story told to therapists who specialized in PTSD.

Yet for the two eldest MacKilligan sisters, a house surrounded by bears wasn't nearly as worrisome as figuring out how to handle what they considered "family."

"But I don't want to!" Max snapped back.

"I don't care!"

"Fine!"

Charlie disconnected the call and Mads dropped the phone on the table. That's when Finn noticed she had her phone in a tough, black plastic case to protect it from falls and other abuse. No cutesy cover like the ones Nelle and Streep had. Nelle's cover was so covered in diamond-like sparkles, he wondered if the gems were actual diamonds. And Streep's was very pink and had the Hello Kitty logo, so he debated whether she'd stolen it from a younger cousin or something.

But Mads and Tock had cases that would allow their phones to be dropped from great heights; which made sense since Mads had been dropped from a great height right onto Keane's SUV and Tock had been dropped from a great height into an incinerator.

"Just like that?" Keane asked Max, appearing very suspicious.

"Just like what?"

"You're going to help us?"

"Unless I never want to hear the end of it until my death? Then yes. I'm helping you." She dropped into one of the chairs and put her feet on the ottoman. "So what do you want, Garfield? For me to steal something? Kill somebody?"

"No! Why would you even ask me that?"

"I don't know. Maybe because you look like a murder-y kind of guy."

"Information," Finn quickly cut in. "We've been told you can get it."

She shrugged. "Maybe."

Keane growled.

"*Maybe*," she insisted. "I can only ask. And I can only ask the Yangs. My mother's people. The MacKilligans won't help. My father has burned a lot of bridges and we're tainted by association. One of you Malones will have to come with me, though."

Finn and Shay both pointed at Keane before he could argue.

"Why me?"

"You represent the family," Finn logically explained.

"And we don't wanna go," Shay stupidly added.

Max scratched her arm and asked, "What do you want to know anyway? Who tried to kill you the other night?"

"No," Finn replied. "We want to know who killed our father. Find that out and you'll probably find out who tried to kill us, too."

"Do you want me to waste whoever killed your father? Because that's actually a job I'll happily do."

"No," Keane said. "That job is ours. But thanks for the offer."

"When can you get started?" Shay asked.

"We have playoffs tonight, and practice in two hours," Mads reminded Max.

"Then we'll start tomorrow." Max stood. "Mads will kill me if I'm not at playoffs tonight."

"Actually, I'll kill you if what happened last night fucks us up for tonight's game," Mads threatened, ignoring the ringing doorbell in her new home. "*This is for the championship!*"

"Why would you blame me for what happened last night?" Max asked

As her teammates gawked at her, Shay went to answer the front door since no one else seemed to be making the effort.

"Anyone send for a lion?" he called out.

"Me!" Streep suddenly screamed, scrambling off the couch. "Me!"

She disappeared around the corner, returning a few seconds

later with a big cat that Mads recognized as one of the Shaw brothers. The annoying one.

Lifting at least six store bags, he announced, "Ladies! I have come to rescue all of you!"

"Rescue us?" Tock asked. "From what?"

"Damaged hair."

"You can't expect us to go out on that court tonight with our hair looking like this, can you?" Streep asked, digging through the bags the lion still held.

"You could have just gone to a hairstylist," Nelle suggested.

"What would a hairstylist know that one with such a beautiful mane as I does not?" the cat asked.

Keane moved in behind the lion, towering a healthy five or six inches over him. He leaned in and sniffed until the lion male slowly turned his head to stare into the eyes of a fellow apex predator. It took all of ten seconds before they shifted and were tearing at each other in the middle of Mads's new living room.

Streep dove in between the males, screaming to her teammates, "*Save the product! Dear God, save the product!*"

Mads touched Finn's arm. "Want to see my backyard?"

"Sure. Is it nice?"

She pushed away from the dining table. "No idea. I forgot to check it out when I bought the house."

As they cut through the kitchen, Finn heard Streep yell, "Get the hair serum! We need the hair serum!"

"She takes her hair care seriously, huh?" he asked Mads.

"You can't win major acting awards without amazing hair. Unless, of course, you're a man."

"Is that written down somewhere?" he teased.

They went through the laundry room and she opened the back door to a good-sized yard. "Awww, sweetie. That's written *everywhere*."

"So what do you think?" Mads asked, looking around the backyard that was now hers.

"It's nice. Good size."

"Is it?" She took another look around. "Our territory in

Wisconsin was acres of land, but the Clan also hunted at night. I don't really need to do that." She glanced over the fence at her next-door neighbor's property. "Although that lovely hive situation they've got going over there . . ." She narrowed her eyes a bit. "I think those are African killer bees. Yum. They make the best honey. It's like angry honey."

"You can't steal your neighbor's honey."

"That would be wrong, wouldn't it?"

"That, and I'm pretty sure Max already does it. I heard the bears complaining outside. I think she went raiding last night after the rest of us passed out. When does she sleep?"

"We stopped asking that question a long time ago. Because I'm honestly not sure she does." Mads gestured to her yard with both arms. "Do I need to do anything to all this?"

"What do you mean?"

"Is it fine as it is? Or is there more I need to do?"

"You should maintain it. Maybe get a gardener."

"A gardener. Okay. Anything else?"

"For your yard?"

"Sure. Or the house."

She waited for him to make fun of her or to tell her how pathetic she was, but after a quick glance away, he suggested, "Why don't I get you a list of things you have to deal with involving your house?"

"A list? There's a *list* of things I have to worry about?"

"Yes. For instance, taxes."

"I pay my taxes."

"Right. But now you'll have to pay taxes on the property."

"Oh."

"And maintenance."

"Why? It looks fine."

Finn faced the house and lifted his head. He growled, very low. So low, Mads could feel it from the top of her head, down her spine, and straight into her toes. She didn't know if she wanted to angry-hiss at him in warning, or hang off his neck like a spider monkey.

After about twenty seconds of his growling, a tile slid off

the roof and hit the ground at their feet. They both gazed at it for a moment before Finn pointed out, "That shouldn't happen. So you're probably going to need some roof repair. Oh, here." He pulled out his cell phone and, in a few seconds, had emailed her a file. Mads opened it and discovered a chart listing all the potential costs for a house of the size Finn owned.

"Just update the stats with the size of the house and property and the costs should automatically update. Then you have spaces next to it with actual costs that you fill in as you pay it. Handy, right?"

"Uh . . . yeah." Mads pointed at her phone. "Why are there flowers on this chart?"

"My niece designed it and she likes to make things festive."

"Niece? Keane has a kid?"

"No. Shay has a kid. She's ten and she likes numbers . . . and charts. And organizing."

"And you let her—"

"I passed it by our accountant. He said it was bizarrely accurate. For an eight-year-old, which was how old she was when she initially designed it. She uses fewer flowers now. She likes things more streamlined."

Scrolling through the disturbing number of things Mads realized she would have to now worry about, she asked, "So . . . do *you* have any kids?"

"No. Why?"

"Just wondering. I mean, no one mentioned that Shay has kids and yet . . . he has a kid."

"He finds children entertaining. I, however, only like my niece. So, I'm in no rush to continue my bloodline. And I'm assuming you don't have any children of your own since you didn't have a permanent place to live until now."

"It did seem like a bad plan to raise a child in someone else's cabinet."

The back door to the house flew open and Shay came down the steps with the coyote tucked under his arm.

"What are doing with that filthy animal?" Finn demanded.

"He seemed to be about to jump into the fight between

Keane and that lion. I decided to keep him out of it. For his own safety." He placed the coyote on the ground and it immediately ran under the house. They all crouched down to get a good look.

"That's clearly where he's been living for a while," Finn noted. "I'm calling animal control."

Mads slapped the phone out of his hand. "No, you're not."

"You can't keep this thing like it's a stray dog."

"It's a dog. And it's a stray. I don't see what the problem is."

They all stood up and Finn said, "The problem is that he's a wild animal living under your house and sometimes in your bed."

"Look around." Mads spread her arms wide and gestured to her yard. "Do you see all the skeletons?"

"Human skeletons?" Shay asked.

"Do you *see* human skeletons?" Finn asked his brother.

"No."

"Then shut up."

"I mean animal skeletons," Mads clarified. "Possums. Racoons. Skunks. Squirrels. They're all over the place. He's protecting my property from pests. What he eats doesn't get into my house. That makes him a perfect *non*-pest animal."

"He'll bring fleas."

"You can give him a pill for that," Shay suggested.

Finn slammed the back of his hand against his brother's shoulder, but Mads ignored the violence and instead said, "See? I can give him a pill for that."

"You're making him a pet."

"No more than people who neuter stray cats who hang out on their property. I'm simply helping him stay healthy in an unhealthy world. And he's keeping the racoons out of my yard." She snarled a little. "I hate racoons."

"Why?"

"I got in a fistfight with one once. And then it turned into a battle with magical spears that took place in front of Odin himself . . ."

Finn shook his head. "Wait . . . what?"

"The thing is . . . I'd also been bitten by my first poisonous snake that same day, so I could have been hallucinating. I've really never been sure . . ." She shrugged. "Still hate racoons, though."

The back door swung open again and Keane walked out in his shifted form with a massive lion gripped in his maw. He dragged the beast into the middle of Mads's yard and spit him out on the grass, then he tried to get the long hairs of the lion's mane off his tongue and out of his mouth.

"Is he just going to leave him there?" she asked Finn.

"Probably. But he's not dead. Eventually, he'll get up and wander away."

Mads smiled up at the cat. "We're in the playoffs tonight. You guys coming?"

"We have team practice."

"Well, if you get out early enough, you should come. It'll be a great game. We're playing against the Detroit Devourers. They're an excellent team."

"Yeah." Finn shrugged. "Sure."

"Wait." Mads frowned. "Do I hear tone?"

"I thought I heard tone," Shay said, which got him a brutal glare from his brother.

Mads narrowed her eyes on Finn. "You don't think women can play sports, do you?"

"That was definitely *not* what I was saying."

"Then what were you saying with that tone?"

He shrugged again. "It's basketball. It's not actually a sport. Not like a real sport. Like football or hockey or even baseball. And I hate baseball. But I don't doubt for a second that women can play sports. I have women on my team. They're great players. And very mean. My coach is a woman. Big Julie."

Finn patted her shoulder. "So I don't doubt *you*. Just the sport you chose."

"I see," Mads said. "Good to know. Now if you'll excuse me, I have to get ready for practice." Mads marched past Finn, pointing at the lion carcass on her lawn. "And do *not* leave that cat in my yard, or I'm going to let the coyote eat it!"

Finn frowned. "Is that supposed to make us get rid of the cat or dismember it for easy digestion? Ow!" he barked when Shay punched his chest. "What the fuck was that for?"

"What is wrong with you, you idiot?"

"Nothing. Why?"

"She asks you to come to her game and you tell her you don't think basketball is a sport?"

"None of us think basketball is a sport. We all hate it. Right, Keane?"

Licking grass to get lion hair off his tiger tongue, their eldest brother still managed to shake his head.

"See? Keane doesn't think it's a sport either."

"That's not the point!"

"Then what is the point?"

"She likes you. That's why she invited you."

"What?" Finn looked at the back door Mads had stormed through to enter the house. "She does? How do you know that?"

"That is not a woman comfortable with other people. From what I can tell she has a total of four friends, all of which are currently putting lion-provided conditioner on their singed hair. Everyone else she's just polite to. But she's been hanging out with you. That means she likes you . . . even though you're an idiot."

Keane now stood next to them as human. He was naked, with a small amount of blood splattered across his face, bite marks on his neck, and claw marks across his chest and legs.

"I hate to say it, but Shay's right."

"You think she likes me, too?"

"No, that you're an idiot."

"I hate both of you."

"But she does seem to like you. I don't know if that means she wants to—" Keane stopped to spit hairs out of his mouth and drag a few out with his fingers. "So much fucking hair with these assholes!" he complained.

"You don't know if that means she wants to what?" Finn pushed.

"I don't know if that means she wants to fuck you. But she does seem to like you. Then again, you did just insult what she considers her life's work."

"It wasn't that bad—"

"I went out with a girl once who, in the middle of dinner, told me three things: that she loved sucking cock, couldn't wait to suck mine, and that football was stupid. I paid the bill and left her cute, cock-sucking ass sitting there in the restaurant all alone. Why?" He jabbed his big forefinger in Finn's face. "Because you don't insult football."

"You're lucky Mads didn't have a drink in her hand. She would have totally thrown it in your face," Shay insisted.

"And you would have deserved it."

Realizing his brothers—for once—might be right, Finn thought about going into the house to apologize to Mads but he was distracted when the coyote skulked out from under the house and ran up to the lion, grabbing its back leg and tugging at it, attempting to drag it away.

"Okay," Keane admitted. "Even I think that's adorable."

Snarling and tugging, the coyote kept trying, even as the lion finally opened its eyes and looked around, eventually spotting the coyote attached to its leg. It shifted back to human and the Shaw brother glared at the Malones as the coyote continued trying to drag him off.

"Seriously?" Shaw demanded. "Are you not done humiliating me? Even after I brought hair products for all your badger girlfriends?"

"They're not our girlfriends," Keane muttered.

"You're just lucky *my* girlfriend's not here," the lion threatened, standing up while trying to shake the coyote off his leg at the same time.

Finn snorted. "Isn't she just a She-wolf?"

Keane glanced down at the coyote still holding tight to Shaw's leg. "So a slightly bigger version of *that*?"

Shaw growled and started to limp toward the back door, but stopped to snarl at Keane, "And if there's even *one* bald spot on my scalp—"

"Blame your genes?"

The coyote wisely jumped up into Shay's arms as Finn and Shay stepped out of the way of the once-again battling cats.

chapter FOURTEEN

When Charlie MacKilligan came out onto the practice field that their pro team used, Finn immediately cringed.

"We didn't have anything that actually fit her?" he asked Keane.

Keane turned away from the tight end he'd crushed beneath his bulk a few minutes before, and looked at the female he'd invited to their tryouts.

He grimaced and admitted, "The only things that fit her were the shoulder pads and jerseys for She-wolves. But pants . . . everything was either too long or too wide or both. She's got legs like toothpicks."

"Oy."

Carrying her ever-present tablet, Big Julie made her way over to Finn and Keane. "Who is that tiny woman?" she asked.

"Charlie MacKilligan," Keane replied. "I already told Coach about her."

"*That's* the female you said you wanted me to see? Why are you so mean, Keane Malone?"

"I'm not being mean. She has potential."

"To get crushed by our entire offensive line?"

"You didn't see her take on a bunch of Chinese tig—*owww! Dammit, Finn! What was that for?*"

"For someone who never says anything, you sure have a big fucking mouth!"

Julie studied the two brothers. "You guys were up to something again last night, weren't you? You're all covered in bruises. I swear, I have to keep all of you in dorms!"

Rubbing his knee and glaring at Finn, Keane said, "Just let us show you what she can do."

"Fine."

"Hey, Charlie," Keane called out. "Line up against those two, would you—"

"Two?"

"Quiet," he barked at Julie before motioning to two of their black bear defensive linemen. "And hold 'em back, okay?"

Charlie looked at the bears, then asked, "Am I supposed to call out numbers or something?"

Julie quickly turned away so her back was to Charlie and whispered to Keane, "So she doesn't know *anything* about football? *At all?*"

"Don't worry about it."

"You do know we're a pro team, right? People usually come to us with at least a basic understanding of the fucking sport!"

"I know it's hard for you, but could you at least attempt to trust me?"

"Fine!"

"Okay, guys!" Keane called out. "Go!"

The two bears looked at each other, and then one called out to Keane, "Are you sure? Seems kind of mean."

"Told you," Julie muttered.

"It's just a drill. No need to crush anybody."

The two linemen got into position and Charlie mimicked them. Again, Finn cringed. She looked so tiny in comparison. Maybe in height the bears weren't dramatically bigger, but in width . . . it was as if she was facing off against those massive redwoods you could drive a car through.

Of course, Finn also couldn't get last night out of his head so he wasn't exactly panicked either.

Julie raised her arm and motioned with her hand. One of the bears called out, "Ready! Set! Hut!"

They charged forward, directly at Charlie, and she . . . stopped them. Flat palms against big, wide chests. She just stood there, holding each bear in place, while the bears sort of kept on running for a few more seconds before they realized that they weren't going anywhere.

When they did catch on and stopped moving, Charlie shoved them back. The entire team, along with the hopeful draftees, watched the two bears fly across the field and through the goalposts.

Not even winded, Charlie looked at Keane, and asked, "Is that what you wanted me to do?"

"Yeah," he said, smirking. "Pretty much."

Mads glared at her teammates, disgusted. "I can't believe you went through practice with those things on."

"What did you want us to do? It was in the directions." Streep sat by her locker, with a bath towel wrapped around her naked body, one leg crossed over the other, sparkly pink flip-flops on, and an extremely unattractive shower cap on her head. A cap that had been on her head since she'd combed that "deep conditioning masque" through her hair. Mads had actually felt bad for the lion who'd brought all those hair products over to her house for her teammates. The masque alone cost over a hundred bucks a tub. And he'd slapped tape on each bottle or tube or tub and put his own directions on them for Mads's teammates. And then he'd been beaten up by a tiger at least twice his size for all his trouble.

And harassed by a full-blood coyote that attempted to drag him under the house as some sort of meal-for-later.

That seemed a little unfair despite Mads's instinctive dislike of lions. They were the species that harassed both the animals within her. Hyena and honey badger. Although hyenas were the true enemies of lions, the badger in her did get pushed around a little should she walk by a bored pride. Of course one of the reasons the Galendotter Clan had moved to Wisconsin was that Detroit had a lot of lions that loved to slap hyenas around. The only one they didn't fuck with was Solveig. Everyone in the neighborhood knew not to start shit with her. Whether they were full-humans, shifters, or cops . . . they all knew. But only Solveig got that kind of respect. And when Mads asked her why she got respect when no one else in the Clan did, she explained it the same way every time.

"I'm Viking."

Mads didn't know why being Viking would matter in modern-day Detroit, but the logic seemed to work for Solveig, if not Mads. What kept Mads safe in the old neighborhood was her game. She could go to any playground court and go up against boys older than her and not, as they put it, "shit her pants." She didn't say much. She didn't start shit. She didn't act better than anyone else. She didn't get in anyone's face unless she didn't agree with a call. Otherwise, Mads was just there to play ball, and she played it well. Her great-grandmother didn't like her hanging out in the neighborhood by herself, but the locals had nothing but good things to say about "that kid" and her "skills" before they purchased some milk and diapers, keeping Solveig's store open during tough times. So Solveig's complaints eventually faded away.

But even better than playing on those courts back in the day was watching the older players. It was learning some of those amazing moves that made Mads one of the best players in the league, and she knew it.

That's why she took basketball so seriously. It meant the world to her. It kept her sane. It got her away from the people who hated her most—her family—and it had just bought her a house in Queens. Most importantly, it kept her and her teammates out of real trouble. Imagine if they *didn't* have a playoff game to go to right now. Who knew what kind of trouble the five of them could get into? It was too horrifying even to think about!

Which was why it appalled her that four of them had gone to their last-minute practice on Staten Island with shower caps on their heads in front of their other teammates like it was normal behavior. It was not normal behavior. It was embarrassing!

Mads watched Streep plucking her eyebrows in a round

mirror, Nelle painting her toenails to match the team colors despite no one being able to see them through her sneakers, Tock filing her claws, and Max asleep on one of the long wood benches. Because she, like Mads, could sleep through anything when she wanted to. She was even snoring.

"Could you guys look any more prissy at the moment?" Mads finally accused.

"We could, actually," Nelle said. "If prissy means adorable and gorgeous."

"It doesn't mean that."

"Did your little tiger make you feel insecure?" Streep asked, smirking.

"He's not my little tiger and *no*."

"You sure? I heard that he suggested women couldn't play sports."

"That's not what he suggested at all."

"Then what did he say?"

"He said that basketball is not a sport."

Everyone in the locker room froze, and Mads could feel all eyes on her.

Tock lowered the metal file and asked, "And you didn't rip his balls off?"

"Why would I do that?"

"Why would you do that? Because there was that drunk kid at our senior week bonfire who suggested basketball was stupid and not really a sport, and you threw him in the bonfire."

"I didn't *throw* him in the bonfire. He tripped and fell."

"After you heaved him in. Luckily, everyone was so drunk, I don't think they remembered it was you. And what about the cheerleader in tenth grade who suggested only lesbians play basketball? You put her in a headlock and held her upside down, shaking her until she sobbed and begged you to stop."

"I didn't like how she talked about the gay community."

Streep snorted. "My girlfriend will really appreciate your thoughts and prayers during our difficult time."

"Oh, shut up."

"And that guidance counselor who suggested you get a *real* job after high school rather than planning on playing basketball professionally?"

"She was wrong!"

"She was full-human! She had no idea about pro shifter sports teams," Tock went on. "You actually lodged a complaint against her. For discrimination!"

"It was discrimination. Against basketball! Because this *is* a real job!"

"You almost got her fired from *her* real job until they understood what you were actually complaining about."

"She would have deserved it!"

"And despite all that, you didn't do anything to some tiger who said basketball isn't a real sport?"

"He plays pro football. I assume he has CTE from all that head banging, which would explain such an irrational statement."

Streep smiled. But the smile annoyed Mads because it was all warm and loving. "You like him," she accused.

"I don't like anybody."

"Is that why we're not friends?" Streep asked, yet again. "Just teammates?"

"Oh, my God!" Tock exploded. "You really need to let that go!" With that out of her system, she grinned at Mads, and said, "And you totally like him."

Keane watched Max's boyfriend reach over his shoulder, snatch the ball thrown by the quarterback out of the air and keep running. A defense tackle came at him, arms outstretched to bring him down, but the jaguar slipped past him like lightning, then sped past a lion linebacker into the end zone.

It wasn't easy to impress Keane, but he was almost impressed. The house cat moved with some grace and unbelievable speed considering he wasn't a cheetah and hadn't played football in quite a few years. But unlike the cheetahs, Max's boyfriend could take a solid hit when he couldn't make it past the defensive line, and he wasn't afraid to tackle guys bigger than him if he was trying to get the ball away from them.

More important, their new quarterback seemed to already have a rapport with . . . what was his name again? He couldn't keep calling the cat Max's boyfriend. Eventually that was going to annoy him. Especially when Keane kept yelling it across the field. "Hey! Max's boyfriend! Come here!"

Julie gasped beside him and Keane turned to see that a group of bears and lions had tackled Charlie during a drill.

"What the fuck?" he demanded of his coach.

"I didn't tell them to do that!" Julie started over to the males and females who'd gotten tired of being tossed around by a hybrid badger who couldn't even shift. They must have quietly decided to gang up on MacKilligan. But Keane realized what a bad idea that turned out to be when a fellow She-lion flew past Julie's head and Keane yanked her out of the way of a grizzly tumbling past like a fast-moving boulder rolling down a hill.

With his mouth open, he watched Charlie toss off all those bears and cats until she was able to stand up and brush herself off. She didn't even look annoyed. Instead, she tried to take off her helmet but it got caught in her curls and she began to yelp. One of the team's African-American She-wolves ran over to help her get her hair untangled and they had a moment of friendly laughter discussing the helmet and their hair. He didn't care so he didn't really pay attention.

"Okay," Julie said, facing him. "How do I hire her? I must have her."

"That's going to be tricky."

"Why?"

"She has another job. An insane life. And the bears in her neighborhood expect her to bake."

"Get high?"

"*No.* Actually bake. Food."

"Oh! Does she work at a bakery? Is her job to bake?"

"No. From what I can tell, her job is to kill. Bad guys. She's not a murderer or anything. Not *my* definition of a murderer anyway."

Julie pushed her mesh cap emblazoned with the team logo away from her forehead so she could scratch her scalp, bury her head in her hands, and sigh long and deep before lifting her head and looking into his eyes. Finally, after all that, she asked him, "Why . . . *why* do you make my life so hard?"

"I honestly don't try to do it. It just happens. But I will say this . . . you're not the only one who has made that accusation. My brothers say the same thing about me all the time."

They waited for their team to be announced so they could run out with their coach. Unlike the shifter hockey teams, they didn't announce each team member individually. Something Mads appreciated. She didn't need all that. A bullshit nickname and stats about how many times she'd been put in timeouts or how many fistfights she'd had or the number of artery surgeries she'd endured.

Basketball was basketball. It wasn't about all that unnecessary drama. It was about the sport and athleticism. Which was all she cared about.

Coach Fitzgerald walked up and down the line of her team, looking them over one last time. She stopped next to Mads.

"Hey."

"Hey," Mads replied, constantly moving. She wouldn't stop moving until the last buzzer sounded.

"I need you and Max to be the assholes tonight."

Mads nodded without even looking at her coach.

"This team has a lot of great shooters, but they're arrogant, with short tempers. Fuck with them."

Mads smiled. "Got it."

Coach patted her shoulder. "That's my angry badger."

The announcer began his introduction of their team: the Wisconsin Butchers. Coach moved to the front of the line and waited for the explosion of yellow and white lights. When it came, she ran out and the team jogged out after her. Mads went into her "zone." It was the space where she ignored all the applause, the cheering, and the hate, and focused on nothing but her team, the other team, the ball, and the net. For the next four quarters, nothing else mattered.

There were a lot of lions on the other team, meaning the players mowed their opponents down like tanks, then exploded with sudden speed toward the basket. The few cheetahs and She-tigers that were also on the team dashed around with ease, slamming the ball into the net so confidently it could be painful to watch.

And yeah, sure, Max might not seem to care about any of this until she was actually *at* the game and in the moment, but that wasn't really true. Every day, she sent out videos of other teams' games. How she got those videos, no one knew or asked. Shifter games were not supposed to be filmed for a myriad of reasons. But Max had them. Even better, the videos focused on the team they would be facing in the next playoff. They'd been watching videos of these players for a couple of weeks.

So when that She-tiger who liked to do those three-point shots sent a ball to the basket, Mads was there to jump up and slap it away. Then she grinned. Or smirked. Or snarled. Or glared. Or whatever else she knew would annoy the particular player she was trying to irritate. Max had sent a list to the team titled "Facial Expressions That Will Piss Off This Team's Best Players."

It was working really well, too. She knew that when one of the She-lions body-checked her right into the middle of the audience when she was about to make her own three-point shot. Not because she had to make such a show-off shot, but because she could.

"Are you okay?" she heard someone ask as they lifted her up over the crowd and got her back to the court. But Mads was too angry to answer or notice who it was. She barely managed to choke back a hysterical laugh. She swallowed, closed her eyes. She would not allow herself to lose it during a playoff game. Besides, her team had already retaliated, with Max wrapped around the head and neck of the She-lion who'd body-checked Mads. The rest of the team was engaged in a general fistfight. But the refs were already stepping in and pulling people apart. The She-lion was out of the game, although they had to pry Max away from her; some of the She-lion's hair dragged out by the fistful. That led to roaring. She-lions complained about the vanity of their males, but the females could be just as bad about their hair.

With the drama over, Mads was given three unguarded free throws.

Tock came over to her and handed her a towel with the team logo on it. Mads wiped the sweat from her face and especially her eyes, which gave her a few precious seconds to put her boiling rage back where it belonged—buried deep down in her soul where all her resentments and disappointments lived.

Blowing out a breath, she handed the towel back to her teammate and walked to the free-throw line. The ref tossed her the ball and Mads began to dribble, carefully lining up her shot until something broke through her usual intense focus.

Low roaring that she felt in her fingertips.

She could usually block out roaring with ease . . . so why was she unable to block it this time?

Holding the ball, she looked over her shoulder, her gaze quickly scanning the crowd until it came to rest on a large group. They were all in matching football jerseys and hats, some of them chanting her name over and over. But it was the trio of tigers roaring at four male lions decked out in the other team's gear that really threw her off.

"Oh, my God," she whispered to herself. "What is happening?"

Finn had been heading to the lockers when Keane grabbed him by his shoulder pads and yanked him toward Charlie and Julie.

"I need you to do some of that fast talking you're famous for," Keane had told him.

"That is not what I'm famous for."

"Whatever it is you do, do it."

His brother had pushed him toward the two females, and immediately he regretted not fighting his brother off.

"I'm not sure being in the same place every day at the same time is a good idea," Charlie was calmly explaining to Julie. "Lots of people try to kill me."

"And . . . why is that?"

Charlie shrugged. "It's mostly because of my father. Because he's done something stupid. Or because my family has stolen something. Or someone's forced me to kill—"

"Okay!" Finn quickly stepped between the two females, taking the team jersey off Julie's shoulder. "Why don't you let me handle it from here, Julie?"

"I'm not sure that's such a good—"

"It'll be fine. Great for the team! We already love her."

"We do?" one of his teammates asked, which was dumb because it just got him a helmet to the head from Shay.

"Of course! Go on, Coach. We'll take it from here. You guys can work out all the details later."

"All right, but—hey!" she barked when Keane pushed Julie toward the rest of the coaching squad several feet away, allowing the entire defensive line and Shay to surround Charlie.

"Are you sure about this?" Charlie asked.

"You did great in the tryouts," Shay reminded her.

"I guess, but . . . what position?"

"Defensive end," Keane told her. "You'll be working with Finn. That way he'll be able to help train you since you have no idea what you're doing."

Charlie looked up at Finn for a few seconds. Then the rest of the line.

"You really think it's a good idea for me to play against guys built like all of you?"

Keane's entire face expressed his disbelief before he reminded her, "You put a grizzly through a wall."

"You told me to stop the guy with the ball."

Taking the jersey from Finn, Keane placed it over Charlie's shoulder. "You'll be fine."

"Any plans for the night?" Finn asked Charlie as she looked her new jersey over.

"I figured I'd suck up the pain and go see Max play. It is a game . . . of some kind."

"Not a basketball fan?"

"Not really. But that could be because everyone at my school kept expecting me to play. You know . . . because I'm Black. So I went out of my way not to like it." She pointed at the training field. "But I like this. It allows me to release all my rage and aggression," she said with complete calm.

"Have a lot of rage, do you?"

"Yes. It's my father's fault."

"You say that a lot. That things are your father's fault."

"That's my father's fault, too. That I say that a lot. You want to come with me to the game?" she suddenly asked. "Mads will be playing."

"So?"

"You like her."

"No, I don't."

"Of course you do. Don't be an idiot."

"I'm not an idiot. And even if I did like her, that doesn't mean she likes me."

"Really?"

"Yeah. Really." Finn let out an annoyed grunt. "You're not one of *those* girls, are you?"

"Pardon?"

"The kind that's always trying to fix up a single guy? Because that's going to really get on my nerves."

"First off, I have never been, nor will I ever be, any *kind* of one of *those* girls. Do you know why? Because I actually have shit to do. Always have, always will. Second, if you want to go through life alone and bitter because you're afraid to make a move on probably the only female on this planet who could ever put up with your annoying ass . . . that's on you. I was just trying to help a Mongolian brother out."

"Again, she may not like me."

"Really? Because I heard you said something remarkably shitty about her precious basketball earlier today."

"All I said was—"

"He told her basketball was not a real sport," Shay pointed out.

"*That's* what you told her?" Charlie said with a harsh laugh.

"Well, it's not really."

"And you still have your skin?"

"It's not that big a deal."

"Tell that to the guy she shoved into a bonfire."

"What?"

"Yeah. It was their senior week. You know, at the end of high school. She'd been dating the guy for, like, two months. He was drunk . . . well, everybody was drunk. He said something stupid about basketball and he ended up in the bonfire. Luckily Tock got him out pretty fast, because the rest of them were laughing so hard, they didn't even try, so he was only a little charred. But Mads almost didn't graduate. Luckily, I'd already had some dealings with the principal over Max and a cheerleader incident . . . so I was able to handle it. But yeah . . . she does not take the mocking of basketball well. So you still walking around with both your balls . . . that means she likes ya."

Charlie was silent a moment before she added, "I get it, though. Basketball was her escape from a shitty life and a shitty family. That's why she's so protective of it and her friends."

"Now you're making me feel bad."

"How cute! I didn't think cats could feel things."

"That's very nice."

Charlie laughed and pulled her new jersey over her head. It was huge; hung to her knees. "Classy! Okay. Come on. Let's go see my sister torture girls way bigger than her . . . and Finn's new girlfriend that he already insulted."

"I was just being honest."

"Don't be honest. Or you'll be alone a lot."

"We're tigers. We're supposed to be solitary."

"You know, all you cats say that, but the cats I've met lately . . . you're always hanging around somebody. And you three"—she motioned to Finn and his brothers—"you live with each other, your baby brother, your sister, and your mother. And have rude aunts who visit. How solitary is that? You might as well have a girlfriend. It'll make you look less pathetic when you're living with your mother."

Charlie motioned to the entire defensive line. "Why don't we all go? That way Finn won't look disgustingly desperate and we can all bond as a team. Won't that be nice?"

She gave them all a big smile and started walking toward the exit, stopping to grab her backpack and motion to the rest of them. One of the grizzlies grabbed Finn's arm and growled, "I want to hate her . . . but I just can't. Why can't I? I can usually hate anybody! I'm a grizzly!"

"I don't know. There's just something about her."

"And even after all that sweating for the last few hours . . . why does she smell like cake and cookies?"

They trooped up a couple of floors to one of the arenas and, because there were seats available and they were on a pro team, they were allowed to go in for free. As soon as they sat down with hot dogs, popcorn, and beer, Finn was immediately annoyed.

"Even our crowds are better."

"I agree," Keane muttered between sips of beer.

Finn glared at some male lions a few rows down. They wore the other team's color and were cheering loudly, forcing Finn to announce equally loudly, "I hate male lions."

"Me, too."

"Yeah," Shay nodded. "They're the worst."

Half their defensive line glared at the brothers. "Hey!" one of their male lion teammates barked.

"We mean you, but . . ." Finn began. "Nah. We just mean you, too."

"Wow," another lion teammate gasped, pointing at the honey badgers. "Look at their hair. It's fabulous!"

"Look how it glows under the lights."

"I bet I know which conditioner they used."

"Dude, you've gotta tell me. I absolutely need that stuff."

"This is also why we hate you," Finn pointed out.

"They're really good," Keane said, gesturing to the court with his hot dog made out of wild boar.

It was the whole group out there. Mads, Max, Nelle, Streep, and Tock. And it was interesting to watch them work as a team under the bright arena lights, doing something that didn't involve . . . you know . . . mass killing.

What was especially fascinating was how much smaller they were than the other team. They were currently playing against two lions, a cheetah, a mountain lion, and a jaguar. But the badgers had fast hands and even faster feet, keeping the ball in play and away from the other team with surprising ease. An ease their opponents didn't really appreciate.

He glanced up at the scoreboard and saw that they were in the third quarter with Mads's team twenty points ahead. He smirked at the team name. Full-humans seemed to use either animal names or names that managed to piss off an entire race of people. But shifters went with honest names. For Mads's team, it was the Wisconsin Butchers. Not exactly subtle, but truthful.

Finn heard the crowd roar and looked back at the court. Mads had the ball and was heading to the basket. A She-lion was blocking the hoop, and when Mads got near she tried to steal the ball. That's when Mads, still in motion, performed an amazing three-sixty spin and passed the ball to Max. The badger, whose ponytailed hair was now a vibrant pink, caught the ball, zipped past a startled cheetah, and slammed it into the net. It was stunning.

The other team got the ball and, during a pass, Mads quickly stole it and started back to her team's hoop. That's when the She-lion body-checked Mads so hard she flew . . . right at him.

"Oh, shit!" Finn dropped his beer and half-eaten hot dog and raised his hands, catching the flying badger hybrid before she could slam her ass into his face and rearrange his nose.

"Look at you," Keane said, something like pride in his voice, "acting like a wide receiver."

"Are you okay?" Finn asked the back of Mads's head.

She let out a weird barking laugh that made most of his team rear back. Except the lion males. All those manes turned toward her and fangs were bared.

Deciding to get her back to the court as quickly as possible, Finn passed her down across the crowd, who eagerly helped, until she was back on the floor. By then she seemed calmer, as did the rest of his defensive line. Probably because they were all distracted by the fight happening between the two teams because of that personal foul. Especially Max, who'd attacked the offending She-lion by wrapping herself around the female and punching her repeatedly in the head.

The male lions wearing the opposing team colors must have been from the She-lion's Pride because they began roaring at Max. Feeling strongly that—for once—the honey badger had a true reason to strike first in this fight, Finn politely asked those particular cats to *"Shut the fuck up!"*

The lion males looked back at Finn's defensive line, which included lion males from other Prides, and the angry roars began. Because that's what cats did when they were angry. The bears, however, kept eating. And so did Max's boyfriend, Zé, who'd tagged along with them to the game. As a jaguar, he should instinctively want to jump in with the lions and roar his little house cat heart out, but nope. He'd just kept eating and, occasionally, yelling out, "Get that bitch, baby!"

Now, the fight was being broken up, and Mads was getting some free throws. Still, Finn and his teammates didn't stop roaring because the other lions didn't stop roaring. At least they didn't stop until they all heard a bellowed, *"Hey!"*

Startled, the cats turned their collective attention to the court floor, where Mads stood holding the basketball and glaring at them.

"What the fuck are you doing?" she asked.

When no one else said anything and he sensed the arena crowd was waiting for *him* to reply, he finally mumbled, "Protecting your honor?"

It was weak, but it was honestly the best he had at the moment.

He heard Keane snort next to him, so he slammed his elbow into his brother's side, enjoying the resulting grunt of pain.

"Oh, my God, you're all so full of shit!" Mads barked. "Now cut it out! I'm working here!" The lion males sporting the opposing team's colors lowered their heads to laugh but Mads snapped her fingers at them and snarled, "You, too."

"Or what?" one of the males asked.

Mads took a step closer. "Do you like your knees where they are?" she asked.

Confused, the lions looked down at their legs, at each other, then back at Mads.

"Uh . . . yeah," one of them finally said.

"*Then cut it out!*" she spat in a voice ten octaves lower than Finn had ever heard. Mads's blue eyes had also turned completely black. It was freaky and disturbing, and all the male lions jerked back in their seats.

Not exactly the kind of basketball-star-against-fan interaction one saw on national TV, to be discussed and analyzed to death on social media for the next twenty-four to forty-eight hours. No. This was definitely a shifter-only kind of thing.

Finn liked it. In football, he didn't get this close to his fans until *after* the games.

Mads walked back to the free-throw line. She closed her eyes, took a couple of deep breaths. Her team began cheering for her again and the crowd loyal to the Butchers joined in. Those who hated them comfortably booed or tried to distract her. But there was no more male-cat-on-male-cat roaring.

One after another, Mads nailed each of those free throws, earning her team three extra points with a shocking amount of ease. After that, she was back in the game until the end of the quarter.

"Still think she's not a real athlete?" asked Charlie, who was sitting in the row right in front of Finn.

"That's not what I said!"

"That's how she's going to remember it."

"Why should she remember that when it's *not* what I said?"

"You know how girls are. We're very sensitive."

"No, you're not! You're the least sensitive people I know!"

"You know what?" Charlie turned around, resting her knees on the seat and leaning toward Finn. He didn't like it. "To apologize for your egregious rudeness—"

"It was not egreg—"

"—you should get some nice flowers from the florist on the first floor and go with the team when they celebrate their win."

"They haven't won yet."

"They will. And you should be ready to go with them. They usually have a dinner or something."

"They have another quarter left. Anything can happen."

"So you don't want to go to dinner with her?"

"I didn't say that either."

"Then get the flowers. An interesting arrangement. Nothing boring you'd give your grandmother. And take a shower. You guys are all funky."

"You think you smell like roses?"

"I know I do. One, because I'm a girl. I'll *never* smell as bad as a male. And two, because the hair product I'm currently using smells like roses, even when I'm sweating. So eff-you." She pointed at Keane. "And lend him your SUV."

"It's his SUV. My hood is still fucked up from where Mads landed on it last night. It looks like I wrapped it around a telephone pole. Sort of."

"We mostly bent it back," Finn admitted. "Enough to drive it home. But it still needs a lot of work."

"Good. See? There we go." She motioned for Finn to leave by flicking the fingers of both hands.

"You're really bossy," Finn pointed out.

Charlie laughed as she turned back around in her seat and

sat down again. "You think I was being bossy? Ask Max how bossy she thinks I am."

When those last few seconds were on the clock, and the Butchers were far ahead in points, they really could have just played a straight game until time ran out. But they were rude honey badgers. So, instead, they played what Mads could only call a really mean game of keep away. They just passed the ball to each other in the most outrageous and ludicrous ways they could think of until, with only three seconds left on the clock, they passed the ball to Nelle. She turned to take her shot and ended up facing a six-two She-tiger who had no intention of letting that happen.

Nelle didn't let anyone get in her way, and shifter sports leagues had unusual rules. Which meant she was allowed to climb that She-tiger like she was climbing an old oak. Once she was on the tiger's shoulders, Nelle launched herself off and slammed the ball into the basket, hanging from the rim for a few seconds before she let go.

The buzzer went off a split second later and the crowd jumped to its feet. Mads and her team charged at each other, realizing they'd not only won the game, but were headed to the championships. Their ultimate goal for the year. They crashed into one another with Max ending up in Mads's arms, her legs around her waist. Tock had Nelle on her shoulders and Streep hanging off her hip. The rest of the team surrounded them, chanting the team call, "Butch-er! Butch-er! Kill! Kill! Kill!"

Max had written the call years ago. Until the badgers arrived, the Butchers had no team call.

After their opponents grudgingly shook their hands, the team returned to the locker room. There was more singing and dancing and chanting until the coach called for quiet.

"I just want to say how proud I am of my girls! It was a hard fight, but we've done it again! The Wisconsin Butchers have made it into the championships!"

There was more applauding and cheering for another

minute or two. Then the coach said, "Now, you ladies get showered up and pretty and dinner tonight is on me!"

Mads turned to her locker, happily stripped off her sweaty uniform, and wrapped a big towel around her body. That's when Streep handed her a white jar.

"What's this?"

"Some of that conditioner I used."

"I am not going out tonight with a shower cap on my head."

"You don't have to. My hair was singed. Twenty minutes tops for you. But you really need this."

"Why?"

"Do you want to look good tonight or not? Especially next to us." Streep turned and flicked her ponytail in Mads's face.

Deciding it was just easier to use the damn conditioner, Mads got in the shower, washed her hair, and combed in the conditioner. While it sat in her hair, she had time to kill, so she shaved her legs before washing everything else. When the twenty minutes were up, Mads rinsed her hair and walked out. She dried off quickly and went to the bar area that had been set up with blow-dryers and curling irons and a makeup section. Mads doubted she'd find the same thing in any of the men's locker rooms but she didn't care. She hated walking around with wet hair. It made her look like death.

She blew her hair out, even hit it with the straightening iron a little bit, and to her disgust . . . Streep was right. Her hair looked amazing.

Mads didn't bother with makeup because she never did. It just wasn't her thing. Once she was done with her hair, she went back to her locker and got changed into a black sleeveless shirt, black jeans, and black boots. She would pick up her dirty clothes the next day since she planned to have a good time tonight with her . . .

Turning around, Mads quickly realized she was the only one in the locker room. Why was she the only one in the locker room? She was the fastest dresser on the team besides Max, who always dressed like she was running from the cops.

Grabbing her backpack, she walked out of the locker room and right into Finn Malone.

"Hey."

"Hey." She looked past him. "Have you seen the rest of the team?"

"They're not here? I thought I was going out to dinner with all of you to celebrate your win." He frowned. "You did win, right?"

"Of course, we won. Wait . . . you were at the game, right? Why don't you know we won?"

"Charlie told me I needed a shower. And to get you these." He shoved a bouquet of flowers in her face. "Congrats on your win."

She snatched the flowers out of his hand. "Those assholes!"

"They're just flowers."

"Not the flowers. This. This is a date."

"We're on a date?"

"We are now. They set us up."

"Oh. Okay." Finn nodded. "So where do you want to go eat?"

"Where do I want . . . ?" Mads wanted to tear the flowers apart and throw them in Finn's face but they were so pretty, she simply didn't have the heart. Instead she asked, "Aren't you annoyed?"

"No. I'm hungry. I'm very hungry. I had to drop my hot-dog earlier when that She-lion body-checked you, and defensive line tryouts were a lot of work because Charlie was just tossing everybody around. So *after* I eat, I might be annoyed. But right now, I'm just hungry. Besides, we should celebrate your amazing ability to be a real asshole on the court. Even Keane was impressed."

Mads smiled before she could stop herself. "It was part of our game strategy for this particular team. That level of dickish-ness is not always necessary."

"It was great. Seeing you slap that ball away from the net constantly. It was irritating the hell out of the other team." He motioned toward the exit with a jerk of his head. "Come on. Let's go celebrate your win."

"Okay. But I'm going to yell at them later."

"Fair enough."

Together, they walked down the hall. And, as they neared the exit where some fans were holding up photos of Mads for her to sign, Finn said, "Your hair looks great, by the way."

"Thanks. I used that lion's recommended conditioner."

Finn stopped walking and just let out a small, annoyed roar.

"What?" Mads asked.

"I just hate those fucking male lions."

"Because they're pains in the ass? Or because their hair always looks so good?"

"Honestly? Both!"

chapter FIFTEEN

Charlie congratulated her sister and her team, but she was in no mood for a dinner filled with animals she would never dine on—zebra steaks? Really? But eating horse was bad? What was the difference? Why couldn't anyone tell her that? Because other than the stripes, Charlie didn't see that big a difference between horses and zebras!—and watching her honey badger sister and her honey badger friends drink more and more deadly snake poisons to "celebrate" their win. So she went home after getting everyone settled for their night of "fun."

After parking her car, she debated whether to go to her rental house first or the Dunn house across the street to see the love of her life. The only reason she didn't go to see Berg first was because she really should check on her baby sister. Although life with her panda had made Stevie a lot more tolerant of having "man-eating bears" around the house, it still freaked her out when they began to "surround us like they're going to eat us all!" Something the bears on this street would never do because they were smart enough to know that if they ate Stevie or Max, they would never get any more baked goods from Charlie.

As it was, she wasn't sure how she was going to tell them that she would be playing football from time to time. If they thought it would cut into her baking time, they might get a little hysterical.

Charlie heard a whistle and stepped away from her car door. She smiled. Berg was sitting on the open back gate of his triplet sister's pickup truck. It was specially reinforced, so it could handle weight up to thirty-five-hundred pounds. Which was good because that's nearly what the triplets weighed together. Not quite, but close . . .

As always, Charlie loved seeing Berg's handsome face. True, it matched the faces of two other people in nearly every way, but it was weird how she could immediately tell the difference between him and his "identical" brother, Dag. Even early in the morning, when she barely had both eyes open, and they were dressed exactly alike for that day's security job, she never kissed the wrong one goodbye.

"Our own mother gets us confused," Dag would complain.

Which would force Charlie to point out that in the brief time she'd met their hippy mother, who loved to smoke the honey-infused cannabis she sold to bears for a hefty sum, "She gets me confused with Max. *Max.* So I wouldn't take it too personally."

"How did your tryouts go?" Berg asked as soon as Charlie put her arms around his waist and buried her head in his massive chest.

"Pretty good, I guess."

"Just pretty good? I heard you put John Hartman through a wall."

"Who's John Hartman?"

"Offensive lineman. Used to date my sister. So she adores you like the sun now."

"I didn't know. They just said—"

"Get the guy with the ball. Yeah. Apparently stories of your tryout are all over the Sports Center. Her hockey team is pissed, though."

"Why?"

"They should have gotten you first."

"I. Can't. Skate."

"They figure, how hard can it be to learn?"

"Very!"

There was the slightest change in Berg's body. The slightest shift in the tension of his muscles. But, for once, Charlie had remembered to take her allergy meds, so she could actually smell what was now standing behind her.

Berg knew he could have grabbed her. Could have held her tight. Could have yanked her onto the back of his sister's truck to keep her away from the two females who'd silently sidled up to them in the dark. He could have done all that.

But where would the fun be? And that was the upside of loving a MacKilligan sister. The fun! The downside, of course, was the worry when they went out at night and you weren't sure they'd come back in one piece or come back at all. Because they faced such daunting nightmares out there in the world. But the upside was the entertaining crazy they brought to a shifter world in which everything had run a certain way for the last ten thousand years or so. It didn't matter if it was Zé dealing with a smiling Max or Shen watching out for an easily startled Stevie or Berg watching a distrustful Charlie. Their lives had not been the same since they'd become involved with the MacKilligans.

That's why when Charlie, with blinding speed, suddenly yanked herself out of his arms, spun, and swung her fist at one of the females standing behind her, he didn't attempt to stop her. He just sat back and watched what Charlie would do next. Because that would all depend on her mood.

Her brutal fist slammed into a nose that had been broken so many times, another hit should not have hurt, but clearly it did. The She-wolf stumbled back, blood splattering the wolf's face and Cella Malone standing next to her.

"*You evil little whore!*"

"Oh, my gosh! It's you!" Charlie put her hands to her mouth in feigned surprise. "I'm so sorry, but you scared me."

"*Liar!*"

"I didn't know what was behind me. I just knew I was unsafe."

It seemed her mood tonight was "taunting innocence."

Charlie didn't get to pull that one out very often. Mostly she had to go with "deadly threat" or "no one leaves here alive." It was nice to see her able to have some fun for once.

"You poor thing. Are you okay?" She reached out to the She-wolf, who stepped back.

It was not something Berg ever thought he'd see. Because this wasn't just *any* She-wolf. This was a Smith wolf. From a greatly feared pack that had whole Southern towns named after them, towns they ran with an iron claw. But even that wasn't the most important thing about this particular She-wolf. She wasn't just a Smith wolf . . . she was Dee-Ann Smith. A former Marine and the most feared wolf anywhere apart from her daddy, Eggie Smith. The pair of them were only spoken about in hushed whispers. And the last thing you wanted was one of them showing up at your door for any reason. Even worse . . . was if *both* of them showed up.

Shifters of all breeds, all species avoided Dee-Ann Smith. Only those who knew her well ever got close to her. And yet, Charlie MacKilligan had nearly killed her once because Dee-Ann had made her mad. The boundary crossed had to do with Charlie's baby sister, Stevie, and that was a fool's move. Max could take care of herself but Stevie . . .

Well, Stevie was unique. Sweet, brilliant, a little fragile mentally, and wildly unstable when it came to her shifting abilities. Although Charlie and Max rarely agreed on anything in life, they did agree on three things: their love of horror movies, protecting Stevie from the world, and protecting the world from Stevie.

When it looked like Dee-Ann was about to interfere, Charlie did not hold back. The only thing that kept Dee-Ann alive was that she was a powerful She-wolf with centuries of good breeding stock behind her. And decades of Marine and Eggie training to keep her alive.

But that shattered nose she was desperately trying to put back in place so it could knit together during the night . . . that was just Charlie toying with her. Because she knew her message had gotten across the first time.

"I'm really sorry. I didn't take my allergy meds—"

Lie. He'd been standing right there when she downed her allergy meds with orange juice and a muffin. Then she'd used her nasal spray.

"—so I can't smell a thing! And I heard something behind us—"

Another lie. The one thing a Smith could do at birth was move without making a sound. Berg didn't want to think about all the times he'd found a bunch of Smiths suddenly standing next to him at some event where he'd been hired as security. It drove him nuts! How could he be doing his job when he didn't notice that Smiths had eased their way in without invites? And then sidled up to him without a sound so he didn't even notice! And yes, he always tossed them out of those venues with way more . . . well . . . let's just say "enthusiasm" than was necessary.

"—so I just reacted. You understand, right?"

"No! You lying little liar!"

"It doesn't matter," the She-tiger said over Charlie's dramatic gasp. "We're here for a reason."

A cat was an odd partner for a wolf to have, but the Marines made for strange bedfellows.

And Dee-Ann Smith and Cella Malone were as strange as anyone could get.

"It'd better not have to do with my baby sister," Charlie said through her teeth, but with a giant smile. "I don't want to get angry."

"This has nothing to do with her," Malone said. "It's all about you and Max. And what you were up to last night in Chinatown."

The fake smile on Charlie's face faded and was quickly replaced by a sly real one.

"Don't know what you're talking about."

"Yeah. That's what the Yuns said. But we don't believe them either."

"Look, I don't know what you want—"

"Cops were all over that part of Chinatown yesterday. There

was blood everywhere. We have our people on it, but we can't have a war between you and the Yuns."

"A war? Are they threatening a war?"

"You took out one of the leader's daughters—did you think that was going to be ignored?"

"I don't know why not. You ignored what happened to your uncle."

Malone's gold eyes narrowed and Smith abruptly stopped trying to fix her nose.

"Excuse me?" the She-tiger snarled.

"Oh, you didn't know? Your family kept that from you? You see, Natalie, the half-sister of the Malone brothers, is also the half-sister of the MacKilligan sisters, which makes the Malone brothers family. And I heard how their father was murdered and his own family—the Malones, namely *you*—did nothing about it. You know, my mother was murdered in front of me and my own father did nothing because, well, he didn't care, so you can see why that would bother me. But the MacKilligan sisters do care. We care, so we're going to help. That's what family does. But seeing that the Malone tigers didn't help family, I just assumed the Yuns wouldn't do anything either. I just thought that was the tiger way or something. I thought the Malone brothers were just different or freaks or something."

Charlie stepped closer to Cella Malone. "But you can tell the Yuns that if they want a war, they can have a war. And I can do to all of them what I did to their precious daughter after she lured *my* sister into a trap and threw her into an incinerator."

Malone blinked. "Max is dead?"

"No."

Malone glanced off, briefly confused. "So the incinerator wasn't turned on?"

"Oh, no. It was on. And if it was anyone other than Max and her friends, they'd all be dead. But it was Max . . . and her friends . . ."

"I don't understand. Max is *not* dead?"

"No."

"But she was in an incinerator."

"Yes."

"That was turned on."

"Oh, yes. Full blast."

"And now she's horribly deformed?"

"No. A few scars, but she already had a few scars so . . ." Charlie shrugged.

With seemingly nothing left to say to anyone, Charlie reached over and gently closed Malone's open mouth, then took Berg's hand.

"You guys have a nice night now," she said before leading him toward her rental house to check on her baby sister.

"Look what that evil bitch did to my nose!"

"How does anyone survive an incinerator?" Cella asked. She kept telling herself that the honey badger-wolf hybrid must be lying. Except Charlie didn't seem to lie about big things. She lied about little things. Like not knowing it was Smith standing behind her and being startled. But when it came to her sisters . . . that woman didn't lie. Ever. "An incinerator that was turned on full blast?"

"I may need actual plastic surgery to fix this! Do you understand that? Smiths don't get plastic surgery, Malone! What am I supposed to say at our next family reunion? Got my nose decimated by a mean little hybrid with daddy issues?"

"It's not physically possible for them to have survived."

"Are you even listening to me, Malone?"

"No!"

They were back in Cella's car. The Trans-Am she'd had in high school and had souped-up all summer so that it was, in a word, awesome! Smith had helped her. The woman knew her way around a car, and they'd had fun working on it. But having to deal with the MacKilligans over the last couple of months had been a nightmare. That family wasn't . . . normal.

Okay. None of them were "normal." But the MacKilligans

and the shifters they chose to associate with were so far removed from normal, it was like they were from another galaxy.
Light-years away from normal.

"What are we going to do?" Cella asked Smith. "If the
Yuns come for them—"

"They'll come! How could they not? It's about honor now."

"Do you actually know something or are you saying this
because you used to watch those Run Run Shaw movies with
your dad when you were a kid?"

"I said that one time and no! I'm talking about the fact that
they are very Americanized gangsters," Smith said. "We'd be
having the same conversation no matter where their relatives
came from because gangsters are gangsters."

"We cannot let them have a full-blown battle in the middle
of the five boroughs and think that the full-humans won't notice. Gang wars they notice."

"Look, when it comes to the Group, we're just guns for
hire. This is for upper management to handle."

"In other words, let your husband and his uncle handle it?"
Cella asked.

"Yeah. That's what he gets paid for. We ain't making
enough to put up with this level of shit! He didn't get his nose
broken!"

"Fine. But you need to stop being a wuss about your fucking nose."

"Really?" Smith pulled off the towel Cella had given her to
help stanch the flow of blood and wiped her hand across her
nose.

"You wouldn't dare," Cella growled out, watching as
Smith had the nerve to slash her blood-drenched hand across
the passenger-side dashboard of Cella's car.

"Now are you worried about my nose?" Smith asked. "Or
should I do the same thing to your backseat?"

"This . . . *this* is why cats hate canines!"

chapter SIXTEEN

They went for fancy, choosing the ultraexpensive Van Holtz Steakhouse not far from the Sports Center. The team must have planned for them to go there, because even though Mads was positive she could hear her teammates somewhere within the four-story building, and the fox hostess instantly recognized Mads from the other times she'd come in with her team after a win, the pair was led to a private dining room that clearly had been reserved by snooty Nelle.

Not that Mads really minded missing out on a big team dinner. This had just been the playoffs. Her mind was already on the championships. If they won that, then they could celebrate together as a team.

The gruff black bear waiter handed them each a menu, took their drink orders, then lumbered out the door.

Giving each other awkward smiles, they disappeared behind their menus, and Mads studied the myriad of options. Cape buffalo. Red deer. Zebras. Giraffe. Antelope. Even wildebeests. She could add a mushroom sauce. Or garlic shrimp. Or an expensive wine. Or a honey glaze. Or . . .

Mads put the menu down. "I don't want any of this."

Finn put his menu down. "I don't either. I feel like I'm eating at Grandmother Malone's house. With the fancy napkins and the glassware you can't break. She kept slapping our hands until Ma slashed her with her claws. The Malone brothers were never invited back to Grandmother Malone's house."

"I've eaten here before but always with Max and the others.

So most of my time is spent making sure they don't kill themselves from the poison-infused tequila they bring or others from
the fights they start. But without anything to worry about, I realize how uncomfortable I am here. That's no fun."

"We come to one of these out on Long Island every
Mother's Day. They have an amazing onion sauce that goes
great with everything, including a regular New York strip. But
without my mom, my brothers, and Nat, it just feels . . . uncomfortable."

They sat in awkward silence, Mads wondering when this
torture would end.

"Wanna make a break for it?" Finn finally joked.

"That waiter looks like he could take us down."

"He's a typical steakhouse waiter. Looks like he's been here
a thousand years. Has a voice like broken granite. Doesn't look
like he gives a shit whether we stay or go as long as we pay for
our drinks and leave him a tip." He grinned. "Where would
you like to eat instead?"

Mads thought for a little bit, but after a robust game, she
really only had one choice. "Do you like Jamaican?"

Finn shrugged. "I never had Jamaican."

"Never?"

"I was born in Syosset. Not a lot of Jamaican restaurants
there."

"That you know of."

"That's true. We weren't exactly looking for Jamaican
restaurants."

"Then want to try it?"

"Is there going to be zebra on the menu?"

"Jerk chicken. Jerk goat. Peas and rice. Meat patties. Those
are really good. And no zebra in the meat patties. Just chicken
or beef."

"Let's give it a try."

They both stood as their waiter walked in with their drinks.
He took one look at them, grunted, and warned as he walked
back out, "You better leave a tip."

Finn shrugged again. "Told ya."

*   *   *

They ended up back in Queens, only a few blocks from her new place and the MacKilligan's rental house. It wasn't exactly surprising that Mads would choose a restaurant in the neighborhood where she'd been staying for weeks, and Finn was just glad to be out of the city.

What Finn didn't expect, though, was not only how well Mads was known by the waitstaff, but how loved. As soon as she walked in, she was greeted with calls and hugs. Everyone was full-human, so there were no mentions of shifter pro basketball playoffs or zebras and Cape buffalo. Instead, Mads simply introduced Finn as her friend and they were led to a small table in the corner that he sensed Mads always sat at.

"Hey, girl," greeted a tall man with shoulder-length dreads, leaning down to kiss Mads's cheek. He placed plastic-covered menus in front of them.

"Hey, Danny. This is Finn. Finn, this is Danny. He owns this place along with his wife, Cherie."

"You sure you comfortable there, my man? Your shoulders look a little"—Danny moved his hands around—"cramped."

"Well . . ."

"You don't mind if we move you, Mads, yeah?"

"No."

"This is Mads's usual table. But you need a little more space. Let's get you a table over there."

Finn stood and Danny watched as he rose until Finn towered over him, which only made Danny laugh.

"Did you really need all this, Mads? Seems like a lot for a little girl like you."

"I thought you were taking us to a new table."

"No need to get snippy."

They moved to the new, bigger table and Finn was relieved that he could actually move his shoulders and stretch out his legs.

"Now isn't that nicer?" Danny asked.

"Don't you have something to do?" Mads asked.

"I'm just making sure everyone's happy."

"Cherie!"

A stunning older woman with amazingly long dreads that nearly reached the back of her knees came out from behind an office door and, without saying a word, silently pointed a damning finger toward the kitchen.

Laughing, her husband moved on; a waiter quickly replaced him to take their drink orders.

Mads mouthed, *Thank you.* And Cherie gave a wink and smile before heading back into the office.

Finn looked around and immediately knew he liked the place. It reminded him of his favorite restaurant, where his family often went for authentic Mongolian food. Not Mongolian barbeque. Those were actually a Taiwanese invention and not remotely "authentic Mongolian." But after their father died, and her family had been forced to go back to their own lives, their mother had needed some comfort food that she didn't have to cook herself. She'd been lucky to discover a little hole-in-the-wall restaurant with a chef transplanted from Mongolia. They'd become fast friends, and he always made sure that Lisa's growing boys had enough food. Easy enough when they were younger, but when the Malone brothers kept growing and eating more and more and more, he did seem to find it a little disturbing. Not that anyone could blame him. Especially when they had their growth spurts. Going from five-six or five-seven to six-two or six-three in the two-week period between family visits to the restaurant would freak anybody out.

"This is a nice place," Finn said after the waiter dropped off lemonade for Mads and passion fruit punch for Finn.

"I love it here. Reminds me of home."

Finn looked around again, lingering on the giant wall mural of Bob Marley.

"*This* place reminds you of Wisconsin?"

"Oh, God, no." Mads laughed a little. "I mean Detroit. I lived in Detroit until we moved to Wisconsin. I spent most of my time in my great-grandmother's store with her. Next door there was this Jamaican fast-food restaurant. She and the owner hated each other, but I liked him. He gave me free food because he thought Solveig was purposely starving me, and he taught me about reggae music."

"You like reggae?"

"Reggae and ska." Her eyes narrowed. "What's so funny?"

"I haven't heard about ska since high school."

"My dad's favorite sister was a huge fan. She got me into it."

The waiter returned with a plate of what Mads called, "Meat patties. They're really good. These are chicken. These are beef."

Finn smiled.

"What?"

"They look a little bit like *khuushuur*."

"Which is . . . ?"

"Fried dough with meat, onion, and seasonings inside. Kind of like these. Although if you get them *in* Mongolia, you might get mutton or camel instead of chicken."

"Camel? Never had camel. But I've had black mamba, so I don't judge."

"Millions of people eat camel as part of their regular diet, so you shouldn't."

Finn tried the beef patty and enjoyed it so much, the waiter brought another plate of beef patties just for him when he finished off the first plate in a few minutes.

"I'm going to order the combo plates for us," Mads announced. "Jerk chicken, oxtail stew, and beef stew. That way you get to see what you like."

"What about the curry goat?"

"I don't like curry."

Finn frowned. "I don't know what that has to do with me."

The waiter came and Mads gave their order before explaining it. "I don't like curry because I can't stand the smell of curry. You get curry, I'm leaving."

"Oh. Okay. So you don't go to a lot of Indian restaurants, huh?"

"No. Which makes Streep insane, because she *loves* Indian food. Apparently I'm ruining her life because she's not able to go out for Indian food with *all* her teammates. That's my fault."

"Streep's an interesting woman."

"Streep's a nut. But she's a shit-hot baller, so I put up with her craziness."

"I think I'll be saying that to the league a lot about Charlie."

A smile spread across Mads's face. "You drafted Charlie MacKilligan to your team?"

"We did."

"That's . . . bold."

"You should have seen her," Finn explained around bites of beef patty. "When she was coming at you, she was like a locomotive and you were just the car stuck on the tracks. But when you were going at her . . . she was just the mountain you couldn't move. The coaches love her and fear her in equal measure."

"That's how I feel about her."

"And yet you don't fear Max?"

She shook her head. "I only fear what Max will do to others. Or any civilians that get in her way. She does not care about civilians in the heat of the moment. So the rest of us have to. Her sister has to. It's a lot of work for all of us."

Their main meal arrived and both of them dove in. After all the physical work they'd each done that day, they worked through their plates of delicious food without much effort. The problem was that Finn was still hungry. Very hungry. Starving, in fact. And about to ask for more when another plate of food was placed in front of him before he could say a word.

"I came in here with the Dunn triplets once for lunch," Mads explained while continuing to eat, her head over her plate, her fork shoveling food in. "They had to close the restaurant down for the rest of the day. They couldn't even open for dinner afterward."

She leaned back and a different waiter whisked her empty plate away and replaced it with a full one. She went back to work and so did Finn.

Mads finished eating after her third plate of food. But Finn didn't until after his fifth. Still, the wait staff and owners didn't say much about it. Maybe because of his size.

About halfway through their meal, a reggae band took the stage at the front of the restaurant. They weren't bad and Mads seemed really happy. He got the feeling that she kept her love of reggae to herself, maybe by listening through headphones when around her teammates. He got that. though. He'd always liked tech music. But it drove Keane nuts and, according to him, made him want to kill the first full-human male he saw. So it made sense for Finn to listen to that kind of music through his headphones. If only to protect full-human males from Keane and Keane from a lifetime in prison.

When the band took a break about forty minutes later, Mads asked, "Want to order dessert and take it back to my house? I don't know if I have coffee but . . . I'm sure I have something."

"Sounds great."

She motioned a waiter over and picked out a few things from the dessert menu, doubling up on the dark chocolate cake since Mads promised, "It's the best. Seriously. The lemon cake is good too . . . but the dark chocolate cake is life changing."

They didn't pay at the table, but up front. Finn gave Mads the paper bag filled with their desserts and sent her outside to his SUV. Danny cashed him out and Finn made sure to break a few twenties so he could tip everyone who'd taken care of them that night. At a young age, he'd worked as a bouncer in enough restaurants and bars to know how important tips were to the waitstaff and bartenders.

When he was done and heading toward the front door, Danny asked, "You hoping I tell Mads what a good tipper you are?"

"I'm always a good tipper," Finn replied. "But you can tell her how charming and handsome I am."

"So you want me to lie to the poor girl?"

Finn smiled. "Only about the charming part."

Mads electronically opened the back of the SUV and leaned in to carefully place their desserts in the rear, trying to find the right spot so the bag wouldn't topple over. She didn't want to lose any of that dark chocolate ganache icing to the containers holding their cake.

"Hey, Mads."

"Mads!"

"Yo, Mads!"

Mads quickly straightened up and looked around. Her head tilted, ears trying to lock onto where those voices were coming from.

"Mads! Come here!"

"Max?"

She reached for her .40 semiauto but then remembered that she didn't have it on her. She didn't like to go to her games armed. It was just asking for trouble with some of the teams they were up against.

Mads moved slowly toward the dark alley, but she could look inside it just fine. The problem was, she didn't see anyone. Not Max. Not her team. Not a dude in military-type gear lying in wait while holding a tape recorder. No one. And yet the voices sounded as if they'd come from—

"Oh, shit!"

Mads spun around, ready to fight. But they'd already grabbed her wrists and forearms, dragging her into that dark alley and slamming her back against the wall so hard she briefly thought she saw actual yellow birds tweeting and flying around her head.

"Hi, cousin!"

"Hey, cous."

The twins that Max had tortured with scorpions on the school bus all those years ago. That event had led to a brief hospital stay they had not forgotten or forgiven. But they didn't blame "the beavers"—Mads had stopped correcting them with "badgers" a long time ago.

They blamed *her*.

Meaning they were delighted that they'd been sent here to make Mads's life hell. Why not? It wasn't like they had anything better to do in between the occasional bank heist.

"Get off me!" Mads ordered, pushing them and nearly getting away. But the pair of them together was a lot of combined strength. They slammed her against the wall again.

"Where is it?" one asked.

"The family wants it back," the other said.

"I don't know. I don't have it."

That's when she got punched by other female cousins who crept in behind Tilda and Gella. She got hit in the face. In the stomach. A few hits to the kidneys. So hard Mads nearly dropped to her knees.

They hadn't even bothered sending the males this time. Except maybe to drive or be lookouts. This abuse was coming from her female cousins, who'd always hated her. Had never wanted her around. And didn't understand why she wasn't left in Detroit with Solveig when they'd moved, or been sent off to live with her father since he'd always seemed to want her.

"We're going to ask you one more time—" Tilda began.

"And then what?"

Gella punched her three times in the face and yelled, "Tell us where it is, you little bitch!"

The roar from the end of the alley had the hyenas breaking out in panicked laughter and whoops, calling to the males nearby. But the way Finn filled up that alley opening with just his shoulders had Mads's cousins immediately releasing her. The weaker ones simply backed away.

But Tilda and Gella had dreams of leading one day.

They didn't attack, though. They were human enough to play it smarter. They sauntered up to Finn as Tilda sweetly asked, "You wouldn't punch a girl, now would you?"

And Finn didn't. He didn't punch a girl. He head-butted her. Sending Tilda tumbling back several feet. Gella came at Finn with claws and fangs out, but he just slammed his palm against her chest and sent her crashing into a nearby wall, causing something on her body to audibly crack.

Finn roared again, and lights came on in nearby upstairs apartments.

Her cousins made a run for it, Tilda having to help Gella up and out. The rest of the Clan had left the twins behind.

Finn walked over to Mads, but before he could say anything, she stomped out. Mads didn't want to talk to him. She didn't want to talk to anyone.

Unfortunately, he didn't seem to get that message.

He caught up to her at the SUV. He didn't grab her arm but he did block the passenger door before she could open it.

"Why didn't you fight them?" he asked.

"There were a lot."

"Bullshit! I saw you take on two tigers with nothing but a baseball bat and your rage. And then you went looking for more. Those were just hyenas. Why didn't you fight them?"

"I wanna go home."

"Why won't you answer me?"

"I want to go home."

"You didn't even unleash your fangs or claws."

"Are you going to take me home or am I going to walk? Is that how you want this date to end?"

Finn pulled his hand away from the door and Mads yanked it open. She got in and he got in on the other side. They didn't speak the entire way back to her house, which was only a few blocks away, but it had to be the longest ride of her life.

Finn didn't understand. There'd only been about six or seven hyenas on her. He hadn't really counted. When he'd found her in that alley, he was shocked to see her just standing there. Taking that abuse. She hadn't put up a fight. She hadn't called for help. She hadn't even told them to fuck off. She'd done absolutely nothing but . . . take it.

True, Mads wasn't as . . . well . . . insane as Max MacKilligan or sneaky as Nelle and Streep. Or as 007 meets Smiley as Tock. But she definitely wasn't a "stand there and take it" kind of gal either. Not from what he'd seen.

Except . . .

Finn pulled into Mads's driveway, turned off the motor, and asked, "*Was that your family?*"

It was the only thing that made sense. The only other person he'd seen her react passively to had been her mother.

Instead of answering him, Mads got out of the SUV and stormed toward her house. Snarling, he followed her to the front door. She stopped on the low stoop and faced him but wouldn't look him in the eyes.

"Thank you for a lovely evening. Have a nice night."

"Mads—"

She turned away from him with her house keys out, but before she could put them in the lock, she realized her front door was slightly ajar.

"Did they break into your house?" he whispered.

"I . . . they . . ."

Mads kicked the door in and charged into the house, flicking on the overhead lights. She took a quick look around the living room. Didn't see anything, so she ran upstairs. Finn kept looking, going into the kitchen, peering out into the backyard. He even went into the basement.

But nothing seemed out of place. Nothing obvious, anyway. He didn't know if Mads would notice anything.

The one thing he did know? He didn't *smell* any hyenas. Not just the general scent of a hyena, but the markings a hyena would have left behind if he or she were bold enough to leave the front door open. And, to be blunt, hyenas left a foul-smell marking. It would have been the first thing Finn and Mads caught as soon as they entered the house.

He came back upstairs and closed the front door. But as he turned away, Mads was coming down the stairs and in her hands was . . . a stainless-steel Viking sword.

She held it as she would an offering to a god: both hands beneath it, the sword laid aloft on her palms. Her eyes wide in shock.

"Where did you find that?" he asked.

"On the bed. Next to the coyote."

"I doubt he was the one who put it there."

She glared. "Funny."

"Did you scent someone else in the house? Because I don't."

"No. I don't. Which makes me think it was someone very good at what they do."

"You've known all along who took that stupid thing . . . haven't you?"

"Probably."

"And?"

Her entire face cringed as she announced, "My father."

chapter SEVENTEEN

"**W**hat am I going to do?"

Finn ducked. "First, maybe you should put the sword down."

Instead of putting it down, she shook it at him. "I should not have this in the house!"

"Why arc you whispering? And give it to me!" He grabbed hold of it and they began to struggle over the Viking sword until Mads suddenly released it and Finn slapped himself in the face.

"That's what I get for head-butting a woman. That was karma."

"Karma? She was a demon hyena happy to beat the crap outta me. And I'm her cousin! You shouldn't feel guilty about anything." She stared at the sword before sadly announcing, "I'm going to send this back to them before this whole thing gets out of hand."

"Your face tells me they don't *deserve* this sword back."

"What does that mean?"

"You look abused. By your own family. At least mine only ignores me and my brothers."

He reached for her cheek, and she slapped his hand away.

"My face is fine."

"You're dripping blood on your hardwood floors. And what's wrong with your side?"

"Nothing."

"Then why are you standing weird?"

"Why are you asking so many questions?"

"Because you're bleeding all over your floor! That coyote is going to eat you while you're sleeping!"

"You have it in for that coyote!"

"*Because he's going to eat you while you're sleeping!*"

They glared at each other until Mads softly growled, "Would you feel better if you could clean my wounds?"

"Yes, as a matter of fact, I would."

"Fine."

"Fine."

She gestured toward the stairs with a sweep of her hand, but he barked, "Just go!" Annoyed at how difficult she was being about all this.

Finn watched her walk up the stairs and he could tell she was definitely walking as if something was wrong. It wasn't her legs that were the problem, though. They seemed fine.

She led him to the bedroom and, sure enough, the coyote was stretched out in the middle of her bed. He didn't even lift his head when he saw them. Just watched them with one eye open as they went to the master bathroom.

Finn placed the sword on the dresser. "I can't believe you let him sleep on your bed."

"Stop complaining."

Finn froze outside the bathroom door and sniffed the air. "Do I smell shampoo?"

"I asked Stevie to wash him if she had time and if he let her. I guess he let her."

"*You had a wild animal bathed?*"

"You had me worried about ticks on my bed! She gave him a flea and tick bath! *And stop yelling at me!*"

Mads flicked on the bathroom lights and immediately grimaced at the sight of herself in the sink mirror.

"See?" he said.

"Shut up."

"Let me look at your side and back."

"It's fine."

"It's not fine. Let me look."

Mads sighed and lifted her shirt just enough so he could easily see. Now Finn grimaced, moving in and crouching so he could examine it closely. They'd pummeled her kidneys.

"You need ice."

"I do not need ice."

"Why are you arguing with me about everything?"

"Because you're making a big deal out of nothing." She faced him. "This is not the first time I've been beaten up by my cousins. This is not the first time I've been hit in the kidney. This is not the first time I've had a wild animal on my bed."

"Your poisonous snakes do not count since they were most likely dinner."

"I had to eat something."

"That kidney looks bad. What if it bursts?"

"It'll heal."

"You don't know that."

"It has before."

Finn gawked at her. "Your cousins burst your kidney before?"

"It had nothing to do with my cousins."

"Max?"

"No. It was Streep that time. We were in Rome. Actually, Vatican City and—"

"Did you rob the Pope?"

"I would never! Besides, any Pope-robbing Streep does is with her parents. This was something completely different and it—"

"Just got out of hand?"

"I don't like your tone."

Finn shook his head. "I'll get you some ice."

"Stop sounding so put upon. I didn't ask you to help!"

The pushy tiger had walked out, but then he'd suddenly popped back into her bathroom.

"'Put upon'?" he asked.

"What? I read. British stuff."

"Do you?"

"Fine. I watch British movies and TV miniseries because Streep has a hard-on for Jane Austen. Which means I stand behind my 'put upon.'"

He rolled his eyes and again disappeared from her bathroom.

Once Mads had a few seconds alone, she dropped her hands on the sink and lowered her head. Only her family could ruin what had been an amazing evening. Her team had easily won the game, putting them firmly into the championships. And although she hadn't liked how her teammates had gone about it, she'd had a date with Finn. A really nice date. Something she hadn't done in a long time. Her last date had been with a full-human who, within the first thirty minutes of coffeehouse conversation, had asked her if she liked anal sex. After she'd headed back to Tock's cabinet for the night, he'd bombarded her with text after text of his dick pics. She'd been so disgusted she'd decided to take a break from dating for a little bit . . . and had sworn off full-human males forever.

This date, though, had given her hope. Maybe she actually had a chance at a long-term thing. But after seeing her fucked up by her own family . . .

Who would want any part of that?

She'd dropped at least two boyfriends over the years who had insisted on meeting her family. She couldn't understand why that was so important. One kept complaining that he felt he "didn't know the real Mads." Of course he didn't! Because the real Mads could shift into a very large honey badger and strip his skin off!

She really should have stopped dating full-human males ages ago.

"Stop looking so sorry for yourself," Finn said from behind her.

"I don't." But when she lifted her head and saw herself in the mirror, all hunched over the sink like that, she did look pretty miserable.

"Face me," he ordered.

Mads turned and lifted her shirt enough so he could view the injured area. Finn leaned over at the waist and slowly swiveled her around so he could easily see where to place the ice pack.

"You found an ice pack?"

"There were a bunch in your freezer. Right next to the frozen food. Lots of frozen meat pies."

"Oh, come on."

He straightened up. "What?"

"Nothing."

"Do I need to get you to the hospital?"

"No, no. Nothing like that." Mads briefly glanced off before admitting, "I love meat pies."

"Holy shit. Is this still about Nelle getting your house set up for you?"

"It's weird!"

He started to say something, but shook his head instead and returned to applying the ice pack.

"You don't think it's weird?"

"I'm not getting in the middle of this." He took her hand and held it against the ice pack. "Hold this a second."

Crouching down, he went into the cabinet under the bathroom sink and immediately came out with a big first-aid kit. He placed it on the countertop and pulled out medical tape. Using two strips from the roll, he secured the ice pack against Mads's wound.

"Is that too cold for you?"

"Nope."

"You sure?"

"Honey badger skin."

"Don't know what that means."

"Can stand up to almost anything. That's why my team-mates survived being tossed in an incinerator."

"I still think *that's* weird."

"Would you rather they'd burned to death so I could be really sad?"

"That's not what I—" Finn's next words were cut off by his own growl of frustration. He carefully grabbed her around the waist and lifted her up on the bathroom countertop.

He used alcohol wipes from the first-aid kit to clean off the wounds on her face.

"Should I worry about you getting the fever?" he asked, discussing the way shifter bodies sometimes healed themselves when gravely wounded.

"I never have," she replied. "Some hybrids do, some don't. MacKilligans don't. But not a lot of honey badgers get the fever anyway."

"Because you're all just so badass?"

"No. I think it's just the way our bodies deal with trauma. Like when we're poisoned. We just pass out for a while. And either we wake up . . . or we don't."

Finn gawked at her for a few moments before throwing the last wipe away and remarking, "Fascinating."

"You asked."

"Sorry I did." He carefully lifted her off the counter and stood her on the tiled floor. "To bed with you."

"I'm not tired."

"Then we'll turn on the TV Nelle wisely put in your bedroom. But you're getting in bed, so you don't randomly pass out, fall down the stairs, crack your hard head open, and—I know it's rare—possibly kill yourself."

"You're worried about me falling down a flight of stairs after I fell off a building and nearly destroyed your brother's car with the impact?"

"And some tough guys get killed by one punch. Strange things happen. Just go to bed. At least until I'm sure your kidney doesn't explode and you start bleeding out."

"Fine. I've gotta pee first."

"Okay. I'll go wait for you out—are you peeing in front of me?"

Mads looked up at him from the toilet she was now sitting on. And, yes, peeing into.

"Yeah. Why?"

"You couldn't wait until I got out of here and closed the door?"

"You saw me beaten up by my own family. We are *beyond* the bullshit games that people play with each other, like pretending we have no bodily functions. Besides . . . it's just pee."

Again, he started to say something but instead simply threw his hands up and stormed out of the room, making sure to slam the bathroom door behind him.

Kind of enjoying his dramatic reaction to her casual Viking ways, Mads finished using the toilet, washed her hands, and walked out into the bedroom. That's where she found him trying to get the coyote off the bed. Much to Mads's growing delight, the coyote seemed determined to stay right where he was.

"It's not moving!" he complained.

"Maybe because you call him 'it.'"

"I'm not giving this animal more respect than I give my own baby brother."

Deciding not to argue that disturbing point, Mads knew she didn't want to go to bed in tight black jeans and shirt. Even a sleeveless one. So she sat on a cushioned bench by the window and began to tug off her boots, gritting her teeth when she had to bend over a bit and her kidney screamed at her to stop. Once she had her boots and socks off, she took a moment to get her breath back and for the pain to stop shooting through her system. She noticed that Finn was now in a tug-of-war with the coyote over the comforter.

Shaking her head, Mads got up and went to the dresser. She opened one of the drawers and, sure enough, she found several pairs of the loose shorts and cotton camisoles she loved to wear to bed.

Damn, Nelle! Why did she constantly have to prove how well she knew them all? That was something Mads would have to figure out later, after she got some sleep.

She pulled out dark blue shorts and a cami and plopped them on the dresser. She was in the middle of changing clothes when she heard Finn yell, "*Why are you naked?*"

"I'm changing for bed."

"Why didn't you ask me to leave the room?"

"Well, I've already seen you naked."

"When I shifted from animal to human. That's different!"

"Is it?"

Finn snarled, turned away from her, dragged the comforter forward and the coyote along with it until he could wrap the material around the coyote and remove all three of them from the room entirely.

"That seemed overly dramatic!" she called after him.

"Shut up!"

Finn dropped the coyote in the backyard, and when it tried to shoot past him back into the house, Finn's roar seemed to scare it off. At least for the moment.

"Shut up the damn cat noise!" one of Mads's new neighbors complained.

"*I will burn your hives to the ground!*" Finn bellowed in warning before going into the house and slamming the door.

He knew he shouldn't take it out on the bears—the coyote was getting exactly what he deserved! Just as seeing a bruised and damaged Mads should have made him feel simple pity for her. But instead, finding her standing there, completely naked, made him horny and hard despite all those bruises. What kind of human being was he?

Maybe his mother's family was right. Their side of the family was more tiger than human. They didn't let things like bruises and kidney damage get in the way of what their heart and loins wanted. The females of their kin were as demanding as the males.

He should leave. Right now. He shouldn't even go back upstairs. He should call Charlie, give her a heads-up about what had happened, and speed away in shame. That's what he should do. He knew it. The coyote knew it. The bear that he could hear next door desperately checking his hives knew it.

He had his keys in his pocket. He had absolutely no logical reason to stay!

"Hey, Finn!" Mads called from her bedroom. "Could you grab a bottled water for me? And a jar of honey-covered nuts, too? Please?"

It was the "please" that did him in. Why did she have to say "please"? And so nicely. Not mocking nice, or manipulative nice, but just . . . nice.

"Fuck!" he growled. "Fuck, fuck, fuck, fuck, fuck!"

He stomped to the kitchen. Got her a big bottled water from the refrigerator. Dug around in the cabinets until he found a whole cupboard filled with cans and jars of honey-covered peanuts and almonds and cashews. He grabbed the peanuts. Then he took all of it upstairs for her.

Finn found her tucked into the middle of the bed with the TV on. A Taiwanese action movie was playing. He'd thought she would be watching ESPN, but was glad she wasn't. He didn't need any more sports tonight. Especially full-human sports.

She was stretched out on top of the sheets, several pillows behind her back. She took the water and peanuts from him and dropped them next to her on the bed. Then she turned those big blue eyes on him.

"Get comfortable," she said, and tapped the bed with her hand. "Sit. You ever see this movie? The fight scenes are awesome."

"Uh . . . I was thinking . . ."

Again, she looked at him with those blue eyes.

"You were thinking what?" she pushed when he didn't finish his thought.

"I should take my shoes off."

"Okay."

He kicked his shoes off and got on the bed, stretching his long legs out.

They watched the movie in silence for a while until she asked, "Water?"

She held the big water bottle in front of his face. "Oh. Thanks." He took it from her and gulped some water down, handed it back. She re-capped it and put it aside.

"What did you do to the coyote?"

"Just put it outside. It's fine. Probably under the house again."

"Poor thing."

"You and my brother."

"Keane?"

"Shay. He's a dog lover, too."

"I could not care less about dogs. But I do appreciate a wild animal that is smart enough to get in and out of a home without messing it up. When you have a racoon in your home . . . you *know* you have a racoon in your home."

Finn put an arm behind his head. "So I guess you're going to tell your teammates about your cousins being in town."

"No, I am not."

Confused, he studied Mads, noticed how serious she suddenly looked.

"Why not?"

"Are you kidding? That's a nightmare I can't wake up from. I'm not saying a word and neither are you. Not a word."

"Wait a minute—"

"No. I'm serious."

Finn let his elbows prop him up. "I don't understand."

"You don't need to understand."

"Explain it to me or I start dialing. Because I think your friends would want to know. At least Tock would."

"I'm trying to protect them."

"Are you kidding?" he asked with a harsh laugh. "You're trying to protect those *broads*? Seriously? There's not *one* of them that I worry about. Not one!"

"But they have families. I can't put their families at risk."

"Isn't most of Tock's family in Mossad? And Nelle's father has bodyguards and I think close to a billion dollars. And Max, oh . . . Max."

"What about her grandfather?"

"He's in a wolf pack, right?"

"Living right next to my much bigger hyena family! They will destroy him! And Streep's family has no protection at all."

Mads shook her head and swiped her hands across each other. "No. We're not telling them anything. We're not getting them involved."

"So what are you going to do with that idiotic sword?"

"We'll just send it back through the mail or something."

"After what they did to you, you're really going to give it back to them?"

"What do you think I should do?"

"I don't know. Throw it out. Or hide it under the house with the coyote."

"So we can put the coyote in danger when they come here looking for that stupid sword? Because they'll eventually find out where I live."

Finn sat up straight and rested his arms on his knees, focusing his full attention directly on Mads.

"Are you telling me that not only are you worrying about your friends, and the families of your friends, but you're also worried about the safety of a random coyote that just happens to be living under the house you just bought a day ago? Is *that* what you're telling me?"

Mads shrugged. "Yes."

"Wow." Finn pressed the palms of his hands to his eyes and lay back on the bed. "Wow."

"It doesn't mean I'm wrong."

"Just . . . no."

"But—"

"No."

"If you'd only—"

"*No.*"

"Well . . . do you want a honey-covered nut?"

"I'm already sitting next to a honey-covered nut."

chapter EIGHTEEN

Mads had no idea when she fell asleep. She just knew that at some point in the night, her side really hurt. So bad, she must have made some sound because Finn told her it would be okay, pressed a fresh ice pack to her side, and brushed her hair off her face. That was the last thing she remembered until she woke up around three in the morning with her head on Finn's shoulder and her arm thrown over his massive chest. She had no idea how she'd got there, but she didn't really mind.

They didn't agree on a lot, but she had to admit that she felt perfectly situated at the moment. Tucked against his body like this.

She also felt something she didn't feel except when she was with all her teammates in a hotel room or on the basketball court. Safe. She felt perfectly safe with Finn Malone.

She couldn't think of any male she'd ever felt safe with. Comfortable, sure. But safe? Nope. Especially while in bed. Which was why most guys said the same thing when they called the next day. "I woke up and found you gone. Where did you go?"

Of course, that was after sex. She hadn't had sex with Finn. She was just lying here. But the fact that she didn't feel like escaping to a cabinet or leaving the state . . . that was new.

"You need to stop doing that," Finn muttered next to her.

She thought he might be talking in his sleep because his eyes were still closed, but just in case, she replied, "Doing what?"

"Rubbing my chest."

She was?

Mads lifted her head from his shoulder to take a look and yes! She was rubbing his chest. Under his black T-shirt no less!

"Oh!" She pulled her hand out. "I'm so sorry."

He smiled even though his eyes remained closed. "No need to apologize."

There wasn't? "Then why did you complain?"

"It wasn't a complaint. I just needed you to stop."

"Was it irritating?"

"Irritation was not the problem."

Mads was trying to figure out what the hell he was talking about when she happened to glance down and—

"Oh!" She fell back on the bed and his arm. "I see."

"I'm a strong man but the tiger inside has its limits."

Mads closed her eyes. Not because she was embarrassed. She wasn't. It was because she was trying to get the outline of Finn Malone's massive cock pressed against his black jeans out of her head. She'd had no idea it was that fucking huge!

Closing her eyes, however, did not help. Now the image was burned into her brain.

"Okay." She sat up. Shook out her hands. Blew out a breath.

"Are you all right?"

Dammit. His low voice wasn't helping either.

"I'm fine, I'm fine." She shook out her hands again. "It's just I'm so damn horny."

"Wait . . . what?"

"It's been a while since I got laid. And winning a game always gets me a little riled up."

"Uhhhh . . ."

"And I had *no* idea your cock was that big."

Finn sat up. "What's happening?"

"So seeing the size of that thing made my nipples really hard and my pussy really wet—"

"Woman! What are you doing?"

"You asked me if I'm all right. I'm telling you what's going on."

"You *just* had a fight."

"That wasn't a fight. That was an assault. And what does
that have to do with anything?"

"Is this the fever? I feel like this is the fever."

"No." She took his hand, pressed it to her forehead. "See?
No fever."

"So then you're just . . . ?"

"Horny."

He pulled his hand away. "With a damaged kidney."

"That healed ages ago."

"I doubt it. I almost rushed you to the hospital. You were
groaning in your sleep and when I checked, the bruise had
spread and there was this humongous lump that just looked terrifying. But when I tried to lift you out of the bed, you grabbed
the headboard and squealed so loud, the coyote started yipping
and the bears on the street started to roar. I was afraid if I took
you outside, they'd eat you." When she frowned, he added,
"They're omnivores. They'll eat *anything*. So I changed the ice
pack and let you settle down, hoping I could take you to the
hospital when you passed out. Then we both fell asleep and . . .
here we are."

"Well, it's fine now."

"It can't be fine."

Mads reached back and yanked the ice pack off her back.
"Look."

She leaned forward, making it easy for Finn to see. She felt
his hands slide across the area that her cousins had hit repeatedly, his fingers brushing over the skin. She had to close her
eyes again because her nipples became so hard they hurt.

"Holy shit. It *is* healed."

"Told you."

"Sure there's no internal—"

"Bleeding? No."

"That's amazing."

"Honey badger."

He sat up again and said, "I just don't want to . . ."

"What?"

"Take advantage of the moment."

"Why are you whispering?"

"I don't know," he whispered again.

"Okay. I get it. If I were in a fever, this would be very wrong."

"Exactly," he finally said in his normal voice.

"Except I'm not."

"True. But the whole experience with your cousins could be emotionally traumatic."

"Could be. Probably should be. But I have been down this road so often . . . I'm sadly used to it. Kind of stopped thinking about it when we were watching the movie. I can promise that I will get angry about it again sometime tomorrow. That's how the pattern goes."

"But at this moment—"

"Not even thinking about it. Because we won a game. We're in the championships. Saw the outline of your cock. Now I'm horny."

Finn started to say something but she was worried he might guilt his way out of this so she cut him off by offering, "If you want, I can make things easier for you by taking the lead here. You know . . . to start."

He took a moment to let that sink in. "Huh."

"You can kind of lie back and . . . not have so many thoughts. Just let that big cat take over. And let my honey badger take the lead."

He frowned. "Your honey badger won't gnaw, will it?"

"It won't. Promise."

"Well . . . if you're sure—whoa!"

Mads pressed her hand against his chest and shoved him back against the bed. She dealt with his jeans and boxer briefs first, dragging them down his hips and legs until she got them to his ankles. Then shucking off the shorts and cami she put on earlier, she scrambled on top of his lap but faced away from him, her legs straddling his hips.

Mads grabbed his cock in both hands. As the outline of his jeans had promised, the size was delightfully massive and she allowed herself to stroke it before settling in and letting her tongue swirl around the tip a few times. Since she loved a good long fuck, she knew it was best to get Finn's first shot out of the way. But because of the size, she also had her work cut out for her. Not that she minded. She did love a challenge.

She started by sucking on the tip first, bringing it into her mouth, pulling out, then sucking it in again. She took her time. Played with it. Let her tongue tease around at the top. She heard Finn groan and felt his hands on her hips. Because of their height difference, sixty-nine was out, but that was okay. She had a feeling he'd take care of her later.

Besides, she was too focused on what she was doing to worry about anything else. She had his cock halfway in her mouth and was determined to get it all the way to the back of her throat without gagging. Wouldn't be easy. Plus, her mouth was already stretched pretty wide.

But she kept going. Taking him deeper and deeper. Loving that his groaning kept getting louder. The hands on her body a little rougher.

What she wasn't expecting, because she hadn't been thinking about it one way or the other, was his two fingers slipping inside her. She was already really wet just from sucking on him, so his fingers easily slid out and when they came back, it was three. He pushed them in hard, and Mads jerked forward, ending up taking all of his cock. At the same time, she growled. Because his fingers inside her felt so good.

He kept fucking her with those fingers, too. Kind of rough, which she liked. Rocking her back and forth, with his other hand rubbing her ass. As he pushed her forward, she came back and arched her ass into his hand. When she did it the fifth or sixth time, he pulled his hand away. Then he brought it down, slapping her ass. Not too hard. But enough to entertain. Enough to keep her attention and make her cry out against his cock.

He tried to pull her off his cock, but she held on and he came in her mouth. He shot three times into her and when he was done, he yanked her off and slammed her onto the bed. Before she could say a word, he was buried face-first between her legs, his tongue taking long, deep strokes. She gripped his hair and planted her heels in his back.

She'd been licked before but never like this. And it took her a few minutes to figure out why. Why she felt wild and overwhelmed and almost afraid of how hard she was going to come. It was his tongue. It was rough. It wasn't a full tiger tongue. That would rip the flesh off. But he'd shifted it enough to give her a rough ride, so to speak, and since she was honey badger anyway, the whole thing was making her toes curl and her body shake.

What was driving her to the edge was that when he reached her clit, his tongue curled around it before letting go. It happened each time. Bottom to top. Curl. And rough.

Nothing. Nothing had ever felt this amazing. And he kept it up for ages. Toying with her. Teasing her. Until she knew he was hard again. He didn't stop, though. He swirled that amazing tongue around her clit, rammed three fingers inside her, slipped his free hand under her ass and squeezed off and on. While all that happened, Mads played with her nipples and let her mind go. Just let her body feel whatever this amazing male was doing to her. When her legs began to shake and her back arched, she didn't fight it. She just let go and came so hard, she cried out and possibly went blind for a few minutes.

When she could see again, Finn was lying next to her and he growled, "I need to fuck you."

"Then get over here and—shit. Condoms."

Finn suddenly sat up. "Shit. Condoms."

Mads scrambled to her knees. "You didn't bring condoms? Not even one in your wallet?"

"I didn't want to look presumptuous."

"Idiot."

"Wait." He raised his brows. "Nelle."

"Oh, no. You don't think . . ."

Together, they both looked over at the end table next to the bed.

Finn had never prayed so hard that a woman he barely knew was truly obsessive. But he was praying.

Mads, beautifully naked, a tattoo of a spear on her left side, crawled across the bed to the end table. When she opened the drawer, she let out an annoyed growl and Finn wondered how fast he could get to the pharmacy and whether it would be faster if he ran rather than driving his SUV.

Then she held up a big box of condoms.

"Oh, my God! She's so insane!"

"Why are you complaining?" he demanded.

She tore off the sticky note attached to the box and handed it to him. He read what was carefully printed on it.

We both know this will be used by you and Finn. —N.

"Do you see?" Mads demanded. "Do you see how crazy she is?"

Still holding the note, he turned and grabbed Mads's face between both his hands. "Can we obsess over the insanity of your teammates later? Please? And instead just be happy there are condoms? Think we can do that? Because you may not have noticed . . . but I just realized, I've never kissed you."

"Because neither of us thought of it before now or because I had your come in my mouth?"

She was a woman willing to deep throat him right out of the box, and he wanted her to have no doubt that he was willing to kiss her before and after she had his come in her mouth.

Still holding her head between his hands, Finn leaned in and pressed his mouth against Mads's. She reached up and gripped his wrists, turned her head, and easily opened up to him. Her tongue slid against his and his cock got even harder, which he hadn't thought possible. It was the way Mads met him on his own ground. He hadn't really expected that. She was so quiet, he'd thought maybe she'd be subdued in bed, too. Not that he would have had a problem with that. Everyone had their own pace, and it could be hard to find someone who was your match. Especially when they were a different species.

And yet, here she was, still kissing him while reaching out for the condom box. He could hear her tearing it open and before he knew it, she had the condom on him.

They were still kissing when she put her arms around his neck and straddled him. She didn't pull her mouth away until she started to settle herself onto his dick and that was only so she could gasp out as she took him inside her.

"Fuck! Yes!" she cried out with a smile as she rocked onto him.

Finn could feel her squeezing him and his eyes crossed from the power of it. To distract himself, he sucked her left nipple into his mouth and began playing with it. He then moved on to the right while Mads got into a nice rhythm riding his cock. When he was sure she wouldn't expect it, he slapped her ass.

That's when her pussy turned into a vise, locking around him each time he slapped her ass again and getting wetter. Her big smile was awesome, too.

What he loved was that he didn't need to go too hard. He liked things light and fun. Not dungeons and darkness. Everyone had their thing and he had no problem with that, but it wasn't for him. Knowing that Mads seemed happy with light fun had him ready to come again. Not until he got her off first, though. He desperately needed to see her come.

Sucking on her breast, he pulled his hand away from her ass and brought it around to the front. He slipped it between them and searched out her clit. He pressed his thumb against it and began to move it in tight circles.

Mads's head fell back and her fingers dug into his hair.

"Oh, God," she groaned. He sucked harder on her nipple. Stroked harder on her clit. And she rode his cock harder. For a little extra, he began flicking his tongue back and forth while sucking on her nipple, and picked up the speed of stroking her clit.

Before he knew it, she was gasping and gripping him tight as she came hard. Her body spasmed at least four times before she finally slumped down on him.

Finn rolled her onto the bed with him on top and began to fuck her hard. Mads's eyes opened and she stared straight at him. She raised her hands and pushed him off. But not to stop him. She grabbed pillows and put them under her waist. "Fuck me from behind," she ordered him, rising up on her knees.

He pushed his cock inside her and she said, "Grab my tits." He did as he began to mercilessly fuck her.

Not only did she pound back against him, ordering him, "Fuck me harder. Harder!" but she played with her clit the entire time so that when he finally came, she came with him. Finn roaring. Mads growling. Both of them collapsing on the bed in a sweaty, snarling mess.

chapter NINETEEN

"I understand that you're upset—"

"Upset? Badgers killed my daughter."

"Your daughter lured them there. She was planning to kill them. You can't now be pissed because they didn't let her. But if you start a war—"

"You'll what?"

The bowie knife slammed into the leather cushion of the office chair, right between Kang Yun's legs.

Niles Van Holtz watched Dee-Ann Smith lean over the head of the Yun mob family, her hand still wrapped around the hilt of her favorite knife. Although he would never understand what his favorite younger cousin saw in the She-wolf as a mate, Van did appreciate the female as a natural killer. Van was born as part of a pack. He never hunted alone. He never fed or lived alone. And he only killed non-prey as an absolute last resort.

But to Smith, everything was prey.

Including a six-hundred-pound tiger and his equally large gangster brothers.

Actually, the only creature Van had ever seen Smith wary of was Charlie MacKilligan, which told him a *lot* about Charlie MacKilligan.

"I don't think you're listening real well to Mr. Van Holtz here, big kitty. He's asking you nice not to make this worse than it already is. We've got cops and feds looking into this— full-human ones—and if you keep this going, they're just going to keep looking more. And considering all the illegal shit y'all do on a daily basis, I'm pretty sure you don't want full-human feds anywhere near your businesses. So do as the man says and stay away from the MacKilligan sisters. Understand?"

Yun glared at her. "Yes. I understand."

"Repeat it back to me. I wanna make sure."

"Stay away from the MacKilligan sisters."

"Perfect."

Smith yanked the blade out of the chair and stepped away.

Yun and several of his brothers and sisters stormed out, the door slamming behind the last one.

Smith sat down in the chair Yun had vacated, placing her elbows on the armrests. She flicked her hands. "What do you think?" she asked.

"I think it's going to cost a lot to replace that leather chair you just stabbed with your tacky knife."

"Hey!" She pointed at the bowie knife. "My daddy gave me this knife."

She was kneading his back with her claws, which had Finn hard before he was even fully awake.

So he couldn't even begin to describe his disappointment and rage when he turned over and found that goddamn coyote lying between him and Mads . . . panting.

"Why is this . . . *animal* . . . in bed with us?"

"He snuck in a little while ago."

"You didn't throw it out?"

"Didn't want to. He was so sweet and cuddly. I think he may be more coydog than coyote."

Finn didn't care if it was more rabbit—he didn't want it in the same bed he was sleeping in. Especially when he was sleeping in that bed with Mads.

"I'm getting in the shower," he grumbled, swinging his legs off the bed. "And I'm throwing it off the bed next time. Until it learns it's not welcome."

Or at least until it learned not to get between them.

Finn was halfway to the bathroom, feeling strongly he'd made his point about the coyote, when he heard, "Next time, huh?"

He stopped mid-step and spun back around, made his way to the bed, and with one hand tossed the coyote off. It yelped but it was fine. Whiney baby. Reaching across the mattress, he grasped Mads's ankle and yanked her to him.

Finn thought of a thousand things he could say. Should say. He ended up not saying any of them. Just kissed her instead. Long and hard, slipping his tongue inside her, putting his arms around her and lifting her off the bed. What he really loved about kissing Mads was the way he could still feel her smiling. She didn't smile often, the Viking. But she did when they were together in bed. Fucking, sucking, or kissing, Mads loved to smile. Which only made him smile. Two of the meanest, angriest predators on the planet finding a reason to smile in each other's arms. Almost romantic if it wasn't for the panting . . .

They both turned their heads at the same time to see the coyote back on the bed, gazing at them.

"I'm going to find out how you're getting in this house . . . and I'm going to block the way, you little fuck," Finn warned him.

"Awww, leave him alone. He's so—oh!" Mads gasped when Finn coldly dropped her back on the bed and made his way to the bathroom and his much-needed shower. "That was bitchy!" she laughed.

When Finn finished showering, he came out to find a new toothbrush on the counter, still in the packaging, and a just-opened tube of toothpaste.

"Did it say 'for Finn' on the toothbrush, too?" he called out to the bedroom.

"You and Nelle can just fuck off!" Mads snapped as she marched past him and into the shower.

Wrapping a towel around his waist, Finn brushed his teeth, combed his wet hair, and headed back into the bedroom. He was expecting to have to go another round with that stupid coyote but, much to his horror, what he had to deal with was his brothers. The pair of those idiots peeking their giant heads into the bedroom.

Were they being creepy? Were they trying to see Mads

naked? Was Finn going to have to kill them and tell their mother that their bodies had fallen off the Staten Island ferry?

"What are you doing here?" he whispered, praying that Mads's honey badger hearing didn't pick any of this up over the shower noise.

"Where's Mads?" Keane asked.

By the ancients . . . he *was* going to have to kill his brothers and dump their bodies off the Staten Island ferry.

"You perverts," he accused.

"No, no!" Keane leaned in. "Her friends are all dead!"

After what had happened with Mads's cousins the night before, Finn wasn't so ready to dismiss Keane's statement as he normally would be.

"What are you talking about?"

"Charlie sent me here to meet Max. But we found them all dead. In the living room."

Now Finn was feeling dismissive. "Are you sure?"

"I know dead. I'm an always hungry tiger. Trust me . . . they're dead. But check it out for yourself."

Finn followed his brothers down the stairs and into the living room. The TV was set to a channel that seemed to be playing one of those shows where women coldly kill their husbands for the insurance money. Bags of junk food and cans of high-octane soda littered the floor. And in what resembled one of those circa 1970s photographs of Alphabet City, Mads's four teammates were strewn across the living room floor appearing . . . dead.

"We checked vitals," Shay said. "No heartbeat. No pulse. No breathing. I know they're hard to kill, but . . . they *really* seem dead."

"And cold."

That caught Finn's attention. It wasn't cold in Mads's house. She had the air-conditioning on low. He'd been planning to turn it up but kept forgetting because he'd been buried so deep inside her, he'd forgotten anything else actually existed.

Now her friends were dead. Maybe . . . ?

Shit.

"Let's get them to a shifter hospital," Finn reasoned. "If nothing else—"

"We tried."

"What do you mean you tried?"

"We were going to put them in the car," Keane explained. "But . . ."

"But . . . what?"

Shay shrugged. "We think rigor mortis has set in."

"*What?*"

Keane walked over to Nelle. Wearing her designer dress, with her arms and legs spread out, she looked like a sparkly starfish. Putting his hands around her waist, Keane lifted her up but she stayed in the exact same pose . . . appearing like a sparkly starfish.

"See?" Shay said. "Rigor mortis."

"If we try to put them in the car now, we're going to have to break their arms and legs first," Keane pointed out. "And if they're not really dead, they're gonna be pissed."

At that point, Finn knew he had no choice. He had to tell Mads. If nothing else, she'd know whether her friends were really dead or not. And if they were dead, she'd know what to do about the bodies. But before he could move, he and his brothers heard a hissing from under one of the couches. Then it was coming at them. Moving with such speed that all they could do was shift to their tiger form and do what cats do when they panic. Something weird.

Finn jumped onto the back of a couch, accidentally knocking a prone Streep onto the floor. Shay made it to a chair. But Keane was looking for a way out, backing up as fast as he could, paws scrabbling across the hardwood floor. The snake came at him with such ease and speed that Finn *and* Shay were both about to launch themselves at the damn thing until a pale, wet foot landed on the snake's back, holding it in place.

Mads reached down and picked the snake up by the tail. It started to turn so it could bite her on the hand, and Finn was already thinking about how he was going to have to break her bones to get her into his SUV when she began to beat the reptile against the floor. So fast and so many times that Finn lost count. When it was limp and blood had splattered all over Mads's feet, she lifted it and began to eat.

Head first.

"What's up?" she asked.

It had been ages since Mads had feasted on Inland Taipan. It was considered *the* world's most poisonous snake. In theory, it could even kill an elephant. Could have dropped these tigers easy. Plus, it was aggressive. So it wasn't like you had to startle it. The taipan would come for you.

And also, in theory, it should be able to put her down just as it had clearly put down her friends. All four crazed bitches fucking up her living room. There was just one difference between her and her friends: Solveig.

When Solveig realized that her daughter and granddaughter had lost any maternal interest in Mads, she'd taken responsibility for her. But she knew next to nothing about honey badgers. Since she'd never seen badgers as a threat, she'd felt no reason to learn anything about them. They meant as much to her as full-humans. It wasn't until she'd gone to the library and gotten a librarian to pull a few books on the subject that she began to understand what she was dealing with. She also understood that Mads could one day protect herself, but only if she got the care and training she needed now.

That's when Solveig had tried to give Mads to her father, but Tova had found out and put a stop to that immediately. Completely out of spite and for no other reason. Solveig knew then that preparing Mads to live for the next hundred years would be on her. That was why she'd thrown Mads into that small vat of scorpions. It was true badger mothers let scorpions sting their offspring to get them acclimated to the poison, but only one at a time. That, however, was not Solveig's way. She just purchased a bunch of scorpions and tossed her great-granddaughter in. When Mads began to cry, she told her, "Toughen up!" When Mads vomited and passed out, Solveig was briefly worried she'd gone too far. Panicked, she'd gone to retrieve the child and rush her to a shifter doctor who could help, but instead she was hit in the face by a scorpion. Because Mads had thrown it at her. Out of rage.

That's when, according to Solveig, "I knew you'd be just fine."

Although Mads always retorted, "You threw me in with a bunch of scorpions? Are you insane? *What is wrong with this family?*"

"Why are you yelling? You lived."

When it came time for Solveig to get Mads used to snake venom, she remembered the story of how the British had killed Ragnar Lothbrok: by tossing him into a pit of snakes. She had no intention of doing that to her great-granddaughter. Instead, she started off by giving her small drops of "minor" poison and putting harmless garter snakes in her crib. According to Solveig, "You started chewing on those like pacifiers by the time you were a month old."

When Mads was forced to move to Wisconsin with her mother, Solveig had already introduced her to four of what were considered the ten most poisonous venoms. As a French chef would introduce a student to the five mother sauces. After meeting her honey badger teammates, Mads had finally been introduced to the rest of those venoms. Mostly through venom-infused tequila. Sometimes through a live snake.

By the time she'd been bitten by a taipan at an illegal zoo, she'd built up quite the toxic storage capacity in her system.

"Are your friends dead?" Shay asked, quickly putting his jeans and T-shirt back on. "We get the feeling they're dead. They seem a little . . . stiff."

"It's the toxins." She held up what remained of the taipan. "It paralyzes. Destroys blood vessels and muscles. Can usually kill a human in about forty-five minutes or so."

"Yet you're eating it," Keane noted, his back to her as he got dressed. It was cute how they were all so shy. Was it because she'd had sex with their brother? So now she wasn't supposed to see them naked and they weren't supposed to see her?

"Honey badger."

"So are they," Finn pointed out, his towel back around his waist. He came to stand beside her, and she instantly began sneezing.

"Dander! Dander!"

"I'm not taking another shower and you're really complaining about my dander while eating a poisonous snake?"

Mads rubbed her nose. It was so itchy now! "What does one have to do with the other? I'm not allergic to taipans." She sneezed a few more times. "I need to get my allergy meds."

"Wait," Finn called out when she started off toward the kitchen where she'd left her backpack. "What about your friends?"

"Teammates. What about them?"

"Are we just going to leave them here to start . . . rotting?"

"Give 'em a couple of hours. If they don't wake up, we'll just bury 'em in the backyard. The poison should do the rest. It'll eat away that flesh before you know it."

Mads watched the Malone brothers' matching expressions of horror and, without saying anything else, she walked away. Not bothering to tell them that an alive Max was now standing right behind them—smiling. Because it was so much fun to hear their startled, panicked roars while she was digging through her backpack for the allergy meds that Charlie had given her.

Finn just wanted breakfast. But before he could make that happen, Big Julie called him, begging for help.

It seemed that news about Charlie MacKilligan's raw talent on the football field had spread throughout the league and now, according to Julie, "Everyone wants her! We have to lock her down and lock her down *now!*"

See? That's what a lot of people did not know. They watched those Animal Planet documentaries about lions on the Serengeti, lounging around all day under the boiling African sun. Then a herd of buffalo wandered by and the females suddenly moved into action with military precision, hunting down food for their entire pride because they couldn't expect the males to get off their lazy asses and help. And to the human world, it seemed as if lions were calm, rational animals. When, in fact, they were as prone to panic as any other house cat.

And it was Julie's She-lion panic that caused Finn to reply, "No," to her demand and disconnect the call. But then she began to call him back over and over and over again. Until Mads grabbed his phone and nearly chucked it out the back door into the yard before he managed to grab it away from her. He grudgingly explained the situation to her and also told her that his plan for the day involved nothing more than getting some breakfast and lounging around the house with her until football practice later that afternoon.

He honestly thought Mads would be charmed by that answer. Why? Because she was one of the few beings on the planet he *wanted* to spend time with. Wasn't that cute? Wasn't that lovable? Didn't she want to have more sex with him? Possibly right now, before breakfast?

"So you're going to let some football conglomerate shove a shitty deal down Charlie MacKilligan's throat without you watching her back? Even after she helped you with Max? Something *I* didn't even do?" Mads asked.

"How did this become my problem?"

"You and your brothers dragged Charlie into this. You can't just let her go to a contract meeting alone."

"Actually I can. It's my right as an American to be selfish and uncaring."

"And it's my right as an American to never touch your cock again. Are you okay with that, too?"

"Are you using sex to manipulate me?"

"Yes."

He scowled and looked away in case he couldn't keep his smile tamped down.

"I don't like that," he lied.

"You like it a little."

Next thing Finn knew, he was packed into his SUV with Mads, Charlie, Shay, Tock, and Stevie. Nelle and Streep had stayed behind at the house because they were still feeling the effects of the taipan snake poison, if the retching sounds from the first-floor toilet were any indication. Keane and Max had gone off in search of Max's Uncle Carl for information.

Of everyone, including those retching in the bathroom, Keane seemed the least excited about the rest of his day.

The only one whose presence Finn didn't understand was Stevie. She just popped up and got into the car, with nothing more than a tiny backpack hanging from her shoulders and a pleasant smile.

Julie didn't want to meet at the Sports Center. She'd noticed sports agents and other team coaches lurking around since she'd gotten in to work early that morning. Finn offered to bring Charlie to Julie's place in Brooklyn, but she didn't want a badger hybrid around her She-lion cousins, who were staying with her at the moment. She feared what would happen, which was smart when dealing with a MacKilligan.

She'd suggested meeting at Charlie's house but he'd looked out the window of Mads's house and seen that the bears had already surrounded the place. Immediately knew that wouldn't be a good idea. Mads's house was out for the same reason. He finally offered his place since his mother would be at work, his baby brother taking college courses, and his baby sister at the summer camp for deaf kids where she was a camp counselor. It would be perfect.

Now he just had to drive them to Long Island, which suddenly seemed like a much longer trip than he remembered.

"Do you like playing football?" Stevie MacKilligan suddenly asked into the silence of the SUV.

"Are you asking me or Shay?"

"Both. Either. Doesn't matter."

Finn decided to answer since Shay was staring out the window and didn't seem in the mood to be communicative. "Uh . . . sure."

"Did your family force you into it as a way for you to prove you're a straight male? Or because they felt you weren't smart enough to do anything else?"

"Stevie!" Charlie barked.

"What?"

"That was rude."

Stevie reached over the seats and patted his shoulder. "I'm sorry."

"No problem," Finn said, already dismissing her question.

They went back to silence for a few minutes, until Stevie asked, "Ever worry about brain damage?"

"*Stevie!*"

"What now?"

"Just shut up!"

"I'm curious."

"Don't be."

More silence until Stevie asked, "Is the rape culture as prevalent in shifter football as in full-human foot—"

"*Oh, my God, Stevie! Stop talking!*"

"We're here!" Finn announced, never so relieved to be home before.

He pulled the SUV into a spot in front of the house and turned the motor off. Everyone got out except Mads, because she was too busy laughing.

"You can stop," he told her.

"I really can't," she squeaked out.

"This is all your fault."

"How is this my fault?" she demanded, wiping tears.

"I don't know. But we both know it is."

He got out, slamming the driver's door behind him, and walked around the SUV. A still-giggling Mads met him on the other side. Julie and the team lawyer were already waiting, standing beside Julie's bright red pickup truck, which she needed to carry around her giant, not-even-fourteen-years-old-yet sons.

"Hello, all!" Julie called out. "This should be fun, right?" She motioned to the team lawyer. "This is Scott. He put the contract together for us."

"This is my sister Stevie. She'll be handling my legal interests for me."

Julie glanced at Finn with a slightly raised eyebrow.

"Um . . . okay," she said, trying not to sound mocking.

Not easy for a She-lion. "Do you have a lot of . . . uh . . . law experience, Stevie?"

"A little. I started when I was about fourteen. My father kept threatening to get back his custody of me, and to be quite honest, I wasn't sure if he could or not and I didn't want that to happen. I felt that if I understood the law better, I would panic less, which was sort of true when it came to family and contract law; not so true when it came to criminal law, but that could be because of my other sister. Surprisingly, though, I did find law in general much more interesting than I'd thought it would be and while I was at Oxford running my own lab, I took some courses and eventually got a couple of degrees in it. Then when I got back to the States, I decided to take the Bar in New York to see if I could pass, which—of course—I could. Took the Bar in a few more states. Passed those, too. Then took the equivalent of the Bar in several other countries, so I could practice law any place I figured I might end up working. Now my whole goal in life is to ensure that no one fucks over my big sister legally while she's throwing her body in front of giant men on a field of death. So, yeah . . . you could say I have a little law experience. What about you, Scott? Harvard grad, are ya? Princeton?"

"Hofstra."

"What now?"

"It's a very good university out here on the Island," Finn explained, not mentioning it was his brother's "safety" school since he kept saying he wanted to move away from the family.

"Well, why don't the three of us have a little talk and let me take a quick look over the contract?" Stevie glanced at Charlie. "Charlie, go wait in Finn's house until we're done."

"Okay."

Charlie walked toward the house and Mads slipped her hand into the front pocket of Finn's jeans. "What are you doing?" He leaned down and whispered, "Not that I mind much."

"Getting the house keys."

Still whispering, "And Charlie just follows Stevie's direction without question? Since when?"

"When it comes to legal stuff. Stevie kept Streep out of prison. Serious prison. In Romania. We *all* listen to her when it comes to legal stuff."

Mads reached for the door, with the keys out, but stopped when she saw it was slightly open. She glanced at Charlie, who gave one nod.

Tock disappeared around to the left side of the house and once she was gone, Charlie quietly eased the door open and stepped inside. As she did, she reached under the light denim jacket she wore and pulled out the gun she had tucked into the holster attached to her jeans.

Mads still didn't have any of her own guns. She knew the sight of her strapping on one of her many .40s might upset Finn. It was a little early in this thing they'd just started, so she'd strapped blades under her green T-shirt when he wasn't around, assuming that would be enough.

Now she kind of regretted that decision. Especially when they reached the living room and Finn's youngest brother was brutally shoved to the ground by three men. Even more concerning was their baby sister, Nat. She was on her knees with a gun pressed to the back of her head. But, like any true honey badger, she was about ready to do something very stupid. Mads could see it in her eyes. Could taste the girl's rage in the air. She was moments from doing something that would get her or her brother killed. And that was something Nat would never forgive herself for. No matter how tough or hard edged a badger she thought she might be.

Charlie took in the men holding the two kids hostage and Mads knew exactly what she saw. These men were young. They were full-human. They were hopped up on something other than the steroids they took to have those ridiculous muscles that the Malone brothers had naturally due to thousands of years of shifter breeding, Irish pagan rituals, and Mongolian warrior-shaman intervention. And they were seriously out of their depth.

Killing them would be easy. And quick.

But an opportunity would be lost.

The one holding the gun on Nat had raised it at Charlie. She had her gun pointed at him. His hand was shaking. Possibly from fear. More likely from a slight overdose. Charlie's hand, however, was steady. She also wasn't sweating. Her pulse wasn't racing. And her pupils were dilated the normal amount for the light they were standing in.

At that point, Charlie gave a small nod and Mads pulled out one of the blades she had holstered to her body. She sent it spinning across the room with a flick of her wrist. She'd learned the skill from Max a decade ago and had practiced ever since. So Mads nailed her target easily, severing nerves in his arm so that the gun he'd held fell from his hand without his being able to pull the trigger.

In horror, he gazed at his now useless extremity, unaware that Tock had crept into the house through the fireplace. She kicked his gun under the nearest couch and had disarmed the others before they even had a chance to think about what was happening right in front of them.

"Mads, get Finn and Shay, please."

Mads walked back to the front door and motioned for the brothers. They were bickering about something on the front lawn but as soon as Finn saw Mads's face, he came toward her, with Shay right behind him. Stevie and the coach and lawyer from the football team didn't even notice, they were so busy arguing over the contracts that were strewn across the hood of the red pickup.

Mads led the cats to the living room, and neither spoke as they took in the situation.

As soon as Nat saw Finn and Shay, she began signing, but Charlie stopped her with a simple finger point.

Once Nat lowered her hands, Charlie looked around the room and asked, "What did you do?"

One of the full-humans began babbling, but Charlie cut

him off with a cold "I'm not asking you." She faced Nat. "What did you do?"

The youngest Malone brother was translating in ASL for Nat and she began to answer the same way, but again Charlie cut her off.

"Don't even try it," she snarled while Dale translated. "I haven't had time to learn ASL and we both know it. And you're not going to sit here and speak to your brothers in a way that I don't understand just so you can *lie* to them, which is what we *both* know you're going to do."

The honey badger in Nat came out, her eyes narrowing dangerously on her half-sister's face as she replied out loud, "I didn't do anything. This is a home invasion and we should kill them all. On principle."

"Principle?" Charlie shook her head. "You are such a bad liar."

"My *brothers* know I didn't do anything," Nat shot back.

Charlie pointed at Dale. "What did she do?"

"Uh . . . noth—"

"*DALE!*" Finn bellowed so loudly that the windows shook, the intruders screamed, and Dale panicked.

"She stole money from drug dealers!" Dale blurted out.

Nat, no longer on her knees, punched her brother in the shoulder. Charlie walked across the room, grabbing both teens by their arms and pushing them down on the couch. She then took a straight-backed chair and plopped it down in front of Nat and Dale. She sat in front of them, motioning to Dale to translate for her while she spoke directly to Nat.

"You stole money from drug dealers? Why? Are you poor?"

Nat glanced back and forth between Dale and Charlie before asking, "What?"

"Are you poor? Does your mother have no health care and she's dying from cancer? Is your family about to lose their home? Is there some compelling reason that you felt the need to steal money from drug dealers? Or were you just fucking bored and thought it would be fun?"

Mads watched Nat struggle with whether she should tell the truth or not. She knew because she'd seen that expression on every badger she'd ever known in her life. She'd probably worn that expression herself. But when it came to Charlie, truth was Nat's best friend right now.

Wisely, the kid owned up. "They were stupid and it was easy. It's been a long summer."

"Easy? Does this seem easy to you?" Charlie asked, gesturing around the living room and the sobbing men on the floor. "You have drug dealers in your house."

"I would have handled them."

Charlie shrugged. "Yeah. I know. But would you have done it without getting your brother killed?"

Dale's hands suddenly stopped moving and he asked, "Wait . . . what?"

Charlie motioned for him to keep translating as she went on.

"And what would you have done with the bodies? Buried them in your mom's backyard? Let the dogs eat 'em?" Charlie quickly looked around. "Oh, my God. Where are the dogs?"

"Locked in my room upstairs. I didn't want them to get hurt. I know how attached Shay is," she added with a little bit of contempt.

"First thing you did right. But let me tell you from experience, even big dogs can't eat that much. Not in the time you have before your mother gets home." Frowning, Finn looked down at Mads, but she just shook her head. This was not the time to start asking questions about how in the world Charlie would know that. They probably didn't want to hear anyway. "And if you're thinking hyenas, do you have them on speed dial? Do you know which ones will actually come over and eat human remains? Because not all will do it. Believe it or not, some have moral compunctions. You've gotta know the difference between spotted hyenas and striped when you call hyenas in to feed. Because if you pick the wrong one, they'll rat you out in a second and you'll end up in jail. And let's make this clear right up front . . . I'll only protect you if you kill someone to protect the life of an innocent or if your life is in danger due to no fault of your own. You start killing people because you're bored and I will make sure you end up in one of those German prisons specifically made for badgers. Do you know why? Because that's what sociopaths do! They kill when they're bored. And I will not spend my life wrangling a sociopath!"

Charlie suddenly pointed a silencing finger at Finn. "And before you say anything, we've had Max thoroughly tested . . . she's borderline. So just leave it alone." She turned her gaze back to Nat. "You are seventeen. You can't be *stupid*! Do you want to end up in a prison you can't dig yourself out of? Because they have them and there are at least three MacKilligans rotting away in them as we speak. One of them in Germany. It's built in what was once known as *East* Berlin and was behind a *wall*. You should look that up sometime if you haven't heard about it in history class. Maybe you can meet your MacKilligan cousin there and both of you can chat over what I'm told is still a very East German–style unpleasant breakfast!"

Nat sat silently for several long moments before she slowly stood, tossed her black hair with the white stripe over her shoulder, and told Charlie, "Thanks for the advice."

And like seventeen-year-olds around the world—because she thought she knew better—Nat ignored her half-sister's words and started toward the men groveling on the floor in her living room.

"Don't tell, Keane, okay?" she sweetly asked her brothers. "I'll take care of all—*arghhhhh!*" Nat screamed as her body flew back into the couch, her hands covering her face, blood flowing from between her fingers.

Automatically, Charlie looked down at her own hands, expecting to see that she'd been the one to punch her younger sister in the face for her rudeness. But, for once, it hadn't been her.

Stevie pushed past Shay and, using ASL, began to rant at her younger half-sister; Nat gawked at her above her blood-covered hands.

Charlie quickly tapped Dale's knee with the back of her fist, prompting him to translate for her.

"Um . . . uh . . . 'Who do you think you are?'" he rattled off in a flat, monotone voice, "Charlie's trying to help you and you're ignoring her. Do you think about anyone but yourself? What if your mother had been home when they came here? What if they'd come at night? What if they hadn't broken into your home but just shot up your car with your mother in it? Or your brothers? What if they set your house on fire with you guys in it? Or blew it up? I can come up with a thousand scenarios of how this could have gone down. Many of them, Charlie, Max, and I have been through because of the shitty decision-making of our idiot father! Do *you* want to be like him? Do you want to be the one we all talk about with hatred when we talk about you at all? When we get a call that there's a body in the morgue that we have to identify, do you want us to hope and pray that it's *you*? And start throwing shit when we find out it's not, terrifying the morgue attendant? Because we're really pissed off it's *not* you! Because our lives would be a thousand times easier if you were dead? That's our father, Nat! That's where you're headed! And if you don't figure out how to harness the shitty MacKilligan in you, then I guess I should just start expecting calls from forty-year-old Nat asking me for gas money!'"

Charlie reached over and tapped Stevie's arm. "That asshole called you again, asking for gas money?"

Stevie waved her off. "I didn't even answer. I just let it go to voice mail."

Letting out a breath, Stevie returned to Nat, and Dale again translated. "'Your family loves you. But if you keep acting like a little asshole-bitch, you will end up alone and bitter and wondering why your life sucks so bad.'"

Stevie pointed at Charlie. "Get outside. The contract is ready to sign. I got you fifteen percent over what you wanted, flexibility on your hours for that other thing you and Max do, and I made that lawyer guy cry a little. So I feel pretty good about the negotiation."

She turned and started to walk out, but abruptly stopped and faced Nat. This time, she didn't use ASL. "And don't *ever* dismiss Charlie like that again when she's trying to help you. Or next time, I'll bite you in half, spit your legs across the room, and make you stare at them while you slowly bleed out."

And with those words, Stevie left.

"What the hell did—"

"No." Mads cut Finn off before he could finish his question.

"But how would she—"

"We don't ask those questions when it comes to Max's little sister."

"We don't?"

"No."

"Why?"

"We know it can't end well for anyone. So we just don't. And you shouldn't either. Okay?"

"Well—"

"Great!"

"My nose!" Nat cried out, blood still gushing from behind her hands.

"It's just broken," Charlie told her. "Don't be such a baby."

Finn moved closer. "Let's see," he prompted.

Nat moved her hands away from her face and all the shifters in the room cried out. Tock actually looked away. Charlie covered her mouth with her hands. Shay nearly retched.

Nat slapped her hands over her face. "What?" she demanded. "*What?*"

"Nothing," Charlie lied. "It'll be fine. Just go upstairs. *Now*. Dale, go with her."

"Why do I have to?"

"Dale!"

As Dale passed Charlie to follow his sister out of the living room, Charlie grabbed his shoulder and quietly told him, "Don't let her look in a mirror. Put a bandage over her nose right away. And don't start crying. It'll pop back out by tomorrow."

"I'm not crying."

"Oh, my God, you're as bad a liar as your sister," she complained, pushing him away. "And bring the money she stole down here once you get the bandage on her, please. Thanks!"

Once the teens were gone, Charlie warned Finn and Shay, "You have no control over her, and it's going to bite all of you in the ass."

"No offense, but we can handle our baby sister."

"She's not a baby. She's a manipulative little viper, aka a teen. And at some point the true MacKilligan in her is going to come out and you will *not* be ready for it."

Charlie started for the front door, but Tock stopped her.

"What about these lovely gentlemen?" she asked.

Charlie studied the full-humans for a moment, then smirked . . . and unleashed her fangs.

Dez put down her phone and looked across her desk at her old partner. Because of polar bears like Crushek and the grizzlies in her department, she'd had to get specially made chairs that didn't crumple under their human weight. The chairs weren't easy to find and cost a fortune, but they were nice looking. And held up really well despite the fact that Crushek didn't simply sit but sort of dropped into his seat as if he was a much smaller man.

"What?" Crushek asked when he saw her expression.

"So I just got a call from Nassau County's shifter division. Seems some drug dealers ran *into* one of their precincts to warn them that monsters with claws and fangs and crazy *woman* strength were trying to steal their money and take over the world. And we need to let the government know and do something about it, otherwise these monsters are going to kill us all . . . and let the hyenas from Africa eat us."

The pair gazed at each other for quite a while until Crushek finally shook that big head of his and angrily sighed out, "Fuckin' honey badgers."

"Okay, so I'm not wrong. That's definitely a honey badger kind of . . . situation we've got there."

"Not even *foxes* cause that kind of problem, Dez. And foxes cause all sorts of problems."

"Is this something we should get involved in?"

"Did you wake up this morning and think to yourself, 'How can I fuck up my day?'"

"I did not."

"Then I say we deal with the nightmares we already have within our city rather than going out to the Island to find more."

"Excellent plan. Coffee and a bear claw?"

"I feel like I'm being attacked with that bear claw thing, but . . . yeah. Sure."

chapter TWENTY

Keane followed Max up a set of backstairs to a small antiques shop on the second floor of a battered building off the Jersey Turnpike.

"You brought cash, right?"

Keane frowned. "You didn't tell me to bring cash."

Max stopped and faced him. "You didn't bring cash?"

"You didn't tell me to bring cash."

She let out a breath and threw up her hands. "Great."

"You didn't tell me—"

"Yes. I heard you," she snapped, continuing up the stairs.

"It's always going to be this way with you, isn't it?"

"What way?"

"Annoying. Trifling. Pain in the ass. You go out of your way to be difficult."

"Not out of my way."

They reached a wood door. Max pulled it open and stepped into one of those packed stores that had so much of everything, Keane could never tell if they were selling antiques or just junk.

"Hello?" Max called out. "Uncle Carl? It's Max. Renny's daughter. Are you here?"

There was a flash in the corner of Keane's eye, giving him only a second to wrap his arms around Max's waist and drop them both to the floor. The gun blast destroyed the stuffed grizzly that had been right behind them.

"Uncle Carl!" Max yelled. "*What the fuck?*"

It took a moment before a voice yelled back, "Did your mother send you here? Well, you can tell her to fuck off!"

"I have no idea what you're talking about!"

Another long pause. "You don't?"

"No."

"Because I heard she took out life insurance on me. A million dollars' worth."

Max dropped her head back, eyes crossing. "I don't know anything about that. I'm not here for my mother. I'm here for information."

"Oh. Okay."

Charlie sat in her sunroom, legs stretched out in front of her, one arm thrown over her eyes. She'd thought about going to bed and taking a nap, but she wasn't really tired so much as miserable and depressed. She wasn't sure a nap would take care of that. At least not for her. She heard liquor was effective for some people, but she'd never been much of a drinker. A beer here or there. Maybe a shot when she went out with friends or her sisters. But anything beyond that just made her think she'd end up a pathetic drunk, spewing anger and hatred in some bar somewhere. That was not the way she wanted her life to go.

"Charlie?"

Not in the mood to move her whole body, Charlie simply lifted her arm to her forehead and opened her eyes. She looked up at Mads and smiled.

"What's up?"

"Just checking on you. Need anything?"

Charlie had always liked Mads. She was just the sweetest kid. And had never deserved the early life she got. Then again, what kid ever deserved a life like that?

"I'm good. Just . . . forget it."

Mads sat on the love seat across from Charlie's chair. "I'm sure Nat will be fine. I think you're forgetting Max's teen years. Of course, you had a lot going on then. A lot more of your dad. Way more kidnappings. Mostly because your dad kept selling your sisters."

"That's all very true. And you're probably right. I did realize something today."

"Meth heads will believe anything when they're high?"

"I already knew that. No. I realized that Stevie's going to
be a great mom one day. We just have to teach her not to shove
her child's nose into its skull."

"I think it's different when it's your own kid."

"Let's hope so."

"Well, if you need anything, just let me know."

"Sure."

She expected Mads to get up and leave. Usually Max's
friends didn't hang around Charlie too long without Max there
to be a buffer. She knew she made them all nervous and she
didn't mind. She'd always sensed she kept them out of any
major trouble by being the thing they had to face if they really
fucked up. So when Mads just sat there, doing nothing . . .

"Anything else, Mads?"

She leaned over a bit to look into the other rooms.

"I think they're out by the pool," Charlie told her.

Mads combed her hair behind her ear. "My cousins came
after me last night. My mother thinks I took something from
the family that I didn't. My father did. I found it in my house.
It's mine by right. Solveig wanted me to have it. But my
mother and grandmother think it belongs to them. I could just
send it back to them."

"And prove to them you're as weak as they think you are?
Don't send them anything. Don't give them anything. You
need to crush them. Now and for good. Or you'll never have
peace, Mads. They'll make sure of it."

"What about the others?"

"The other what?"

"Max? Tock? Streep? Nelle? I go after the family, they'll
come after them."

"And we'll be finding pieces of hyena all along the Eastern
Seaboard. People will wonder for days and weeks where all
these hyenas came from. 'Are people transporting them from

Africa for pets?' the news will ask." She chuckled. "It'll be pretty funny." Charlie laughed a little more until she saw Mads's expression. "Wait. Are you worried about them? After all these years? After you've *seen* what they can do?"

"But what you said to Nat about her family—"

"Sweetie, they're tigers!" Charlie sat up in her chair, her depression and misery forgotten in the face of Mads's irrational thought process. "You shoot up a car full of tigers, you could kill them. You shoot up a car full of badgers . . . you're just going to have a car of pissed-off badgers! And in the case of your friends? Well-*armed* pissed-off badgers."

"What about their families?"

"Their families are all badger dynasties."

"Not Streep's family."

"Why do you think that? Because they're Filipino? The Gonzalez family have been a badger dynasty for centuries. In fact, her family has been ripping off the Vatican since the Philippines became Catholic in the 1500s. Not only that, but her family managed to infiltrate every Philippine government since then. Not because of any political aspirations but because they really like money. And gold. They love gold."

"Why didn't Streep ever tell me?"

"I think she thought you knew."

"Why would I know any of that? I was raised by hyenas."

"And I was raised by wolves. You live by the hand you're dealt. You want my advice? It's time to be who you truly are. Who Solveig knew you were. It's time to *crush* that family of yours, Mads Galendotter. Not completely wipe 'em out. I'm not a heartless monster . . . most of the time. But make it clear to them that you're not to be fucked with ever again. Show them who the true Viking is now that Solveig is gone."

"Okay." Mads winced. "The whole thing is scary, though."

"Life is scary. That's why I'm going to make brownies."

The two females stood, but before they could head toward the kitchen, a loud bang at the big windows shocked them both. A black bear from the neighborhood stood at one of the sunroom windows, gazing at them.

"Did I hear someone say brownies?" the bear asked.

"Sorry about that," Carl said, placing mugs of coffee down on the table in front of Max and Keane. "We've all been a bit jumpy since your mother came back."

"I don't know why. She never said anything to me about having a problem with any of you."

"No problem with her sisters maybe. But with her brothers, she sees dollar signs. She's out to get us all."

He put a plate of fudge-covered Oreos in the middle of the table. Max reached for one but Keane had taken the entire plate and had already gone through half the cookies.

"Dude . . . seriously?"

Carl went back to the cabinets, grabbed the rest of the box of Oreos, and dropped it on the table. Max grabbed several in case she didn't get a chance later.

"If that's true, she hasn't said a word to me," Max insisted. "And I wouldn't do something like that anyway."

"Not even for your mother?"

"I love my mom, but I'm not going to start killing family members so she can collect insurance. That's just tacky."

"Really?" Keane asked around a cookie in his mouth. "Tacky? That's the best you can come up with?"

"It's tacky."

Carl dropped into a chair at the table. "I've also heard that the Yuns are out to get your psychotic sister."

"They don't even know Stevie."

"Not Stevie. The one with the big shoulders."

"Charlie? They're going after Charlie?" Max snorted. "Good luck to them."

Carl looked at Keane. "And you're here about your father."

"Yes."

"I hate saying this but . . . I don't know anything about his murder."

"Oh."

"It's been kept surprisingly quiet. Usually you can at least hear something from foxes. They can't keep a secret to save their lives but, for once, they're not talking."

Keane's massive shoulders dropped and Carl actually looked a little sad that he was unable to give the big cat any information. That's when he said, "You know, my brother might be able to help you. He knows a lot of people I don't."

"Which brother?" Max asked.

"Jacob."

"Oh, I like Uncle Jacob."

"I'll tell ya what. I'll text him. Give him a heads-up you guys need to talk to him. Now I don't know exactly where he is and he probably won't tell me. I think he may be on a . . . ya know . . . job."

"Right," Max said, knowing that among badgers the word "job" could mean a myriad of things.

"Once he knows you need to talk to him, he'll let you know where he is."

"Thanks, Uncle Carl. That's really helpful."

Carl shrugged. "Honestly, sweetie, I'm just glad you're not here to kill me for the insurance money."

Max glanced at Keane before asking her uncle, "Is that becoming a common thing in our family? Because I feel like it's something I should be informed about."

Mads was shooting baskets in Charlie's backyard when Max and Keane returned from their meeting with Max's uncle.

"How did it go?" Charlie asked, handing plastic baggies filled with dark chocolate brownies out to the bears patiently waiting on the other side of the fence. The bears had originally been in the yard, but Finn and Shay began roaring at their presence when the first batch of brownies came out and there was a small scuffle that could easily have turned into a big scuffle. Mads became worried when Stevie scrambled up a tree, hiding in the leaves like a baby bear. Charlie had tried to calm everyone by telling them there were more brownies on the way, but no one was listening . . . until Streep had pulled out the scorpions.

"You guys don't want scorpions?" she'd asked, holding up a big, shiny black one. "They are soooo yummy! And putting up quite a fight. This one has stung me about six times!"

That's when the bears scrambled over the nearby fence while Finn and Shay jumped into the pool.

"What?" Streep asked the bears. "You really don't want one? The poison gives it a nice little zip. Especially with the crunch!"

It always helped that none of the locals knew anything about scorpions and snakes. The really poisonous ones had to be secretly brought into the country and badgers would often build whole dinners around the event, pairing excellent wines and tequilas with the specific kind of scorpion they would be enjoying that night.

Honestly, these big black ones might as well be wine in a can as far as the badger community was concerned.

"We found out nothing," Keane announced.

"Not exactly true," Max quickly cut in. "Uncle Carl didn't have much to tell us. But he passed us on to his brother. I'm just waiting for a text from him. Hopefully he'll have more info."

"*Any* info."

"I warned you it would be like this," Max reminded Keane. "That we might have to talk to more than one badger. That we might have to travel a little bit. Especially since no one else has had any information about your father in all these years. You just have to be patient." The cats all stared at her. Even Finn and Shay, who were still floating in the pool in their jeans, T-shirts, and boots. "I know. As soon as that came out of my mouth, I knew it was a stupid thing to say."

Max turned away and walked toward the house.

"Where are you going?" Nelle asked.

"I have to pee."

Keane closed his eyes. "She couldn't just say I'm going to the bathroom?"

No one replied because they all knew the answer.

"Don't feel discouraged," Mads told Keane. She thought about patting him on the shoulder, but she didn't feel like reaching up that high. "There are no straight lines when it comes to badgers."

"She's right," Nelle said, stepping back as Finn and Keane got out of the pool so she wouldn't get the chlorinated water on her shoes. "And you guys should get a bag together with a change of clothes. You'll probably have to travel." She looked off for a moment, then added, "You know what? I'll see if my father will loan us one of his planes."

She began to tap on her phone.

"Your father has so many planes he can just . . . loan us one?"

Nelle glanced up at Keane, and chirped, "Uh-huh."

"You going to come with us, too?" Finn asked Mads.

"Until practice starts for the championships . . . okay."

"Seriously?" he demanded. "The championship is more important than—"

"Yes!" she replied before Finn could even finish. What surprised her was that all her teammates joined in at the same time. Because they had no delusions about her loyalties either.

Finn grabbed her around the waist and hugged Mads close, which she normally wouldn't mind except that he was soaking wet from the pool. Laughing, she halfheartedly tried to push him off. Neither stopped until Max ran out of the house.

"He texted me back!" she cheered. "I heard from Uncle Jacob! He said he'll meet with us." She stopped in front of the group and grinned.

In fact, Max stood there and grinned for so long that Keane finally barked, "*When?*"

"Don't yell at me!"

"That was not yelling. You'll know when I'm yelling."

"Daddy says we can use any jet that's available," Nelle said, smiling. "And there are an array. Would you like me to list them?"

"How rich are you?" Shay asked.

"Very," she replied, not missing a beat.

Staring at her phone, Max asked, "Any that can do, well . . . long distances?"

"Yes." Nelle raised a brow. "Why?"

She cleared her throat. "Uncle Jacob is not exactly around the corner." Keane growled and Max immediately became defensive. "*It's not my fault!*"

Nelle placed her hand on Keane's arm. "Everyone calm down," she ordered, using her best soothing voice so that you never really knew it was an order. "Instead of making this a chore, we're going to make this fun. Together. We'll take one of Daddy's best jets, we'll go meet with Max's uncle, get what information we can, and then we'll go someplace fabulous for dinner. Like Paris. Or Rome. We'll be back before you know it!" She looked over at Charlie, who was still handing out brownies. "Charlie, do you think you and Stevie want to go?"

"Not me, sweetie. I think I still have a warrant out in Paris I haven't dealt with. Stevie? You want to go with—"

"No, thank you," came from one of the trees. "I am currently attempting to manage a new and hopefully short-lived irrational fear of flying—you know, because of climate change? I fear sudden and brutal storms whipping up that will cause damage to the engines, and all the passengers plummeting to untimely deaths. As well as my more rational fear of terrorism in this current political climate."

When only silence followed that statement, the tree shook a little, and Stevie's small head popped out from the leaves. "Not that you guys have anything to worry about," she immediately backpedaled. "You guys will be fine. I'm . . . I'm . . . sure. Absolutely fine."

With still no reply, she cringed and ducked back into the solace of the tree.

"Anyway," Nelle continued, "everyone should go pack *one* overnight bag and meet me at the airport. I am this very moment texting you the address." She looked up at Keane. "And stop looking so angry. I promise! This will be fun, fun, fun!"

*   *   *

"*Is this really fun, fun, fun to you?*" Keane bellowed before diving behind the remains of a blown-out building.

"*If you ask me that again,*" Nelle yelled back, firing the submachine gun that had already been packed onto the private jet she'd borrowed from her father, "*I will kill you myself!*"

Finn wasn't sure how they'd actually ended up here, but here they certainly were. In the middle of a goddamn war. Not a known war. Not the kind of war you'd see on the nightly news while sitting down for dinner. This was some Eastern European thing that was sneaky and illegal and involved backhanded government deals that every government involved would deny later.

And Max's Uncle Jacob was right in the middle of it. He apparently was a mercenary. That was the "job" his family meant.

Finn heard screams and saw women and children trying to run away from a group of armed men attempting to chase them down. Finn looked at his brothers and they shifted.

Mads landed hard on the ground, her machine gun knocked from her hands. A full-human male grabbed her leg, dragging her close. She kicked him in the face, breaking his jaw. He stumbled back and she lifted her leg so she could grab a blade from her holster. Mads flipped forward and plunged the blade into the man's chest, but immediately had to yank it out again because another man was coming at her. She was still low to the ground, so she cut his inner thighs, turned back to the man she'd stabbed in the chest, and cut his throat. Returned to the man standing and cut him low across the belly.

As his insides fell onto the floor, she ran back to her gun and grabbed it up just as the door to the small house she'd run to was kicked in. She opened fire and dashed over the bodies in time to see three massive tigers take down armed men so that women and children could make a desperate run for safety.

"This way!" Mads yelled out in very bad Russian, motioning with her hand. She knew the people she was yelling at weren't Russian but it was the best she could do, and she hoped they understood enough. If nothing else, they seemed to grasp her gestures. Tock then used her skills with explosives to clear space behind them.

When the dust settled, they heard Max shout, "Here! Over here!"

The team ran toward her and Mads whistled for the big cats. To her surprise, Finn spun and faced her. He bumped his brothers and they followed her as she ran to Max.

Inside a dilapidated office building, they found Uncle Jacob. He was tall for a badger, a true soldier. He kept firing out a broken window while casually conversing with Max and Keane.

"I remember your father! Quite a cat. Big bastard! Mean! But knew how to get the job done! Can't say I know who killed him. No one would talk about it! You. Bomb girl. Blast those boys over there, would you? Thanks, dear girl. Anyway, you know who might have more info . . . your Uncle Billy, Max! He was in Prague last I heard! Try him!"

"Exactly how many uncles do you have?" Keane asked as the private jet made its way to Prague.

"More than I thought," Max admitted.

"Sure you guys don't want to choose something from the Zhao family plane armory?" Tock asked, gesturing to the gun display. It had been hidden behind a panel, and it was not the only one. Apparently most of the family's jets had them.

The brothers politely declined. They knew how to use guns but such weapons always seemed excessive when they already had claws, fangs, and, when they shifted, nearly a thousand pounds. Finn didn't hold it against the badgers for adding weapons to their fangs and claws, though. Not that they necessarily needed any enhancement. He'd watched them fight earlier. When they lost a weapon or ran out of bullets, they moved to hand-to-hand combat with ease and they kicked ass. He was guessing that it was a form of krav maga that Tock had taught them, modified to take advantage of their badger rage and willingness to strip off an enemy's skin at a moment's notice.

"We're not going into another war, are we?" Shay asked, staring out the plane window. "I am not in the mood for another firefight. That's the second one I've been in, in . . . like . . . three days. I might get PTSD. I may have to get a support animal."

"You are not getting any more dogs!" Keane snarled.

"Of course not!" He scratched his neck. "But I heard goats are good."

"You get a goat, I'm eating it," Finn warned. "While it's alive and screaming."

"You sick fuck—"

"It's not a war zone," Max promised, probably thinking of her younger sister's words and not wanting two tigers to get into a fierce battle on a plane that could suddenly go down. Sure, as badgers they might survive a crash . . . but they also might not. "I never knew my Uncle Jacob that well. But my Uncle Billy is definitely not a soldier, and he's not going to be fighting for anyone."

"So we'll be in and out?" Keane asked.

"In and out!"

"Thirty seconds!" Billy Yang yelled, moving from case to case and smashing each one with a crowbar. "Go! Go! Go!"

Mads refused to get involved, so she stood by Finn and his brothers, waiting while Max yelled questions at her uncle and her teammates . . . "helped" Billy's associates.

Streep and Max handled the watches. Nelle and Tock, the diamond necklaces and bracelets.

"Twenty seconds!"

"Do you know anything?" Max asked Billy again.

"Um? Yeah! Bosnia."

Mads felt Finn's entire body tighten beside her and all three brothers straightened up.

"What about Bosnia?" Max asked. "Was he in the war there?"

"No. Not at all. Ten seconds! *Wrap it up!* He was there for something else! I don't know what! Maybe Larry knows! All right, team! We are out!"

* * *

Wearing a five-million-dollar-diamond necklace, two-thousand-dollar shoes, as well as designer sunglasses and dress, Nelle strutted through the art museum that was housed inside an old castle. She had a fur stole wrapped around her shoulders and yelled at everyone in Cantonese while the rest of them followed her in black suits and dark sunglasses.

It was a brilliant performance Nelle was putting on, but at this point Finn wasn't surprised by anything she might do. She'd managed to steal the necklace she was wearing from the Prague jewelry store's safe while Max's Uncle Billy and his team smashed the shop's cases and grabbed its mid-level wares. She'd also come out with several diamond-encrusted watches and rose gold bracelets she knew her mother would like. How and when she'd gotten into that safe, Finn had no idea. He just knew he was impressed.

While Nelle loudly interrupted what turned out to be an auction of works by the Swedish artist Carl Larsson, demanding to purchase a piece that had already been sold to a local billionaire, Max's Uncle Larry was in the museum's basement switching a recently loaned Monet out with a recently forged copy.

"Niece!" he greeted, when he saw Max. "You're not here to kill me for the insurance, are you?"

"No! How common is this with you guys?"

Laughing, he hugged Max. "What are you doing here? Hoping to get your own Monet, are you?"

"No. We are not here to stay. Just to see you. Very quickly. Super quickly."

"About what?"

She filled him in on why they'd flown to Sweden and the badger frowned. "Why did Billy send you to me?"

"You don't know anything?"

"Honey, I don't have to. Your Uncle Russ knew him. Sent flowers to his funeral and directly to the widow. I know he actually looked into what happened."

Feeling as if his heart had stopped in his chest, Finn turned to look at his brothers.

"Are you sure?" Max pushed. "Russ knew him?"

"Positive. He was really upset. But you know Russ. Ma always said he had that weak gene."

"You mean sympathy?"

"And the other one."

"Empathy?"

"Yeah. That one, too. But Russ is definitely the one you should talk to." Larry shook his head. "I do not know why those boneheads didn't send you right to him."

"Because both sides of my family are full of idiots?"

"Pretty much."

"So any chance Uncle Russ is in Norway or Iceland or Valhalla? Or anywhere within a thousand-mile radius of where we are currently standing?"

Max's Uncle Larry cringed and Finn already knew the answer was a solid "No."

"Last I heard," the older badger said, "he was in the Congo, protecting gorillas from poachers."

"*Africa?*" Max demanded, her voice breaking a little. "He's in Africa?"

"Even from here, that's not a short trip," Keane muttered.

"Can we just call him there?" Max practically begged. "I mean, even if I felt like being in a jet for twelve to fourteen hours, my friends and I have some . . . lingering issues involving a few African countries. *What?*" she demanded when Finn and his brothers stared at her.

"You think *we're* paranoid?" Larry asked, looking at his cell. "Russ will never tell you anything over the phone. Now, let's see. I'm looking at the last few texts with the family. Blah, blah, blah. About the gorillas. How amazing they are. Yeah, it looks like he is definitely in the Congo, fighting poachers"—he glanced up and added—"which I think we all know means wiping them from the planet. Okay. I think I have his exact location coordinates right here and . . . oh!" He lowered his cell. "Russ is in Brooklyn now."

"Sorry?"

"Yeah. Got a little confused. Forgot he came back from the Congo about a month ago."

"And none of your brothers knew that?"

"I'm not sure they cared enough to remember. You know . . ."

"The sympathy gene again?"

Larry shrugged. "Yeah."

"Don't go anywhere," Max said into the phone. "Understand? Just stay there until we come to talk to you." Suddenly Max's fangs unleashed. "I am *not* coming there to kill you for the insurance money! Just do as I say and stay in New York! Okay, fine. Even better. We'll meet you at your job. That's perfect."

She disconnected the call and was about to throw her phone when Streep snatched it out of her hands. The last thing they needed was for her to lose their connection with her family.

"Is your mother planning to kill all her brothers?" Tock asked as one flight-crew member poured wine and another put out cheese and cracker plates with sides of honey.

"Dude . . . I honestly don't know. I don't know what she's doing. But clearly they are all worried."

"But if she asked you . . . ?"

"No, Streep, I would *not* kill my family for my mother. And the fact that I have actively attempted to kill my father several times does not count because that had nothing to do with my *mother*. I did that on my own. I also need to add there was no money to get when it came to my attempts to kill my father. Because he is a useless, worthless man."

"But your uncle will see us when we get back?" Keane asked.

"Yes. He will. He's nice, too, so I believe him."

Finn returned from the bathroom and dropped into the seat next to Mads. "I can't believe there's a shower and tub in the bathroom here."

"And scented oils," Mads told him.

"Is that what that rose smell was?"

"No, that was the fresh flowers they replaced while we were out."

"Wow." He looked around and smiled at her. "This is kind of awesome."

"Thank you," Nelle said from the plush leather seat she reclined in, a copy of the most recent Italian *Vogue* in her lap. Unlike the rest of them, Nelle hadn't changed back into her "real" clothes after their time in the museum, pretending to be someone else. That ridiculously overpriced designer dress was one of her regular dresses. She'd had another just like it, but one of her nephews had spilled grape juice on it, so she'd asked the *designer* to send her a new one even though it was from two seasons before. Why? "Because you know it's my favorite and I love it! And legally I'm not allowed to beat my nephew to death for fucking up the old one."

"I said it was an accident, Auntie!" the sixteen-year-old had yelled back from another room.

And three days later, delivered by messenger, the dress she currently had on arrived.

"I designed the look and feel of this particular fleet of planes for my father," she bragged.

"Did you also do that without asking him if you could?" Mads wanted to know.

"American Jesus Christ! Is this about me decorating your house again?"

"It was rude!"

"It was necessary! Because we all know you were never going to do it!"

"She's right," Max chimed in. "You were never going to do it."

"How the fuck do you know?"

"I know because you rented that place for six months one time, near where we used to practice, and you remember what happened there."

"Oh, come on. I was eighteen."

"You were twenty-four and you had nothing in the place

but a mattress, a cardboard box, and an old black-and-white TV that you put on the cardboard box."

"Where did you even *find* that TV?" Streep asked. "I thought those TVs were in massive trash heaps, slowly destroying our planet."

"You barely had any lights!" Max went on. "It was like a pit of despair and even I hated going there. And once I lived in a dirt hole in the woods for three days."

"Why?" Keane felt brave enough to ask.

"To see if I could."

"Of course."

Finn didn't know how commenting on enjoying being in a private jet rather than crammed onto a commercial flight with a bunch of complaining full-humans had led to a fight between honey badgers, but here they all were.

Although he'd kind of known it would be coming. Hard to decorate a person's house without their knowledge or approval and not have them get a little pissy about it.

"Seriously?" Mads demanded. "*None* of you guys think Nelle coming into my house and putting in furniture and clothes and appliances is remotely weird? On any level?"

"Nope," Max easily replied.

"Not at all," Streep said.

"I told her to do it," Tock suddenly admitted.

Uh-oh. It was like the air had been sucked out of the cabin. Even though Finn had no doubt that most of Mads's shifter genes were honey badger, he still had a definite feeling that a few hyena ones had slipped through. If nothing else, it would explain how her lovely neck seemed to get longer and sort of drop, then swing out while her eyes looked up at Tock in dangerous warning.

"You *what?*"

Nelle stood. "I think I need to use the conveniently placed shower—"

"*Sit down!*" Mads barked.

Nelle sat back down.

"I think I was quite clear," Tock said.

"*You* told her to do all that creepy shit in my house?"

"I did."

"Because I'm poor?"

"In what world are you poor? That hippy aunt of yours ensured you'd never be poor as long as you don't give your shit away."

"Is this about the Kandinsky again?"

"You also have a Warhol, a Basquiat—"

"Well, I'd never give away the Basquiat. He gave that to her on her birthday."

"It doesn't matter whether you'd give it away. It's that you have it. You have millions of dollars' worth of artwork in storage units spread out all over this country due to your Buddha-loving aunt."

"Buddha?" Shay asked.

Mads shrugged. "She used her love of Buddha to replace her intense love of cocaine. It was the eighties and there was a *lot* of cocaine." She refocused on her teammates. "But it doesn't change the fact that you should have talked to me first."

"Why?" Tock asked. "You weren't going to do it. I really didn't think you'd notice. Not during playoffs." She glanced off. "I guess we should have waited until the championships."

"Tock!"

"Look, we are all nearing thirty. It was time for you to act like an adult."

"Couldn't you all have just taken me shopping or something instead?"

"No!"

"God, no!"

"Heaven forbid!"

"I'd rather set myself on fire . . . again."

"You hate shopping," Tock explained, "unless the new Jordans are out. And then you just go and stand in line with everyone else. That's not exactly the act of shopping."

"Whereas," Nelle interjected, "I love shopping and I know exactly what you like. I just had to look up a few things online, send my ideas to my personal shoppers, and you were set. That way you didn't have to worry about it. I was truly trying to be helpful. Not shove your nonexistent poverty down your throat. Since that seems to be what you're harping on."

"And the creepy factor."

"What's so creepy? That you're easy to buy for? Jeans. Basketball tanks. An array of unattractive basketball sneakers. It's not exactly brain surgery."

"You also bought me underwear."

"Sports bras and Hanes for Her. They come in packets." Nelle looked at her teammates. "*Packets.*"

"The condoms?"

"From what I surmise, they have not gone unused."

"With a note on the package."

"That was just funny. Max would have done the same thing."

"I probably would have," Max agreed with a small shrug.

"It would have only been weird if you'd picked one of the other two," Nelle said, pointing at Keane and Shay. And when Finn's brothers only gawked at her, she added, "Oh, come on. You three are practically interchangeable. The Dunn triplets are easier to tell apart because at least one of them is a woman.

"And I'd like you all to keep in mind," she added, "there are very few people in this world that I would do this sort of thing for: you ungrateful bitches; my father, because he is amazing and brilliant and adores me; my eldest sister, because she never once threw an axe at my head or set the dogs after me; my mother, because I wisely fear her . . . and . . . yeah. That's it. And that's how you know you guys mean so much to me because . . ."

Nelle's words faded off and Finn looked over to see why she'd stopped talking. That's when he saw that Streep was sitting on the edge of her seat, hands clasped in front of her, eyes practically bulging from her head.

"Say it!" Streep finally pushed, with a huge, impatient smile. "Say it!"

"Say what?" Nelle finally asked.

"Say that you love us all."

The females reared back from Streep. It was as if she'd grown a second head or suggested doing something disgusting with dolphins. There was even a loud, simultaneous "Ewwwww!"

"We risk our lives for each other! We spend so much time together! Happily! We are as close together as five people can be who are not fucking. Why won't you just say we are all friends and that we love each other dearly?"

Nelle leaned over and took Streep's hand. Smiling warmly, she said with great feeling, "You guys are my dearest, closest associates. And I tolerate all of you greatly."

The eager grin Streep had on her face faded away and she snatched her hand back.

"All of you are mean, petty cunts, and I don't know why I waste a bit of my precious time on you!"

With that, and with as much dignity as she could muster, Streep stood and walked toward the bathrooms in the back of the jet. Once one of the doors slammed shut, the badgers exploded into laughter. Max fell onto the floor; Mads into Finn's lap. And Nelle had actual tears in her eyes while Tock had trouble getting her breath back.

"I can hear you laughing at me, you evil bitches!" Streep yelled from the bathroom. "And I will never forgive you!"

Of course, that just made them all laugh harder.

"Streep is right, you know," Keane said, staring out the window. "You *are* all evil bitches."

chapter TWENTY-ONE

Shay studied Max MacKilligan for several seconds before asking what they were all thinking. "How do you not know your own uncle has a PhD in zoology? And is currently in charge of a well-known zoo? With his specialty being gorillas?"

"I don't know," Max replied.

"Uh-huh."

"I guess he never told me. He was one of the few Yang members who actually spoke to me. He'd write me letters. Some came from Africa."

"Did the letters include pictures of him with gorillas?"

She blinked. "Sometimes."

"You didn't think that was weird? Your honey badger uncle just hanging around a bunch of gorillas?"

"Well, when you put it that way . . ."

"I'm just pissed this uncle was only ten miles away from the *first* goddamn uncle," Keane growled.

Mads couldn't be angry at Max about anything, though. She was just glad to be back in the States. All that flying around and bouncing from country to country had made her homesick. Surprising since she'd never felt as if she'd had a home. Now, though, she had her own house. That was a start to a home. But first she had to be there longer than a day or two.

They were all waiting in the Africa section of the New Jersey zoo that Max's Uncle Russ ran. It supposedly had an excellent breeding and rehabilitation program.

"How are you holding up?" Finn asked Mads as she gazed

into the hyena exhibit. He'd eased up behind her, and she'd never heard a sound. Despite her honey badger hearing.

"I'm doing pretty good. You know, before we went—"

"On Mr. Toad's Wild Ride?"

She laughed and pressed her shoulder against his. "When you get in the middle of a small war, it is a bit of a wild ride. Anyway, I talked to Charlie before we left. Told her about my family coming after me."

"And she said you should handle them the way she handled your grandmother back in junior high?"

Mads turned, resting her elbow on the exhibit railing. "How did you know that?"

"She managed to keep Max MacKilligan out of prison and out of the morgue for years. There's only one way to do that. By taking no prisoners. Which seems very Viking to me."

"It is very Viking. Although my people did take prisoners so they could sell them as slaves, but I don't like to talk about that."

"That's probably for the best, considering the diaspora that is your friend group. Do you have any ideas on how you're going to stomp your family into the ground?"

"It's not just the family, though. It's the entire Clan. And whatever I do, it'll have to be right the first time."

Russ Yang, PhD, ordered them into his tiny office with the brusque manner of a Marine sergeant.

"You're sure your mother didn't send you?" he asked Max.

"I am *not* answering this question again."

"Fine. I'm trusting you, Max. Don't let me down." He looked over at Finn and his brothers, and Finn saw a small smile turn up the corner of his lips. "Damn, you boys are built just like him. But you all have your mother's face. How's she doing?"

"Well," Keane replied. "But she also wants to know who killed our father."

"I'm not surprised she doesn't know. Your mother didn't know half of what your father did."

"Because he was cheating on her?" Finn asked.

"Your father?" Yang shook his head. "Never. He just wasn't exactly what he said he was. A part of himself he couldn't reveal. For her safety. For yours. I only knew because of the people we had to deal with from time to time in the Middle East and Africa."

"Are you saying our father was a poacher?" Shay demanded, his voice filled with disgust.

"Oh, no! Absolutely not. Your father worked for the CIA. He was a spy."

It was the blank stares on the Malone brothers' faces. The way they simply stood there, staring at Max's uncle. She'd never seen cats so confused before.

Finally, it was Keane who roughly asked, "What the fuck are you talking about?"

"It's true. He was in the CIA. Not even the shifter division of the CIA but the full-human, uptight CIA. Recruited straight out of high school. I don't think even his siblings knew."

"How did you know?" Finn asked.

"There was a bit of a dustup in the Congo. I found him half-dead in a river. Dragged him out. Realized what he was and took him to safety."

"Which was with the gorillas?" Mads guessed.

"Exactly. We kept him safe until he'd gone through his fever and his body mostly healed. When it was time to get him out of there, I couldn't find any Americans to help, but there were a few Mossad in the area handling something else." Yang suddenly looked at Tock and smirked. "When you get a chance, tell your grandmother I said hi."

Finn looked back and forth between Yang and Tock. "Her grandmother knew my father?"

"Spies always know spies. But whether she knows who killed your father . . ." He shrugged. "That's the thing."

"What is?"

"I don't know if his death had to do with a specific job.

You know, a spy-versus-spy incident. That they would have wrapped up nice and neat in a bullshit story that would have most likely satisfied you boys and your mother. When that didn't happen . . ." He let out a breath. "He'd contacted me a few weeks before it happened. Left me a message. Said he needed to talk. But I was on a book tour, raising money for the zoo and the gorillas. By the time I was back in the country and able to meet with him . . . he was . . . dead."

Yang walked around his desk and briefly looked out the extremely tiny window that let only the barest amount of light into the room before facing the Malone brothers again. "I will say this. His three sons agonizing over his death is not what he would have wanted for any of you. He loved you kids. All of you. And he never would have wanted you to put yourselves at risk. I say that because I know he would have wanted me to say that. I also know that he was the most vengeful motherfucker I'd ever had the deep displeasure of knowing," he added with a grin. "The ones who'd nearly killed him in the Congo? Not one of them existed longer than a month after he'd made it out. He hunted down each and every one and made them pay by fang and claw, because guns and bombs just weren't good enough for him when it came to revenge."

"It's over too fast," Keane said.

Yang's eyes lit up when Keane muttered those words and his grin grew impossibly wide. Mads knew the zoologist had heard them before from Keane's father. More than once.

"Absolutely nothing terrified your father's enemies more than when they'd really pissed him off. Because he didn't stop. He never stopped. And looking at you three—all I see is the tribal version of that rage. Genghis Khan riding across the steppes."

"Our mother's tribe existed long before Genghis's people were even born, and my mother's people exist still," Keane told Russ Yang. "And you're right. We won't stop. We'll never stop. Until we strip the flesh from the bones of whoever killed our father."

*   *   *

Without a word being spoken among the entire group, they got back into the two SUVs they'd taken to Jersey and headed back to New York. But they didn't go to Finn's house. In silent agreement, they went to Queens and Mads's house.

When they parked on the street in front of her home, everyone got out. Still silent. But Keane didn't make it past the hood of the rented SUV he'd picked up while his was in the shop. He simply stopped and dropped his arm on the hood and his head on his forearm.

Streep immediately went to him, gently rubbing his back. "Oh, sweetie, don't cry," she sweetly soothed.

Keane lifted his massive head, eyes dangerously narrowed, and snarled, "I am *not* crying. And get off me!"

"I don't know why I bother with any of you!" she snapped, stepping away.

"I'm just so tired," Keane said, his head resting again on his forearm. "Part of me was hoping we'd know enough by now for me to go out, kill the guy, and go home to sleep. That was literally my whole plan for the next twenty-four hours. But instead, we learned that Dad was—"

"CIA." Finn leaned against Keane's SUV. "I can't believe Dad was in the CIA."

"Why is that so unbelievable?" Streep asked.

"Because he was a Malone," Finn and his brothers said together.

"Everything is for the family," Keane explained. "That's how we were raised. That's why we felt so betrayed when they did nothing after Dad was killed."

"I hate saying this," Tock weakly suggested, "but you may have to talk to someone in the government about—"

Finn felt bad because they wouldn't even let her finish her sentence. They started loudly groaning at the mere thought of trying to get any information about anything from the government.

"I am still trying to get a new trash can for the house," Finn told her.

"That's local government."

"You act like federal government is better."

"No, but if you can talk to the shifter divisions of the CIA—"

"But Dad was in with the full-humans."

"That doesn't mean our kind didn't know what was going on with him. My grandmother always knows where all her people are—shifter and non."

"You could also talk to *your* connections," Shay said, gazing down at Tock.

"That's not a good idea."

"Why not?"

"You do not want my grandmother involved in this. At all."

"So you're afraid of your grandmother?" Shay pushed.

"No. But you should be."

"Can I make a suggestion?" Nelle offered as she hopped over to Keane and leaned against his back so she could remove one of her high heels and shake it out.

"What are you doing?" he demanded, trying to look over his shoulder to observe.

"I have something in my shoe."

"You couldn't lean against the car?"

"You were right here. And stop complaining! There are men who'd kill for me to do to them what I'm currently doing to you."

"What men? I want names."

"What's your suggestion, Nelle?" Mads asked.

"You guys take a break. Not a long one," she quickly added when they opened their mouths to instantly disagree. "Just a couple of days. To sleep. Play your football. You all seem to like that. Anything that will allow your brains to reset."

Finn gazed at Keane. "She's not wrong."

"Of course I'm not wrong. When am I ever wrong?"

"When you bought me pink Hanes For Her," Mads tossed in. "I only wear black."

"And when Mads needs a break," Nelle continued with a smile, "she enjoys being ungrateful."

"That's a nice idea and all," Keane grumbled, "but I don't know what you think would actually distract us from the murder of our father."

"Hey, Mads," Streep said, pointing out to the street. "Isn't that your pet coyote?"

"He's not my pet."

"Yes, he is," Finn muttered.

It took a second for the coyote to pass the SUV so they could all see him. But once he did, they noticed that he had something long and cumbersome hanging from both sides of his mouth.

"What is he holding?" Keane asked.

"Huh," Mads said before replying, "that is a hyena leg. The coyote is holding a hyena leg."

"From a recently killed hyena," Tock added.

Shay went out into the street and looked for a blood trail. He found it and began to follow, with the rest of them trooping behind.

They made a left at the corner and kept going until Max said, "This is cat terri—"

Which was all she got out before a lion roar exploded around them, warning them off.

"How do they get away with that?" Tock wanted to know. "There are full-human streets and businesses all around here!"

Male lions seemed to come from every house, every yard. And they were not happy to have honey badgers in their territory. Not happy at all.

"You need to go."

"What did I do?" Max demanded when it seemed to dawn on her that the lions were speaking to no one but her.

"Where's my father's watch?"

"I know you stole my car!"

"I had ten thousand dollars in that bedroom safe!"

"Hey, hey, hey!" Max said, palms out to placate. She waited a moment before she added, "You don't know any of that was me."

One of the lions unleashed a mini-roar and big fangs sprang

forward, but Finn stepped between them, pushing his fellow cat back.

"That's not going to happen," Finn warned.

"Why? What are you three going to do?"

Finn told him honestly. "Tear your throat out."

"Okay." Mads quickly pushed herself between the males. "Before this gets out of hand, I have one simple question and then we're gone: Did you guys happen to see a hyena hanging around here?"

The lions looked her over, and one asked, "Are you a cop?"

"I play basketball."

Another male snapped his fingers. "Wisconsin Butchers! You guys just won the playoffs!"

"Yeah!"

"Would you sign my ball?"

"Hey!" Finn barked.

"He means his basketball."

"I know. I still don't like it."

"And in answer to your question," said a lion male with lots of black hair in his mane, "yeah. We saw six hyenas hanging around. We could smell 'em. We tracked them down to the bears' street, but we don't like them being that close to our cubs. So we went after them."

"And?"

He glanced at the others and, after most shrugged, replied, "Five got away, the sixth . . . did not."

"Do you still have the body?"

"It's being cremated. There's really no way to adequately explain how a hyena got its throat ripped out on your property. Not even to New York cops. Although some street coyote did get a bit of the body before we could get it in the back of Clem's car."

"Keep anything from it?" When his eyes narrowed with distrust, Mads again said, "I play *basketball*."

"Right." He reached into his back pocket and pulled out a wallet, handing it to Mads. She immediately yanked out the driver's license.

"Wisconsin ID." She looked at Finn. "My mother sent scouts. To my *house*."

"You're not hyena," the lion noted.

"It's a long story."

"Which I think it's about time you filled us in on," Tock said.

"Yeah," a young lion male agreed. "It's time to tell us what's going on."

With his fangs out, Shay snarled, "*She's not talking to you!*"

"Well, you don't have to be rude about it!"

It was not a long story to tell, since everyone knew bits and pieces anyway. But once Mads was done, she felt better. Although she did have to take the sword away from Max because she nearly took Keane's head off when she kept swinging it around.

"What do you want to do?" Tock asked, while sitting on Mads's floor and attempting to wrestle the hyena leg from the coyote.

"I want to forget my mother and grandmother exist, but that's not possible because they won't leave me alone. And just give him that leg so he can bury it under the house, Tock!"

"You could send the sword back," Streep reasoned. "But, honestly, I still think they'd come after you."

"I know," Mads said, watching the coyote run away with his prize. "I just don't understand why."

"You represent what they will never be," Nelle explained. "They are hyena. Down to their core. Although they do lack the intelligence I've seen in most hyenas. Your great-grand-mother, however, was Viking. *You* are Viking. And the Galen-dotter Clan in Norway is Viking. Being able to shift into hyena is simply another weapon for you. Like having a sword or an axe. As long as you live and breathe, you are a threat to your mother and grandmother because you are more fit to rule the American Clan than they are."

"I don't want to rule the Clan. I don't want to rule the

family. I don't need them. I got you guys. They don't have my back."

"Because to Tova you're not hyena. But to Solveig, you didn't need to be. You were badger, but more important, you were Viking. That's all those Norwegians care about."

"You already have a plan," Finn prompted. "Don't you?"

Mads shook her head. "It's too . . . it's crazy. It's like a Max plan."

Max frowned. "What's that mean?"

"That's what you need right now," Tock said. "Something so ridiculous and insane that no one in their right mind would ever think of it or do it. A Max plan."

"Hey!" Max complained. "I'm getting insulted."

"No, you're not," Tock told her.

Max grinned. "Nah. I'm not."

Mads looked at the Malone brothers. "I'll need your help. All of you."

"Who do you want us to kill?" Keane asked. "I'd prefer not to kill the old lady, though."

"No, no, no." Mads shook her head. "Not exactly that. I need your connections."

"Oh, God," Shay groaned. "You need the rest of the Malones, don't you?"

"Actually, the last thing I want or need for this . . . are tigers."

chapter TWENTY-TWO

"**K**yle!" Charlie called out, putting his warm oatmeal and bacon on the kitchen table. "Breakfast!"

Stevie looked up from her computer. "What are you doing?"

"Calling Kyle to breakfast. I know he's eighteen now, but I still like to make him breakfast sometimes."

"Kyle isn't here. Kyle hasn't been here for the last five days. He's been with his family in Seattle."

"Are you sure?" Kyle was another onetime child prodigy like Stevie who'd been staying in their basement and paying rent. He was a brilliant artist and jackal who'd taken over their garage with his artwork. He was also arrogant and annoying and rude, but that just made Charlie like him more. How could she not when he managed to tick off everyone who came within ten feet of him? That was a skill even Max didn't possess. And the extra rent didn't hurt either.

"I'm positive. He's been texting me regularly to complain about his family, the Seattle weather, and the state of world politics. He also wants to make sure you won't rent his room out to someone else."

"Huh. I never noticed he was gone."

"Okay. So not only do I need to wait to be a mom, but you need to wait to be an aunt."

"Oh, come on. The kid's eighteen. I'm sure I'd be much better with a baby."

Charlie heard the front door slam open and a familiar voice

cry out, "Help! I need help!" She waited while big feet ran down the hall toward the kitchen.

"See?" Stevie pointed out. "Neither of us moved, even though we heard someone screaming for help."

"We were supposed to move?"

The Malone brothers' youngest male sibling, Dale, ran into their kitchen. "I need your help!"

Charlie held up her phone. "You couldn't call?"

"Charlie!" Stevie snapped.

"Nat's been kidnapped!" the kid said.

Charlie and Stevie exchanged glances before Charlie asked, "Sure she just didn't run away because Stevie shoved her nose into her face?"

"Valid question," the kid replied. "And I would have thought the same thing. Just one problem."

"Which is?"

"My brothers aren't home. They went off with your sister Max and the other badgers. They're not even in the state!"

"Okay . . ."

"Look, my sister is not going to dramatically run away without an audience. My mother's not even home right now. She's with my aunts at the Jewish rec center playing Texas Hold 'em. I'm telling you, my sister would not do the big stomp-away without someone there to give a shit. And I am *not* that one."

"Maybe she just went out with friends," Stevie reasoned.

"I've texted her all morning—she hasn't texted me back. She *always* texts me back."

"When did you last see her?" Charlie asked.

"She walked with me to school, where I take my advanced college courses."

"Why?"

He cleared his throat and began looking really shifty.

"Just tell me, kid, we don't have time for this."

"She was drinking last night and didn't want Mom to smell it on her."

"Drinking what?" Charlie asked.

The kid cleared his throat again. "Liquor."

"Liquor with what?"

He threw his hands up. "She has some badger friends, okay? And yes, she likes her vodka mixed with some snake poison. What were you doing at seventeen?"

"Not drinking poison-infused vodka."

"Isn't that because you liked your poison mixed with tequila?"

"You are *not* helping, Stevie."

"Can I get on with this?" the kid yelped.

"Fine. Go ahead."

"Anyway, I was walking up the stairs and when I looked back, she was talking to this Asian guy. Totally her type. I didn't think much about it until I texted her from class and she didn't text me back."

"What do you mean 'her type'?"

"Tall. Good looking. *Breathing.*"

Stevie snorted, but quickly lowered her head.

"And to keep our mother off her back, tiger," he added.

Wide-eyed, Stevie looked at Charlie, and Charlie knew that her baby sister was thinking the same thing.

"Tiger? Was this Asian guy Chinese?" Charlie asked.

"How the hell should I know? I can tell you he's probably *not* Mongolian."

"How would you know that?"

"Because that would make our mother *too* happy. And she will never make our mother *too* happy."

"Okay, okay. Fine. So the kid's Asian."

"Wait. What does it matter if he's Chinese or not?"

"It probably doesn't."

"Probably? Why probably?"

Charlie pulled out her phone and turned away from the kid. She quickly went through her contacts until she found the name she was looking for. The phone rang twice on the other end and when it connected, she only got a "What?"

"When Van Holtz spoke to the Yuns, what did they say?"

"They said they'd leave you alone."

"What specifically, Smith? For most people, words have meaning. What were their words?"

"Lord, let me think. He said . . . 'We'll stay away from the MacKilligan sisters.'"

"You're sure?"

"Yes. I'm sure. Why? What's going—"

Charlie disconnected the call and again faced the kid. "What's your sister's legal name?"

The kid blinked. "What?"

"On her birth certificate? What's her legal name? Is it MacKilligan? Is our father down as *her* father?"

"It's complicated."

"We're smart." Charlie pointed at Stevie. "She's a genius. We can figure it out."

"Dad was already dead when she was born. So Mom didn't put anyone down as the father."

"But she didn't give her the name MacKilligan either."

"No. She was a Malone. Raised a Malone. Even though no one on the Malone side but us was happy about it."

Charlie closed her eyes and asked, "Did the rest of your family tell anyone that Nat was *not* a Malone? That she was, in fact, a MacKilligan?"

"Uh . . . well . . . I think so. I think I remember my mom complaining that the Malones told everyone they did business with that she wasn't blood related. It's a big deal for them."

"Who do the Malones do business with?" Stevie asked.

"Criminals," the kid easily replied. "A lot of leg breakers in my family. You want someone's legs broken because they owe you money and you don't want them accidentally killed . . . you bring in a Malone."

"The Yuns promised they wouldn't strike against the MacKilligan sisters," Charlie explained to Stevie. "So they went after Nat . . . because she's not a MacKilligan. Legally, she's a Malone."

"Oh, my God," Stevie said, beginning to pant. "Oh, my God!" she said again, this time a little louder.

She slammed her hands onto the table, giant claws bursting out of them and her voice exploding with rage as she roared out, "*Oh, my God!*"

Charlie waited until the windows stopped shaking, the glasses, plates, and pans stopped dropping onto the floor, and the chairs stopped skittering across the room. Then she looked up at the terrified young tiger who was hanging from a now partially broken cabinet door like a panicked house cat and said, "You should go home now, kid. Keep your phone on—we may have to call. But we'll handle it from here."

Tova pushed open the door of her home and stepped barefoot onto the grass. She held a cup of coffee as she started walking toward her daughter's trailer, shoving out of her way a male who'd gotten too close. He apologized and kept moving, which was what Tova expected. If he'd done anything else, she'd have torn off his face.

As Tova was about to knock on Freja's door, she heard one of her grandnieces behind her.

"Tova! You need to come out to the south field."

"Why?"

The girl smiled. "You won't believe who's here."

Tova headed back to her trailer to put on her clothes and steel-toed boots. She motioned to the other trailers. "Get 'em up. Get 'em all up. Now!"

They dragged Nat out of the trunk and Kang Yun pointed toward a doorway that led into a long hallway. It was an empty warehouse made of concrete. Some place that Nat did not want to be, but so far all they'd done to her was shove her around and try to scare the shit out of her.

Not that she wasn't concerned. She was definitely concerned. These tigers were pissed about something and she knew her kind well enough. True, she was mostly honey badger, but she knew her brothers and mother. She knew tigers. They were vengeful, angry fucks and for some reason these particular vengeful, angry fucks were pissed at *her*. She knew she hadn't done anything to them herself, but for whatever reason, she was their means to an end.

The problem was, she hadn't reached her full shifter potential yet in order to properly fight back. She could unleash her claws and begin digging but she wasn't at the point yet where she could dig herself completely out of the building in less than a minute. That took some training and practice and she had neither. Same thing with her shifting.

The tigers did seem to know she was deaf but were unaware that she could read lips. Something she might be able to use. People tended to underestimate those they considered to have a weakness, not realizing that her body had compensated for her loss of hearing in other ways.

Two males held her bare arms tightly as they dragged her through the warehouse until they reached a room and threw her inside. They closed the door and stepped in front of it, facing her. Then they waited. She stood on the other side of the room and said nothing. Simply watched them.

The smaller one started to sweat first, wiping his forehead a lot. His partner noticed and asked, "What's wrong with you?"

"I don't know. I don't feel so well."

"Suck it up. The boss is in a bad mood." He glanced at Nat. "Poor kid doesn't even know what's about to happen to her. Unlike her, we *will* hear her screams."

"Sure she can't hear?"

"Yeah. I'm sure."

Now the taller guy wiped his forehead. "Is it me or is it getting hot in here?" He looked down at his hands, studied the palms. "Do your palms feel sweaty, too?"

"It's like my skin's on fire."

"Yeah. Mine, too."

The smaller one pointed at Nat. "What's she smiling about?"

"When will you get the money?"

"I . . . I . . ."

Joey didn't know what to say. He didn't have the money.

And he'd already borrowed from everyone he knew to pay off all his old debts. He still hadn't paid his rent and he wasn't sure how much longer he could keep that from the wife. As it was, she thought he *had* paid the rent. But he'd thought this time the horse was a sure thing. He'd looked into the horse's eyes! He'd thought for sure this time . . .

Now he had the biggest man he'd ever seen standing over him, telling him if he didn't pay up money he didn't have he would not just break his legs, he would *demolish* his legs.

Joey had always thought he was a big guy. He was a big guy! Six-three, three hundred pounds, and, like his dad and granddad before him, he worked on the docks. But the guy staring down at him with weird gold eyes . . . he was bigger. Way bigger. Taller. Wider.

Joey always thought he was mean, too. Joey sent most of the guys who came around demanding money on their way with a swift kick in the ass while he and his union boys laughed about it. But this guy. This guy was definitely meaner. Colder. Impatient. Joey didn't think he'd be kicking this one's ass anywhere.

"I asked you a question."

"Uh . . ."

"Hey! Malone."

It was a woman's voice. Coming from behind the mountain in front of Joey.

The mountain turned and said, "You? What are you doing here?"

She walked around him and Joey saw her and another woman. The first one was Black. Only about five-nine, but with big shoulders. Cute, though. The other one was tiny. Blond, thin, in a little sundress one of Joey's daughters might wear. Neither of them seemed to belong on the docks. And they definitely didn't seem like the kind of girls who should be talking to the mountain.

"I've been told," the Black one said, "that you do work for the Yuns."

"Look, I'm not about to get—"

"They took my sister. I need to know where they would have taken her."

"I'm not getting in the middle of this. Not against the Yuns."

"I'm sorry if I was unclear. You don't have a choice."

The mountain sort of laughed. "Really?"

The Black one suddenly grabbed the mountain. By the hair, twisting him down, so that he was forced to look up to her. Her other hand, she pressed against his neck, and warned, "Move and I'll rip it out."

The mountain stopped struggling.

"The Yuns took our half-sister. They plan to torture her and kill her. This would also be the half-sister of the Malone brothers. Your cousins. While you should be worried about what I will do to you, you should really be worried about what *the Black Malones* will do to your entire family when they get back to New York. Because we both know that if anything happens to their sister, they will never stop until the entire Malone bloodline is wiped clean from the planet. So I strongly suggest you answer me."

Joey could see the mountain struggling. He didn't want to answer, and Joey knew why. Ratting out the Yuns was a quick way to end up in the East River. But before the big man could make up his mind, the tiny blonde leaned over and screamed right into the mountain's face, *"TELL HER!"*

The containers that surrounded them, which needed to be lifted by very powerful cranes, shook from the force of the girl's roared words.

That's when the mountain blurted out an address somewhere on Staten Island.

He was released, and the blonde started walking away. The other didn't follow immediately, though. She stared at the mountain a moment before heading off, tossing a warning over her shoulder as she did. "If that kid is hurt or dead because you didn't give us the information right away, I promise you'll never see me coming."

Realizing that this mountain of a man had let those two

women stomp all over him and was still looking weirded out and panicked, Joey swung on him before he could get his senses back. He hit him right in the face, too. Should have knocked him out.

Instead, all the mountain did was turn his head slowly to glare down at Joey. He didn't even blink. Or move. Or appear harmed in anyway.

Then he did something truly unsettling. He growled.

That's when Joey knew he was well and truly fucked.

Tova stood next to Freja as Mads came over the hill with her new Oriental boyfriend and his Oriental brothers. They were big tigers. All three of them.

Some of her clan were in their human forms, but some were loping back and forth, sending out their whooping call. Some laughing. So Mads would not forget what she was dealing with.

"Do you have it?" Freja called out to her worthless daughter.

Unlike her fertile sisters, Freja had always had trouble conceiving. It hadn't really bothered her. She didn't like children. But if she wanted to take over, to rule when Tova moved on, she knew she'd need a daughter of her own to watch her back. She'd heard about the tough genes of honey badgers. She'd thought at worst she'd get a disturbing mix of hyena and badger. Instead, she got a weak little badger with a love of basketball. Ghetto trash with ghetto-trash friends. The Clan would have found a way to get rid of her a long time ago if it hadn't been for Solveig.

But Solveig was gone now. No one to protect little Mads anymore except three tigers and her crazy badger friends. They might not be standing right next to her, but Tova wasn't fooled. She knew those bitches were around somewhere. Maybe under her feet. She knew they could dig. She was ready for their little tricks and moves. Even the probability that they would use weapons because their little claws and fangs weren't strong enough to go up against hyena jaws. Tova's Clan had weapons of their own. Just in case.

"Well?" Freja pushed when the badger just stood there. Not saying anything.

"I'm not here to fight you," Mads finally said. "I'm just here to tell you that it's over. It ends here."

"What ends here?"

"The harassment. The stupid fights over swords. It's just . . . done."

Tova dropped her head. "Lord!" she muttered to one of her nieces. "That girl is sad."

"Okay," Freja said, her voice full of sarcasm. "It's done. Because you want it done. Because we're upsetting you."

"No. That's not why. Because I'm doing what Solveig always wanted to do but never tried because she thought it was too crazy, even for her."

Confused, Tova raised her head, watching the first one trot over the hill.

His big mane waved around him, thick legs standing tall and powerful, massive chest moving in and out with each breath, instincts kicking in at the mere sight of the clan standing in front of him.

At first, Tova kind of laughed. Admiring the balls on the girl to come up with this crazy idea, with or without Solveig. But that laughter died in her throat when more males kept coming. Filling up the hillside. Lion males as far as the eye could see. More male lions than she'd ever seen at one time in all her life.

More male lions than she had hyenas in her entire American Clan.

This wasn't a warn-off. As she'd thought it would be when it looked like the girl had only brought a few lions and her pet tigers. This was a wipeout.

"You wouldn't," Tova snarled at her.

"Better hide the children," Mads Galendotter growled out, her badger fangs extending past her lips. "I'm not sure I'll be able to keep them from going that far."

Then the evil bitch threw back her head and unleashed a

Viking scream Solveig would have been proud of, sending all those lion males charging straight at Tova's entire Clan.

Charlie pressed her foot on the gas and drove straight ahead, ignoring the bullets that kept slamming into the windshield. She'd borrowed a work SUV and those vehicles were mostly bulletproof, allowing her to continue driving forward until she rammed the cats protecting the front of the building, shoving them into the wall and then right through the concrete.

She didn't duck down until she realized the top of the SUV was being partially sawed off and worried her head might go with it. There was definitely no coming back from a decapitated head. Even for a honey badger.

Once she cleared the wall and the near loss of her head, Charlie spun the wheel hard and hit the brakes. She grabbed the machine gun next to her and started shooting before she even straightened up. When she did sit up, she had already taken down five tigers and was gunning for three more when something slammed into her from behind. This one had shifted into his cat form. His forelegs slammed onto her shoulders with a brutal force that should have crumpled her like tin foil.

Her father's freak genes, though . . .

Charlie reached back with one hand and grabbed the tiger by the extra skin of his neck and flung him into the tiger launching himself at her from the front. They slammed into each other and landed in a muddle of claws and fangs. She jumped out of the wrecked SUV and cleared the empty mag, quickly replacing it with a new one from the vest she was wearing. She started firing again at the males rushing in from a doorway.

There were a lot of them. And it was clear they'd been waiting for her. So Charlie wasn't exactly surprised when she got hit twice in the back, just above the vest she had on, knocking her to the ground. She rolled over and started to clear her empty mag again but a hand reached down and yanked the weapon from her hands. He slammed his foot against her chest. A rib cracked and Charlie yelped out in pain. He kicked her in the side a few times, then grabbed her ankle and began dragging her toward the open doorway.

Mads heard her mother scream orders as the female hyenas attacked from all sides. She didn't shift and neither did they. Instead, they came at her swinging. But Mads blocked their blows with her arms and struck back with the blades she had tucked under her T-shirt. She slashed one across the face, another across the shoulder. Someone kicked her from behind and she rolled forward, came up standing. She spun around and brought the blade down, nailing a cousin in the chest.

The rest shifted and scattered; lion males took off after them.

She knew blood had sprayed across her face, and she had it on her hands and white T-shirt. Slowly she faced her mother and grandmother with her arms spread wide, a blade in each hand.

Mads said nothing. There was nothing to say. The only thing her family could do at this point was flee.

They did.

The banging coming from inside the SUV stopped the man dragging Charlie toward the hallway. He looked back, gold eyes narrowed. He shook his head and started dragging Charlie again. Another bang had him tossing Charlie against the wall and aiming his machine gun at the back of the SUV. He shot at the vehicle a few times. Paused. Shot it some more.

Charlie rolled to her stomach, got onto her knees. She pressed her hand to her chest and forced her ribs back into place so she could breathe a little better. Once breathing was no longer a challenge, she pulled out the .40 holstered to the back of her jeans and put a round in the chamber.

As soon as she did, she had to duck, because the back door of the SUV was flipping across the room as an angry, roaring Stevie emerged from the trunk.

The male tried to fire again when he saw the giant, tiger-striped honey badger but Stevie didn't even see him. She was too busy stepping on him with her giant paw as she got out of the vehicle, crushing him into the ground. Leaving nothing but his flattened, bloody remains behind once she'd stepped away.

In the past, when her meds weren't quite right and she had no real control over her emotions, this incarnation of Stevie would have been an explosion of panic and fear. But that fearful Stevie no longer existed and right now she was too angry to be afraid of anything, it seemed.

More men charged out of the doorway, completely unaware of Charlie. All focused on Stevie. She gave Charlie a short nod before doing what Stevie did best . . . freak everyone out.

This time it was by running across the room and up the wall to the ceiling. She hung on there for a moment until the men began shooting at her. Then she ran across the ceiling, keeping their focus on her.

Charlie ran through the doorway, searching for Nat. She shot on sight any male who came at her. When she reached the end of the hall and could go neither left nor right she heard screaming.

Following the screaming usually worked, so that's what she did. The sounds took her to a steel door. She carefully tried opening it but it was locked. Charlie took a few steps back, angled her shoulder in and down, positioned both hands on her gun, and ran.

She rammed the door and took it off its hinges with the first hit, sending it across the room. Inside, she found Nat on her knees, holding Kang Yun by his arms and spitting at him.

No. That wasn't right. Well, it wasn't wrong either. She was spitting at him. Not like a scared, angry teen, but like a spitting cobra. Yeah. Exactly like a spitting cobra.

And it was Yun who was screaming.

Nat released the cat and he fell back, writhing and rolling over and over, his hands desperately wiping at his face.

Charlie looked around the room. There were at least six male tigers, all dead. Each of them in a different state of contortion and decomposition. There was only one thing that caused a human body to react like that: the world's worst snake venom.

Grabbing her sister by her T-shirt, she lifted her to her feet and raised her arm. She sniffed Nat's palm and her forearm.

"You can release poison through your pores?" Charlie asked Nat, looking her right in the face. "And spit it? Like a reptile?"

"Only after I drink it. I don't digest it. It just sits in my system."

Charlie let out a breath. "You know whose fault this is, don't you?"

"Dad's?"

"Dad and his fucked-up genes."

The doorframe cracked and Stevie shoved her massive, tiger-striped badger head in. The legs and torso of a man still hung from her mouth, but he'd stopped kicking. When she looked around and saw nothing but dead males in the room, she spit her "toy" onto the floor and gawked at her younger sister.

Charlie jerked her thumb at Stevie and said to a wide-eyed Nat, "That's also Dad's fault."

To Finn's surprise, some of the hyenas had guns and started using them when they realized how dire their situation actually was. Not that he blamed them. The problem was, the weapons didn't really help. As he walked around, lion males tore hyenas to shreds like cruel boys ripping apart their little sisters' stuffed animals.

Eventually, the hyenas that weren't killed right away started to run for their lives. Probably smart, because it had turned out to be way easier than Finn had thought possible to round up a bunch of lion males for this. All Keane had to do was put a call out to the lions in his football league. They'd only received "yes" replies and the males showed up at the airport less than twenty-four hours later on their own dime. Apparently running down hyenas for amusement was something lion males did whenever they could. Whether on the Serengeti or in Brooklyn on a Saturday night. So to be able to take on an entire clan for another player's badger girlfriend—because Mads was now officially Finn's girlfriend as far as the league and Finn's brothers were concerned—was an "honor."

What was strange to Finn, though, was that he hadn't seen any of Mads's teammates since this had all started. They'd disappeared when Mads and the rest of them had headed toward the trailers and hadn't been spotted since. He just hoped they weren't about to blow the place. He wouldn't put it past them, but he really didn't want to have to make a run for it.

Once Tova and Freja turned tail, the whole thing was pretty much over. The hyenas that were left just took off. They grabbed the kids—who had not been harmed in any way—got in their trucks and cars, and were gone.

Finn went looking for Mads and found her staring out over a small man-made lake. She was covered in blood and had a few bruises, but not nearly as many as she'd had the night her cousins had ambushed her.

He put his arm around her shoulders from behind and kissed the top of her head.

"You okay?" he asked.

"I'm fine."

"Think they'll be back?"

"Don't know. Don't care. I just know they won't be bothering me. And I never have to come back here."

"This was never your home."

"It really wasn't. Detroit was my home. Solveig was my home. Those parks and those basketball courts were my home."

She grabbed his forearms with her hands and just held them. They stayed like that for a long time until they heard a truck pull up and the badgers got out.

"Where did you go?" Mads asked when she saw her friends.

"Had to get some stuff for you," Max said. "And now you owe us. Because oh my God!"

"What are you talking about?"

Tock carried a metal box from the back of the truck. One

of those safe boxes people had in the bottom of their closets for important papers when they didn't want to deal with a big safe.

"We found this in the hoarder house."

"You went in there?" Mads took a step back. "I can't go anywhere with you guys until you shower."

Finn covered her mouth with his hand because that was way rude.

Tock opened the box. "Deed for this property. It was owned by Solveig." She reached into the box again. "Copy of Solveig's final will, signed and witnessed blah blah blah, leaving everything to *you*. Including this property."

"I don't want this property."

"Then sell it to my grandfather," Max said. "The wolves will love it. They can expand the Pack and keep the hyenas off it."

"Oooh. And make it a sanctuary for full-blood wolves," Streep eagerly suggested.

"Anything else?" Mads asked. "Hidden treasure worth millions?"

"Dear God, you have a Basquiat!" Nelle snapped.

"Oh, what? Now you're going to bring that up every day?"

"There is one more thing," Tock said. She went back to the truck and returned holding a battered cardboard box with a few grease stains that might have come from pizza.

"What's that?"

"Solveig's ashes."

Mads's entire body tensed. "How . . . how do you know that? Are you sure? You can't be sure."

"Little kid hiding in the house pointed it out to us. I think she liked to play in there. I also think she saw where the adults hid it. So when I asked, she showed me."

"I'm surprised they didn't flush the ashes down the toilet."

"What if they needed them later to use against you? Especially if you ever found out you owned the property."

Mads stretched out her arms and Tock carefully placed the box into her hands.

"Thank you," Mads said.

"My friends," Streep added.

"What?"

"Thank you, *my friends.*"

Mads, Tock, Nelle, and Max stared at Streep until she snarled and stalked away.

"Evil bitches!" she yelled over her shoulder.

Dez and Crushek gazed at the set of legs in one corner of the room, walked out, went down the hall, and found the torso and head that went with the legs in another room. The doorways of both these rooms had been torn down by something enormous and strong. Like construction equipment. Or Godzilla.

There were more destroyed walls in the building. There were more bodies. Some had been torn apart. Some had been shot. All of them were Asian and male. They were also gangsters with very long criminal records who had worked for the Yun family.

In fact, Kang Yun was in one of these rooms. Dead. At least Dez was pretty sure it was Kang. A good chunk of his face was gone. Like someone had thrown acid at it. But she wouldn't know for sure until the M.E. had a look.

"We're never going to figure out what's going on here, are we?" she finally asked Crushek.

"Nope."

"I mean with the Yuns, the badgers, and the other . . . tigers. It's just going to stay a mystery to us, isn't it?"

"Probably."

"Is it something that should keep me up nights?"

"Not really."

"And why is that? Just so I'm clear."

Crushek pointed at one of the dead. "That guy there. I busted him myself for human trafficking. My least favorite thing. The Yuns bailed him out and paid for a top-notch lawyer to get him off."

Dez nodded. "Good enough for me. Hungry?"

"Always."

EPILOGUE

When Mads said she wanted to have a "little ceremony for Solveig in Detroit," Finn had really thought she meant a little ceremony. What was happening at this moment was not a little ceremony.

It was a massive street fair in honor of "the crazy Viking." A title of honor Solveig had earned over the years that she'd lived and worked in her Detroit neighborhood. From what Finn had learned walking around that street fair and talking to people, Solveig was never friendly or nice, but she could be kind. Helping those who needed it without being condescending or giving speeches. She seemed to understand what people were going through and she just acted.

People on her street were going to miss "the crazy old white lady with the scary tattoos." They'd pulled out all the stops for the street fair. A stage was built for all the bands that would attend, including music from reggae to soul, blues to jazz and rap to hip-hop. There would be something for everyone. There would also be food stalls and trucks, a farmers' market, and people selling their jewelry and clothes.

Finn and his brothers had thought they'd be there a couple of hours and then go back to the hotel to get in some pool time. But the whole thing was way more fun than they'd expected, and at some point, his brothers went off to flirt with some really good-looking women and Finn went to find Mads.

He should have known where she'd be because the street

fair was right next to the park where she used to play basketball as a kid.

That's where he found her playing with her teammates against some locals, who were getting their asses handed to them by a "bunch of girls."

Yeah. "Girls."

Finn found a spot on the rickety bleachers, trying to pretend they didn't creak when he sat down, and that everyone didn't kind of stare at the six-seven Asian dude they didn't recognize. Especially when Mads did her thing on the court and he cheered her on at every turn. She played it straight, too. None of the shifter stuff she had to do when playing against a six-two She-tiger or a seven-one She-bear. Here she could just go back to the fancy moves that she'd done when she just wanted to be on the WNBA. Those moves, combined with her teammates' play, had the crowd wildly entertained and the opposing team of men pissed.

When Max shot an amazing three-pointer that clinched the game and had her teammates jumping on her, Finn got up and went out onto the court. He put himself between the badgers and the full-human males. He could see how embarrassed they were to lose to a bunch of girls and how quickly their embarrassment could turn into what he liked to call "a situation." He found "situations" only happened with full-human men.

Shifter males knew better.

But before he could get too worried about it, his brothers were there. Just the presence of the three of them together prevented any problem; the situation resolved itself. And Mads and her teammates had no idea.

Together, the group went back to the fair to get food and drink; Mads was still holding on to the winning ball. She seemed prouder of this win than of winning the playoffs.

"I take it back," he said to her as they waited on line to get jerk chicken and beef patties. He had his arm around her shoulders and she had hers around his waist. And he actually enjoyed feeling like someone had a little bit of a claim on him. The pair of them looking like an actual couple. He usually hated that.

"Take back what?"

"Basketball *is* a sport. But only when *you* play. You and your teammates are . . . awesome."

"Thank you. I'm sure Michael Jordan, Scottie Pippen, and LeBron James would argue the whole 'only a sport when I play' thing—but whatever. I love the sentiment."

"I can't believe how fast this whole thing was pulled together."

"I think the event planners started right after Solveig died. They'd tried to get in contact with Tova about it but she'd ignored them. When I called about arranging something, they told me what was going on and I just jumped in. Later tonight I'll be sprinkling some of her ashes around. Leaving a piece of her here. Another time, I'll go to Norway. Leave some of her there. But I'll keep some for myself. So she'll always be with me."

"We'll go together. I've never been to Norway."

"You still planning to be around then?"

"I'm not going anywhere. You going anywhere?"

"Only for away games."

"Oy," they heard behind them and Finn saw Tock approaching them. "You two."

"What about us?" Mads asked.

"I don't know. You're just getting on my . . ." Her words faded away and she suddenly asked, "Is Shay standing behind me?"

"Yes," Finn replied.

"Why are you being so creepy?"

"I'm not being creepy," Shay replied. "I'm just standing here."

"You're not just standing there. You want something. What do you want?"

"You still going to help us with our father?"

"We said we'd help you."

"But are *you* going to talk to your grandmother?"

"I already told you, you don't want me to talk to my grandmother."

"Why?" Shay asked. Because Shay was that annoying.

"Can't you just trust me on this?" Tock asked.

"I don't know you well enough to trust you."

"Don't you have a dog to pet or something? Look over there. Look at that friendly dog. Why don't you go play with that one?"

"The two-hundred-pound pit bull with the spiked collar being held by what seems to be a possible gang member of some sort? You want me to play with *that* dog?"

"Yes. Go put your hand right in front of his face. I'm sure he'd love it."

Finn faced forward again and said to Mads, "Or we can go to Norway tonight. There's nothing stopping us."

Mads carefully sprinkled her great-grandmother's ashes around her old store and thanked Solveig for all she'd done for her in this life. Then she promised to meet her in Valhalla one day, but not anytime soon.

She walked across the street to those waiting for her and right into Finn's arms. He hugged her tight and she let him. Something she didn't normally do. She'd always found being hugged suffocating. Even when it was meant to be friendly. This, however, she really liked.

"You okay, Mads?" Tock asked.

"I'm great." She pulled out of Finn's arms and looked at her friends. Although she'd never call them that when Streep was around because it was just too much damn fun to piss her off by calling them "teammates" instead. "Thanks, you guys, for coming. It really means a lot."

"You want to go back to the hotel now?" Nelle asked.

"Or," Max tossed in, "stay and listen to the crappy reggae set that's coming up on stage?"

"Crappy?" Mads barked. "Did you just say *crappy*?"

Laughing, the group headed back for more food and dancing but Mads felt a tug on her arm and turned around to see Finn looking at her. She moved in close and they stared at each other for a long time, neither saying anything because it was unnecessary.

When the music from the stage hit her and she realized it

was a band she loved, she went up on her toes and he came down. They kissed and Mads knew that she wouldn't spend the whole night at this street fair. Not when there was a big bed waiting for them at the hotel.

She pulled back, her hands stroking down his arms before she grasped his fingers with hers and pulled him toward the dance floor.

"One thing," he said as he followed her.

"Yeah. What's that?"

"When we get back, you need to get that coyote its own bed."

Nat's mother let her gaze bounce back and forth between Charlie MacKilligan and Stevie MacKilligan, trying to understand what they were saying to her.

"So you think that *my* daughter should live here with you now?"

"Not all the time, but yes."

"My *seventeen*-year-old daughter? Should live with a couple of twenty-somethings—"

"Three," Charlie corrected. "Three twenty-somethings."

"And their boyfriends," Stevie added.

"Although I spend most of my time in the house across the street with my boyfriend's triplets. He's a grizzly."

"Uh-huh."

"My boyfriend's a panda," Stevie said with a wide smile. "But we wouldn't take this responsibility lightly. We would watch her closely."

"Uh-huh. So my seventeen-year-old with you three, your three boyfriends—"

"And sometimes the badgers from Max's basketball team."

"Right." Stevie nodded. "But just badgers from the team."

"I'm back!" a voice called from the front of the house, and a few seconds later Kyle Jean-Louis Parker stormed through with all his luggage, heading toward the basement. "I couldn't do it! I couldn't stay with them a minute longer! I am an artist! Possibly, one day, the greatest artist that will have ever lived. I can't trap myself with the tiny minds of my family! I need freedom! So I'm back! I will be in my basement, watching reality TV and attempting to forget the horrors of this week with those . . . peasants!"

He stomped off, marching down the stairs, and Lisa Malone said, "You want my seventeen-year-old daughter to live with you three, your three boyfriends, badger basketball players, and that *stunning*, blond, long-haired jackal who is . . . how old?"

"Eighteen."

"Eighteen. And why in the history of the universe would I do this stupid thing to my daughter?"

Charlie moved her coffee mug aside and stretched forward a bit on the kitchen table before carefully explaining to Nat's mother, "I just discovered that your daughter can unleash venom through her pores and spit it out of her mouth. Like a reptile. Actually, the way she spits it out of her mouth is *exactly* the way spitting cobras do it."

"Exactly," Stevie repeated. "I looked into her mouth and compared it to images of a spitting cobra. Most of the time, her mouth is normal. But when she shifts because of a dangerous situation *and* has poison in her system, it becomes the inside of a spitting cobra's mouth.

"Although, now that I think about it," Stevie went on, her gaze suddenly focusing on the small kitchen window behind Charlie, "we should test other snake poisons on her and see if the inside of her mouth changes to match the inside of each individual snake's mouth."

"That," Charlie said, "would be a good idea."

"That would be fascinating, wouldn't it?" Stevie agreed, grinning at Charlie.

"Would it?" Lisa asked.

Charlie looked at Nat's mother and realized it would be best just to be direct with her. Straightforward. No point in beating around the bush anymore.

"See, Lisa, the problem here is that you weren't just impregnated by any badger. You, like our mothers, fucked Freddy

MacKilligan. And, like our mothers, you've cursed your child with fucked-up Freddy MacKilligan genes."

"I'm a scientist—world-renowned, actually," Stevie explained. "And would normally consider my sister's thoughts insane. But the more evidence I see . . . the more I believe she's right. Freddy MacKilligan has fucked-up genes."

Charlie put her hand over Lisa's. "And understand, the problem isn't that Nat has this weirdness. And it *is* weird because she's half badger and half tiger. I have no idea how that reptile part got in there. The real problem is that she has no real control over it. She just unleashes it when she feels in danger. Or pissed. Or simply annoyed. Which she feels any time she drinks some snake venom–infused vodka. All you need is a guy to pat her ass during a teenage party and the next thing you know, you're looking at a very serious situation. And I am sure you're thinking you can just tell her not to drink. Sure! Why not? But think about yourself when you were seventeen. Was that really an effective strategy? And that's where I'm hoping we can help."

"That's why we're offering to have her stay here for a little while," Stevie said. "Not all the time, but back and forth. Here and there. But you know, spend enough time around us so that we can help guide her."

"Teach her how to be a honey badger without going to prison," Charlie suggested.

"We just want what's best for her."

"And for you not to get hit in the face with a mouthful of black mamba venom when you two get into a mother-daughter spat over cleaning her room. Or you can do what you've probably been doing and pretend everything is just fine. That you don't see what's going on. Don't see that your daughter's different."

"My family tried that with me for a while," Stevie said. "Then one day my mom dropped me off at Charlie's mom's house. To meet my sisters, she said. And she never came back. I haven't seen her since. It was for the best, but it still hurt."

"Deal with it now," Charlie promised, "and we'll all get through it together like family."

Lisa leaned back in the kitchen chair and slowly nodded her head. "My boys won't like it, but . . . but . . . What is that noise?"

"That is your daughter. She is building a nest in the walls."

"Why?"

"Don't know. My hope is that she's not laying eggs like a snake, though." Charlie took Lisa's hand. "But whatever she's up to, we'll find out together. And then we're going to make her stop." She turned toward the wall behind her. "Because I'm renting here! I do not *own this house!*"

Lisa stared at Charlie for a moment before pointing out, "You do remember that she can't hear you . . . right? When you yell?"

Charlie winced and admitted, "Yeahhhh . . . that's going to take me some time to get used to. Because usually I just yell at Max and Stevie when they screw up. Mostly Max." She shrugged. "Always Max. But don't worry. I will do my best to keep in mind that she's—"

"Deaf?"

"I was going to say not Max. But sure. Deaf, too. I'll keep both in mind. Just for you."

"How comforting for a mother entrusting you with her child."

"See?" Stevie happily cheered. "We're already working like a family! This is gonna be great!"